PATIENCE CAN COOK A STONE

M. B. Gibson

M. B. Gibson Books
BLACKVILLE, SOUTH CAROLINA

M. B. Gibson Books
2728 Reynolds Road
Blackville, South Carolina 29817
www.mbgibsonbooks.com

Publisher's Note: This is a work of fiction. Names, characters, places, and incidents are a product of the author's imagination. Locales and public names are sometimes used for atmospheric purposes. Any resemblance to actual people, living or dead, or to businesses, companies, events, institutions, or locales is completely coincidental.

Book Layout ©2017 BookDesignTemplates.com

Ordering Information:
Quantity sales. Special discounts are available on quantity purchases by corporations, associations, and others. For details, contact the "Special Sales Department" at the address above.

Patience Can Cook a Stone/ M. B. Gibson. -- 1st ed.
ISBN 978-0-9972234-4-6

In Memory of my Grandmother,
Mary Edith Beckett Pryor

Dedicated to my Daughters,
Emily, Sara, and Hannah

We have it in our power to begin the world over again.

–THOMAS PAINE

Contents

Chapter One 1

Chapter Two 11

Chapter Three 19

Chapter Four 25

Chapter Five 35

Chapter Six 42

Chapter Seven 51

Chapter Eight 61

Chapter Nine 68

Chapter Ten 79

Chapter Eleven 84

Chapter Twelve 94

Chapter Thirteen 105

Chapter Fourteen 114

Chapter Fifteen 121

Chapter Sixteen 129

Chapter Seventeen 137

Chapter Eighteen 151

Chapter Nineteen 161

Chapter Twenty 168

Chapter Twenty-One 172

Chapter Twenty-two 183

Chapter Twenty-three 196

Chapter Twenty-four 207

Chapter Twenty-five 216

Chapter Twenty-six 227

Chapter Twenty-seven 235

Chapter Twenty-eight..246

Chapter Twenty-nine..256

Chapter Thirty 265

Chapter Thirty-one 275

Chapter Thirty-two..285

Chapter Thirty-three..295

Chapter Thirty-four 302

Chapter Thirty-five 309

Chapter Thirty-six..322

Chapter Thirty-seven..331

Chapter Thirty-eight 344

Chapter Thirty-nine 356

Chapter Forty...369

Chapter Forty-one 381

About the Book 383

Acknowledgements..387

ABOUT THE AUTHOR 389

Chapter One

APRIL 3, 1780
ORANGEBURGH DISTRICT, SOUTH CAROLINA

Thomas de Barnefort's creaking knees and rheumy eyes trumpeted his advancing age. As the fragrance of jessamine, magnolia, and wisteria floated on the evening breeze, the master of Kilkenny Plantation limped past the cabins of servants, most of whom were enslaved.

"Evenin', Mr. Tom," called one after the other as he passed.

Nodding, he hobbled toward the end of the quarters to the house of the Dillons. Joe and Nan came from Ireland, like himself, though not as criminals. Nor were they indentured. They arrived free. His cousin and partner, Sir Richard Lynche, had written in '67, asking him to find a place for the couple. He gave no explanation, but upon meeting young Nan, his wife detected the high brow and gray eyes of the Lynches. A love brat, most likely. Surprising for a man who'd been strait-laced, even as a lad.

The Dillon cabin mirrored the rest, bolstered by two-foot brick pillars to create a crawl space beneath the floor. The airflow helped keep the cabin cool. Four wooden steps led to the porch where the couple sat on small, crudely carved stools.

Nan perked up. "Mr. Tom, fine evening, ain't it?"

1

"It is." He sat on the top step and glanced at the window. Open shutters allowed a cross breeze through to another window in the back. Four little heads peeped above the sill.

Joe leaned forward. "The last sheep was shorn as the sun slid behind the trees. We've many-a fleece to see us through 'til next spring."

Thomas sighed. It was not sheep he'd come to discuss.

Doubt crept into Joe's voice. "Is all to yer satisfaction, then, Mr. Tom?"

Thomas patted Joe's knee. "Of course. You're doing a fine job. Are you still content with Thunder? Is Ketch working out?"

Joe had a knack with the animals. Thomas had assigned two fellows to help him tend the flock. Thunder worked with him full time, with Ketch as an extra pair of hands during the spring shearing. The wool provided clothing for everyone on the plantation.

"They work hard, sir. You can rest easy about them."

"Good to hear." Thomas took a deep breath and looked at Nan. "I've news from the old country. Duncullen to be exact."

Even in the encroaching darkness, he sensed Nan's tension. Her voice was tight. "Not Jack."

He remembered the simple farmhand well. "No, Nan. No word on Jack—good or bad. It's Sir Richard himself." He swallowed. "Seems his heart gave out. They say he was again raving about Alistair Moore dragging him into hell's fiery pits when he keeled over, dead. Such a fruitless waste of intelligence and talent."

"'Twasn't fruitless." Nan clenched her fists. "He murdered me Uncle Nolan and Father Alistair Moore. The fruit was rotten to the core."

Joe wrapped his larger hand around hers.

"Yes. Well." Sadness tightened Thomas's heart. "For better or worse, he's met his Maker."

Nan sighed but said nothing. Likely for the best.

Thomas stood. "I'll leave you both to your thoughts."

Joe rose as well. "Thank ye for coming with the news."

He nodded. "See you in the morning." Heading toward the Big House, he heard the tittering of the children inside the cabin.

"Who died, Mama?" asked the oldest, Mary Edith.

"Back on yer pallets, the lot of ye," barked their mother.

While his cousin's demise saddened Thomas, he had another concern. Richard Lynche had secretly financed this plantation, enabling Thomas to escape his own overbearing father. Though an absentee owner, Lord Ethan had somehow managed to smother Thomas from across the sea.

At Kilkenny, he and Richard were equal partners with Thomas free to run the enterprise as he chose. He owed Richard more than he could ever repay, but what to do with his share? The answer was not simple. Over the years, Richard had managed a tenuous hold on his sanity. He never married and had sired no heirs.

Perhaps a portion of the land for Nan and her family. He shook his head. His wife, Anne, would never stand for it. Why did she despise the young woman so? Nan was a steady worker as were her older children, Mary Edith and the twins, Baby Eveleen and Nolan. Even Daniel, at age five, ran errands and helped around the barn.

He'd mention his thoughts to Anne once they'd crystallized. No use creating a whirlwind until his decision was firm.

✞

Joe Dillon heard the scamper of his children's feet as they scurried to their pallets. Once Mr. Tom was out of their hearing, he stretched his hand, inviting Nan to join him on the step. The darkness engulfed them as she snuggled under his arm.

"So, the old villain is dead at last," Nan whispered.

Joe did not miss the catch in her voice. His rough hand caressed her cheek where he found a tear.

"I don't know why I even care about the blackguard." Nan sniffed. "I despise him. Or I did."

"Because ye've no chance now. No chance to know him nor scream yer rage if ye choose." He lifted her face toward his. "Or reconcile."

She tried to smile. "Is it yerself that's crazed or is it me? Would I look for him to sail the seas, travel that rickety stagecoach through forest and swamp, only to pull up here so I could spew me venom?"

"Maybe so he could hold ye, tell ye he loves ye with all his heart."

With a stuttering intake of breath, she said, "Ridiculous."

"'Tis. Yet our hearts still yearn for it, don't they?"

Joe felt the presence behind him before he heard the padding of bare feet. Mary Edith moved like a cat.

"Mama? Who died?"

Nan sat up and threw back her head. "By Saint Christopher's toes! Ye've got the biggest ears on Kilkenny, Mary Edith. Maybe all Orangeburgh District."

And, Joe knew, the most tender of hearts. He waved her over and placed his arm about her waist. "Someone from yer ma's younger days, darlin'. Back in Tipperary." To Nan, he added, "She should know. She's soon to be twelve."

Nan leapt up. "Not yet." She lurched from the steps to the ground below and waved her arm in the air. "Ach. Tell her then. I'm off for a walk."

Joe sighed. When riled, Nan never could keep from escaping into the forest or fields. "Not that way, me love. Too late, 'tis, for the woods. Toward the Big House."

With a growl, she turned and marched in the opposite direction. Joe watched her form melt into the darkness.

"Sit, Mary Edith." Once beside him, Joe stroked her loosened hair. "The man who died was Mr. Tom's cousin, Sir Richard." He took a deep breath. "He was also yer grandfather."

"My grandpa? A sir? How could that be?"

"Ye know of yer grandma, Eveleen." He swallowed. "She never married. The man was a gentleman and she, a servant. He refused her."

Mary Edith drew in her breath, aghast. "Cruel, he must have been. No wonder Mama hates him."

"Ye should never hate, turtledove." His eldest daughter shot him a look, reminding him how fast she was growing up.

The girl licked her lips. "That means Mama—never mind. I didn't say nothing."

That hated word—bastard.

What if, now, Mary Edith looked upon her mother with new eyes? He regretted telling her. "Keep such thoughts to yerself."

✿

Thomas smiled as Wilbur, the plantation's oldest servant, stepped from the Big House to help his master climb the veranda steps. The irony of leaning on a fellow seven years his senior did not escape him.

Like his neighbors, Thomas preferred the term "servant" to "slave," finding it more refined and truer to the life they led on Kilkenny. Whether enslaved or free, wages amounted to good food, warm clothing, and satisfactory boarding. The Dillon family could leave whenever they wished, but why would they? They were treated no better than the other servants, and still found Kilkenny provided comfort and contentment. As, he was sure, did all who toiled on his farm.

They reached the top of the steps. "Mr. Carlton be waitin' on ya inside, suh."

Thomas sighed. His oldest son was a source of both pride and disappointment. "Thank you, Wilbur. Off to bed now. I'll need you no further tonight."

"Yes suh, Mr. Tom."

Thomas crossed the wide veranda. He paused, then opened the front door. Once he stepped into the house, Carlton's whiskey-laced breath struck him full force.

"Father, there y'are."

"You've been to McHeath's Tavern, I see."

Carlton placed a hand on his father's shoulder as though in camaraderie, but Thomas suspected it was more to steady himself. "Where I've heard outstanding news."

"If I may shut the door first."

"Ah." Carlton reached behind and closed it for him. "This can wait no longer. John McHeath has it on fine authority that the formidable Sir Henry Clinton, general of the British army, has reached the outskirts of Charles Town and begun his siege."

"Why can't they fight this blasted war in the North? They promised to leave us be if we remained neutral."

Carlton rambled as though Thomas hadn't spoken. "General Lincoln and his rebels are trembling inside the walls of the city with their cowardly tails tucked. It's time we squashed those traitors like the cacarootches they are." He howled with laughter.

Grimacing, Thomas broke away and headed for the staircase. "Good night, son."

"There's more. They captured Thomas Farr and forced him and his insufferable brat to herd their supply train's cattle. What an indignity for the Speaker of the House of Representatives! How I'd love to watch those dumb oxes stumbling over cow turds."

Thomas stopped. "Carlton. Go to bed."

"But Father—"

"If you will, give me one night of silence to mourn my cousin's loss."

Carlton stumbled forward a few steps. "Ha! That madman should have been kept in a cage."

Thomas's face burned. "You know nothing of Richard Lynche! Without him—I insist you go to bed!"

Caring little if he'd been obeyed, Thomas yanked himself up the staircase with the banister. These forays to McHeath's Tavern were becoming too frequent. At the top of the steps, he nodded to the hall boy, Oscar, who struggled to stay awake beside his wife's chamber. Thomas crept past the open door as quietly as he could, to no avail.

"Husband, come in for a spell."

Could this evening become any more trying?

Thomas had lost affection for Anne years ago, before they first boarded the ship to America. When living at Duncullen Estate with Richard, she and his father had concocted a dastardly scheme to have his cousin committed to an asylum. He'd tried to forgive her betrayal, but the deceit never stopped.

He stuck his head through the threshold. "Yes, my dear?"

"No, sweet man. I mean for you to join me." When he hesitated, she frowned. "For a time. I'm feeling nostalgic with the loss of poor Richard."

Was he to believe she'd unearthed compassion for the man? Anne scooted to the far side of the bed, creating room for him beside her. It wouldn't be for long, and he preferred to avoid the emotional battering his denial would provoke.

Once he lay down, Anne reached for his ear and rubbed it like she'd done when they first married. It had been so long, it caught him unawares. A tear sprang from his eye.

"Oh, Tommy, I've missed you so!"

Her old pet name for him. Wistful since the news of Richard's passing, it was too much. Fearing he'd regret it, he rolled into Anne's arms.

"My darling husband." She kissed his brow, his cheeks, and at last, his lips.

His defenses melting away, he wiped his eyes and chuckled. "We were so happy when we'd first arrived at Duncullen. Relieved to be away from our parents' glare."

"We were." She ran her well-kept nails through his thinning hair. It tingled and relaxed him much as it had at age twenty-five. "We're not so old, you know, that we can't start again. Stay with me tonight."

"How did we go so wrong, Annie?"

"It doesn't matter. We have the rest of our lives to make up for it. With poor Richard gone, we're on our own now. Alden will likely stay in Charles Town once he's finished reading law with Mr. Talbot."

Thomas flinched at the mention of their younger son, who was possibly surrounded by the British. Surely, Talbot removed Alden and himself from the peninsula before General Clinton and his army got so far. Loath to spoil this rare moment, he'd not mention it to Anne. It and his new plans for Alden could wait until morning.

"Carlton and Rosabel will soon marry," Anne went on. "We can leave our responsibilities to them. We'll sit on the veranda and bounce grandchildren upon our knees."

Thomas smiled at the image. He wearied so easily now, and Carlton had inherited his good head for agriculture. Rosabel would make an obedient wife, which was not what his son needed. She had a warm heart, though, and would be a fine mother.

Anne continued to run her fingernails over his scalp. "With Richard leaving no heirs, it will be simpler for Carlton. He has so much ahead of him. His stalwart loyalty to King George may be well-rewarded once this absurd rebellion is over."

Smiling, he decided to mention his thoughts on Alden and the Dillons after all. There'd never be a better time. "Annie, I plan to change my will. I'd like Alden to have a share of the plantation so he can practice law right here with us."

Her fingers froze, but he plowed forward. "I'm also thinking of a hundred acres for Nan and Joe. Down by Turkey Creek."

"Well, that's something to consider." She resumed her caresses. "While I've not always gotten on with the woman, it only seems fair. Roll over, sweetheart. Let me rub your back."

Thomas's heart leapt as he rolled to his left side. This was far easier than he'd ever dreamed. "You are my old Annie, after all."

✤

Well, Anne thought, there's no fool like an old fool.

She'd feared Thomas would hire a solicitor to track down some lubberwort of a cousin, too many times removed, to inherit Richard's share. But this plan was so much worse. Paving the way for Alden to return to Orangeburgh District would be disastrous for all involved. Carlton was chomping at the bit to run Kilkenny Plantation with the order and discipline that had eluded her soft-headed husband.

Thomas and Alden together? The foolhardy ideas they'd come up with boggled the mind. Alden's naive idealism fit well in urbane Charles Town, though not at all in the raucous crudity of the backcountry.

As far as even one acre for Richard's bastard, that smug draggle of a woman, it would be over Anne's dead body.

With the scratching of his back, the room resounded with Thomas's snores, as she knew it would. She gently rolled him from his side to his back. His face was smoother. Relaxed. His mouth curved at the ends as though he dreamed of something pleasant.

"Yes, my dearest. Sweet dreams."

Anne lifted her pillow and, with arms that were stronger than they looked, pressed it over her husband's face.

Chapter Two

Jaw set, Nan strode up the path. When she nearly caught Mr. Tom lumbering toward the Big House, she slipped to the right and into the meadow. Under a sliver of a moon, she'd not be seen. Preferring the safety of darkness since a young girl, she'd always moved with the stealth of any night creature.

Rounding the manor house, she headed to the sculptured gardens, the pride of Kilkenny's mistress. If Nan were seen walking the pathways through the shrubs and small trees, she'd be flogged. Again. She made her way to the round garden building and plopped onto its wooden bench.

Nan's heartbeat slowed to its normal pace. Joe was right, as he often was. How many times had she thought she'd put the pain of being fatherless behind her? Or the bitterness of later discovering the villain Sir Richard had turned out to be. Maybe with his death, she'd finally be free of that anguish.

Yet, what of Mary Edith? They'd planned to tell the children of their past once they were old enough to appreciate it. Now, Joe decided the time had come. Nan wrung her hands. Could she bear to scrape the scab from that wound?

She breathed deeply to quiet her mind. Amongst the fluttering clicks of a nearby frog, she heard crickets and katydids. Small, furry creatures scuttled through the grasses.

Her thoughts drifted to Miss Anne, or Lady Anne as the shrew insisted all servants call her. Such a fool! Nan remembered the unflattering stories told by Duncullen's housekeeper, Biddy. When Nan decided to leave Ireland, Biddy made it clear in her delicate way that Anne de Barnefort was an upstart who craved the prestige of the quality.

Only a few years past, annoyed with what she saw as Nan's haughtiness, Miss Anne had hissed, "I know who you are and what you are, you churlish hedge-born harpy!"

Nan hadn't held back. "I've heard about yerself as well."

Anne sneered. "That's right. You lived a while at Duncullen, so you're familiar with the lord of the manor, his quirks and aberrations. Perhaps you didn't know he had visits from his father—his dead father! I heard him with my own ears, pleading to be left alone by mere shadows." She mimicked Sir Richard in a taunting voice. "'Stop laughing at me, stop laughing at me.'"

"Ye'd best watch yerself, mocking yer betters as ye are."

That gibe cost Nan a flogging. The old hag had insisted on ten lashes, but gentle Mr. Tom reduced it to three. The scars still burned her soul.

She knew her father had been off the hooks, as was his mother before him. Mr. Tom had said he was so even as he died. Was that her fate as well, one she could pass on to her own children? Jesus in Heaven, let it not be so!

Joe understood her need to get away when her blood rose, but he'd worry if she were gone too long. As she stood, a swish of air caused her to spin. The bulging eyes of an enormous barn owl confronted her. Outstretched talons charged her throat. Its ungodly scream brought terror to her heart. She plunged to the ground. It swooped low over her prone form before soaring back into the trees.

Heart thundering, she crept to her feet. It meant to carry her away, she was sure of it. Old folks said owls foretold death. Her eyes brimmed with tears. Did her father's spirit find her here, after all? Or was this the beginning of madness?

Nan stole back toward their cabin. All were in for the night. Terrified of another attack by the owl, she stuck closer to the Big House.

Passing by, Nan heard raucous snores coming from the mistress' second-floor chamber. Mr. Tom? That was curious since all knew Miss Anne did not share a bed with her husband. Unease held Nan to the spot before she headed once again toward the quarters.

Several yards past the veranda, she heard the first cries from the Big House. Her already-rattled nerves lit up. Was it Miss Anne or Little Oscar? It was hard to tell, but the distress was real. Nan turned back. She clambered up the tall veranda steps two at a time and burst into the house. She found Oscar calling for Mr. Carlton, who stumbled in confusion from his room to his mother's chamber door.

Nan climbed the staircase and stood in the same doorway. Her hand flew to her mouth as the young lad squalled.

Mr. Carlton was bent over the bed, shaking the lifeless form of Mr. Tom. "Wake up, Father! You must wake up!"

It was then Nan saw Miss Anne perched upon her settee in her dressing gown, hands folded. Her face revealed nothing until she glimpsed Nan.

"Get her out!" Anne's face contorted with rage as she thrust a stubby finger toward the door. "I want this strumpet out of my house!"

❖

Carlton had sobered quickly when Little Oscar appeared at his chamber door. The boy was in such hysterics, Carlton couldn't make out the trouble. Finally, he caught the words "Mr. Tom" and "got no life left." The rock that had clunked into his stomach at that moment remained there still.

He'd headed to his father's chamber only to have Oscar stand before Mother's door and wave him in. So unusual for the two to sleep together, but there his father lay, his skin already wearing the ashen gray of death.

Mother sat in a corner in her nightclothes, strangely serene.

That was earlier. Now, the black servants had gathered around the veranda, wailing into the night. Echoes bouncing from the trees sent a chill clear through him.

Mother reclined on the parlor's divan in her satin robe, Oscar asleep at her feet. She rubbed her brow as if determined to smooth the wrinkles. "It's bad enough, Carlton, when they carry on in their quarters, but here? And for your father?"

Wilbur was upstairs with the young African, Thunder, preparing Thomas de Barnefort's body.

His father's body. The words had an imaginary quality, as if it were some cruel joke. He could not fathom life without him. "They're showing respect. Chasing the spirits from hell who might try to snatch Father's soul. They want him to get safely across the river."

"Balderdash! Must we be subjected to such heathenish behavior? They're worse than Ireland's superstitious ruck."

While he objected to his father's laxity with the bondservants, their pleas for his safe passage into heaven—though quite primitive—touched him. They saw him as one of their own. "It's known as a 'sit up,' Mother. A lot like Irish wakes."

"I know what it is, Carlton. It means we must endure this commotion all night long. How can I grieve surrounded by that primeval screeching?"

She hid her sorrow well.

As the longcase clock chimed once, Carlton regretted such an ungracious thought. Each must deal with grief in his own way. Gazing out the window, he watched some slaves dance while others wailed. "We'll get word to Alden first thing in the morning. He'll be distraught if the burial occurs without him, yet we'd best not wait too long for his return."

When his mother made no response, he turned. She massaged the fingers of her left hand with her right, a sign she had something on her mind.

"I saved you, Carlton. Your father told me this evening, with Richard gone, he wanted to add Alden to his will as your partner. To live with us at Kilkenny."

Carlton frowned. "Alden has no desire for life in the back parts. Father knows—knew that."

"He wanted him to practice law closer to us." She sat up and patted the cushion beside her. When he joined his mother, she placed her hand on his thigh. "It's no secret you're my favorite. We think alike, don't we? Alden was your father's. He may have missed having one so like-minded around." She took his hand. "Now, we'll never know."

She was right. It was no secret, but to have the words spoken aloud that Alden was his father's pet caused his chest to sag. True, he and Thomas agreed on practically nothing. Carlton found his father too soft to make Kilkenny flourish. It embarrassed him when other planters, with raised eyebrows, sneered at Thomas de Barnefort's theories about his labor force. He burned at the thought of them laughing behind Father's back. Carlton had warned him. Many times. But Thomas de Barnefort cared nothing of the opinions of his peers.

The other planters never mocked Father's agricultural acumen. He had a natural understanding of how things grew and thrived—animal and vegetable. The problem lay in the pampering of those beneath him, encouraging them to forget their place. When the bonded saw how Kilkenny treated its slaves, it encouraged defiance on other plantations. At least that was the fear.

Carlton had battled with his father, laying out point by point how they'd wasted money on cabins many white men yearned to own. Their servants ate as well as wealthy travelers stopping at McHeath's Tavern. New clothing was distributed before the last had worn thin. All encouraged their inborn laziness.

Thomas was unshakable. Carlton could hear him as though he were standing beside the hearth, his arm laid across the mantle. "Who built the cabins, son? Who planted the food and raised the sheep? Why should they not share in our bounty?"

Carlton's eyes welled with tears. He'd desired nothing more than to prove to his father his approach was superior. Now he'd never have the chance.

Out of nowhere, his mother's words reverberated in his mind: I saved you, Carlton.

He leapt to his feet. "You saved me? What do you mean by that?" Nausea rose in his throat.

She smirked. "You are the sole owner of Kilkenny now. Sir Richard had no heirs. Chances are, no one was aware of his involvement here outside Father and himself." The smirk inched its way into a smile, making his skin crawl. "The will remains intact. Alden will receive his share in the cash that's been set aside for him."

Fear clutched his throat. He waffled, unable to ask: What was Father doing in your chamber? What have you done?

He swallowed. "I'm weary. Let's talk no further tonight."

✦

The African, Thunder, tried to bite his lip, but could hold back no longer. "Why am I here, doing dis?"

The old manservant, Wilbur, looked at him in disgust. "You don't want no part in preparin' Mr. Tom's body? After all he done for you?"

Thunder scowled but didn't answer. He'd arrived in America at the age of twelve and was brought straight to Kilkenny. Yet, in the dozen years he'd been there, not once had he entered the Big House. A shepherd didn't belong in this oversized wooden structure devoted to the gluttony of his captors. Too much food. Too much drink. Too many riches. Sweat trickled and gathered in the small of his back.

Wilbur glanced at him. "You young, Thunder. And strong. I'm an old fella. I can't lift Mr. Tom's dead weight like I could as a pup." He sniffed as he petted the graying hair of the departed. "Mr. Tom deserves the best we can do for him."

Thunder's blood simmered. He turned away.

"What eatin' you, boy?"

The young slave nodded toward the corpse. "Because of Mr. Tom, I never see my family again. I am not a man. I am like a horse or mule." He paused but decided to go further. "Wilbur, you are like his pet hound."

The old man's voice quivered, and his hands shook. "So, that's how ya see it. Ya must not-a noticed how other servants 'round here live. We got good homes, shirts on our backs instead of rags, and our bellies be full. We blessed by this man here."

Thunder frowned at Wilbur's eyes, awash in tears. "If a man owns much cattle and horses, he feed dem well. He brush der coats and stroke dem. Yet dey are not men; dey be animals. If dey do not suit him, he sell dem. He will sell me. He will sell you."

"Grab that towel, ya cold-hearted brute." Wilbur snatched it from Thunder's hands. "I'll hear no more talk 'gainst Mr. Tom."

With the cloth, he blotted his old master's remains. "Poor ol' fella. Don't listen to this fool. You with Jesus now. You be lyin' in the arms of Jesus."

Thunder's heart pounded in his chest. He'd said too much, yet he couldn't resist one more remark. "Mr. Tom is gone. We got Mr. Carlton now."

May Allah have mercy on you, Wilbur. And on me as well. Thunder held his hands, palms open, before his face. He prayed. *Hasbun-Allahu wan na 'mal wakeel.*

Chapter Three

Nan's eyes burned. Once news of Mr. Tom's death flooded the quarters, everyone spent the night grieving, singing, praying, and shouting until some, especially the children, dropped to the ground, asleep.

Joe carried young Daniel to their cabin in the wee hours with the rest of the Dillons trailing behind. Nan lay awake until the first hint of day, haunted by the eerie omen. She'd thought the owl swooped toward her because of Sir Richard, but now what to think? Had her father appeared through the owl for his cousin, Thomas? Who would be next?

Once the sun peeked above the horizon, the work of Kilkenny had begun. Joe had left before sunup to drive the sheep to their pasture. Lambing season was soon upon them and the ewes needed extra grain. Nan said nothing of the owl.

Later that morning, she returned from the pantry with a basket of nutmeg, cinnamon, and mace. She inhaled the scent of freshly cut pine as Kilkenny's carpenter, Jeb, planed a simple coffin. Nolan, ten years old and Jeb's apprentice, mixed soot with lanolin distilled from last month's shearing to create a dubbin for blackening the wooden box.

Nan glanced toward the Big House where Mary Edith and Baby Eveleen, who most just called Baby, were beating carpets. With neighbors expected to pay their respects throughout the day, the house required a thorough cleaning. Who knew how many would make the journey? The rebellion had made enemies of many-a former friend. Yet, they must be prepared with the proper trappings of mourning as well as ample food and drink.

In the cookhouse, several worked furiously to prepare the arval, sweet funeral cakes for mourners to eat during their visit. Some would take a few home as well. Nan shifted the basket of spices to her other hip. Five-year-old Daniel sat outside the kitchen tossing knucklebones with little Oscar.

"He was fit like a fiddle 'til Lady Anne lay over him," she heard Oscar saying. "Then he couldn't breathe."

"Why she do that?" Daniel asked.

Oscar cocked his head to one side. "She wanta sleep on top of him, I think."

Heat rose to the tips of Nan's ears. That shameless old bawd! Forcing her husband into a bit of basket-making at his age. She give the poor fellow a heart attack and done him in!

Disgusted, she thought about Miss Anne's cold-heartedness the night before. 'Twas no more than well-deserved guilt, Nan thought as she stepped into the stifling heat of the kitchen.

The plantation's cook, Ruth, looked up at her arrival. With a bit of cloth, she wiped the sweat from her brow. "Ya finally back with the spices. Them ovens is ready. We got no time to spare."

Nan set the basket on the large table. She grabbed the metal grater from its peg on the wall and began mincing the cinnamon bark. Old Mama Juba sat in the corner, rubbing currants dry in a cloth. She was generally considered too old for labor, but every hand was needed to get these cakes baked.

Mama Juba's face resembled the shriveled currants in her towel. Nan remembered the day the old slave had arrived at Kilkenny with her son. Though she was already too feeble to be much help, Mr. Tom hadn't the heart to split the woman from her boy. When he bought Ketch, Mama Juba came too.

Yet, her mastery of herbs and roots had been a blessing to black and white alike. Everyone knew her remedies had snatched more than a few from the grave's ledge.

"I tol' ya, Ruth, six crows was in that tree outside the smokehouse. 'Someone's gonna die,' I tol' ya." The old woman growled. "And you just a-snortin'."

Ruth used her large hands to mix flour, sugar, and cool butter in a wooden bowl. "I went outside myself to count them birds. They was only five of 'em, meaning sickness. Not death."

Mama Juba grunted. "I guess that's why the master's stone cold, awaitin' his coffin."

Ruth whispered to Nan, "How would she know how many birds they was with them webs in her eyes?"

"Nothin' wrong with my hearin'," the old woman barked.

Ruth pushed her bowl across the table. "Nan, throw that ground cinnamon in here. This batter gonna ruin if we don't get some cakes in the oven. Come on, Mama Juba. Them currants be dry enough."

Mumbling, Nan carried the bowl to the old woman so Mama Juba wouldn't have to pull herself up from her stool. "'Twas more than an extra crow in a tree that kilt him."

"What's that?" asked the old woman, scraping the currants into the bowl.

Nan glanced at Ruth and raised her eyebrows. "I said, 'God between us and all harm,' Mama Juba."

The old healer touched the amulet hanging around her neck. "Somethin' ain't right 'round here. I heard screamin' in the night. Might-a been a owl. Might-a been one of them witches you tol' about, Nan."

"Banshees?"

"That's right. Them banshees."

Nan felt a shiver up her spine. "A fairy, she is, not a witch. Some say she's young and beautiful, others claim she's a hag. Either way, her wailing in the night will chill yer bones."

"And she come to tell folks of a death, ya said."

"She does. But I heard the screech of a barn owl in the night meself. Likely, that's what ye heard."

Mama Juba leaned forward, peering into Nan's eyes like she could see clear to her soul. "So, ya heared it, too. Spirits be afoot. That's the truth."

✦

Carlton smoothed the parchment he'd found in his father's desk. "A nighttime burial, he says." He glanced at Wilbur, who was blowing his nose once again. "Only family and servants are to attend. Isn't that how your people inter your dead?"

"Gotta git buried at night." Wilbur jammed his handkerchief into a pocket and gazed out the window. "Slaves can't stop work 'cause of dyin'. Wouldn't nothin' git done."

Carlton smirked. "Little vexed me more than Father's penchant for humility. Even in death, he belabors the point." He ran his finger over the will's instructions. "Only Mother is to dress in mourning, it says. Appropriately," Carlton added with a hint of sarcasm. "Tell the servants common dress for them, Wilbur. I and the other gentlemen will need black armbands. The women, a knot of black ribbon."

"That's good, Mr. Carlton." Wilbur cocked his head to the side. "A wagon comin'. News do travel fast."

As the old servant stepped outside to greet the condoler, Carlton approached the window. They'd yet to get the house in order; Father's coffin was still under construction. How crass to come so early! His frown deepened as the wagon neared. McHeath's horse and cart from the tavern. Ketch had returned from there an hour earlier with two barrels of ale and a keg of whiskey. Who could this be?

Carlton squinted. He recognized the brown-headed individual beside the driver. A bit broader in the shoulders and a countenance more assured, but it was he. How could his brother, Alden, be arriving so soon? He'd sent Ketch with the letter to Mr. Talbot just hours ago. It had to be lying on McHeath's bar still. He hustled onto the veranda and down the steps as the wagon pulled up.

Wilbur was already there, weeping. "Mr. Alden, how you know to come? It's God's blessin' you here."

Carlton ran past the old man and grabbed his brother's arm, pulling him from the wagon. Alden had grown an inch or two taller than he. "You're here."

Alden's blue eyes were awash in tears. "They told me at the tavern as soon as I stepped from the stage. It was last night?"

He nodded.

"A few hours. Couldn't Father have held on a few more hours? What happened?"

Carlton's stomach twinged at his suspicions about his father's demise. "He's been getting feeble, yet it was sudden. His heart gave out."

Wilbur was wringing his hands. "He with Jesus now."

After dismissing the driver with some coins, Alden embraced the old retainer. "What'll we do without him, Wilbur?"

"I don't know, suh. I sure don't. I'd best tell yo' mama you here."

While Wilbur mounted the veranda's steps, Alden followed until, in despair, he dropped onto them about halfway up. He looked at Carlton. "I don't know whether to curse God or to praise him."

"What?"

Tears spilled. "What I had to tell Father would have broken his heart in any event. At least he was spared that."

"Alden!" Their mother loomed above them from the top step. Her thin, grating voice pierced Carlton's chest. "Whatever is this about? Tell me this instant!"

Face drawn, Alden reached inside his coat. He handed a letter to Carlton, who broke the seal and opened it, then read aloud.

"My dear Mr. de Barnefort, it is with great disappointment I release forthwith your son from my tutelage. While his intellect is sharp, it is wasted by trifling with undesirables who truck in rebellion. I can no longer devote my energies to one who will eventually swing from the gallows for treason against our King. You have my sincerest condolences. Mr. Abel Talbot, Esquire."

Chapter Four

Carlton's stomach churned as his mother tramped down the steps and hovered over his brother. "What is the meaning of this?"

Alden looked up at her with red-rimmed eyes. "Hello, Mother. I've missed you, too." He sighed. "The letter speaks for itself. I stood beneath the Liberty Tree and listened to the Patriots seeking freedom. I'm not ashamed of it."

"Liberty Tree?" Anne de Barnefort slapped her son's face hard enough to rattle his head. "You selfish ingrate! Word of your treachery will be all over Charles Town to say nothing of Orangeburgh District. You disgrace me, your brother, and the name of your dear father!"

Carlton's jaw dropped. Should he step in? Say anything?

Alden's cheek burned scarlet from his mother's blow. He stood, his sad eyes hardening, and spoke as though chastising a headstrong child. "You know little of what you speak. When Father came to the city, many times we found each other beneath that same tree."

Their mother grabbed the lapels of his coat. "Liar!"

Carlton woke from his stupor and bounded up the steps. He pulled the outraged woman off his brother, who stood stoically by. "Come now, Mother. You need a little lie down. Don't let anyone see you like this."

As he wrestled his mother into the house, Carlton glanced at Alden with raised eyebrows, who nodded in response. They would talk in private later.

✦

Despite the pall over every servant of Kilkenny, the mid-morning's spring air held the aroma of new life. With the sheep tended and grazing peacefully, Joe Dillon sank to the ground and rested his back against a tree. Despite the birds' lyrical songs, his chest ached with the loss of Mr. Tom. A decent man who treated Joe not so much as an equal, but with respect.

Life was strange. First, they learned of the death of Sir Richard Lynche, an old enemy. Now Mr. Tom, a treasured friend, had gone the way of all flesh. Joe sensed the end of a season, or something like it, in his life. The old ones were no more. What would come with the new?

Thunder ambled over to join Joe in a well-deserved break. With Ketch helping to ready the house for guests, Thunder and Joe picked up extra chores.

Remembering Nan's comparison of them, Joe smiled to himself. "Yer strong, Joe," she'd said. "Lean and ropy. But Thunder is a strapping man, with muscles aching to burst from his skin."

While there was no doubt the African was robust and hard-working, Joe appreciated his quick mind. The two had spent many hours discussing the ways of the world. When the younger man dropped to the ground beside him, Joe noticed his furrowed brow and tightly pressed lips.

"A sad day for us," Joe said, "with the loss of Mr. Tom."

Thunder glared at Joe with unusual intensity. "You are my brother. I tell only you what I feel."

Surprised, Joe nodded.

"How will I work for a man like Carlton? You know what he done."

Joe's heart ached at the agony in his friend's eyes. "'Twas long ago. He was young and stupid. Ye must put it aside."

"I cannot. To look at him, I see only Minda's bright face." He closed his eyes. "I want to tear his throat."

Joe considered placing a hand on Thunder's shoulder but dared not. Anger bristled from every fiber. It had been six years since a drunken Carlton had ravaged Minda, the sweet lass Thunder had set his sights upon.

He remembered how Thunder and Minda lit up at the sight of one another. The giggling couple warmed the hearts of all the servants as a daily reminder of young love's glory. Until Carlton was seen one night, staggering from Minda's cabin.

The young girl became sullen and aloof. It was no secret what had happened, but the servants could do and say nothing. Mr. Tom punished Carlton, but what good did it do? A swelling belly replaced the glow on Minda's face.

Thunder was beside himself. A man gelded, Joe had thought. Things could not be worse. Yet, that was not to be true. Nine months later, little Oscar was born, ripping his mother asunder. Minda did not survive. Nor did a huge part of Thunder. Only his anger and hatred thrived.

"Allah commands dat I turn from de ignorant. I must forgive, but I am weak. If I stay, I will kill him."

Despite his own life spent avoiding violence toward man and beast, Joe sympathized with his friend's lust for revenge. The outcome, though, would be more than vengeance. It was Thunder's own death wish, for there was no other possible result.

The African's jaw clenched. "Mr. Tom, he keep me away from dis pig, but now I must look at his face. Every day. My wish for killing does not fade; it grows stronger."

Joe rose to his knees and grasped Thunder's shoulders. "Ye'll think these things no more, do ye hear? Ye'll have no dealings with Mr. Carlton. I'll... I'll see to him meself. Ye have me word."

Joe saw a flicker of hope in the young man's eyes. Or did he just wish for it?

Interrupted by the sound of swishing grass, Joe looked up to find Ketch approaching.

The surly slave stopped before them, arms folded. "I shoulda knowed the two of ya'd be shirkin'." He glared at Thunder. "Young Master Carlton be needin' ya back at the house. He ain't gonna put up with yo long face neither, boy. It's a new day now."

Once Thunder bowed up at him, Ketch scuttled back toward the Big House. Joe scowled. So, it was "Master Carlton" now, with Ketch already licking his feet. No doubt it was a new day.

☦

Arms crossed, Anne glared at her son from where he'd placed her—on her bed. "Carlton, I am a grown woman. You'll not toss me aside like old, useless baggage."

"Mother, there's no need for crudity." He knelt before her and took her hand. "You are distressed and there's much to be done. Allow me to do what you've always claimed I am suited to do—run this farm with firmness and competence." His brows lifted. "Or had you meant to run it in my stead?"

Anne stared into his eyes, but could not determine if he was teasing or, in truth, probing her intentions. If she hoped for any control at all, she must reassure Carlton. She squeezed his hand. "Of course, you know best. It's been a trying night."

He stood. "Thank you, Mother."

As he was departing, Anne called out, "Send Becca to me. Or at least Little Oscar."

Carlton put his finger to his lips. "Rest, Mother."

What did that mean? Would he send for her maid or not? She knew Becca was with Wilbur, preparing the armbands and black knots for any mourners who arrived. Who would that be? It was hard to tell friend from foe in these troubled times, especially since Thomas never took a firm stand in support of King George. The blasted shilly-shally! He demanded only to be left in peace. Now Alden proclaimed Thomas had consorted with traitors in Charles Town. How many had spotted him under the Tree of Treason, as she considered it?

Anne glared at the mourning gown Becca had earlier draped over her settee. Black, her most despised color. It paled her so, she'd be wearing her own deathly pall. And knowing this, Thomas instructed she and no one else was to wear it. Clearly, he'd derived great pleasure from composing those funeral instructions, laughing at how miserable she'd be in the woolen weeds. A year and six weeks was considered proper, but what did they know of proper in the wilds of Orangeburgh District?

Her muscles relaxed. Maybe she would sleep after all. In the very spot Thomas had expired only hours ago. As her eyelids lowered, her lips curved in satisfaction.

☦

"Lady Anne." A gentle touch on her shoulder. "Lady Anne!"

Anne opened her eyes to find Carlton's betrothed, Rosabel Gatch, looming above her. Once Rosabel saw she was awake, the girl dragged a wooden chair to the bed and sat with hands folded as though in prayer.

"Oh, my poor Lady Anne," she whimpered. "My heart is heavy with sorrow. Dear Mr. Thomas is gone. I can only imagine your heartbreak."

Anne clamped her eyes shut and willed her soon-to-be daughter-in-law away. Instead, the round-faced girl with porcelain skin grasped her hand and pulled it to her cheek.

"I am here for you, Mother. May I call you Mother?"

That this witless creature call her Mother was, itself, penance enough for all her sins. Opening her eyes once again, her mouth stretched into what she hoped was a smile. "Of course, my dear. But do let me up."

Rosabel stood. She clutched Anne as though she were too feeble to rise on her own. The shaft of sunlight pouring through the window indicated it was midday. Anne had slept three hours, at least.

"Who's brought you here?" she asked the younger woman. "Isn't your mother still off visiting her sister?"

"Yes. I am with my father who is downstairs speaking with Mr. Odom. Mrs. Odom is abed with some unknown ailment." Rosabel whispered. "It's the grief, some say, since her boy was kicked in the head by their mule. I'm sure it's a sin to say, but he should do his mother a kindness and depart to the other side. He's been insensible for five months now."

"Sara's always been a bit of a hysteric. Bring me my dress, Rosabel."

The girl scampered to obey and served her as a lady's maid would. The lass might not be as objectionable as Anne had thought.

"What of Carlton?"

"I've not seen him, Lady—Mother. He was already tucked away in Mr. Thomas's study when I arrived. Wilbur is not to disturb him for any reason."

"What in the name of all that's holy?" Anne moved to her toilette table. "See what you can do with my hair. I cannot abide my wig today."

With widened eyes, the little fool poked about Anne's hair.

Anne snatched the brush. "God's bones, Rosabel." She completed the grooming on her own before the two descended the staircase.

✚

In his father's book-lined study, Carlton stood behind the desk and watched his brother pace.

"He was in her bed?" Alden asked. "How long had that been going on?"

"It hadn't." Carlton's stomach twisted, fearful of where this conversation could lead.

Alden stopped and peered at him with head atilt. "So, after years of barely civil discourse between the two, Father and Mother lie beside each other out of the blue, and his heart ceases to beat. It just quits?"

"It would seem so." Carlton picked up his father's will, desperate to change the subject. "I have ordered—"

"What does Mother say about it?"

Carlton squirmed. She said she saved me, he recalled, from Father's whims and from your interference.

The heat rose in his neck. "Oddly enough, Alden, I hesitated to ask her what she and her husband found to do in their marriage bed. After all, he'd only moments before departed for the World Beyond as he lay in her arms."

Alden collapsed into an upholstered chair. "Something's amiss. I don't trust the old harpy."

Carlton slammed the paper onto the desktop. "She's our mother! Have some decency about you. Perhaps Talbot's right about your association with ruffians." Truth be told, if he knew all, Alden would trust her even less.

A tear rolled down Alden's cheek. "I wish Father were here. I could explain everything to him face-to-face. I rehearsed my defense on the stagecoach the past two days, all for naught." He rubbed his eyes. "I feel so empty. I don't know what to do."

"I know." Carlton realized he could make Kilkenny Plantation the greatest farm in the colony of South Carolina, but without his father to witness his success, it would be forever diminished.

Damn you, Mother.

With no evidence with which to lay such blame upon his mother, in his bones, Carlton held her responsible for Father's death. Aloud, he rattled off the provisions in the will concerning the burial. Alden bobbed his head in consent to each arrangement, seeming too weary to care.

"Enough of this." Carlton set the will on the desk. "We should speak to our guests."

He strode across the hall to the parlor where Mother sat on the divan, the fawning Rosabel hovering behind her. Alden followed. Phineas Odom and Walter Gatch loomed over Father in his coffin beside the hearth, mumbling about heaven knew what.

He watched Phineas, then Walter touch his father's chest, as was the custom. Many in the backcountry believed when a murderer laid hands upon his victim, the corpse would bleed. This custom vindicated the neighbors of wrongdoing. Would Mother touch her poor husband? Carlton closed his eyes, wishing he could ban all such thoughts from his head.

Rosabel glanced up and scurried toward him, stopping short at the sight of Alden.

"Why, Alden, could it be you?" Her clear ivory cheeks reddened, creating small circles like a china doll. She lowered her head and peeked from under her lashes. "You've grown up. I hardly recognized you."

Carlton was stunned when she ignored him and stepped toward Alden with her hand held out. "My poor dear, I am so sorry about your father. He was the kindest of men."

Alden lifted her hand to his lips. "Sweet sister, how we will miss him at Kilkenny."

Carlton growled. Both Alden and Rosabel turned toward him. Apparently remembering herself, his wife-to-be rushed to kiss his cheek.

"My dear Carlton, I'm here for you." The light seemed gone from her eyes.

He huffed as he took her hands in his. "Of course, you are. It's been quite difficult. For Mother, as well. Why don't you sit beside her while the men talk?"

Flustered, she glanced at Alden. "Yes, yes." She pattered across the room and dropped beside his mother, who was glowering on the couch.

Their older guest, Phineas Odom, turned to Alden. "How fortunate you've arrived at this moment. Thomas would be pleased to know you're here for your mother and brother."

Walter Gatch piped up. "How is that, Alden? General Clinton scare you off? I hear he's rib-roasting those rebels in Charles Town right nicely." He elbowed Odom in the side. "The sooner we get rid of Gadsden and the rest of them firebrands, the better we'll all be."

Carlton had crossed his arms and was nodding in agreement when he noticed the throbbing vein in Alden's neck.

His brother pulled himself upright. "Are you calling me a coward, sir?"

Gatch looked surprised, then his eyes narrowed. "You tell me, son. Am I?"

Carlton's heart raced as his mind floundered, struggling to know what to do. To his relief, Rosabel leapt from the couch and grabbed her father's arm. "Daddy, please! On such a day?"

Mother also sprang up. "Carlton! Alden! I need to lie down. Take me to my chamber." Both sons ran to support her and lead her from the room.

Carlton noticed the Dillon girls, eyes wide, standing in the doorway with their serving trays. The older one carried cups of ale and the younger, funeral cakes.

They rushed into the room with their trays. "Arval for your journey home?" Mary Edith asked.

Mounting the steps, he ground his teeth. Alden! The bastard had wasted no time in shaming the de Barnefort name. Without a doubt, word of this would spread through the village like smallpox.

Chapter Five

"Hush," Mary Edith hissed. "What if someone hears ya?"

Under Becca's direction, they had placed black crepe over the mirrors. Clocks were stopped and covered. Every inch was dusted and swept. When mourners began to arrive, the girls served them ale or whiskey, along with the freshly baked arval. Wilbur gave out the armbands and crepe knots he'd prepared. During a lull, the girls hid in the study to play their favorite game—spying on the gentry.

Baby's eyes lit up. "I can't help it, Mary Edith. Mr. Alden is so handsome." Giggling, she covered her mouth with her hand.

It'd been two years since Mr. Tom's younger son had been back at Kilkenny. Mary Edith remembered the skinny lad who left, but he'd returned a man.

"He's like the prince in a story." Baby grew serious. "He's ... noble."

At the sound of padding feet, Oscar toddled up to Baby. "Lady Anne said come."

She turned to Mary Edith. "You see about her."

Mary Edith wagged her head. "Oh no. She called for you, Baby. You're her favorite."

Oscar tugged on the girl's sleeve. "Now. She say now."

With a sigh, Baby handed her tray to her sister and trudged up the stairs behind Oscar.

Mary Edith returned both trays to the rear of the house, re-filling one with drinks and cakes. Back in the parlor, she found

Mr. Tom's sons alone, with no current visitors. She served each man another cup of McHeath's famous whiskey. Alden guzzled his, then snatched a second one.

"Come now," Carlton warned him. "We've a long day ahead."

Mary Edith resisted shaking her head in disgust. How many times had she heard Mr. Carlton stumbling by their cabin, sputtering and swearing? Once, he puked right outside their window, the stench causing Mary Edith's stomach to churn for the rest of the night.

Gazing toward the coffin before the hearth, she allowed her eyes to settle on the lifeless form of Mr. Tom, the closest to a grandfather she'd ever known. He often stopped to tousle her hair and slip each of the Dillon children a sweetmeat. After which, he'd pop one into his own mouth, touch each child on the nose, and say, "Our secret."

The memory tightened her chest. And to think what she'd learned of her actual grandfather. A villain, it seemed, compared to this kind man.

"Girl!" Mr. Carlton's voice called her back. "See to the guests."

She hustled to the door where Wilbur gave the tavern keeper and his wife their mourning gear. Mary Edith held up her tray. "A drink for you, then? A cake in memory of Mr. Tom?"

John McHeath, a short, dark man, snatched a mug of ale and strode into the parlor, calling out his condolences. In the foyer, Mrs. McHeath pressed her lips together as she stared at her wringing, gloved hands.

Wilbur spoke up. "Missus, the lady be restin' in her chamber. Mar' Edith, take her on up."

Mrs. McHeath lifted her head and smiled. Mary Edith warmed to her gentle, pale-blue eyes. "This way," she said.

At the door to Lady Anne's chamber, the girl stepped inside. The mistress sat ramrod straight in the bed, ordering Baby, "Right there, you numbskull. I saw it in that corner."

Baby was on her hands and knees under the chamber window, searching for something.

Mary Edith cleared her throat. "Mrs. McHeath to see you, ma'am."

Lady Anne slumped onto her pillow and lowered her eyelids. "See her in."

Mary Edith willed herself to stare ahead, loath to reveal her distaste for the woman in the bed. Stone-faced, she mumbled to Mrs. McHeath. "You can come in, missus."

The tavern keeper's wife froze to the spot. Mary Edith raised her eyebrows. "It's fine. Lady Anne will see you now."

Head down, Mrs. McHeath shuffled only inches into the room.

Lady Anne sighed. "I cannot see you. Come close to the bed."

The visitor did so but spoke in a whisper. "I offer my condolences to you and your sons. I do call upon the Almighty for Mr. Tom's everlasting peace."

The mistress of Kilkenny reached out her hand as though she were feeble. Mrs. McHeath grasped it within both of hers.

Lady Anne's voice trembled. "You pray for a man already in the sight of God. Lift your petitions for me, for I am filled with sorrow."

"Oh, yes!" cried the tavern keeper's wife. "My heart breaks for you."

Mary Edith felt her stony face melt into an expression of pure disgust, until she saw Lady Anne's hardened eyes catch hers.

"Why are you standing there, gawking? Get me a cup of tea, girl. And one for this woman."

The signal was given. The visitor could stay. Mary Edith dipped into the curtsy she was taught. "Yes, milady."

As she left, Baby was hauling the spindle-backed chair to the bedside for Mrs. McHeath, whose face lit at the offer. Descending the staircase, Mary Edith couldn't decide whether she pitied a shy, timid woman or was sickened by some groveling lickspittle.

Likewise, she could not abide her mistress' haughty airs. Perhaps the kindness of the man lying in his coffin made Lady Anne's behavior more intolerable. Nonetheless, she had to keep her feelings to herself.

Remembering Lady Anne's expression when she'd let down her guard, Mary Edith's stomach roiled. Had her face revealed the hatred she felt?

Dear God, she prayed, let Lady Anne forget what she seen.

It was late afternoon when Wilbur sent Mary Edith and Baby back to their cabin. He instructed them to be ready for Mr. Tom's burial shortly after dusk. Only family and servants would attend. A proper Christian funeral would be held the next time an itinerant preacher came through.

As they approached the quarters, Mary Edith said, "I'm gonna visit Mama Juba, Baby. Tell Mama I won't be long."

"You best not be late. You'll get a whipping for sure!"

"Don't you think I know that? Just tell her."

Mary Edith ducked through the door into the darkness of the old woman's cabin. Even though the sun had not set, Mama Juba kept her shutters closed. She sat on a wooden chair behind a table, clasping her stone amulet. Smoke rose from a small clay pot before her. The scent was familiar, but Mary Edith couldn't place it.

"What you burning, Mama Juba?"

"That's cinnamon, Mar' Edith. For to take my prayers straight to heaven."

Mary Edith sat on a small keg opposite her. She inhaled the spicy aroma of the curling smoke. Maybe it would take her prayer about Lady Anne to God. She fixed her eyes on the smooth stone Mama Juba held. It had a cross scratched into it with a rusty nail. The old healer had fastened the amulet around her neck with a leather strip threaded into a bored hole.

She'd once explained to Mary Edith, "It keep me safe and ward off all bad fortune."

Mary Edith watched the healer's lips move. "What you praying for today?"

"The spirits, they skittish, Mar' Edith. I ask them to protect all us here on K'Kenny. I ask safe passage for Mr. Tom." She let go of the amulet and picked up a segment of a clay pipe's stem from the table. She twisted it in her gnarly hand.

Mary Edith shifted on her seat. "Why you got that old pipe piece?"

"For the burial. After the white people done preachin' and prayin', and the box put in the hole, they'll each throw on a bit of dirt. Then, they go back to the Big House. That's when the real send-off starts. But you don't need to worry none about that. You'll head home like the white folk."

"How come, Mama Juba? Is it bad?"

"Bad? Lawd, no. It's fine, real fine. Just too raucous for white people."

"Tell me," Mary Edith begged.

"Well, once the family's gone, Amos and Hercules'll get their drums. Ida and Lydia will shake the rattles, them ones they made from gourds. All this while Thunder shovels the dirt atop Mr. Tom."

Mary Edith shivered to think of the dirt smothering their old master. Tears threatened to fill her eyes.

"Once that done, each one gonna put somethin' on his grave, somethin' he might need. A bit of food, small jug of wine. He love that wine, don't he?" She grew quiet for a minute or two. "This here pipe stem, that's what I'll put on the mound. He enjoyed a good pipeful, too. Um hm, I believe he'll like that."

"I don't have nothing, Mama Juba. What should I put on his grave?"

"I can't tell ya that, chile. You gotta figure that for yoself." She set the pipe stem back on the table. "Next, come the dancin' for Mr. Tom's homegoin'. We dance 'til we too tired to dance no mo'. Then home we go."

Mary Edith's heart filled with sorrow. She leapt up, ran around the table, and into Mama Juba's soft arms. She had not yet cried, but now tears flowed. "I can't believe he's gone. He treated us so kind. Who's left to sneak us a lemon stick now?"

"He ain't gone. He crossed over, but his spirit be around, helpin' us what's left on Earth. Ya ever see the sun flickerin' on the water?"

"Uh huh."

"That's him. And all the others who gone before, lettin' us know they ain't forgot about us." She pushed Mary Edith to her feet. The old woman's rough thumbs wiped her tears. "You git on, now, 'fore your mama loses that temper of hers."

Mary Edith kissed the healer's wrinkled cheek, only to realize it, too, was wet. "I love you, Mama Juba. Don't you never cross over."

"Chile, long o'long, short o'short, we all die." She shoved her away. "Go on."

Low clouds rolled in, creating breezes that cooled the now-darkened sky. Mary Edith sped home, knowing too well the tongue-blistering that awaited her.

Chapter Six

Distant thunder rumbled as Anne, her two sons on either side, approached the family plot. Two small graves lay in the clearing next to a small rill that emptied into Turkey Creek. A weight rested on Anne's chest. She remembered the little boy she'd lost at birth, and her only daughter, who'd struggled for three months before succumbing to the hostility of this world. Two more lost babes lay at the plantation her father-in-law owned at Georgetown.

She shivered at the gaping cavity awaiting Thomas's coffin. Hercules, too small a darky for such a name, led five other servants who served as pall bearers. Anne sighed as they approached the grave and lowered the black coffin into the even blacker hole. A current of icy air swirled about her. She drew her shawl close, aware of how fleeting the time until she made a similar journey.

Alden steadied her when Carlton released her arm to stand at the head of the grave. Rosabel stepped into his place with Walter Gatch behind her. All other attendees were servants. The moaning, the whimpering, the muddle of unwashed bodies began to suffocate Anne.

"Begin, Carlton," she snapped. "Begin this instant."

Even in the darkness, she saw him recoil at her words. He waved his hand, beckoning Jimmy to bring his lantern. Carlton opened the prayer book and began to read, "Man that is born of a woman hath but a short time to live and is full of misery.

He cometh up, and is cut down, like a flower; he fleeth as it were a shadow, and never continueth in one stay."

For no apparent reason, her heart pounded in her chest, drowning out the rest of Carlton's words. She found it difficult to breathe. Time raced until Alden's voice snapped her back to the present.

"Mother?"

All had stopped and were waiting for Anne. "Of course," she mumbled and took the few steps to the dirt pile. Lifting the least she could get away with, she flung rust-colored clods atop the coffin. As Alden and the Gatches followed suit, Carlton continued, "We therefore commit his body to the ground; earth to earth, ashes to ashes, dust to dust; in sure and certain hope of the Resurrection to eternal life."

Once the prayers ended, Carlton closed his book, picked up a handful of soil, and sprinkled it atop the grave. "Goodbye, my dear father," he said, his voice cracking. "You will be forever missed."

Such sentimentality! And from Carlton, so like herself.

Alden then stepped to the top of the grave and cleared his throat. With neither book nor paper, he recited, "Cowards die many times before their deaths; The valiant never taste of death but once. Of all the wonders that I yet have heard, it seems to me most strange that men should fear; seeing that death, a necessary end, will come when it will come."

Carlton cocked his head to one side. "Julius Caesar?"

Alden nodded and returned to Anne's side.

It occurred to Anne that she, too, must speak. "Am I, his wife over three decades, to have nothing to say?"

Rumbling thunder preceded a nearby flash of lightning. Drizzling rain dotted her face.

Alden leaned closer. "Certainly, Mother, but say it quickly."

"Becca, where is that umbrella I told you to bring?" Anne had purchased the unusual item years before in a small Parisian shop. Her maid snatched it from young Mellie and ran it to her mistress. Anne opened the umbrella and thrust it toward Thunder.

"You there, African. Hold this over my head as I speak to my husband." Anne looked to her sons in turn. "In private. All of you, stand away. Out of earshot. This is between my beloved and myself."

Once the others were far enough removed, Anne took a deep breath, then another. "Well, Thomas. It's come at last to this. It pains me to think of our beginnings. Remember the gala at Garvanlea? I'd hoped to catch the eye of your brother, Jonathan. Did I never tell you that? Yes, it was Jonathan I'd hoped to wed, for he was the eldest and heir, after all."

Hopefully, Thomas writhed within the pine box at that revelation. "But Jonathan barely glanced my way while you, Thomas, lit up at the sight of me. A fairy tale of a romance, really. All you lacked was a title.

"Your father and I determined we'd see to that. You could have been Duncullen's ideal lord, you know. Noble, stately, with your innate talent for agriculture. But you would have none of it. As always, you thought only of yourself."

The rain picked up, and she tightened her shawl around her shoulders. "We were right about Richard. He was unfit. Surely you can see that now. He died a raving lunatic who belonged in an asylum, not the Irish Parliament!"

She sighed. "Instead, you cast me as the villain in Richard's story. How I suffered when your eyes no longer gleamed in my presence. Yet, that was not the worst. You became a tyrant, forcing me to come to America or face the disgrace of a deserted woman. I have not forgiven you. Nor will I.

"First, it was the disease-ridden rice paddies of Georgetown. Two of my babies withered and died there. I blame you and always will." She waved her hand, indicating the surrounding land. "But to drag me to this godforsaken wilderness, away from any semblance of society, was the straw that broke the mare's back. I despise you, Thomas. You destroyed my hopes and dreams—my very life. I would not let you destroy Carlton's."

Clenching her fists, she spoke through gritted teeth. "I did the right thing. Your association with traitors in Charles Town proves it. You were determined to destroy this family. You should've known I'd never allow it. To save the name of de Barnefort for Carlton, you had to die. So burn, Thomas. Fuel a fiery blaze 'til the end of eternity!"

φ

Thunder's heart hammered as the old crone wiped water dripping from her chin. These were not tears. As the storm strengthened, raindrops had blown onto her cheeks and rolled along the deeply etched lines leading from her flared nostrils to her thin, downturned lips.

It was her words that stole his breath. She killed him. This wicked woman killed Mr. Tom, her own husband. Thunder realized she was not aware he understood English, explaining why he was the only person to witness this confession. True, he'd known not a word when he'd arrived a dozen years earlier, but had it not occurred to the hag he was capable of learning?

His heart pounded. If she ever guessed he grasped every bit, what might she do to him, a mere slave? A woman who so calmly killed the father of her children. He yearned to flee from this cold-hearted murderer but hid his fears behind a frozen face. Crashing into his thoughts, Carlton's voice made him jump.

"Mother! It's pouring now. We must go inside before all of us become bedridden with fever."

Thunder watched in awe as Miss Anne transformed her face from evil killer to forlorn widow. She was the devil.

Lightning sizzled across the blackened sky. The woman turned to the others. "Alden, retrieve the umbrella from this ape. My grief is such that I must take to my bed immediately."

Once the family was near the house, Thunder emptied his lungs of air. While the other slaves prepared for their part in Mr. Tom's burial, the African stole away to his cabin. He had much to ponder this night.

♰

Carlton followed the cacophony created by barking dogs and bawling calves separated from their bellowing mothers. For the first time in the fortnight since Father's death, he arrived on his favorite horse, Hector, at the cow pens. He found the manager and his cow-hunters branding the distressed calves in a split rail corral. A crude shack nearby served as shelter for the cattlemen.

As he trotted up to the fire, two of them slung a squirming brown and white newborn to the ground. Carlton shuddered at the red-hot iron K lying in the coals. Hopefully, it went unnoticed.

He remained mounted, which forced the slaves to look up to him. "A simple gesture," Phineas Odom had advised, "that reinforces their place in the world. And yours."

Father would dismount before speaking to the herders, or any servant. He believed in looking a man in the eye. Carlton pursed his lips. Fine for sharing cigars and brandy in a friend's parlor, but foolish when firmness is required. He straightened his shoulders and lifted his chin. "Geoffrey, how many new ones this spring?"

The old cow pen manager stood from beside the bawling calf, swiping his ragged hat from his head. Of course, Carlton would have to replace him. Walter Gatch mentioned a white man was preferred for such a position.

"Hard to say for certain, suh. So far, look like ninety. Maybe more. Jimmy be beatin' the bushes for stragglers."

Carlton nodded. The cattle were free range by day, herded back inside the pens at night. "That's quite good. Once the branding is done, we'll want more open land for grazing. You and the boys burn off a couple acres by the southwest creek. I plan to expand our herd." He frowned and deepened his voice. "Do you understand?"

Geoffrey nodded. "I do, suh. We can do that in a few days. We sure can."

One of the herders stood beside the manager, glancing up, then casting his eyes down. The other pair knelt on the ground, pinning the calf that would soon wear Kilkenny's mark. None of them seemed to know where to look as they waited for their master to speak.

Good, Carlton thought. Mr. Odom had instructed him to keep them a little unsure and on edge. Unfortunately, he could think of nothing more to say. "Carry on," he barked before turning Hector toward the Big House.

He was determined to follow the advice of Mr. Odom and Walter Gatch, whom he now considered peers. Each had stopped by to instruct him on the proper handling of servants. Something he did not learn from his own father. They warned him of impudence, which was likely after the way Father had spoiled them.

"Don't hesitate a minute!" Walter had told him. "The first sign, put 'em to the whip 'til they know how to treat a white man. If not, you mark my words, you'll have trouble all your days."

Carlton carried his crop at the ready, but thus far had found no insolence at all. It worried him. What if he were incapable of recognizing it? He'd be a laughingstock, no better than his father.

However, the changes he'd made since Thomas's death reassured him. Aside from added pastureland, he'd instructed they clear land for indigo, a solid cash crop. Father had refused to grow it, claiming it diminished the quality of the soil. Carlton was skeptical. He planned to cut cedar trees for shingles. They could be marketed through Charles Town once the present difficulties were resolved.

Carlton inhaled the warmth and freshness of the spring air. It had always been his favorite season and this day exemplified its beauty. Pale green bundles of new growth, soft breezes, and colorful wildflowers spread their sweet fragrance. Even the calves proclaimed a new start.

Carlton's foresight would make Kilkenny the greatest plantation in the backcountry. This ludicrous rebellion could not last much longer. Indigo, beef, shingles. Trade would increase, and he would be at the forefront of financial expansion.

Reports asserted the British siege was tightening. They were close to reclaiming Charles Town from the traitors. Word had come that the king's ships had overwhelmed and destroyed Commodore Whipple's inadequate fleet. Touted as equal in naval warfare to Britain's greatest admirals, Whipple had lost every ship in his flotilla. He now rotted in a prison hulk.

British General Sir Henry Clinton had offered terms to the rebels' so-called general, Ben Lincoln, who'd refused them.

The full power of the greatest army would shortly bring the city to its knees.

Carlton sighed. If but that were his only concern. Mother rambled about the title King George would bestow upon him once this insurgency was squashed. Carlton feared for her mental faculties. Nobility hadn't existed in South Carolina since the Crown bought out the Lords Proprietors fifty years before. The prattle she'd spoken all his life now took a more ominous tone. Was this the foolishness his father died for? He could barely look at "Lady" Anne.

Heading toward the stables, Carlton scowled at the sight of his brother reading a book in the gardens. Alden had made no move to re-establish his Charles Town connections, for obvious reasons. Yet, neither did he contribute to the workings of Kilkenny.

Carlton turned Hector into the barn's aisle and dismounted. Father's will stipulated a sum of money to be transferred to a bank for Alden's use. Yet, what bank was secure in these turbulent times? Spanish gold pistoles, Portuguese joes, as well as bills of credit for beef and wool had been set aside for Alden in a metal box. It lay beneath a pair of bricks in the study's hearth. Father had made a point of showing both his sons this hiding hole at the same time. He wanted to ensure they felt equal in his eyes.

Carlton's chest tightened. The sting of Mother's comments about his father's attachment to Alden returned. What was his brother up to, anyway? Both his new mentors, Odom and Gatch, had warned him of the danger his traitorous brother posed to his stature in the colony. But neither man displayed the hysterical vitriol of his mother.

"He's my son, but he's made his choices, Carlton. He will destroy us all! Ban him from Kilkenny. Disavow him firmly and in public. Each day here, he eats away at our prominence. I have risked too much."

Even the memory of her screeching chafed his eardrums. Her next words cut like a blade. "You're proving to be as weak as your father."

Carlton straightened his back, envisioning the noble image he likely bore as he strode across the courtyard. Alden was his brother, but his treasonous sympathies must be renounced. As the master of Kilkenny, he would see to it. Soon. He'd do it soon.

Chapter Seven

"I cannot denounce them, Carlton. Don't ask it of me."

Hands folded, Alden sat in the chair across from his brother, who was perched behind their father's desk. He remembered Thomas once telling him, "To my cousin, Richard, a man's desk represents the man. I wonder, at times, if that's so."

In this moment, Alden was sure Sir Richard was on the mark. Unreasonable as it was, the sight of Carlton so brazenly sitting in Father's place was an affront. Then the pompous request that he submit to Carlton's ethics—his fingers itched to curl into fists.

A cold draft caused him to shiver. He looked about the study for the source but found none.

Oddly, Carlton seemed unaffected. He leaned his elbows on the desktop, his head cocked in that condescending way of his. "These are dangerous games you play, brother, and it brings me no pleasure to say it. You and I were born in America, but we must never forget our loyalties are to the king."

Alden lifted his chin. "I've learned enough law to know our rights are flouted for England's own ends. What of the excesses we've suffered? Restrictions on where we can settle. Outlandish duties on—" He counted on his fingers. "—sugar, clothing, coffee, wine, paint, paper, and glass. To say nothing of tea!"

Carlton rose and stood beside the hearth. He lifted a pipe from the mantle—surely, it wasn't Father's—and began to pack it with a pungent tobacco. "You blame the king for measures put forth by his ministers? What would you have us do? Throw tea into the harbor like those barbarians in Boston? Better to be ruled by a monarch than a mob."

Alden bristled. "I will not sit by while our liberties are stripped from us. How much will you tolerate, Carlton? Will you sing 'God Save the King' as Lobsterbacks sit in that chair you vacated, their boots propped on the desk? Or will you wait until they slaughter your beloved beeves and sheep? Rip the turnips and sweet potatoes from our garden?"

Carlton lifted a straw from the mantle, held it against the coals below, and lit the pipe. Once kindled, he inhaled, then blew the sweet, smoky scent of their father. "And from what is it you demand liberty? A well-ordered society? Do you crave anarchy where any man may be dragged from his bed, then tarred and feathered for daring to defend the Mother Country?"

Alden stood, his nerves on edge. What was it? Nostalgia for Father or the way Carlton was usurping those mannerisms for himself? In either account, even to Alden, his own voice sounded frenetic. "Anarchy? Like the days before the Regulators? Where was your well-ordered society then? The royal government didn't give a fig's end what happened to the people in the backcountry."

Carlton's mouth twitched. "There are problems, yes. But the king will put things right. You must believe that."

Carlton's haughtiness was too much to stomach. But two could play that game. "You are aware there is no such thing as the divine right of kings, aren't you? The earliest kings were likely the slickest in a band of thieves. William the Conqueror was a bastard, for the love of God."

"What's that? Blathering from Thomas Paine's ludicrous pamphlet, *Common Sense*?" Sneering, Carlton plopped back into his perch behind the desk. "A more ill-named rag was never written. Good, at least, for wiping my arse."

"Think about it." Alden paced from window to bookcase and back again. "Charles I was a tyrant by anyone's measure. He was beheaded for the preservation of liberty, a more vital concept than any one man. Even you can grasp that."

The twitching of Carlton's mouth grew more pronounced. "And what a fine result we got from that. The infamous Oliver Cromwell, so heinous they dug up his grave to hang the corpse! Is that your solution? To take a bad situation and make it abhorrent?"

Alden's heart pounded. That twitching. As a boy, he took it as fair warning to retreat. But he was no longer a cowering child, and he would not back down. Hands propped on the desk, he leaned forward until their faces were inches apart. "That is all in the past. Today, King George is the tyrant. It is he we must defy!"

Carlton's face burned red as he sprang from his chair. It tumbled backward, crashing into a cedar chest. "That is treason, Alden! Treason! How dare you utter those words? Mother was right. You are determined to destroy us all."

"Mother said that?"

"Get the hell out of this house!" Carlton shouted. "Never come back. You're a traitor who will hang until you're dead, but you'll not take us down with you." He went to the hearth and pulled away the bricks, exposing Father's hidden box.

"I don't care about that money."

Carlton pulled the box from the hole and thrust it at Alden. "Shove it up your shithole, for all I care. Just get out!"

⚓

"Watch yerself." Nan's stern tone was belied by her smiling eyes. She couldn't mask her delight.

Baby Eveleen's waggish imitation of the so-called Lady Anne had everyone in the loom house cackling. Holding a freshly cleaned fleece over her chest like a quilt, she pursed her lips and lifted her chin to feign looking down her button nose. Joggling her finger toward the loom on the far wall, she said, "Right ov-ah there, you dim-witted ninny."

She pointed from one spot to another. "Not there! Over there. No, no, no! There. Why has the Almighty seen fit to surround me with such driveling imbeciles?"

Nan swelled with pride. Such a clever girl! Laughter sent tears down her cheeks. Mama Juba's chest bounced up and down. Mary Edith pressed her lips together, hoping to hold back her chuckles only to burst forth in a loud snort. This set the whole room giggling once again.

Baby continued. "What is it you say? My de-ah Carlton is coming to see me?" She then drooped her shoulders and put on a weak-eyed, pouty face. She lifted a limp, quavering hand. "My dah-ling son, my poor heart has been smashed to tiny bits. Yet, King George has sent not one word of comfort for my unending sorrow."

"What she think she see?" Mama Juba asked Baby when all got quiet. "When you runnin' after them haunts in her room."

"She claims there's mice, but there ain't none."

"Um hum. Sounds like them little shadows that swim around yo eyes when ya get to be an old granny like me. Some call 'em webs. Make ya think ya see things."

"Aye," Nan said. "Me friend, Old Will Bridge, used to claim his eyes played such tricks on him."

Baby leaned in close and whispered. "The old hag's got more webs in that big ol' head than her eyes."

When Nan reached over to pop Baby, she glimpsed Daniel and Little Oscar climbing the wooden steps into the clapboard shop. Large enough for the big loom and two spinning wheels, its loft held fleece, wool carded into rolags, and spun yarn.

"Hush now," Nan warned. "Small pitchers have wide ears." No one could trust five-year-olds to keep their own counsel. Everyone sobered.

"Come by Mama Juba, chillun." The old woman waved the lads over. "Help me tease out this fleece so these gals can get to cardin' it."

Mary Edith and Baby returned to combing the woolen fibers through nailed paddles, bundling it into rolags. Later, the untangled threads would easily spin into yarn. Nan carded high quality fleece with paddles of finer teeth. Her rolags would create a softer yarn for the family's use.

The finished bundles were tossed into large baskets woven by the women, whose skill had been passed down from Africa. Nan was in awe of such beauty and craftmanship. The cook, Ruth, had tried to teach Nan to weave the pine straw vessels, but hers looked no better than what Oscar might do. Perhaps she was too harsh with herself, but Nan didn't think so.

Her true talents lay with fleece. She'd been carding wool with her ma since a wee lass in Tipperary, and often claimed she'd go to her reward with paddles in her hands.

As the morning wore on, Baby left for the privy. In short order, she came flying into the loom house, breathless and wide-eyed. She struggled to speak. "Something...I don't know...something's happened."

Nan's heart pounded. Her paddles fell to her lap. "Well, what is it, lass? Spit it out."

"I stepped out the jacks when Becca run up, her eyes red and tears on her cheeks. She said them boys, Carlton and

Alden, was fighting. It was bad, she said. Furniture was crashing and they was screaming at each other."

"Mary, Joseph, and the wee babe." Nan rolled her eyes. "They act no better than sea-dogs on a shore leave bender."

"Becca told me Lady Anne just a-smiled during the ruckus. She said, ''Bout time Carlton run that boy off.' That's no way for a mama to talk about her son." Baby's eyes watered.

Mama Juba's brows drew together. "With Mr. Tom gone, I don't know what gonna become of us."

Baby sniffed. "When I was running back here, I heard the Big House door slam. Mr. Alden ran down them steps two at a time. A pack, he carried, and a box under his arm. I think a gun, too. He stamped over to the stables, not speaking to no one. I come back here as fast as I could go."

Hearing a horse's whinny, they scrambled to the door. Peering out, they watched Mr. Alden gallop past as though chased by the King of Hell himself, his hat pulled low over dangerous eyes. The items Baby described were strapped to his steed.

Mama Juba gripped her amulet as she shivered. "Evil's astir."

A gust of frigid air swept through the open door, causing them all to gasp. Heart thumping, Nan slammed the door against the swirling villainy surrounding them.

She wondered aloud, "What's to befall us?"

☥

The wind whipped Alden's tears across his cheeks and into his ears as he raced his roan, Enbarr, down the two-rutted road toward the village. Where he was headed, he couldn't say. His mind reeled with Carlton's words, his mother's scorn, and his father's absence.

Before reaching the McHeath's Tavern, Alden veered off the road toward White Oak Springs, where pure water bubbled beside Turkey Creek. He needed to clear his head, come up with a plan.

Dismounting, he tied Enbarr to a branch and removed a canteen from his pack. Before filling it, he set it on the damp ground and bent over the pool surrounding the spring. Overheated with emotion, he splashed cold water on his face until his passions cooled enough for rational thought.

Grabbing the canteen, he filled it, guzzled, and filled it again. His chest heaved as he sat on a nearby log. How had he come to this?

A month ago, he was reading law under the dotard, Talbot, dodging another upbraiding from the prig about sneaking off for a mug of ale with his mates. The British were closing in as the solicitor made plans to evacuate, as it turns out, without Alden. But he'd had a family and a home where he'd felt welcome and, for the most part, loved. Now he had nothing but a box of scrip and a shredded heart.

Truth be told, he'd known a showdown with Carlton was inevitable. It had been building for a fortnight. His brother's snide and venomous tone surprised him, nonetheless. Brothers argued and fought, didn't they, but they remained brothers. They stood beside each other against the world. Where was the loyalty to blood over—what? Politics, social standing, greed?

It was Mother, however, who'd hurt him most. They were not close, it was true. But he was sure, even when she didn't like him, that she loved him as a mother did her son. His heart clenched. How quickly she'd turned on him. He'd climbed the stairs to her chamber, mentally forming the argument he'd make after she insisted he stay and apologize to his older brother.

That insistence never came. She'd scowled and said, "You've chosen to lie with vermin. Did you think you were welcome to spread their stink here?" With that, she rolled to her right side where she'd no longer have to look at him.

His mouth had dropped as he searched for a response. Then, all the fight drained from his body, leaving him hollow. His father was dead, and his mother was casting him off.

Now, astride a log with no company save the humming insects and gurgling stream, it slammed him like a hammer on an anvil. He was an orphan now, with no family and no home. He dissolved into sobs.

Spent, he took several deep breaths before Enbarr began whinnying and pawing the ground. Alden sat up, alert to the sounds of two men, a mule, and perhaps a wagon as they approached. He inched toward his horse as soundlessly as he could. Reaching for his rifle, he glanced to find George Collins aiming his Carolina musket inches from Alden's head. George's grandfather emerged from the woods in a cart. Hands held open, Alden stepped away from his horse.

"Hold on there," the old man said. "That you, Alden de Barnefort?"

"It is, Mr. Collins. I have no quarrel with anyone."

The white-haired fellow bobbed his head. "Same as his pa, George." He addressed Alden. "A fine man, your pa. Knew when to step up and when to step back, like us Collins. We take no sides in this sorry war neither."

George lowered his gun and stretched his right hand toward Alden. "Meant no harm. Can't take chances these days."

Alden grasped the hand. "No offense taken. I was reaching for my own rifle." He smiled. "It's been a few years, George."

"We were real sorry to hear about Mr. Tom, weren't we, Grandpa?" He dipped his head toward Enbarr. "You heading back to Charles Town? Things are right testy down there."

Alden's body sagged with renewed sadness. "No. Not quite sure where I'm headed."

The two Collins looked at each other. "So, Carlton give you the boot," Old Mr. Collins said. "You ain't joining up with the rebels, is ya? It's looking bad for them boys."

George ran his hand over his jaw. "We come from McHeath's Tavern. Ben John and his gang are right keen after news brought in by the stage. Looks like some who was trying to bring supplies to General Lincoln in Charles Town was stopped cold at Biggin Creek Bridge. You know, down by Monck's Corner. Ferguson and his Loyalists caught the rebels by surprise. They lost a fair number of men, horses, and every bit of them supplies."

"Charles Town is cut off," Mr. Collins called from the cart. "I don't see no hope for them fellas now."

Alden hadn't thought he could feel any worse. "I have many friends there," he said.

"I'm sorry, son. It's all over but the praying, to hear Ben John and McHeath talk about it."

George jerked his head, indicating he and Alden should walk further down the path. "Grandpa," he called back, "how about you fill up our jugs whilst I talk with Alden here."

"Stay out of it, George. You promised."

"I know, Grandpa. I'll just be a minute." Once out of the old man's earshot, George stopped Alden. "I'm all he has left. He won't make it without me, being eighty-five years old."

Alden nodded.

George continued. "We heard talk of what happened with you in Charles Town. I can guess why you'd be heading off.

Best not go to McHeath's. They're drunk and fired up. Would love a good hanging if they could find the least excuse. And to them, you're looking pretty rope-ripe."

Alden swallowed. "I'd prefer to seek out like-minded people, but don't know who to trust anymore."

"I don't want Grandpa to know I have this information, but Tarlton Brown from Brier's Creek has rounded up some fellows. They're quartered at Cracker's Neck. You remember where that is?'

"By the river south of Silver Bluff."

"That's right. Give the tavern a wide berth. If you start now and ride fast, you can get there before dark. You can trust the folks nearby to guide you."

Alden placed his hand on George's shoulder. "You're a good man. May they cut out my tongue before I confess who sent me."

George lifted one side of his mouth in a grin of sorts. "Hopefully, that won't be necessary. But make no mistake. The dangers from man and beast are rife. I bid you Godspeed, Alden. May we meet again in peaceful circumstances."

Chapter Eight

Carlton's mouth twitched at the whining of his betrothed, Rosabel Gatch.

"But where will he go?" she whimpered. "It's been three days. Alden's the only brother you have. You cannot throw him out."

She'd started as soon as she stepped into the foyer with her father and Phineas Odom. Walter Gatch snickered. "Now, Rosabel. That's a matter between two men and no concern for your tender heart."

With his neighbors present, Carlton struggled to control his rage. "My dear, your worry for my brother appears unseemly to me. Are my own difficulties of no interest to you? It is I you are to marry, not my brother."

To his shock, Rosabel stuck out her chin. "Difficulties? You have a roof over your head."

The impertinent, mewling shrew! Every fiber of his body yearned to slap the insolence off her face.

Gatch's jaw dropped. "Rosabel! Your womanly passions have gotten the better of you. Go to the gardens and pray before you disgrace yourself further."

The girl burst into tears and scurried out the back door. Outraged, Carlton felt no sympathy for the harpy, only disgust.

Walter Gatch placed a hand on his shoulder. "You've no father left to help you with the ways of women, so I'll share a bit of advice. Now, Rosabel's a fine girl, but she gets her hackles up now and again. You gotta put your foot down. Don't let them tears sway you."

Little chance of that.

"Rosabel don't tend to need much scolding," her father went on. "You might need to cuff a more vigorous lass now and then, but a sharp word sets my Rosabel right."

Phineas Odom, who had stiffened and stepped away during the exchange, seemed to relax once the girl left their company. "Walter is correct, son. Their spirits rise with their blood. I've found they settle down upon the appearance of a new moon."

Carlton forced a smile onto his face, if for no other reason than to end this revolting conversation. He'd a lot to learn of the female mysteries, which he supposed he'd find equally distasteful, but he'd no stomach for it now.

Carlton stretched out his hand. "Shall we retire to the parlor? I've uncorked a bottle of Madeira in anticipation of your visit."

When all three men were served and seated, Phineas Odom raised his glass. "To your father, in whose honor we move forward with the strengthening of his legacy."

"Damn, Odom," Gatch said. "You can sure come up with some fancy words."

The older gentlemen sipped while Carlton drained, then refilled his glass. The wine's warmth surged through his body.

"First, some good news," Phineas Odom said. "We've found a capable man to serve as your overseer. He hasn't the experience we might have liked, but he understands the need for strong supervision among the lower races. He'll not back away from whatever situation arises."

"Who is it?" Carlton asked.

Gatch set down his glass. "You know John Reeve? He works at the mill a few miles down the road from Phineas."

"I can't say I do."

Walter Gatch leaned forward. "You know him! Comes into McHeath's Tavern from time to time. Short fella with eyes about sunk into his head."

"The boorish one with the broken nose?"

Phineas nodded. "He's opinionated but knows how to handle his underlings."

Carlton became uneasy. Reeve didn't last thirty minutes inside the tavern before he was reducing another man to pulp. What would Mother think? He hated the idea of Reeve skulking around his property, but what if he refused Odom and Gatch's offer? He'd appear no more stalwart than his father.

"Fine. Fine, then." He gulped another glass of wine, rose, and refilled each man's glass. When he returned to his chair, the unease had increased.

Odom rubbed his thumb over the rim of his glass. "We have, perhaps, a more important issue to broach." He looked to Gatch, whose nod suggested he continue. "I know you are aware that things are going our way in Charles Town."

Carlton brightened. "Yes. It won't be long before the world is put right again."

"Adzooks!" Gatch slapped his knee. "That young Brit, Banastre Tarleton, caught them rebels with their pants down. They're saying at McHeath's that the king's men found a darky skulking through the woods with a letter telling exactly where to find the rebel troops. Now, what half-wit gives a message like that to his slave? Might as well tie it around the neck of his hound dog."

Carlton smirked. "Wave a chicken leg in the air and all their spies come running."

Phineas Odom laughed. "Don't disparage the Patriots' stu-
pidity. It's like stashing a grenade inside each of their caps. It's
only a matter of time before they blow themselves to bits."

"With the rout at Monck's Corner," Carlton said, "Charles
Town is left without ammunition or food. We capture the city,
and the backcountry will rally behind the king."

"We can't count on that. There's work left to be done,"
Phineas said. "It's true, once Charles Town is defeated, the
British can run off every rebel in the colony, but not alone.
Now is the time for right-minded men to disinfect our land of
treasonous vermin."

Carlton's disquiet disappeared. His time had come. As
Mother claimed, his reward may be great.

"Your father chose to be neutral," Phineas Odom said. "That
was unfortunate. But in the meantime, those of us who believe
in our Motherland have sacrificed for the king. So far, we have
supported our Loyalist brothers with food, horses, arms. We
hope you will make similar offerings for the good of the land."

Here was his chance to atone for his father's negligence.
More than that, he could gain recognition for his dedication to
King George. Carlton pulled back his shoulders. "I leap at the
opportunity to contribute whatever I can."

"Bravo!" Odom called out, raising his glass in a salute.

Gatch leapt from his chair and slapped Carlton's back. "Well
done, lad!"

Awash in satisfaction, Carlton smiled, surer than ever his
time was upon him.

"When will you leave?" his future father-in-law asked.

"Leave? Where?"

Phineas Odom chuckled. "Why, to Charles Town, of course.
Major Patrick Ferguson is combing the colony for valiant

young men like yourself to drive the pestilence from our countryside."

Carlton's heart skipped a beat. "But...but, I can't leave Kilkenny. You want me to leave Mother alone, unprotected?"

Gatch stepped away from Carlton's chair. "Son, we got you a man to run things around here. A good man."

Panic flowed through his veins. "Good for keeping slaves in line, not protecting the honor of a fragile woman like my mother. It cannot be done."

Odom and Gatch glanced at each other. Odom said, "Your devotion to dear Miss Anne is commendable, but I believe she is stronger than you think."

"I am needed here. The militias need beef and wool. I cannot trust a hotheaded dolt who swills like a tinker to keep this homestead afloat."

"Come now, lad," Gatch said. "What man doesn't enjoy a nip of McHeath's whiskey, eh? You get a bit rammaged yourself now and then."

Carlton's fists clenched. "I will not forego my duties to my family. As you said, my father's memory and honor are at stake!"

Red-faced, Gatch waved his arms. "Bugger it, man! You've a duty to your country and you sit there whinging about your father's honor? I'm not sure you're man enough for my Rosabel."

Odom stood. Carlton did not miss his raised eyebrows directed at Walter. A warning?

"Whoa! Hold on, Gatch. You're too harsh with the lad. He's been through a lot since we lost dear Thomas and now, out of the blue, we've thrown this new responsibility at him." He turned to Carlton. "A bit of time to think?"

Feeling faint, Carlton latched onto this lifeline. "Yes. I must admit, my head is spinning. More time, certainly."

Gatch growled, but Odom held up a hand. "We'll leave you now, son, in the confidence you'll do the right thing—the manly thing."

Both men bowed—Gatch, reluctantly—and took their leave.

✦

Jimmy sat before the fire where he and the other cowhunters were brewing tea made from wild mint. He breathed in the spring air. Rain was on its way. The clopping of a horse's hooves turned his attention to the north where Master Carlton, as he was now to be called, arrived on ol' Hector.

About five yards away, the master pulled up on the reins, climbed off, and handed them to Amos. He pointed at the manager, Geoffrey, and beckoned him. The old fellow hoisted himself from the log beside the fire and hobbled behind the young, strutting Carlton to where no one could hear.

This didn't sit well with Jimmy nor the other cattlemen. They looked from one to the other, lines of concern carved into their faces. No one dared speak, not even a whisper. A good breeze had kicked up and sounds traveled far in these parts. They all knew, though, this couldn't be good. Mr. Alden had been gone about a week and things had been right tense on Kilkenny.

The young buckruh, as his kind called a white man, spoke to the manager about ten minutes before calling to Amos, "Bring my horse here."

Once Amos delivered the animal, their master swung his leg over Hector with great swagger. *He want all us to see what a dandy rider he be*, Jimmy thought.

But, of course, he said nothing. As Mr. Carlton rode off, he was more concerned with Geoffrey who ambled back and squatted before the others. Jimmy took note of his ashen face as he told them he wouldn't be the manager no more.

"Master Carlton done hired himself a white overseer—Mr. Johnny Reeve from over by Cooper's Bridge. He worked the mill down there."

Jimmy looked from one to the other. "Who that?"

"Lawd," said Solomon, "that rascal's no better than a slippery canebrake rattler."

Amos, who'd remained standing, took off his hat and ran his fingers through his hair. "They say it don't take much to vex that man. Heard tell he damn near killed a white fella by Craig's Pond. Didn't like the look on his face."

Geoffrey lifted his head. "I'll be the driver, still in charge of y'all and these here cattle, but this Mr. Johnny gonna be the overseer, watchin' out for all us workers. Us cow-hunters, Joe Dillon and Thunder, and Jasper with the hogs."

"What about Ketch?" Jimmy asked. All the cattlemen groaned at the mention of the foot-licker.

"Don't know," Geoffrey said. "Mr. –I mean Master Carlton ain't said nothin' about Ketch."

Hercules spit. "Aww, we'll be right. We keep goin' the way we been unless this Reeve fella sidles up. He can't be ev'rywhere at once. And if things happen that ain't to his likin', I say ev'ry sickness ain't for tellin' no doctor."

Geoffrey's face was grim. "Anything I see go wrong, be with the cattle or you fellas, I gots to tell. I don't, well, Mr. Carlton didn't say exactly, but I don't trust that scowl he wore one bit." He leaned in. "Between us, he scared. 'Fraid he can't run this place. I seen it in his eyes. And scared people, they get mean." He sighed. "Face it. Mr. Tom is gone and his like ain't never gonna be back again."

Chapter Nine

Mary Edith first heard the hysterics in Lady Anne's voice as she was cleaning the ashes from the parlor hearth. Her heart pounded. Baby Eveleen was attending the mistress in her chamber, and the rancor in that woman's tone was more poisonous than usual.

"How dare you insult me, you ill-bred measle!"

Baby's voice wobbled, thick with tears. "There ain't nothing, Lady Anne. Your eyes are tricking you. I swear it."

The wretched wail that followed left Mary Edith cold. She knew that cry. Baby was hurt. Against all good sense, she bounded up the stairs and barged into the mistress' chamber. Baby huddled in a ball at the foot of the bed. Above her, the red-faced woman plunged a two-pronged fork into her sister's back again and again as Baby shrieked in agony.

The old woman's arm was raised for another strike when Mary Edith rushed forward and grabbed her wrist, stopping her mid-jab. Baby crawled away while Mary Edith clenched the arm. Her grip tightened as her heartbeat thudded in her ears. What to do now?

Lady Anne's scarlet face puffed with rage. Veins throbbed within her crepey neck. "Release me this instant! I will have you beaten into a bloody puddle!"

The woman tried to purse her lips as though she wanted to spit on Mary Edith. Instead, her face contorted. Her mouth drooped. She tried to speak, but the sounds gushed out as though her tongue had fattened. Eyes shutting, Lady Anne tumbled backward to the floor, dragging Mary Edith on top of her.

Baby squatted by the window, bawling with barely a gulp of breath. Mary Edith released the withered arm and scrambled to her feet. She struggled to breathe. Her vision blurred, but she heard Wilbur and Becca shouting as they clambered up the stairs and entered the room.

"You killed her, Mary Edith. You killed her!" Baby was saying.

Becca rushed over and slapped her across the mouth. "Hush, ya little fool! She ain't dead."

It was true. Wilbur knelt beside their mistress whose chest was heaving. The old woman grunted and snorted, fighting to draw air into her lungs.

"Help me, Becca," Wilbur said. "You too, Mar' Edith. We need to get her onto the bed. Baby, hush your hollerin' and send Ketch for Master Carlton right away. You fetch yo mama."

Baby stood like a pale statue of herself.

"Git, girl!" Wilbur yelled. As she tore from the room, Mary Edith glimpsed bright red stains spreading through the back of her sister's shift.

Becca and Mary Edith stood on either side of Lady Anne. Wilbur moved toward her head. With every ounce of their strength, they lifted the dead weight onto the bed. Mary Edith stepped back and stared in horror. The grunting had stopped. Only the shallow movement of the mistress' chest showed any life at all.

What had she done?

✢

Nan cringed with Baby's every gasp. Soothing scents of plants and herbs hanging throughout Mama Juba's cabin did nothing to calm her this day. Baby was perched upon a stool with her back exposed, allowing the old healer to work her magic. A magic greatly needed.

Even in the dimness of the hut, Baby's wounds were angry, swollen pairs of holes scattered across her back. It sickened Nan to see her child's clear, soft skin marred in such a violent way. She wavered between breaking into sobs and plotting her revenge on a bedridden old hag, too cruel to deserve life.

Mama Juba placed senna leaves smeared with lard over each pit in Baby's skin. "Some of these holes be deeper than others. We gotta see how they do. Don't let no dirt get inside these marks, Baby."

The ten-year-old gasped in pain as another leaf was placed over her inflamed puncture. "I won't, Mama Juba."

Somehow, her daughter's determination to remain strong left Nan more heartsore than if she'd wailed. A child should not have to endure this.

"I don't know what get into that woman. She got some demons, for sure." Mama Juba sighed big. "Don't let no one say you nor Mar' Edith done this to her, chil'. That old woman done it to her own self."

Baby spoke in a small voice. "Is Mary Edith gonna get flogged, Ma? She was trying to save me."

Fury bubbled inside Nan. "Let 'em try to whip me child. I'll snatch that cat o' nine tails and turn it on any clod who risks it."

Mama Juba glared at Nan. "Another foolish white woman lettin' her blood get too high." She pointed to a pot cooling beside the fire. "You best drink some of this sassafras tea. You be needin' a good spring tonic to clean that blood of yours. You gonna get yoself kilt."

"We're neither slaves nor indentured. That she-devil does not own a-one of us Dillons. She'll soon learn what's coming to her if she hurts me young ones again."

Wilbur poked his head into the cabin door, his eyes revealing they'd seen too much. "How she be?"

Mama Juba added another greased leaf. "She gonna need to lay on her stomach for the rest of the day. Tomorrow, too. You see to it, Wilbur. They can't make this chil' work no mo' today."

He nodded as he climbed into the room and walked over to Baby. "I so sorry, Baby Eve." With tear-filled eyes, he petted her hair.

Baby looked up at the old man. "I'll be right, Wilbur. Don't worry none." She flinched as another leaf was laid.

Wilbur wiped a tear from his cheek. "Lawd, Lawd. This a sad day at K'kenny. Lady Anne been knocked insensible. She can't talk. She can't move herself. She can't even give herself a sip of water. I don't know how she even alive."

Nan hugged herself with her trembling hands. "What they saying about Mary Edith? They dast not blame her!"

"That's the curious thing," he said. "When Master Carlton get there, he just lookin' at his mama, head cocked to one side. He says she got herself siderated. 'What's that?' I ask him. 'Hit with the stroke of God,' he say. 'The stroke of justice.'"

Nan felt a part of her fear drain away. If the affliction came from God, surely Carlton would not punish Mary Edith.

"I ask him what that meant," Wilbur was saying. "He shake his head. 'Send someone for Silas O'Bannon. Tell him about the apoplexy. She need to be bled.' I sent Mar' Edith on that task. Got her out the Big House."

"That's why I make this sassafras tea. To clean out that woman's blood." Mama Juba clasped her amulet, as was her habit. "But I tell you all this. The devil is loose around K'Kenny. Evil is flyin' through the trees, in the windows and out the doors."

Nan shivered. In her soul, she knew the truth of the old conjurer's words.

Mama Juba stared at nothing and spoke as though the others weren't there. "We under a curse. Master Carlton know why these dark spirits be here, how his mama come to be struck down. That they seeped into her body, rose up her blood, troubled her heart. He know."

She blinked and looked from one to the other. "I got much work to do."

Nan stared at her daughter's back, now covered in senna leaves. In her mind's eyes, she still saw the girl's skin pocked with fierce, fiery holes. The vision of Baby's mutilation was burned into her eyes, and she would never un-see it.

✦

Carlton sat in the dining room, slurping his supper of catfish stew. It had been five hellish days since his mother had been struck with apoplexy. As a penance for her sins, she did not die, but had to be fed, clothed, and cleaned like an infant. Worse, she was mute. With no movement save the force of her grunts and wildness in her eyes, she was unable to express the intensity of her suffering. Everyone had to speculate on her wishes. But did he really care?

He was more concerned with the millstone her affliction had tied around his own neck.

Shoveling another spoonful into his mouth, Carlton's indifference toward his mother surprised him. Had it been months ago, would he have shown concern? He suspected so, but it was hard to say. Now, he saw only a self-serving shrew causing pain to all around her.

And the poor Dillon child! What kind of person stabbed a little girl, servant or no, with the prongs of a fork? It staggered the imagination. He'd struggled with the obligatory visit to the cabin, the child on her belly, covered with Mama Juba's remedy. Although he made no apology as such, he was at a disadvantage before Joe's understandable anger. Nan didn't hide her contempt, but what could he do? Tie her to the whipping post for insubordination? Even Walter Gatch had agreed such a display would cross a line.

Carlton looked up from his bowl to find Becca standing beside him. He ran his sleeve across his mouth. "What is it?"

"I sorry, suh," she said. "It's Lady Anne. She made a frightful mess in her bed and Wilbur and me be needin' ya to help us move her. So's we can clean her up."

He slammed his spoon onto the table. "Damnation! Can I not eat in peace?"

"I sorry, suh, I sure am. Me and Wilbur can't lift her."

He stood. "I am aware, Becca." He headed for his mother's chamber. Before he placed a foot on the first stair, her foul stench caused him to gag.

"Master Carlton, yo mama got the flux," Becca said.

Without responding, he started up the staircase. The entire floor reeked of her excrements. How was he to sleep? Though he knew it was unfair, a disgust for his mother permeated his body.

Entering her room, the woman he'd adored as a lad sat propped upon her pillow, her face sagging on one side. The bag under one eye was grotesquely elongated as her mouth stretched into a permanent scowl. Drool leaked from the corner of her lips. Seeing him, her eyes widened. While he'd tried to mask it, she'd noticed his repulsion.

At that, he'd felt a twinge of guilt, but it was short-lived. While he held his mother upright, the servants scrambled to disrobe, clean, and redress her. They stripped the bed, which was padded with cloths to protect the mattress, and replaced the linens. All the while, a rage bubbled inside Carlton like a pot of water on the verge of a rolling boil.

This could not go on!

Once he laid his mother upon her fresh sheets, he turned to the servants. "I refuse to live like this. Clear the library furniture and move Lady Anne to the first floor. I want her carried to the latrine behind the house from here on out."

Old Wilbur wrung his hands. "Master Carlton, I can't carry this poor lady and Becca can't neither."

"Damn you, then! Figure out a way!" He strode down the stairs and out to the stable. After ordering Ketch to ready his horse, he paced until the moment he could leap onto Hector and tear across the fields to McHeath's Tavern. It had been far too long.

⚘

Despite the lateness of the day, several horses were tied before McHeath's. The two-story wooden structure housed a tavern on the first floor, which served as a courtroom if the circuit judge came through. John and Catherine McHeath lived in quarters on the second floor. Also above the bar, a large room with eight straw pallets was available for any travelers who stayed the night.

Carlton climbed the three steps to a porch and headed into the bar. All heads turned. Ben John, a ruffian to be sure, but a Loyalist nonetheless, called out, "What have we here? The prodigal son? Come back to join the pigs for one more wallow in the mud."

Five or six of his compatriots burst into laughter. Carlton's face burned. Matt Birch attempted a proper bow, with his left leg stretched before him and the wave of an arm. The rest of the boors mimicked Matt, tripping up two of them and renewing the uproar. Carlton bit his lip, fighting to control his temper.

John McHeath's eyebrows rose and he called to the fellows, "A little respect, now. The lad's lost his father."

Ben John held up his wooden cup. "A toast, then, to Carlton's good fortune!"

Grunts, raised mugs, and slurps followed.

Carlton thought his head would explode. "Up your arses, you goddamned lobcocks!"

A gangly fellow named Elijah frowned. "Ye ain't done nothing but snivel and moan about the man since I known ye."

"And with your pea-brain, you conjured up the idea I wanted him dead? Bloody ignoramus!" He searched the room for something to beat the man with.

"Now, now," McHeath called out. "These boys are cracking on you, Mr. Carlton. Don't take nothing they say too serious." He scowled at the mob, daring them to say another word. "This man's grieving."

Carlton's fists opened and closed. The men grumbled but turned back to their drinks.

McHeath brought him a pewter mug of rye whiskey and led him to the rocker before the hearth. "Sit here, Mr. Carlton. They won't bother you no more."

His hand shook as he took the cup from McHeath. Taking a long swig, he turned from the others to stare into the fire. The prodigal son. How many times had he bolted from the plantation—and his father—to this very tavern? He'd considered himself a man, independent of his father's judgments and expectations. This mob who now mocked him had embraced him as one of them.

Or had they? Did they embrace him only to laugh or scorn once out of earshot? His stomach twisted. Instead of a man, he'd been a fool amongst fools. It sickened him.

He no longer belonged here. His grog could be ordered from McHeath and delivered to his home, but to rub elbows with this raff was beneath him now. Even they seemed to know it and had distanced themselves instinctively.

An overwhelming loneliness engulfed Carlton. Who was to be his friend? There was nobody. Not a one. A shroud of sorrow surrounded him. After draining his mug of whiskey, Carlton banged the vessel on the arm of his chair. "McHeath! Will you leave me dry over here?"

The tavern keeper scuttled to him with a jug and filled the cup to its brim.

Carlton nodded and took another large swig. The harsh, yet restorative fluid splashed into his stomach, then spread its warmth throughout his body. An outburst from Matt Birch startled him from his reverie.

"One more round, McHeath, for the heroes standing before you!"

The band of Tories held out their mugs to be filled.

McHeath scowled. "I've spotted you four rounds for your bravery. You took revenge on two scoundrels, to be sure, but the fifth drink you buy for yourselves."

The men scoffed and jeered. Elijah lifted his haunch and farted toward the barkeeper.

"One for Ben, at least," Matt demanded. "We rounded up the rebels who tormented sweet Lauren DeLoach. Elijah and Davey stripped them naked and tied them to the branch of an old oak down by the Lower Three Runs."

McHeath rolled his eyes. "So you said—a dozen times now."

Carlton mentally urged the story on. Which rebels did they string up?

Elijah pointed to his chum. "And you know how good Davey is with a bullwhip. He only had to hold it up before Wyman Heape started blubbering."

Davey lifted one side of his mouth in a smirk more than a smile. "That don't stop me none. It proves they's the no-good cowardly scum we thought they was. Forty lashes, I give each of 'em, well laid on."

Forty? Carlton's father had never allowed more than ten. He could only imagine the raw, bloody backs of those lads. Wyman was only sixteen. The other fellow must have been Luke Farrell. He'd never seen one without the other.

Matt slapped Ben John on the back. The leader smiled, exposing a number of missing teeth.

"But that weren't nothing," Matt said. "Just as we was about to leave, old Ben here pulled out his flintlock pistol and shot them both in the head. Bam! Bam!"

Carlton started at the violence of the words, his heart skipping a beat.

Elijah nodded his head in Carlton's direction and laughed. "That'll teach any other fools who want to mess with a fine Tory woman with four young'uns." He spoke to Carlton. "They took all her furniture, stripped the beds, pilfered everything—leaving the little ones without a stitch of clothes. Even Lauren herself had no more than a shift to wear."

They all looked to Carlton for his reaction. His heart pounded.

"The bastards—they got what they deserved." He nodded to McHeath. "The next round is on me."

A roar arose as they lifted their soon-to-be-filled mugs toward him in a salute. Carlton returned the gesture with his own cup, drained it, and took his leave.

As Hector carried his master homeward, Carlton knew. He was not born with a warrior's heart. Any form of military service would be disastrous. But how could he avoid it?

Chapter Ten

Just past dusk, Thunder headed back to his cabin from the privy. Only a few in the quarters remained outside. Darkness fell quickly once the sun slid behind the trees.

He heard the clopping of horse's hooves. Carlton was returning from the tavern early. Thunder took larger strides, hoping to avoid any chance encounter with the yellow dog. Joe Dillon had been true to his word, stepping between him and Carlton whenever their new master approached. Not once had he been forced to speak to the man he despised.

Carlton slowed his horse as he approached. He looked Thunder's way and, without warning, yanked on Hector's reins, stopping right in front of him.

"You there, African."

Heat rose from Thunder's neck to the crown of his head. There was no escape. He dropped his eyes. "Master Carlton, suh."

The man dismounted and wiped his mouth with his sleeve. His speech was slurred. "The answer to my problem is standing right in front of me." The devil poked his finger on Thunder's chest. "Why didn't I think of this before?"

Thunder's jaw tightened. "I do not know, suh."

"Starting tomorrow, you will no longer work with the sheep. I want you in the stables, close to the Big House."

His throat closed, making it difficult to swallow. He struggled to take in a breath. Living closer to Carlton and his murdering hellcat of a mother would undo him, he was sure.

"You will be ready whenever Wilbur or Becca calls." More poking. "Lady Anne must be carried to the latrine, and you're the one strong enough to do it."

His voice croaked. "De sheep, suh."

"Ketch will take your place." Carlton lurched toward the Big House, forgetting Hector. He spun around, nearly toppling. "Get the horse back to the barn."

Thunder took the horse's reins and stumbled toward the barn. This could not happen. He was now expected to carry the black-hearted witch in his arms while the man who ravaged and killed his sweet Minda hovered day and night.

How long before his rage overtook his desire for good? How long before he committed murder himself?

☥

"I can't stay long, Mama Juba." Mary Edith peeked out the old woman's door. "I told Wilbur I had to make water."

"Things is bad, is they?" the healer said. "My heart be sick 'bout Thunder, havin' to live underfoot of Mr. Carlton like he do. And haulin' that old crow to the backhouse is hard labor, missy."

Mary Edith giggled. "Lady Anne's not taking it too well, herself. You should see the fire in her eyes when Thunder comes to haul her in and out of the house." She shrugged. "But what can she do about it?"

"Ain't nothin'. She gots to put up with it. I worry more for our boy, Thunder."

"He don't talk much, Mama Juba. He wears a stern face. That's all I know. He done all his talking last night in our cabin."

"What you mean?"

"He come to tell Da about the new ways, and he was blame near crying. A big ol' fella like that."

"All size men cry sometimes, Mar' Edith."

"Well, he wailed about killing Mr. Carlton and called Lady Anne evil, straight from the bowels of hell!"

"He ain't wrong." Mama Juba rubbed her chin. "'Cept about killin'. I gotta help that boy 'fore somethin' bad happen." She waved her arm at the girl. "Run on, now, 'fore you in a mess, too. Stop by later. I'll need ya to do some gatherin'."

φ

Thunder's mind wandered as he mucked out the barn. He already missed the open spaces he was accustomed to. This new task closed him up with the stench of beasts and humans alike, with no room to breathe.

More than open spaces, he missed Joe Dillon, who, from his first day at Kilkenny, had taken him under his wing. So far from his homeland, he'd become like a newborn, relearning so many things. While the Fulani were cattlemen by nature, Mr. Tom had allowed Thunder to work with Joe. He was the only one the young African trusted when he first arrived, frightened and distressed.

Joe Dillon was more like an older brother than a father. He taught without scolding and listened without judging. He was the one Thunder dared tell he could read and write—an ability that scared the white men more than any other.

Of course, he could not read the language of this land. As a boy, he had attended the madrasah only a short time, but the reading and writing of the Qur'an came easily to him. He liked to write the Arabic characters in the dirt when no one was looking.

That was how Joe caught him. Yet, illiterate himself, Joe was more fascinated than intimidated. He'd asked so many questions about Thunder's life within the Fulani culture, the then fifteen-year-old found himself telling his story.

He explained it was against the law of Islam that one Muslim sell another into slavery. Several leaders had no qualms selling those of other faiths, though, who were captives from skirmishes and wars.

"My leaders sell more and more men, women, and children for guns, powder, and cloth. Dey say to keep our people safe from slavers. Yet, to buy dese guns, dey sell others."

His eyes stung at the memory. "My father speak to our leader who try to sell our servant, a man of our own faith. He tell all who would listen of de wars, dey fight dem only to get captives. He say, 'Now you want to sell our brothers,' speaking of our servant. De leader, he angry with de words and order him to keep quiet. He say, 'Your servant is a dog who does not pray. He more a kafir dan a believer. He must go!'

"My father, in his anger, run toward our leader—to do what, I not know. The leader pull his sword. He run my father through." Tears fell from Thunder's eyes. Though years had gone by, the anguish never eased.

He tapped his chest. "Dis man, he say I, my mother, my sister also speak against our faith. We must be sold with our servant."

Slavers had carried them all to the sea where they were forced to work until their ship's departure. Though separated from his mother and sister, he didn't worry. He was sure they would all be ransomed by their kinsmen. Yet, none came. He was not to see his mother, sister, nor even the servant again.

Thunder still had nightmares about the seemingly endless journey over the water. While he yearned to return home, the thought of one more voyage tormented by dread, disease, and death brought terror to his heart.

Shoveling manure into the bucket, he remembered the story Joe Dillon shared of his own youth. He told Thunder of his desire to become a holy man—a monk. In secret, young Joe met with such a man, Brother Timothy, who taught him many things. But when Joe Dillon's father learned of this, he grew angry. The family was poor, and Joe was needed to help keep food on the table. With much sadness, Joe Dillon slipped into the night to tell Brother Timothy they could no longer meet. Upon his return, he found his home ablaze with flames reaching into the dark sky.

"Me whole family was inside," Joe had told him, "with no way to get them out. The men who'd done it were still there, watching the flames roar from every window and door. Why would they do such a thing—burn a family to death? I still don't know."

Thunder was struck by the agony in Joe's eyes.

He went on. "A coward, I hid behind some bushes while me family burned. Me dear ma and da, two little brothers and a wee sister. I still see their faces and, some nights, dream of them screaming me name, pleading for help. Part of me wishes I'd burned alongside them." He picked up a stick and dug a small hole in the dirt. "I stayed amongst the ashes two more days, but there was nothing left. I wanted to die but was forced to live."

Thunder was heartsick. "Same for me."

"I traveled many miles and found work. There, I met Nan. Only she knows me story. And now you."

"I never break your trust, my friend." He'd looked at Joe and added, "More dan my friend. My brother."

Chapter Eleven

Mary Edith slung the half-full burlap sack over her left shoulder. Traipsing through the woods, she found the pine bark, needles, and cones Mama Juba needed. She'd yanked a half dozen snakeroot plants from the ground and threw them into the sack as well.

Plenty of dandelions and flowering horse nettle were growing in the sheep pasture. Hopefully, she'd find her da there, too, grumbling about Ketch now that Thunder was moved to the stables.

Mary Edith loved these errands away from the Big House, especially since Lady Anne had become bedridden. Though, as Lady Anne's favorite, Baby felt the heavy weight of that burden. Which was fine. Mary Edith found pride as the one Mama Juba picked to teach the ways of the root.

"Yo born with a shirt, Mar' Edith," the old woman had said. "That mean you chosen by the Lawd for conjurin'."

Ma had told her a caul covered her face at birth, but her mother wasn't convinced of any special standing with the Almighty. "'Tis a sign of good fortune in life, that I do know," was all she'd admit to.

Approaching the edge of the woods, Mary Edith's breath caught in her throat. About three yards away, a long snake with a triangle-shaped head slithered through the sandy soil. Save her pounding heart, she remained statue-like for several moments after it passed.

Once her brain re-awoke, she realized her treasure. Snake dirt! Mama Juba could make wisdom powder with that. From her pocket, Mary Edith snatched the swath of deerskin she used to protect her hand from the horse nettle's stinging hairs.

She spread it like a kerchief and scooped as much of the dust as it could hold. Pulling up the corners, she twisted the hide. Hanging from a tree nearby was a thin vine to wrap around the top, securing the packet.

In her excitement, she ran straight to Mama Juba's cabin, leaving the dandelions, horse nettle, and her father behind.

Mama Juba set a clay jar on the table. She and Mary Edith poured the snake dirt from the bundle to the container.

"I'm sorry about the dandelions and such," Mary Edith said, panting. "I'll run back out."

"No, chil'. It too late in the day for that. You brung the most important part. This here pine and snakeroot is what we need to uncross the house, and maybe Lady Anne herself."

Mama Juba suspected someone had placed a cross, which was a spell or curse, on Kilkenny. "Could be on all us or jus' the family, I don't know yet. Sometimes the spell come from the outside, sometimes from the heart of the victim herself."

"Lady Anne? You mean she could talk again?"

"Can't say. I tol' ya, we don't know where the cross come from, but we gonna find out."

Mary Edith shivered. Who hated Mr. Tom and the de Barneforts enough to curse them? Who would have crossed Lady Anne? Ma would do it if she had the power, but it seemed to Mary Edith all the troubles started when Mr. Tom died.

Mama Juba removed the plants she'd brought from the sack and separated them. "Now, if the grand lady could stand herself up, I'd put her on a cloth and throw the bones. That's how ya divine what's goin' on with a body. I'll show ya that one day."

Mary Edith's head spun at the thought of all the hateful wailing Lady Anne would do if she recovered. Who would be blamed for her treatment over these last days? Baby? Mr. Carlton? Thunder? Or herself, for snatching the harpy's arm mid-air?

Mama Juba placed the pine needles, bark, and cones in a bucket. "Tomorrow, we gonna use these needles and cones to smoke out the curse. Then we'll give the mistress my snake-root tea."

"But what if the crossing bounces back on you—or on me?"

"Now chil', ya know that won't happen. Not if we doin' this for the right reasons. And we is!"

Mary Edith looked at her feet. All magic work had to be justified or it could ricochet onto the conjurer. Yet, how could she be justified if her deepest wish was that the woman never speak again? Or even better, that she die? Sure, Lady Anne was evil, but wasn't wishing someone dead also wicked?

Mama Juba tilted her head. "Now, what's wrong with ya? Ya still shook from seein' that snake? Go on, then. Tell Ketch I need him, then head home." She lifted Mary Edith's chin. "Ya done good."

Fighting tears of shame at her own sinful thoughts, the girl raced from the cabin.

⚛

Mary Edith thrashed on her pallet, haunted by nightmares. In one, the snake she'd watched in the woods slithered toward her. As it got nearer and nearer, she froze to the spot, willing her legs to flee. They refused to obey. The snake slid up her left foot and coiled itself around her leg, reaching her thigh.

As with her disobedient feet, her throat would not give voice to her screams. She stretched out her arms, appealing to her parents a few yards away. They only watched, smiling. Looking down, Mary Edith peered into the serpent's eyes. They reflected an eerie light. Blood raced through her body as its mouth widened, exposing fangs and a flickering tongue. Then it spoke in a whispery voice.

"Are you jussss-tified?"

She awoke with a start, bolting upright on her pallet. Her heart banged against her chest, leaving her breathless.

Ma shifted. "Lay down, Mary Edith," she mumbled. "'Twill be daybreak soon enough."

She obeyed but, tormented by doubts, sleep never came. Should she help Mama Juba with her works, knowing her bitterness toward Lady Anne? No justified conjure could hurt them, but Mary Edith could not wish the old cow well. Her scorn could cause the work to rebound, bringing pain to everyone she loved.

She prayed to God, his Son Jesus, and to the ancestor she'd never met, Eveleen Scully. Ma talked about Mary Edith's grandmother all the time, describing Eveleen as gentle, but strong enough to calm Ma's wild streak. As she prayed, Mary Edith pleaded with them all to tell her what to do.

But when the sun finally showed its face, she had no answers.

✦

At Mama Juba's request, Nan agreed to take part in the uncrossing, only to save the innocents on the plantation. "The shrew, Anne, cannot suffer enough to suit me," she claimed.

While she did not have the gift, she could be the arms and legs of Mama Juba, too old and crippled to move fast or far.

She noticed Mary Edith, who, instead of listening to Mama Juba's instructions, was staring at the small table in the corner of the cabin. It held two burning tapers made from animal fat and a bucket from which gray curls of smoke carried the woodsy scent of burning pine. "Are ye listening, lass? Ye should know better than meself how grave this be. Where's yer head?"

"Mama Juba's altar to the ancestors. Why don't we have one for our spirits?"

Nan's temper rose. "Jesus, Mary, Joseph, and the wee donkey! Are ye sure, Mama Juba, she can do the magic?"

"Somethin' ain't right." The old conjurer folded her arms and frowned.

With jutted chin, Mary Edith blurted, "I can't feed no tea to Lady Anne. I don't want nothing to do with her."

This wasn't like Mary Edith at all. Nan looked to the old woman. "Her sleep was troubled."

Mama Juba pursed her lips. "Gal, you jus' tote this bucket of pine smoke around the house and say the prayers. Ya can do that, can't ya? Yo mama can't talk to the spirits like you can. That's all you need do. Nan will do the rest."

Seeing Mary Edith's wringing hands, Nan chewed her lip. She turned to Mama Juba. "What now?"

"We gotta cleanse." Mama Juba handed a chicken foot to each of them. Mary Edith began brushing herself downward, starting at her head. "Nan, you do like Mar' Edith. Keep the strokes goin' down. That's the onliest way."

Nan swiped the foot down her body from her head to her feet. When she finished, she saw that Mary Edith had taken one of the candles from the altar and blown it out. She was circling it around her head.

Mama Juba blew out the other one and handed it to Nan. "Run that 'round yo head three times."

Nan started to do so when the old woman barked at her. "T'other way, Nan!"

She reversed directions.

When finished, both candles were replaced on the altar and relit. Mama Juba looked out the door of her cabin. "There they go. Wilbur and Becca is headin' to the kitchen like we planned." She looked at Nan and Mary Edith. "It's time."

She handed the smoking bucket to Mary Edith. The handle was wrapped in thick cloth to protect her hands. "Ya know what to do, gal."

Mary Edith took a deep breath, nodded, and left the cabin.

The conjurer laid a hand on Nan's shoulder. "I done put the magic in this snakeroot tea. It won't taste too bad with all the honey in there." She placed a corked earthenware pitcher in Nan's hand. "Now, ya gonna need to put this in Lady Anne's fancy china cup before ya spoon it to her. Becca says she'll clamp them lips shut if'n ya don't."

In Nan's other hand, Mama Juba placed a small leather sack closed with a drawstring. She said another prayer over it and made sure Nan knew what to do. "Ya come back empty or won't none of this do a lick of good. Y'hear?"

After stashing the cloth bag in her apron pocket, Nan carried the jug to the Big House. Upon entering, she saw Mary Edith making her way through the parlor, swinging the bucket like a priest incensing a church. The girl mumbled as she dispensed the magic. Nan could hear little of it, but caught the names Eveleen and Nolan, her own mother and uncle. Or could she have meant their namesakes, Mary Edith's sister and brother? With the talk of ancestors, Nan believed it was the first.

She went to the cupboard and chose a delicate cup and saucer of pure white, painted with dainty flowers of red, yellow, and orange. So thin and fragile, it was, she feared her rough fingers would crush it. Setting it on the sideboard, she poured the magic tea from the crude pitcher, then stuck her finger in it. Still warm. Placing a silver spoon on the saucer, she made her way to the library where Lady Anne rested.

As she neared, her stomach ran wild with the fidgets. But once she spotted the old crone propped in the bed, nervousness ripened to rage. With the house servants at dinner, Nan was alone with the hag who stabbed her Baby. It was a rare moment in her life when she could say what she wanted. What could the harridan do in her condition?

Nan eased herself into a cushioned chair beside the bed. Lady Anne's eyes betrayed her fear, but the woman quickly recovered. Eyebrows furrowed, she peered through narrow slits. It occurred to Nan all would be lost if Lady Anne refused her tea, so she forced a smile she hoped appeared kindly.

"Well, Lady Anne, I'm coming in place of Mama Juba with some of her best healing tea. The poor old soul can't climb steps, I'm sure ye know." Nan took a deep breath. "She put plenty of sweetness in this brew, milady, so it'll go down smooth."

She dipped a spoonful, held it before the woman's drooping lips, and waited. After the two women held eye contact for several seconds, Lady Anne opened her mouth. Nan almost laughed with relief. Not trusting herself, she fed her the tea in silence.

When only two spoonfuls remained, Nan looked Lady Anne in the eye. "We've come a long way, the two of us." She slipped in another sip. "Ye left Duncullen when I was a wee lass, so we never met, but I know all about ye." She poured the last drops into the spoon and tipped them into Lady Anne's mouth.

"Done! May this tonic work its magic." Nan set the cup and saucer on her lap. She heard Mary Edith's footsteps above as the girl made her way through the second floor. "Will we have a few words about the old days before I leave?"

Lady Anne frowned.

"Ye know Joe and me lived at me father's estate before our voyage to Carolina."

Her eyebrows arched.

"Aye, I know Sir Richard was me da, though a poor one. But I've always wondered about you. Did ye think yer devilment at Duncullen went unnoticed by servants? They had eyes. They had ears. They saw ye skulking about the hallways, spying on me father. Biddy herself—ye remember the housekeeper—told me all about it. How in yer villainy, ye convinced Sir Richard to send off me poor ma, no more than a lass. 'Twas you who gave the command, in fact."

Lady Anne donned her arrogant sneer and grunted in disgust.

The woman's disdain boiled Nan's blood. She stood, dropping the cup that shattered into tiny bleached shards. "Ye were vile then and yer vile now. Ye claimed me ma trifled with Jack, a man-child with a pure heart! Aye, I knew Jack. It surprises me none ye didn't recognize the good in him, yer own heart the color of soot!

"Ye despised the kindness in yer own husband, so ye destroyed him, too! Climbing atop him at yer age, ye bawdy old draggle-tail. Ye disgust me!" Nan's rage was reaching a dangerous level, but she didn't care.

The mistress' eyes widened, the fear returning.

"And then to stab a child in her back! Ye've no right to live, ye nasty wench. Everything ye touch turns to pain and suffering." Nan's chest heaved as she reached into her apron pocket. Mama Juba had more for her to do.

Willing herself to calm down, she pulled the leather sack from her apron and yanked the string open. "One last treatment from Mama Juba." She reached into the bag and pulled out a handful of soil. Starting at the feet, Nan sprinkled the dirt onto the invalid.

Lady Anne opened her mouth wider than Nan had thought possible. From her throat came a fierce and savage growl. Her head thrashed from side to side as though instead of dirt, Nan drizzled hot embers.

Goose-skin arose up and down Nan's arms. Without thinking, she drew back in horror, but remembered Mama Juba's warning. "No matter what happen," she'd said, "don't get turned aside. Use every bit of that dirt."

Nan reached into the sack for another handful. She continued dusting from the woman's knees to her belly. The groaning and snarling were ungodly, but she continued upward until, stopping at Lady Anne's neck, she'd emptied the bag. The soil seemed too potent to risk on the old woman's face.

Hands shaking, she stuffed the empty burlap into her pocket. The grunts waned until they were no more than whimpers. Turning, Nan found herself face-to-face with Mr. Carlton. Her heart stopped. Speechless, she struggled to read his face.

"What did you pour onto Mother?"

Her voice broke. "'Twas a remedy, Master Carlton, sent by Mama Juba. She can't come herself, sir."

"Yes, but what was it?"

"Grave dirt, sir. Dust gathered at midnight from Mr. Tom's grave."

He cocked his head to one side. "Hmm."

Without another word, her young master turned on his heel and left

Chapter Twelve

Carlton stepped from the Big House to a chilling wind. He descended the veranda steps where the new overseer stood yards away. His stomach gnawed at the sight of Johnny Reeve. He had delayed this moment as long as he could, claiming he needed to write new procedures. There was no point bringing on the new man before they were finalized, he reasoned.

A few days earlier, a disgusted Walter Gatch had run out of patience. "Reeve's given his notice at the mill. Another might snatch him up if you're not careful."

"Has he another offer, then?" Maybe the problem would take care of itself.

"Naw, but with all the men getting called upon for the militia—"

"Send Reeve here the first of next week," Carlton had snapped before Walter could remind him once again of his own military obligations.

Sure enough, on an early May morn, the lout showed up at Kilkenny. "Let him wait," Carlton had told Wilbur. "I'll have my breakfast and see to some business first."

He'd been awake into the wee hours the night before writing out the man's duties by lantern light. He carried them to the courtyard.

"Mornin', Carlton," Reeve said, holding his hat in his hand and swinging it back and forth. "Ain't seen you at McHeath's in a while."

Carlton couldn't contain his disgust. "I beg your pardon. You will address me as Master Carlton. To which point, I hardly know you, so we will keep our discourse within the professional realm."

"Oh. Clearly. The professional realm."

The man's sarcasm did not go unnoticed. Carlton crushed the parchment he held in his hand. "You will keep a civil tongue, or I'll dissolve this arrangement at once."

Reeve's face dropped. "Right."

The man's hasty retreat bolstered Carlton's confidence. "I have written all my expectations on this paper for you." He inwardly smiled at the stunned look on the man. "Of course. You can't read any of this." He laughed. "What was I thinking? I'll read it to you."

In his mind, he grew two inches. Let the cur try that smug attitude again. "First and foremost, you will have no jurisdiction over the Big House, kitchen, or gardens."

"Jur—what?"

"Jurisdiction, man. No authority. No...rule. As a matter of fact, but for the stables, I don't want to see you near here again. Unless I send for you, of course. Your duties shall include supervising the cattle, sheep, pigs, cedar shingles, and farming enterprises. Which should keep you quite busy." And away from him and his mother.

Reeve spat into the dirt. "Meaning no harm, but the boys at McHeath's say you got a white fella here already name of Joe Dillon. They's wondering why he ain't your overseer. He simple or something? I mean, since I'll be his boss and all."

"Joe is capable, and you will have no trouble from him. You can tell the boys I'm looking for a firmer hand."

Reeve held up a whip in his other fist that Carlton hadn't noticed. "Well, I'm your man, that's for certain."

Carleton swallowed, then read from the paper. "The over-seer is not expected to work in the field or pasture but must always be with the hands. He will see that all of them leave their houses thirty minutes past daybreak. Once, or more, a week he will visit every house at night to see that all are inside in a timely manner."

"I can do that. Won't put up with no stragglers."

"Do not fall into a regular routine but proceed such that you may be expected at any moment. That way, they're out of kil-ter, always on guard for your arrival."

Reeve cocked his head to one side and squinted at Carlton through deep-set eyes. "Before we go no further, Master Carl-ton, sir. How'm I gonna handle business 'round here if I ain't to come near the Big House, what with you off fighting and all?"

Carlton sucked his breath. He'd not go off fighting, that much he knew. But how he'd get out of it, he hadn't deter-mined. Before he responded, Nan Dillon carrying a basket of vegetables captured Reeve's attention.

The man's dark eyes widened. "Now there's a fine-looking woman. Yes, sir. A fine-looking woman."

"That's Nan Dillon, Reeve. A married woman. Keep your own counsel where the female servants are concerned. You will have Saturdays off to see to your needs, but you must be back on the property by nightfall."

Reeve wasn't listening. He leered as Nan bent to retrieve some cabbages that had fallen from her basket. Carlton grew concerned. Would there be trouble with Joe Dillon?

Then, it came to Carlton. The obvious answer to all his problems.

φ

As the sun peered over the horizon, Alden de Barnefort crawled from his brush hut and swept the leaves from his clothes. He'd slept fitfully; the night was cold for May. Birds created an early morning chorus at the Cracker's Neck encampment, not far off the Savannah River. He scanned the cluster of shelters constructed with sticks and leaves, not easily spotted in the forest. Some, like Alden's, were built for one person while others were large enough for three or four men.

The soft glow of cookfires tended by wives and sisters of the militiamen dotted the landscape. Camp followers. The women performed many duties to keep the Rangers functional, preventing the unit from falling into disarray. Yet, men did the cooking.

Not far from Alden's hut, a young fellow, Seth Richardson, formed small loaves from flour and water mixed in a wooden bowl. He handed them to the lieutenant, Tarlton Brown, who crouched before a fire, placing the firecakes on a warmed rock.

Alden pulled his coat closed with one hand as he approached with his tin cup. Tarlton Brown rose, once again stunning him with his great height. He stood well over six feet and, with reddish hair, made an easy target for eager Tory riflemen.

"Morning." Tarlton nodded toward a stand of trees. "We moved the water barrel over there."

Alden had been part of the Cracker's Neck Rangers for three weeks. He'd discovered an instant kinship with the lanky man. Despite Tarlton Brown's lack of formal education, the lieutenant had an innate intelligence about matters military and political. Alden felt sheepish around this battle-hardened veteran. While he'd passed his time in Charles Town debating philosophic principles, this man had been fighting for freedom since '75 when war first broke out in South Carolina.

Returning to the fireside, Alden sipped the cool water and enjoyed the brisk air which would warm up by mid-afternoon.

The bland aroma of firecakes made him homesick for Ruth's sweet bread straight from Kilkenny's kitchen. Alden could almost taste the buttermilk, brown sugar, and dripping melted butter. A delight he'd taken for granted.

He shook his head. Kilkenny was no longer his home. He had no home but Cracker's Neck and dreaming of what no longer existed was useless.

"Hallo, Seth," he said. "Those firecakes are making my stomach rumble."

The lad continued forming loaves. "No salt today."

Of course not.

Tarlton squatted to remove the cooked cakes and place them on a wooden trencher sitting on the ground. He nodded toward the food. "Have one."

Alden crouched alongside and reached for a loaf. He snatched his hand back, fingers burned.

Tarlton laughed as he lifted three more from the hot rock. "Live this life long enough, your tender hands will harden." He placed the raw slabs of dough Seth handed him onto the rock. "I talked it over with Captain Inman. Some of us'll be heading out in a few hours. It'll be a hard ride to Georgia. Word is Ben John and his mob are causing more trouble over there."

Some of the men had their blood up over the murders of Wyman Heape and Luke Farrell. Tarlton had told the Rangers the two had been fools to torture a mother and her children, Tory or no.

"Flog 'em," Wyman's brother, Obie, had called out. "No one's denying they deserved that. But those mongrels shot 'em in the head. It's cold-blooded murder, pure and simple. They can't get away with it!"

Alden reached for a loaf, now cooled, and ripped off a bite. He refused to think about brown bread. Glancing up, he noticed a deep frown on Seth's face.

Finally, Seth spoke. "What time we leaving, L'tenant?"

Tarlton chuckled. "You in possession of one of them new-fangled pocket watches?"

Seth lowered his eyes and stared into the mixing bowl, now empty.

"Midmorning. That's all you need to know." Tarlton handed the fellow one of the baked loaves, then spoke to Alden. "Your first mission. Nervous?"

It was true. Alden had participated in foraging raids for food which presented their own risks, but this was his inaugural military conflict. "A bit."

"This ain't the first time we've gone to Georgia. Back when we were fighting the Brits in Savannah—'76, I believe it was— we set off in an open boat, eager for the fray. Some Tories on-shore rained iron hail upon our heads, but we gave it back just as fierce."

He pulled back his shirt and pointed to a spot on his left breast. "One ball struck me right there."

"Damned close to your heart," Alden said.

"Providence was with me. The ball was near-spent and raised no more than a blood blister." Tarlton laughed.

Alden's heart raced as he struggled to find the humor.

Seth's face brightened. "We sent them running last time, didn't we, L'tenant? Last month on the Ogeechee Causeway, the Brits come at us with slaves and overseers alike from Governor Wright's plantations and others thereabouts, but it done no good. We give a few of 'em a taste of Georgia Parole."

"What's that?" Alden asked.

"No parole at all! We shot 'em dead."

A shiver ran up Alden's spine.

"We won't cross at Two Sisters like last time, Seth. That ferry's been destroyed," Tarlton said. "We'll take Burton's Ferry across the Savannah and give Ben John and them good measure."

Seth's eyes widened. "Burton's Ferry? Ain't that risky?"

Tarlton grew serious. "Everything's risky."

✦

Summoned by Master Carlton, Joe Dillon headed toward the Big House. He didn't know why he was called but was determined to use this opportunity to warn Carlton. This new overseer bore watching.

As he neared the back entrance, Carlton stepped from the house, stopping several inches above Joe. Inwardly, Joe rolled his eyes. He'd known highborn men, both fine and crude, and this ploy for advantage was oafish.

Crossing his arms, Carlton said, "I have need of your services, Joe."

"Aye, milord." He slipped into the title of his youth. "First, allow me to say this new overseer has me vexed. Ketch brought the man to the sheep pasture and tried to explain where the best water could be found. Reeve slung that whip of his right across Ketch's face."

"I'm sure there was good cause."

"'Tis for you to say, milord, but his reason was that Ketch spoke without permission. He drew blood, he did." It took a lot for the rest to pity Ketch, but there was a rumbling among the herders.

Master Carlton's face grew dark. Joe couldn't tell whether it was Reeve's behavior or his own impudence that disturbed him.

"We've something far more serious to discuss." He drew in a deep breath before continuing. "First, I want to remind you of all you owe the de Barnefort family. My cousin, Sir Richard Lynche, paid your passage to America, and my father took you and Nan in when you had nowhere else to go. You've been treated like family."

Joe sighed. Richard Lynche would have paid double to rid himself of the daughter so like his first love, Eveleen. Nan was a daily reminder of his cruelty toward her. Mr. Tom had taken them in and provided a good home but living in the servants' quarters was a far cry from being family.

Carlton continued. "It's time you repaid the kindness that's been shown you all these years. Don't you agree?"

Again, Joe, Nan, and all the children had worked as hard as any slave for no more than food, clothing, and shelter. Yet, he nodded, unhappy with the direction of the conversation.

"It has come to my attention that we need to send a representative from Kilkenny to—how shall I say this?" Carlton looked above in search of his words. "To maintain the security and freedom so generously afforded us by our King, George III."

Joe's head started to spin. "What are ye saying, sir?"

Carlton placed his hands on his hips. "I've overestimated you. To put it more simply, it is our obligation to fight against this ungodly rebellion and quash it once and for all. A British colonel named Ferguson is seeking men to rout the Patriot scum, and you are to join the Loyalist militia in the name of the de Barneforts of Kilkenny Plantation."

"Master Carlton, yer father and I had an understanding. I'm a peaceable man who will not harm man nor beast without just cause. I cannot, in good conscience, fight a war beyond defending me family and friends when attacked."

Carlton's jaw clenched. "This is a defense of friend and family. Surely, you've heard of the assaults these scoundrels have made upon innocent women and children. Many from right here in the District."

Joe's eyes burned as he fought tears. "I have. And if any of these marauders set foot on this land, I will give me heart and soul to its defense. But it is against me beliefs to seek out such violence."

Carlton seemed to struggle for words. When he finally found them, they were brutal. "I don't believe you understand. I am ordering you to serve in the militia."

Joe pulled back his shoulders. "Sir, we Dillons are grateful for all yer family has done, but we ain't no slaves. We're free. Ye cannot order me to do nothing."

Carlton's eyes darkened. "But I can kick you off my land. You and Nan. Those young children. If you refuse me, I want you all gone from my sight by midday."

"Ye don't mean that, sir."

"I demand your answer now!"

Joe felt weak from head to toe. Where would they go? How would they live? The very roads were dangerous during these lawless days. Both Patriots and Tories attacked men, women, and children, then asked questions later. His mind settled on little Daniel, so young and happy. Mama Juba, Thunder, Ruth, and Wilbur—more family than fellow servants. Dare he take all this away from Nan and the children for a principle?

Joe could barely catch his breath. "This new man. He's a brute no better than Ol' Scratch Himself. Who's to see to me family while I'm gone?"

Carlton's shoulders relaxed. "Why, I will protect them. I give you my word."

Joe could only think of Minda. How well was she protected by the likes of Carlton?

He seemed to read Joe's mind. "I was a foolish and rash boy, I know. But I am responsible now that Father is gone, and I will take that obligation to my grave. As you trusted my father, so you can trust me."

Joe's stomach wrenched as he thought of Nan's beautiful face, her caring eyes, and saucy tongue. How could he leave her? Yet, could he stay if it meant the family was thrown to the wolves?

"I will do it."

✢

An overwhelming burden had been lifted from Carlton's shoulders. Joe Dillon would take his place in the militia while his own standing in the community remained intact. Such an arrangement was not unusual. Several men of means paid others as substitutes in the field of battle. Of course, Joe could not serve as an officer as he would have done, but Kilkenny was where Carlton's duty lay.

He became giddy as his control over his life grew. He had found solutions to every problem dumped upon him. Yet, what would Phineas Odom have to say? Or worse, Walter Gatch?

Just as quickly, he had another revelation. He would marry Rosabel as soon as propriety allowed. She visited the Big House twice weekly and doted on his mother. Though how she tolerated the surly cow, he couldn't fathom.

It didn't matter. Marriage now would alleviate the remaining burden of his mother while distracting Walter Gatch from Carlton's avoidance of the fray.

His genius confounded even himself.

✢

After smearing bear grease over his skin to ward off stinging insects, Alden stood around the water barrel with other Rangers filling their canteens.

Out of the corner of his eye, Alden saw something flash through the woods. A man on a horse, but who?

"You see that?" Levi Anderson pointed while the others scattered to grab their guns. Militias like theirs could be ambushed by local Tories at any given moment.

Tulius Dew called out, "That was Seth Richardson, y'all. I seen him clear as day."

The men gathered around Tulius in the middle of the camp. Tarlton Brown ran over. "Where's Seth headed? Who knows?"

"He's got a little honey on the Georgia side, I do know that," a black-haired man said.

"Whereabouts?" Tarlton asked.

"Not sure, L'tenant," the black-haired fellow answered. "Not far from Burton's Ferry, I believe."

Tarlton and Levi shared a look.

Tulius stroked his chin. "Her father's a Tory by the name of Cooper. Hers is Jean or Jane, something like that."

"Jane Cooper?" a tow-headed lad said. "I know her. She's a looker."

"Know where she lives?"

"Sure do," the boy said.

Tarlton Brown pointed out a party of a dozen or so men, including Alden. "Mount up."

Chapter Thirteen

As soon as she saw Joe's drawn face approaching the kitchen, Nan recognized trouble. Her hands and feet grew cold. "Don't tell me."

Joe entered, took her hand, and kissed it. "We'll go to our cabin, me love, and talk there."

Nan looked around the room for someone to save her. Yet, Ruth stood stock still, her face frozen, while Mellie wrung her hands within the skirts of her apron. Becca stepped into the building, spotted them, and scuttled back to the Big House, a hand over her mouth.

"Come," Joe urged, his voice so gentle, it hurt.

Holding his hand, she stumbled along the lane as though sentenced. Every horror she'd experienced in her life churned through her memory. Her mother's death in a lonely, abandoned cabin, Uncle Nolan's headless body rolling on a cart past the house after his execution, her newfound father's madness on full display as he screamed of being dragged into hell.

What now, God? I can take no more.

Her feet felt leaden as she dragged them up the steps into the cabin. Joe led her to the chair beside their table, sat, and lowered her onto his lap. Nan leaned against his shoulder, her mind emptied. She refused to speculate what was to come.

"I have to leave ye for a while, Nan. Not for long, and then I'll be back."

"Leave me? Why?"

"Mr. Carlton is sending me to fight this war in his stead."

Nan leapt to her feet, and to her surprise, found herself sucking in deep breaths as she giggled. "Oh, ye give me a fright, ye did. I thought one of our children—never mind. Of course, ye'll not fight. Yer a man of peace, everyone knows that."

The tears rolling down her husband's cheeks stopped her short. "Ye told him no, didn't ye? That ye'll never fight in some war that's no concern of ours."

He looked away. "Carlton gave me no choice. I have to go."

"No choice? We're freeborn, Joe. Of course, we've a choice. No. The answer has to be no!"

Joe looked into her eyes. "Yer still so beautiful, aren't ye? No different from the day we met. Yer me whole life, Nan, you and me little treasures. For the love of ye all, I will go."

Her fear blazed into anger. "'Tis not for me ye do it! Don't blame the wee ones, neither. If ye go, ye do it for that bastard of a coward, Carlton, and I'll tell that weasel so meself!"

His face crumpled into sobs as he dropped his arms onto the table and lay his head upon them. His shoulders shook with the depth of his grief. Nan was stunned. She could count on five fingers the number of times she'd seen Joe cry.

Sitting beside him, she ran her fingers through his hair, massaging his scalp. "All will be well, Joe. We'll explain to the almighty Master Carlton he'll have to find another dupe."

Eyes swollen, Joe lifted his head. "Do ye reckon I hadn't thought of that, love? I've explained it all. He doesn't care." He opened his mouth to speak, but instead, pressed his lips together.

"Say it, Joe. We've no secrets between us."

His hands balled into fists. "He'll evict us, Nan. Put us on the road."

"He'd never do that."

"I saw it in his eyes." His jaw tightened. "He'll do it."

Nan stood once again and paced the cabin. "So, we'll be on the road. At least we'll be together. We can find a plot of land, start again." The thought terrified her, but not as much as losing Joe, even for a time.

Joe rose and placed his hands on her shoulders. "'Tis a dangerous world right now, and I won't have our family suffer for me own beliefs. What good are beliefs if yer family's homeless and starving?"

"Ye'll not fight for the bloody king of England, I know that. The very ones that killed Uncle Nolan and Father Alistair? Who thrust innocent families into starvation?"

He didn't answer, only hung his head.

"Ye took an oath to the Levellers to stand against the brutality of that very same king, or did that mean nothing as well? Are ye no more than a traitor, then, to yer brothers-in-arms who give their lives for the Irish poor?" She thought of her beloved uncle who, it was said, stood upon the gallows before jeering crowds. He declared no regret over any actions he took to stop cruelty toward the downtrodden. Joe's effortless surrender to the mealy-mouthed Carlton de Barnefort sickened her in comparison.

Joe's face was as white as a sheet of parchment. "'Tis done, Nan. I've made me decision and given me word."

The determination in her husband's eyes and finality of his words seared her like Geoffrey's branding iron. She lashed out at the intense pain they caused, pounding Joe on his chest. "Ye had no right! I hardly know ye, ye yellow coward! I hate ye, Joe Dillon! With all me heart, I hate ye!"

Joe held her tight, but he was no match for the power her rage produced. She ripped herself from him, fled the cabin, and into the woods. Joe shouted her name, but she refused to lis-

ten. She would run, she decided, until this nightmare disappeared.

✛

Alden rode south amidst his comrades through the forest of
pines, oaks, and cypress that followed the Savannah River.
Although an excellent horseman, knowing his enemies could
be hiding behind any lichen-covered tree on either side of the
river tightened every muscle in his body. In particular, his
neck and shoulders. Any movement, no matter how slight,
caused him to grasp his loaded rifle in its scabbard. The menacing hum of mosquitoes around his ears did nothing to ease the
tension.

With little time to lose, the riders kept a steady pace. About
three hours into the journey, Alden's senses heightened. Something felt amiss. His heart raced, and he could hear the blood
rushing through his ears.

Lieutenant Tarlton Brown, leading the squad, held up his
hand. When the rangers slowed to a walk, Alden heard it. An
agonized wail from the woods. It could have been a woman or
a boy. Squinting, he saw the small, crude cabin fifty yards away
amidst the brush. The lieutenant nodded, and they crept toward the hovel. Alden's chest rose and fell as he gasped for air.
The smell of mud and rotting vegetation beneath Enbarr's feet
permeated his nostrils. Only one word screamed in his mind—
ambush!

Like his compatriots, he pulled his rifle from the scabbard
as soundlessly as he could. They closed in on the cabin as the
moaning grew more intense. Every nerve in Alden's body was
raw. The lieutenant reached the porch, leapt from his horse,
and entered the structure. The others remained mounted with
guns at the ready, scanning the area in all directions.

"Oh, Sweet Jesus in Heaven," they heard Tarlton call out. "It's the Widow Johnston. I need some help in here."

Levi Anderson and Tulius Dew dismounted and ran inside. Alden followed. The woman lay sprawled on the dirt floor, blood oozing from her head above the right ear.

Tarlton knelt beside her. "We're here, Mrs. Johnston. You'll be fine now." He looked at Tulius. "Get something to wrap around her head."

The man left.

"Who are you?" the woman whispered.

"Tarlton Brown from Brier's Creek, ma'am. Billy Brown's boy. We're Patriots."

The woman closed her eyes. "Makes no difference. Both sides are brutal."

"Help me get her up," the lieutenant told Levi. "If we can lift her onto your horse, can you take her to my homestead? My mother and sisters will nurse her."

Levi ran his arm under the woman's neck and shoulders. "Mrs. Johnston, it's Levi Anderson. Miss Sarah Brown and her girls will take good care of you."

As they lifted her, she passed out. Tulius returned with a strip of linen donated from one of the men's shirttails which he tied around her head. Alden then helped the other three carry her to Levi's horse.

Once beside the animal, Alden ran to Enbarr and grabbed his canteen. He poured water over the woman's pallid face until she came to. They raised her onto the horse, and Levi climbed behind.

"Luckily, my family lives only two miles from here," Tarlton said. "Godspeed, Levi."

With his arm around the woman, Levi clicked his tongue and led the horse toward the northeast.

Tarlton's eyes narrowed. "I only pray it was Tories that attacked a helpless woman and not one of our own. The world is going mad. No one is safe."

With that, he remounted, and they continued on their way. Within another hour, they neared Burton's Ferry. They approached with caution as Tories and Patriots skirmished there on a regular basis. Tom Burton had declared himself neutral and, since the ferry was critical to both sides, he was mostly left in peace. Yet, it would not be surprising to find Ben John and his yahoos in the vicinity.

They were in luck. Old Tom and his boy were on the Carolina side of the river with no one else in sight. The lieutenant paid for their passage with one of the coins Alden had donated to their cause. Old Tom looked it over, bit down, and waved the men and horses aboard. The thirty-foot barge allowed them to cross in one trip.

A few of the men picked up poles to help push the ferry through the easy current and unruffled waters of the Savannah. Watching lazy turtles nap on fallen logs and an occasional fish take a playful leap into the air, Alden could almost forget the savage purpose of the crossing.

"You seen any young whipper-snappers coming through in a hurry?" Tarlton asked the ferryman.

Old Tom looked up from manning the ropes that guided the river crossing. He sneered at the lieutenant, then spit into the waters. "You know better than to ask me that, ye bloody blackguard."

Tarlton sighed and looked away. The tow-headed boy, whom Alden learned was named Hiram, called out, "Y'all might wanta pump ship. It won't be far once we get to the other side."

All the rangers unbuttoned their pants and pissed into the Savannah. Obie Heape leaned over to him. "Best to pee now. You don't want to piss down your leg once the action starts." Alden followed suit.

Once the barge was secured on the sloping bank of the Georgia side, the men mounted their horses and made their way onto solid ground. Tarlton tipped his hat to Burton as he passed, but the grizzled man only grunted in reply.

It was mid-afternoon, and clouds began to gather. "We're 'most there," Hiram said.

The squad picked up the pace when they hit the open fields surrounding Cooper's house. Tension that had eased on the ferry returned to Alden with a vengeance. Heart pounding, he panted like he'd swum across the river. Like the rest, he slipped his rifle out with one hand as he held Enbarr's reins in the other with a white-knuckled grip.

Once the Rangers reached the large clapboard house, Seth Richardson bolted out the door, leapt off the porch, and sprinted toward the woods.

"Get him before he reaches the trees," Tarlton shouted.

Several shots rang out, but Alden heard only a ringing in his head. He held his rifle in front of him, but had he pulled the trigger? He couldn't be sure. He saw everything as though through a spyglass. Time moved at a snail's pace. Seth flailed, his arms waving overhead as he stumbled, then crashed to the ground. It felt more a dream than reality, as though Alden was observing the skirmish outside his body.

His hearing returned with a jolt as someone yelled, "There goes the old man. Don't let him get by!"

More shots, but Alden was too stunned to pull his trigger. Old Mr. Cooper went down in a field about two hundred yards from the house.

Alden looked back at the fallen figure of Seth Richardson. The lieutenant and a few others rode toward him, and Alden joined them. He dismounted. There, in a heap, lay the lad who'd fixed his breakfast just hours before, now riddled with blood-soaked holes. Alden's head began to spin. Had a bullet from his gun made one of those holes?

The stench of dust on his lips and the sulfur of gunpowder mixed with the sweet rusty iron of a young boy's blood. Even worse, the lad had pissed and shat himself as he died. Alden's stomach roiled. Surely, this was the aroma of hell.

Alden's eyes burned, but no tears would come. At daybreak, Seth was a young man in love, with dreams and desires. Now he was nothing. He didn't exist. Merely a lump of flesh that would soon begin to rot.

Anger welled within him. What were they doing? Each was fighting for what he believed in. Neither side deserved to die like this. Alden took Enbarr's reins and walked away from the others.

"Hey," Tulius called.

"Let him go," the lieutenant said. "Let him go."

As Alden moved to an open area in search of some space and fresh air, he heard shouting from near the barn. The old man was alive but hollering as the men carried him to the house. A young girl—Jane?—stood on the porch and wailed.

"He's only hit in the heel, miss," Obie told the girl. "Your pa's gonna live."

But that didn't soothe her. Her squalling intensified, creeping into Alden's very marrow. Out of nowhere came a long-forgotten memory of Wilbur, his father's manservant, dabbing his eyes.

"Sorrow be catching," he'd said.

Alden's own emotions threatened to overtake him. He feared if he succumbed, he would crack. He pulled up his shoulders, determined to block any further thoughts of the young lovers from his mind.

Seth had made his choice. It was over.

Chapter Fourteen

The Rangers wasted no time vacating the property, leaving Richardson for the Tories to bury. They were back on the South Carolina side of the Savannah River in less than an hour and a half from when they'd left it. Such a short space of time, Alden thought. He'd lost an innocence he'd never regain.

Once in the woods, the lieutenant pulled everyone up. "I'm going to my family home to check on Levi and see if we can learn anything from the widow. Y'all return to camp. Tell the captain I'll be back in the morning."

"Right, Lieutenant," they all responded and started up the trail to Cracker's Neck.

"Alden," Tarlton called out, "you come with me. A hot home-cooked meal and soft pallet will do you good."

"I'm fine, Lieutenant," he said, not sure it was true.

Tarlton nodded. "I know. Come on."

It wasn't long before the two reached the sizable log home of the Brown family. They dismounted and entered the house, laying their guns against the wall inside the door.

Tarlton's small, energetic mother, Miss Sarah, and his sister bustled about, urging stew and ale upon the men. A young slave scurried to the kitchen house and back, seeing to their every comfort. Alden learned the sister's husband was fighting near Charles Town with a brother, Bartlett.

Alden had visited lively households while in Charles Town, but never one as boisterous as this. It sharply contrasted the subdued upbringing he'd had with only Carlton to share his childhood.

A sixteen-year-old brother, Manden's continuous questions faded into incoherent babble when another sister stepped into the room. Alden was mesmerized. Was it the thick black curls she'd allowed to tumble down her back, her smooth, warm skin, or those dancing eyes?

She glanced his way. Caught gawking, Alden could feel the heat rising from his neck. But their eyes locked, and instead of indignation, the girl smiled, causing her eyes to twinkle and her entire face to glow.

"Suzanne!" Tarlton held out his arms for an embrace that swallowed the slight girl.

Alden wondered how such a delicate creature could be the sister of a long, lanky specimen like Tarlton Brown.

Her brother brushed a stray hair from her face. "Where's Levi? I thought he was with you, seeing to the widow."

Suzanne shot a sidelong glance at Alden, which flipped his heart. "Mama has the widow buried in quilts in the back room."

Her mother frowned at the girl. "Levi and your father rode to Adam Wood's place. His son came by and said there'd been suspicious activity that way."

"I begged to go with them," Manden said. "I'm sick of being treated like a child."

"When you're seventeen and not a day before," his mother said.

"What, Manden, and leave the women here unprotected? Mama, I wish you'd mentioned this earlier." Tarlton turned to Alden. "We'd best ride over and see if they need any help. We have an agreement with the Woods to watch out for each other."

Alden had risen from his seat when the whinnying of horses stopped him cold. Tall as he was, Tarlton peered out the crack in the logs above the bolted door. The tension in his shoulders melted away. "It's Pa and Levi." He threw open the door. "We were about to bring reinforcements—me and Alden de Barnefort."

The men entered the house, stamping mud off their feet onto the wooden floor. "Tom de Barnefort's boy?" An older version of Tarlton approached Alden and shook his hand. "A good man. I was sorry to hear of his passing."

"Thank you, sir." It always surprised Alden how much better the old-timers knew each other, even over a large area, than his generation did.

"What was going on Adam Wood's way?" Tarlton asked. Everyone stopped for the answer.

"Seems like it was one fellow trying to steal some turnips out the garden. We fired a couple shots and that was the end of it."

"Thank the Lord," Miss Sarah said. "Sit down, you two, and eat."

Levi went to Suzanne and reached for her hand. "How's everything here?"

Alden felt a punch to his gut. Was there something between the two?

Suzanne placed her hands behind her back. "Fine, Levi. Mrs. Johnston is still asleep."

Levi took his place at the table and joined the others who were feasting on a rich, flavorful venison stew. "Your cook, Tina, is a wonder," he said. "Food fit for royalty."

Levi spoke like one of the family. Another spate of jealousy washed over Alden.

Tarlton's older sister, Liza, laughed. "Tina knows the best herbs to use. I don't know how she does it, myself."

The conversation grew animated as the family relaxed into what Alden guessed was familiar teasing and taunting of one another. Tarlton's father, Billy Brown, was the jovial ringleader of a large, happy family. He had taken a small break from his company of militia south of Burton's Ferry.

"We're getting plenty of action near King's Creek. Shots fired across the river 'most every day. Tarlton, you and Levi oughta consider connecting with us down there. It's a good deal closer to home than Cracker's Neck."

Tarlton shoved another spoonful of stew into his mouth. "Might do that. What you think, Levi?"

"I'd feel better if we could check on the women more often." He glanced at Suzanne, smiling shyly.

Alden looked the girl's way. Her beautiful brown eyes created a fluttering in his stomach. She flashed him a hint of a grin, then stared into her bowl.

Once darkness hit, Mr. Billy Brown announced they should all get some sleep. Alden, Levi, and Tarlton planned to leave at daybreak. The old folks slept in one room while the sisters bedded down in the room with the Widow Johnston. Tarlton was frustrated that the injured woman never woke. He was determined to ask about her attack. Miss Sarah forbade him to disturb her.

The younger men, including Manden, made pallets for themselves in the Great Room. Alden lay awake long after the room resounded with snores.

The charming Suzanne was a welcome sight after the day's horrors at the Cooper place, but what about Levi? He was a good fellow, quiet but steady. Everyone in the Cracker's Neck

Company knew he was humble, brave, and dependable in a fight.

Yet, Alden wished he didn't exist.

He had finally fallen into a deep sleep when the barking of the family's dogs roused him. Tarlton and Levi rustled in their bedrolls as well. Within a few minutes, a loud rap rattled the door. Levi, Manden, and Alden sat up.

Tarlton leapt to his feet. "Who's there?"

Several voices—it was hard to say how many—answered, "Friends."

One went on, "We've come from Sister's Ferry. We're General Lincoln's men and our term's finally up. We've travelled far hoping to reach our homes, but we're bone-weary, friend. Can we stay the night?"

Tarlton looked around the room from one to the other. "I'm sorry as I can be, boys, but we're full up with company."

Like the others, Alden rose to his feet. He could hear whispering among the men outside the door. Finally, the spokesman called in. "Sure, sure. How 'bout a torch of fire, at least, so's we can camp down by the creek?"

"What you think, Levi?" Tarlton whispered.

"Well, them fellows are due for a discharge. What'll it hurt to hand them a torch?"

Tarlton nodded. While he removed the bolt, Manden grabbed a green stick set aside for that purpose and wrapped a rag around the top. After dipping it in some bear fat, he stuck it in the fire until it lit. Tarlton took it from him and unlatched the lock. He opened the door, passed out the torch, then slammed the door and latched it.

"You spooked?" Levi asked.

"Something don't feel right," Tarlton mumbled and peeked out the crack at the top of the door. "I can see them pretty good now they've got that torch." He backed away as though stung. "Bloody hell! It's Matt Birch, that bastard of a Tory."

He handed all of them, including Manden, their guns. "As Pa likes to say, I was damned near shuffled off this mortal coil."

"We all could have been slaughtered," Alden said.

Manden held his shotgun with both hands. "God is with us tonight."

Upon hearing the men approach once again, Tarlton laid the heavy wooden bolt across the door. Alden hoisted his rifle and aimed at the entryway.

"Hallo," the leader called out. "How about some water?"

Tarlton and the others pointed their guns at the door. The lieutenant shouted, "Get some blasted water from the well in the yard!"

"Tarlton Brown, you shit-eating son of a bitch! By God's blood, may a plague take you, your bastard of a father, and the whore who birthed you!"

Other voices joined in the cursing. "We'll burn this bloody pigsty to the ground with you and every mongrel in it!" and more evil slanders.

Alden's heart was in his throat when the pack of them rammed against the door as a unit, hoping to tear it from its hinges. Again and again, they hammered into it until it should have splintered into a thousand pieces.

Alden could hear the women screaming while Mr. Billy forced them all to shut their gobs. "You're making targets of yourselves!"

Once they gave up battering the door, a glimmer reflected from the fire caught Alden's eye. He told the others to duck as a gun blasted through a crack in the wall beside the door. Gun barrels poked in and out of the crack, firing repeatedly. A piercing screech from the back room caused all to turn.

On the floor lay the body of young Manden, his neck shattered as blood spewed from the wound.

"Jesus in heaven!" yelled Tarlton.

Footsteps of the attackers could be heard in retreat. Levi and Alden reached the door together and threw the bolt aside. Unlatching it, they rushed outside firing at the killers as they ran off, pivoting for a few last shots.

The two gave chase until it was useless. Turning around, they found Tarlton had joined them.

He had his powderhorn and hunting patch slung across his shoulders. "Vermin! Bloody lowlife scum. We've plenty of powder and ball, but they skulked into the dark like the wretched cowards they are."

"They ain't men, Tarlton," Levi said. "And they ain't soldiers. They're stinking, yellow curs and we'll get them. For Manden, we'll get every one of them!"

Chapter Fifteen

Though grief stricken, Joe Dillon's heart swelled as he looked from one of his children to the next. As they chewed on cornmeal pancakes Nan had prepared, their glum faces reflected the early morning firelight. Ruth had brought Joe a short link of sausage and sorghum syrup from the kitchen. He divided the meat so each had a bite.

The usual chatter was gone. Who knew how long before they shared a meal again? Joe forced the food down his clenched throat.

Nan had spoken little since learning he would serve the British as Carlton's proxy. Twice over the last two days, she'd erupted into tongue-lashings that cut him to the quick. He knew her well; later she'd be overwhelmed with remorse. Yet, in the moment, he suffered.

He brushed a tear from Baby Eveleen's cheek. "All will be well."

Her voice cracked. "What if I never see you again, Da?"

Joe placed his hand on her chin. "Ach, I'm like a burr from the fields that's stuck to yer shift. Ye'll never rid yerself of me."

She leapt from her seat and, still sore from Lady Anne's attack, wrapped her arms around his neck. "I never want to be rid of you."

The tramping of boots across their wooden porch startled them all. In marched Johnny Reeve with neither a knock nor a word. Joe sprang to his feet.

"I'll thank ye to announce yerself before entering our home," Nan spat from the other side of the table.

Reeve ran his sleeve under his nose. "Long as I'm boss 'round here, I'll go where I please." He turned to Joe. "Sun's about up. The master wants you on the road."

"Watch how ye talk to me wife, Reeve. She's a proper woman and ye'll treat her as such."

Reeve took a step closer to Joe. "Or what?"

Carlton's voice could be heard from outside. "Or you'll have me to deal with."

The overseer's eyebrows popped up. "Right you are, Master Carlton." He ran onto the porch followed by Joe. Nan and the children pushed through behind him.

The sky had lightened in the east, allowing them to see Carlton's clenched jaw as he stood in the lane. "I thought I made myself clear, Reeve. If not, I can be clearer."

"No need, sir. No need." The overseer scuttled down the steps. "I'll see if that brute in the stables has readied the horse."

Joe scowled watching the lowlife scramble off like the fidgety rat he was. He walked down the steps and into the lane. "I said so before, Master Carlton, the man bears watching."

"I promised you I'd protect your family," Carlton said, "and I will do so."

While the man seemed confident in his own words, Joe took no comfort. Never had he placed any store in Carlton's ability to think beyond his own fortunes. A damned spoiled scoundrel, he was, who'd no right to put Joe in such a position!

His heart torn asunder, he struggled with an emotion he'd rarely felt. Hatred for Carlton de Barnefort.

The master of Kilkenny reached into his jacket pocket. Removing a sealed parchment, he handed it to Joe. "This letter is to be delivered by you and you alone to Major Patrick Ferguson. Let no one deter you, Joe. Tell any of his underlings who it is you represent and demand to see the major."

Joe took the letter and turned it over as a pair of roosters announced the dawn.

"Can you remember that name?" Carlton asked.

"I can." Joe's disgust sat bitterly upon his tongue.

"Ride my horse to Charles Town but turn it over to Ferguson once you arrive. As a gift from me. A steed that fine is fit only for an officer."

"I understand." Joe turned his attention to the approach of Thunder with Hector, Carlton's favorite horse. Stunned, he glanced at Carlton who owned other spirited steeds, but none as gallant as Hector.

When the horse reached them, Carlton stroked Hector's muzzle, speaking in low tones as one would to a favorite child. Joe noticed that tears filled the man's eyes.

"Care for Hector as you would your own, Joe." Carlton placed a hand on his shoulder. "It's time you left. As we discussed, follow the stage road, but be wary of villains of all stripes. May God protect you." He'd barely spit the words before hustling back to the Big House.

"He will not let us see him cry." Thunder wiped his own eye. "It is well he left. He should not see my tears either." He set his hands on Joe's shoulders and spoke low enough that only he could hear. "I do not know how I can stay. My anger swells, and soon I will burst."

Joe inhaled. "Stay strong, old friend. Yer faith has served ye well. Hang on tight to yer God. And I'll do the same."

"I will try, my brother."

"Wait now!" Mama Juba lumbered down the lane. "I got somethin' for ya."

"What in the world, Mama Juba? Ye said yer good-byes last night with the rest of them," Nan called out. She sent Mary Edith and Nolan to support the old woman as she rushed toward them.

All the servants had given Joe a warm, loving send-off at sunset the evening before. Until Johnny Reeve dispersed them, of course.

Mama Juba stumbled once she reached the others, only to be caught by Joe and Thunder. Panting, she labored to speak. "I...it's a prayer bag...a mojo." She held up a small cloth sack closed with a drawstring. "Got snake dirt. For protection. Devil pod and garlic." She looked to Nan. "Now I need a snip of hair from each of ya."

Nan nodded. With a small knife, Mama Juba cut a lock from each of the children, spoke a few words over it, and placed it in the red bag. Last, she added a curl of Nan's red-brown hair, bringing a lump to Joe's throat as he watched.

Closing the bag, the old healer presented it to him. "You don't take this off for nothin', ya hear? It hold all the magic I know to keep ya safe and bring ya home to Nan and these chillun."

Joe leaned over, allowing Mama Juba to place the string around his neck. He kissed her forehead. "I don't know much about yer ways, but if a prayer lifted from a heart as big as yer own can bring me back, I'll not be long."

Mama Juba tried to answer, but words seemed stuck in her throat. She turned back toward her cabin and waved her hand in the air.

Joe's emotions mushroomed until he could stand no more. "I must be off."

Arms crossed and chin raised, Nan said, "'Tis yer choice. Don't say ye were forced to go." Her lower lip quivered. "Ye can still do the right thing."

His heart would have ached less if she'd grabbed it and squeezed it to pulp. "This is best, Nan. Please know that."

She spun away. "I don't know it!"

Heartsick, Joe turned to the children. "Come here, Daniel." He kissed his younger son on the head. "Be good for yer ma." The child grabbed his leg and would not let go. He motioned to Baby, who ran to him and hugged him about the waist. Joe said, "I'll come back to ye. Ye'll see."

"Don't make promises ye can't keep," Nan said.

He forced himself to continue. "Mary Edith, me turtledove. Help yer ma all ye can."

"I will." Her face was awash in tears. "I'll look to the stars and pray for you every night."

Baby stepped back allowing him to hold Mary Edith against his chest. "Knowing that will give me great comfort, darling." He beckoned to his older son. "Nolan, lad."

The boy stiffened, fighting so hard to be a man.

"I leave knowing ye'll watch out for yer ma and yer sisters," Joe said. "Yer a good son and I'm proud of ye."

Nolan lost his fight. He dissolved into the ten-year-old child he was and clung to Joe, sobbing. Straining to regain control, he stepped back. Joe gently untangled Daniel from his leg.

"Nan?"

"I wish ye well, Joe. I can do no more than that."

"A kiss, then?"

She pecked his cheek. "Is there nothing I can say?"

"That ye love me?"

She backed away. "I'll love ye more if ye stay."

Helpless before her scorn, his shoulders slumped. He turned and mounted Hector. "I love ye all more than me own life. Never forget that." He watched Nan in hopes she'd thaw towards him, but she remained stalwart.

Clicking his tongue, he signaled Hector forward. At a walk, he turned back several times and waved to Thunder and his children, who huddled together. It was Nan's sweet smile he yearned to see, but she would not give it.

Finally losing all hope, he shook the reins and tore off at a gallop.

✦

Unyielding before her cabin, Nan was certain her anger would soften Joe. Surely, he would relent. They could handle anything, if only together. As he rode away, he turned several times, silently appealing to her. Yet, she held firm, sure he'd give in and return.

But he didn't. He spurred the horse and galloped away at a tear, looking back no more. Realizing she'd lost, she screamed and bolted after Joe, but it was too late. He'd gone too far. Stumbling, she fell headlong into the road, scratching her face and hands on the rocks. Empty inside, she lay there, struggling to catch her breath.

Footsteps pattered until her children surrounded her, crying her name. Thunder broke through and lifted her to her feet. The children clutched her arms and trunk, steadying her.

She looked up to the tall African, his own eyes reddened. "He left me, Thunder. What'll I do? He left me."

"You a strong woman, Nan. You wait for him, eh?"

In her mind, she called out to Joe the words she should have said. "I love ye with every gasp of breath, every beat of me heart." Why hadn't she spoken them aloud?

Joe had been by her side when she lost her mother and uncle at fifteen years old. They'd been through good times and bad ever since. He was her calming spirit in times of trouble, her shoulder to lean on when weary. Now, she was lost.

Trudging to their cabin, Nan caught sight of Mr. Carlton astride a different horse, trotting toward them. The sight of him smugly propped in the saddle caused her blood to boil. He pranced around Kilkenny, safe and sound, while poor, tortured Joe—.

Her temper exploding, she rushed the horse, causing it to rear. When it regained its footing, Nan pounded the thigh of its rider. "Ye bleeding coward! Ye'd no right to take a man from his wife, from his young ones! Yer scum, no more than scum!"

Nan wailed as arms about her waist wrenched her from Carlton, whose horse danced in confusion. She turned to see that Thunder had stopped her onslaught. The commotion drove people from their cabins which brought Johnny Reeve running.

Nan glanced at Carlton's face, twisted with rage. Her stomach churned at what would likely come next.

Pointing at her, the master of Kilkenny bellowed at Reeve. "String this lowborn hellion up! Ten lashes, goddamn it. No, fifteen!"

The slaves drew in closer, calling, "No, Master Carlton! She just lost her man! Have mercy, sir! Have mercy!"

Reeve growled. "You gotta show a wench like this what's what. Thirty lashes, sir, well laid on."

Carlton scanned the howling crowd imploring him for pity until his eyes landed on Nan. "I made a pledge of protection and I plan to keep it. Let it never be said I was incapable of mercy. Five lashes." He dismounted and walked his horse back to a tree on the south side of the stables.

Moaning and squalling, everyone in the quarter was ordered to watch the punishment. Reeve shoved Nan along, calling for Ketch to bring him some rope.

"Send me children home," Nan pleaded. "Don't force them to watch this."

"You shoulda thought of that a little earlier," Reeve said.

At the flogging tree, Reeve pulled her arms around it, binding them with the rope Ketch brought. He then ripped her shift, exposing the flesh of her back. Nan fought the panic rising in her throat. It was not the first time she'd been tied to this tree, but her horror was as severe.

At the sound of her children crying her name, she determined she'd bear it with all the strength she could muster.

Her breath heaved when Reeve approached her, checking how securely she was tied. He leaned in and whispered in her ear. "Don't worry, missy. I'll make sure you never miss your man."

Nan twisted, attempting to spit on him, but the slaver dribbled down her chin. Reeve's expression turned vicious as he shoved a knotted rag into her mouth.

"You just made this ordeal a whole lot worse."

The first lick was bearable, but each succeeding lash bit deeper into her muscle. She bit down on the knot in her mouth as she counted. One...two...three...four...five.

Six, laid on with added vigor. An extra stripe for refusing his vile advance.

Her head swam with a ringing in her ear as she was cut down from the tree. Her mind could only repeat, "I love ye, Joe. Come back. I love ye."

Chapter Sixteen

Choking back tears of fury, Thunder cut Nan from the tree. He lifted her in his arms as Jimmy and Ketch rushed forward to help. They held her from either side, hoping to avoid the swollen red stripes on her back. Jimmy pulled up her torn shift to cover her nakedness.

Thunder caught sight of the overseer's smirk, the disturbing gleam in his eye as he locked eyes with the African.

Dis man, he love to cause pain. He will come for me next.

Thunder's muscles burned with an urge to snap the man's neck. His head pounded at the sound of Carlton's tight voice.

"Reeve! Come here this instant."

The three slaves carried Nan, who moaned in pain, to Mama Juba's cabin. Her weeping children followed behind. Still, they could detect Carlton's wrath as he spoke to the disobedient overseer.

"You will follow my commands, or I will take the whip to you myself!"

Reeve growled. "You ain't got no call to talk like that in front of them darkies."

Carlton glared at the man, then spun on his heel, and stalked toward the Big House.

"He afraid of dat man," Thunder whispered to the others.

"That's what Geoffrey say," Jimmy said. "I think that white man, Reeve, know it, too."

Reaching the healer's cabin, they climbed the steps and shuffled through the door.

The old woman dabbed her eyes with her handkerchief, then pointed to the cleared table in the middle of the room. "Put her here." She frowned. "On her stomach now. Keep yo mind about ya."

They did as they were told. Thunder stepped back, his aching stomach gnawed more from the calamity that surrounded him than emptiness. He felt gelded, a limp witness to the suffering of those he loved.

Thunder crouched beside the table and spoke to Nan. "I tell you dis. You are brave, like my father. He speak his mind, but lose his life. Was dat wise?" He petted her head. "I cannot say."

Becca stood in the doorway. "Thunder, you needed in the Big House. Lady Anne wantin' to go to the privy."

His anger surged. "I will come for de cow when I am ready."

All in the room gasped.

"Watch yo'self, man," Ketch said. "You be strung up next."

Mama Juba turned to her son. "This a bad day, boy. Keep yo mouth shut, ya hear?" Her eyes became teary. "There be evil 'round this place I can't stop. Lawd knows I tried, but the conjure's pow'ful. We all keep what's said in here to ourselves."

Ketch swallowed. "I know that, Mama."

"Be sure you do." She waved her arm. "Now, the rest of y'all git on out of here. Let me help this woman. Chillun, go about yo chores. I got yo mama now and she gonna be fine. Just fine."

They all filed out the door except Thunder and young Nolan. The lad stood beside Nan, grasping her hand. "I'm the man now. I gotta stay."

Nan moaned. "Go, son. I'll be well."

Mama Juba shook her head. "Boy, there ain't nothin' you can do. Run along and help Jeb."

With questioning eyes, he looked to the old woman.

"Go on," she said. "Git! Come back in the evenin'."

Nolan's chest heaved, and he released Nan's hand. His feet dragged as he headed for the door. Thunder followed.

Dis de first time, the African thought, but not de last. Nolan's manhood will shrivel away like all de men who work dis plantation. Like all de men in dis cruel land.

◈

"Stop that jumpin'!"

Nan lay as still as she could as Mama Juba tended to the stripes on her back. While the welts were tender to the touch, the open gashes stung like she'd jabbed a hot knife into them.

The old woman grumbled as she placed the lard-covered leaves on Nan's back. "I'm gonna have to plant a senna bush 'longside my yams and turnips the way you Dillons get yo backs tore up."

Nan threw her head back in agony. "Aaah! Yer rough with me, Mama."

"Not so rough as you been with yo chillen." She placed the next leaf more gently. "The sorrowful looks on them sweet faces would break the heart of the devil's nastiest demon. You didn't give that no thought, now did ya?"

Nan's chest burned, but she gritted her teeth and said nothing.

Mama Juba placed the last of the leaves on her back, then went to the hearth. "And Thunder callin' you brave. I had to ball my hands into fists to keep from slappin' that fool."

Carrying a steaming cup and a wooden spoon, she pushed a small stool with her foot until it was beside Nan. After she sat, she dipped sassafras tea, blew on it, and fed it to Nan. "Lemme tell ya somethin'. You got troubles, sure. But yo man still livin', with no greater wish than to be here with all us. Yo chillen is alive and well in y'own house."

"Me ma used to say I feel things too much." Her uncle had said her temper would be the death of her, but she kept that to herself.

"Strong feelin's ain't no 'scuse. Little ones be countin' on ya. 'Til Joe get back, you all they got."

What did Mama Juba know of what she'd seen and smelt and tasted of cruelty? She told her what she'd told her ma. "Some things are worth the risk."

"And some things ain't! How you feel when the risk is yo babies gettin' sold away from ya? One by one, ya watch them go. You no more to the man than a bitch losin' her pups."

Nan lifted her head, brow furrowed.

"That's right. All six of my babies sold away soon as they Oscar's age or thereabouts. I ain't never seen none of them again." She spit her words like bile from her tongue. "They may be fine, they may be dead. I'll be gone and buried and won't never find out."

Nan lay her head on the table. Her body felt filled with sand. The old healer hadn't ever mentioned these children. Nan had lost one before he was born, but to have him ripped from her arms—.

"How could ye bear it?"

"Oh, I was like you. Six times, I scratched and bit to keep that slaver from taking my chile. Four boys and two little girls." She dipped out more tea. "Their tiny arms stretching out for me, cryin' my name. Two or three of the men had to hold me back. I kicked and clawed. I screamed from a place so deep ... but off they rode in the back of that wagon anyhow. I'd-a killed someone if I could.

"Like you, I got thrashed. For what? My babies still gone. The last two, they give them to another woman as soon as they weaned so's I wouldn't get attached. Ha." She wiped tears from her chin. "What they know about a mama's love? They let me hold onto Ketch. He a runt and not worth much."

Nan's eyes blurred. She touched Mama Juba's arm. "I didn't know."

"What's the use talkin' 'bout it now? I only tellin' ya 'cause yo chillen right here. And they need ya. They sufferin', Nan. And all you done was add to it. Ain't nothin' gonna change."

While the tea was normally soothing, her stomach wrenched. "I know 'twas senseless, but I didn't care. He sat upon that horse so cocky, so ... puffed up." She sipped the tea Mama Juba fed her. "I'm afeared. Afeared of meself. Me own father—an arrogant brute like Mr. Carlton, he was—he went raving mad. I saw how he talked to the air when no one was about. He'd wail of being dragged into hell by Father Alistair, the kindest of men who'd never damn another soul to the fiery pits." She sighed. "There are days, like today, when I understand the man. I feel things so fiercely that..." She swallowed, afraid to say the words. Would that give them life?

"You scared you brainsick like him."

Nan nodded.

Mama Juba ran her calloused hand along Nan's cheek. "If you is, I is, too."

At the risk of the healing leaves falling from her back, Nan lifted herself and wrapped her arms around the beautiful angel.

✤

Thunder trudged toward the rear of the Big House where he found Wilbur beckoning him from outside the door. "Where you been? The mistress getting agitated."

His blood was still high. "I am here now."

Wilbur didn't seem to notice. "Lawd, help us today. Master Carlton call me down to the kitchen. He worked up about somethin'. Becca went on ahead. Just take Lady Anne to pee and bring her right back."

Without another word, the old retainer hustled toward the kitchen house, shaking his head and mumbling to himself.

Thunder entered the house. His loathing was even stronger than usual. In the library, the crone lay like a lumpy old sack on the bed, her smell as musty as one already in the grave.

Aware of his presence, Lady Anne twisted her head to face him. Her eyes burned with anger. Still unable to speak, she squalled like an injured beast, eager but unable to rip into its attacker.

Who was she to be offended? He fought the urge to strangle her. Glancing over his shoulder to be sure they were alone, he advanced on her sickbed.

"You want to harm me, but you cannot. You were once a li-on of a woman, but now you too feeble to piss by yourself. You are nothing." He stepped closer. "And your son, he is nobody. Like you, he act strong, but he is ... how do you say it? He has lilies in his liver. Yes. He shivers like a rabbit for all to see."

The woman growled, her eyes flashing.

"I say dese things and what can you do? Cry out to your son? Take a switch to me? No. You can do nothing. Your son rape a beautiful soul, causing her death." He reached over and snatched her from the bed. "You did not know we have souls? Oh yes. We are children of God as much as you." He carried her out of the house. "Now the worm sends a real man to war while he cowers at home."

Thunder remembered the *sharo*, a festival of his people where young men proved their worth by withstanding a public caning. With each strike, they called out for more, determined to endure whatever came. Failure was more than shameful. It meant they were not fit to marry. Thunder was sent away only a few years before his time, but he was sure he would have shown great strength.

"In my land," he went on, "Carlton be called a disgrace to your family. No man at all."

The old woman's head thrashed in his arms. Her skin, normally the color of thick fog, displayed a flush of red amid twisted features. For an instant, he feared he'd provoked another fit, but, in truth, he didn't care.

Instead, a foul blast of watery stool and the warmth of acrid urine cascaded down his torso and legs, causing him to cry out an old Fulani curse. He staggered forward, nearly dropping the hag. He gagged from the stench. Lady Anne wore a contented look.

"You a filthy woman," he told her.

Becca, followed by old Wilbur, raced toward them, calling, "Thunder, what happened. Oh, Lawd-a mercy! I told ya not to take so long. You lucky Master Carlton gone to see Mr. Gatch for a spell."

Wilbur stopped short when the stink hit him. "Ki! Bring the lady to the well, Becca. This can't wait for the wood tub."

Thunder, carrying the old crow, also headed toward Wilbur.

"She ain't gonna like that, Wilbur," Becca called. "You know she hate the cold water."

The old man shook his head. "We can't help none of that. She foul!"

"De colder de better," Thunder yearned to say, but kept it to himself. Once beside the well, he held the pale, scraggy woman upright while the two house servants stripped her down to her shift.

Wilbur hauled the bucket up from the bottom of the well. "I'll wash her," Wilbur told Becca, "while you get somethin' so's to dry her off and another gown. And hurry! She could take sick. We riskin' the ague every minute she out here."

Thunder shook with rage.

"Hold still, boy," Wilbur said. "This po' woman shiverin'."

Dis is my life, Thunder realized. I am covered in de dung of de white master.

Chapter Seventeen

Furious, Thunder poured bucket after bucket of well water over his shirt and pants, yet the stench of his mistress remained. Was he destined to carry Lady Anne's stink for the rest of his days? He came from a proud people. Surely, this was not his fate.

He thought of his father's courage when he'd challenged the cruel leader of their people. Yes, the price was high for his entire family, but Thunder remembered his father with pride. Even a woman, Nan Dillon, had shown bravery as she confronted Carlton, the murdering coward.

But what of me? What courage have I shown?

He was a beast of burden, called upon to shovel horse dung and carry old crones who covered him with their filth. No more than a dumb animal, a disgrace to his ancestors. With his sweet Minda, there might have been a chance for happiness, but no longer.

He could leave, run away to the British army. Most knew of their offer of freedom in exchange for fighting alongside the king's soldiers. Word had spread of slaves in the area who'd made the effort. Too many were found and dragged back to be branded, flogged, or worse. Yet, some were never heard from again. Likely, they lay dead in a desolate swamp, but perhaps they'd made it.

My life is worthless now. My peace may be found in death.

Returning to the barn, he saw he was alone. Facing east, he lowered himself in prayer. To the best of his ability, he performed *Istikhara*, a petition for the guidance of Allah. As he said the necessary prayers, he grew fearful he'd forgotten too many of the words.

"Have mercy on me," he added. "I wish only to serve You."

Bowed in submission, tears came to his eyes as he prayed in Arabic, "'O Allah! Behold I ask You the good through Your Knowledge, and ability through Your Power, and beg out of Your infinite Bounty. For surely You have Power; I have none. You know all; I know not. You are the Great Knower of all things.'" Heart pounding, he breathed deeply. "Do I go or do I stay? In Your time, send me Your sign. I will follow it, even if it means I remain at Kilkenny."

Though the thought sickened him.

At the sound of shuffling boots, Thunder leapt to his feet and grabbed a pitchfork. He stepped into Hector's now-empty stall and began to muck it out.

A small cat-o-nine-tails at his side, Johnny Reeve walked toward him. He hacked and spat inches from Thunder's foot. "Head out to the sheep pasture. I'm needing Ketch elsewhere."

Thunder looked Reeve in the eye, his head cocked. "Is dis what Master Carlton say?"

The overseer lifted the whip and shook it. "It's what I say and what you gonna do!"

The clearing of a throat caused both men to look to the barn door. There stood Becca, her hands twisting in her apron. "Thunder, you gotta come to the Big House. Lady Anne gettin' restless again."

Turning to Reeve, Thunder jammed his pitchfork into the earthen floor inches from the overseer's feet.

Reeve stepped back. "Watch yourself, you bloody ape!"

Staring straight ahead, Thunder strode past him toward the Big House.

Becca trotted beside to keep up. "That man wanta kill ya. I seen it in his eyes sure as I breathe. What we gonna do 'round here?"

Thunder said nothing, but he knew. Allah's sign had come.

✦

Seated in the Gatch home, Carlton scanned his surroundings. While no squalid peasant hut, the home was modest by Kilkenny standards. A log structure of a story and a half, it held a parlor, dining room, and two bedrooms. As usual, the kitchen was a separate building in the back. He glanced at the hutch where Walter poured drinks. The creamware dishes, he thought, while nice, were nowhere near the quality of Mother's fine porcelain from Ireland.

Walter Gatch handed a glass of port to him, his wife, and Rosabel. Before sitting, he lifted his own glass. "We drink to our daughter and her betrothed, Carlton de Barnefort. May the joining of our two families bring great joy and prosperity to us all."

Carlton sipped the wine, which spread much-needed warmth through him on this most wretched day. Why had he sent Hector with Joe Dillon? He had other fine horses he could have contributed. Truth be told, the grief Joe's family displayed at his parting shook him to his core. Didn't they realize sacrifices had to be made? Were they to be immune? And the display by Nan Dillon was off the hooks! To say nothing of Reeve's insubordination. He took a longer swig.

"I must ask." Mrs. Gatch set her glass on a side table. "Why are you here?"

"Mother!" Rosabel's alabaster skin glowed like a burning ember.

Mrs. Gatch showed no such embarrassment. "It's a reasonable question." She looked toward Carlton. "Of course, you are welcome any time, even unannounced."

Rosabel leaned forward. "Oh, do say you'll stay for the midday meal."

"He'll stay," said Walter.

Carlton was in no hurry to return to Kilkenny. He addressed Mrs. Gatch, the only one who'd made no offer to share her meal. "That's very kind, madam. I accept your invitation."

The older woman sighed. "Well, that's settled. I'll ask again. What drags you away from a fine feast at home to sample our humble victuals?"

He turned toward Rosabel with a gaze he hoped looked earnest. "Dear Rosabel has been such a comfort to me since the passing of my father followed, as you know, by Mother's pitiable affliction. I've been lost, you might say, and Rosabel has been a bulwark for me in the face of these horrific tragedies."

Rosabel's blue eyes glistened. Was she teary? Her pink lips parted. In awe, he hoped. Carlton felt emboldened.

"I trust I may open my heart to you both," he told her parents. "I am in despair every time my darling Rosabel leaves Kilkenny. I ache for her lovely face and kind words." He sighed with every ounce of drama he could muster. "Dare I ask it? My greatest wish is that she join me as my wife. Right away. With no clergy in this area, I would like to live as man and wife with the understanding that a ceremony will take place as soon as a priest appears. As is the custom."

He figured he'd have to fake the moist eyes only a man truly in love could display, but there was no need. After the morning he'd had, this was more emotional than he'd imagined. "There. I've said it. I beg your mercy on my deplorable state."

Rosabel leapt from her chair and rushed to him, kissing him on the cheek. Glancing at her father, her face fell, and she returned to her proper place.

Carlton's confidence washed away at the sight of Walter Gatch, who stood up with legs apart and arms crossed. His brow created an overhang that darkened his eyes.

"Tell me straight. You're gonna take Rosabel away from her family, place her in Kilkenny with none but your invalid mother to wait on hand and foot, whilst you're off fighting the rebels? You shoulda been on your way to Major Ferguson by now. I wasn't gonna say nothing about you dragging your feet. But this?"

Carlton leaned forward. "Walter, you've got me all wrong. I've met my obligation to the king. As we speak, my man, Joe Dillon, is on his way to stand in my stead."

Walter's eyes flashed. "One of your hands? The Irish fellow? How's he supposed to lead the yahoos they're rounding up? You're needed because you're a gentleman, you damned fool. We're needing an officer in the Loyalist militia. And here you sit!"

The obvious difference in their station flew all over Carlton. He stood. "I will not be spoken to in this manner. I have done what I believe is best for my king and for my family, and I refuse to be questioned in this way."

Walter took a menacing step toward him, causing him to flinch.

"Get out of my house. You ain't fit for my only daughter!"

Rosabel sprang from her chair and clutched Carlton's arm. "Papa, no! I love him." She turned to Mrs. Gatch. "Mama, make him stop."

The older woman took a deep breath. "Now, Walter, think. Who else is Rosabel gonna marry?"

The affront was too much. Carlton peeled Rosabel's grasp from his arm and stormed from the house. He snatched the reins from the hitching post and started to mount his horse when Rosabel dashed through the door, hysterical.

"No, Carlton! Don't leave!" She reached him and wrapped her arms around his waist. "I love you. He'll calm down, I promise. Don't leave."

He couldn't imagine tolerating Walter Gatch another minute. "What does it matter?"

She looked up at him, her eyes pleading. "It does. It matters."

He petted her hair and felt, for the first time, a true affection for the girl. What would he do without her? Not only because of his troublesome mother, but for him. Was this what being in love felt like?

"Are you willing to come to Kilkenny as my wife?"

"Yes, anything!"

He thought for a second. "After your parents are asleep, can you meet me at the big tree where we picnic sometimes? It's not far. I'll wait, and if you come, I'll bring you home as my bride."

She looked into his eyes. "Nothing will stop me."

✦

Having made his decision, Thunder wavered between a strong resolve and a gnawing unease. He returned his petulant mistress to her bed. Instead of leaving the house, he stole toward the front where Carlton's study was located. Through the open door, he saw a quill pen on the desk and knew he'd found his target.

After creeping into the room, he slowly closed the door. Its squeak was slight but as grating as a screech owl to him. He rounded the desk. Opening drawers, he located a sheet of parchment and placed it on the flat surface. Lifting the quill, he dipped it in the inkwell. He had been a boy when last he touched a writing tool, but it felt natural in his hand.

He began to write a verse from the Qur'an when a splotch of ink marred the paper. He shook the nib into the bottle and tried again.

"Kifayat li hu allh. ealayh taetamid ealaa almursalun."

"Sufficient for me is Allah; upon Him rely the reliers." As Thunder completed the last marks of the verse, he heard the stamping of boots on the veranda outside the open study window. The grunting indicated it was Mr. Carlton.

He blew on the barely dry ink and replaced the pen. He heard the large front door open and the echoes of Carlton's footsteps in the hallway. Risking the smearing of the sacred words, he rolled the parchment and stuffed it into his shirt. The thudding of boots against the wooden planks signaled the master's approach.

"Who shut this?" he heard Carlton mutter under his breath.

Barefooted, Thunder slipped to the wall behind the door. His heart felt ready to explode at the now-familiar creaking of the study door. He heard Old Wilbur.

"Master Carlton, there ya be. I'm needin' to talk to ya about yo mama, suh. We done had a time with her this mornin'."

"Bloody hell!" Mr. Carlton said. "What is it now?"

The voices of the planter and his old slave faded as they moved to another part of the house. Likely the library where Lady Anne was abed.

He could hear their low rumblings as he slid through the now-opened door, into the hallway, and onto the veranda. He could barely breathe from the danger of leaving out the front door like a white man. He hustled to the safety of the barn where he hid his parchment scroll under some hay. Then, he returned to work.

Never had he been so happy to sling shovelfuls of manure.

✞

When Tarlton Brown and Levi told the Cracker's Neck Boys they'd be moving to his father's line company, Alden volunteered to join them.

The lieutenant seemed less than happy about the idea. Before leaving camp, he took Alden aside, wasting no time in revealing his concern.

"Let me make this clear. My sister, Suzanne, is promised to Levi."

Alden's heart sank, but he wasn't surprised by the news. "Levi's a good man."

"And he'll make a fine husband. He's like a brother to me."

"Right." Chagrined, Alden struggled to maintain his composure. His admiration of Suzanne must have been painfully obvious. He returned to his brush hut to gather his meager belongings, but more to avoid the accusation in Tarlton Brown's scowl.

Once they reached the redoubts south of Burton's Ferry, Mr. Billy Brown was proven correct. Shots had rung out from both sides of the Savannah River every day since they'd arrived. Alden couldn't speak for the Tory side of the water, but no Patriot had been killed or even hit, except a new fellow, Brandon, from south of the river.

He'd been grazed across his upper arm. "That was only inches from my brain."

"If it'd gone through one of your ears, it would've missed altogether," called out a man named Colding.

"Joke all you want, that was too close. A little to the right," Brandon said, "and there's my heart."

Others laughed at the amount of force required to pierce such an obstacle.

"Damn," Brandon said. "What I need is some of that rum I hid by Hershman's Lake. A few swigs of that would set me right."

"Hershman's Lake?" Benjamin Green licked his lips. "I know where that is. My family's nearby. What you got there?"

"Three jugs of the good stuff buried by a particular tree. Only I know which one." Brandon touched his arm, then winced. "But I could describe it to you."

Alden brightened. A swig of the brown elixir would soothe his nerves rattled by fitful salvos of gunfire. Along with Colding, Benjamin Green, and Tarlton Brown, Alden volunteered for a foray to the south side of the Savannah River. After procuring a sturdy, dugout canoe, the four headed down King's Creek. Reaching the river, they paddled upstream.

"Only a whisper, boys," Tarlton Brown said. "We needn't disturb any wild creatures on the Georgia side."

The scatterings of Tories to the south did not dull their enthusiasm for the mission. The four oarsmen made quick work of the gentle currents.

"Not far, boys," Benjamin Green said. "Just around this bend up ahead."

But they were not to reach that bend. As if on cue, a gang of thirty or more Tories arose from the brush. Dozens of musket, shotgun, and rifle muzzles were trained at their heads.

"Ambush," whispered Tarlton.

One of the Tories called out. "You done come to the right place. Row over here a spell and we'll consider sparing your lives."

"Hell, no!" yelled Colding.

"If'n you don't, we'll shoot every one of you fellas full of holes. The snakes and gators'll appreciate gnawing on your carcasses, bitter though they'll be."

"They'll kill us either way," Alden said to the others. They maneuvered the canoe to face down river and paddled feverishly for the Carolina bank.

Lead balls whistled past, many plopping into the water beside them. Colding dropped his oar and reached for his gun.

"Damn you, man!" Tarlton shouted. "There's too many of 'em. Pick up that blasted oar!"

A ball whisked by Alden's ear, bringing goose flesh to his scalp.

Colding released his gun and snatched the paddle, but Alden never saw it pierce the water. A sharp impact on his left shoulder lifted him from his seat, causing him to tumble overboard. An agonizing burn bit into him as the freezing water stole his breath. Flailing, he latched onto the side of the canoe with his good hand. Lead balls splashed into the water on all sides.

Still gasping, he saw Colding collapse into the bottom of the canoe. Within seconds, Green fell beside Colding. Were they dead? Tarlton Brown continued to plow his oar into the water, pushing the canoe ever-closer to the shore.

I'm going to die now, Alden thought. In his mind's eye, he saw his bloated body floating down the Savannah River to the sea.

He struggled to focus. To his shock, he saw his father, laughing while Alden struggled to mount a small donkey, only to slide off the other side. In an instant, he was beside Turkey Creek, wailing at a young Carlton to get out of the water. A small alligator's eyes peeked above the surface only yards from his big brother.

He was beneath the Liberty Tree with like-minded young men, calling out his determination to give his life, if necessary, for freedom. Now he would do so. He glimpsed the beautiful Suzanne.

Alden's feet scraped the river bottom, reminding him he was still alive. Tarlton Brown yelped as he twitched this way and that. With difficulty, the giant of a man leapt from the canoe, yanking it toward the underbrush. Alden moved to its stern. The bullets that still flew seemed to give him extraordinary strength as he pushed the boat ashore.

Once within the thicket's cover, Alden dropped to the ground. He flinched when he touched his wounded shoulder. His hand came back sticky and red.

Tarlton Brown pulled off his shirts and looked them over. "Three shots."

Alden glanced at the man's naked back. "You're marked by welts, but no blood."

"That's good," Tarlton said. "It hurts like hell."

Alden rose and looked in the canoe. Colding lay insensible but breathing. Several bloody holes were splattered across his shirt. Awake, Benjamin Green pushed himself to his knees. A large pool of blood stained the lower back of his hunting shirt.

"We need a wagon, Lieutenant," Alden said. "I'll be back as soon as I can."

"No," Tarlton Brown said. "You stay. I'm most able to go." Without waiting for a response, he disappeared into the woods.

Gasping for breath, Benjamin Green said, "May a plague take me before I strike out on such a fool's folly again." His weak laugh dissolved into quiet sobs.

Alden felt wetness on his cheeks as well.

⚘

As dusk fell, Thunder took the leather bag from Mama Juba. In the fading light of her cabin, he pulled the drawstrings apart and peered inside to find the scrap of paper he'd passed to the old woman earlier.

The healer grunted. "I took the rest of that parchment and burnt it up. Then I took the ashes and set them in the wind. Y'ain't puttin' me in danger 'long with yo fool self!"

He closed the bag and placed the strings around his neck. "Dis carry de word of God. I will wear it everywhere I go." He kissed Mama Juba on the brow.

"Wherever ya go? What ya up to?"

The sound of Reeve humming as he strolled through the quarters caused them to hold their breaths. If Thunder were discovered outside his own cabin after dark, there would be hell to pay—for them both.

Once the overseer was near the Dillon place, they exhaled. But they dared not risk a word until he'd left the lane.

Mama Juba pushed Thunder toward her door. "I don't need to know nothin' else 'bout yo African ways. Jus' git on out of here."

He held her arm, yearning to express his love for her, but no words came. "'Night, Mama," he said and slipped into the growing darkness.

He returned to his cabin one last time. The familiar scent of wood, smoky ash, and woolen blanket brought an ache to his chest. He took the bare minimum—a cup, a spare shirt worn through, and a sheathed hunting knife he'd pilfered from the barn—and rolled them into the blanket. He tied the bundle with a leather thong. After one last look, he sneaked from the cabin and began his journey east. He'd travel along the stage road, but not on it, toward the rising sun.

✦

The old woman kept watch before the rear window of her cabin. Her eyes widened when she saw a bent figure creep into the black of night. Shaking her head, she crept to her shelves and climbed upon a stool, reaching to the highest shelf for a clay pot. She removed the lid. With great care, she carried it from her cabin, padding to where the figure had been. There, mumbling under her breath, she emptied its contents over the low-lying brush.

Soundlessly returning to the cabin, she replaced its lid and returned the pot to the shelf. Brushing aside a tear, she lay down to sleep.

☥

Thunder inhaled the brisk freshness of the night air. The soothing chirps of crickets and katydids kept him company as he wended his way toward the road to the village. It would be safe to travel the path at night, he was sure. Rarely was anyone about after dark. Once at Red Hill, like Joe Dillon, he could connect with the stage road toward Charles Town. His veins flowed with excitement. In his imagination, he could taste the freedom he knew as a boy.

Lost in his thoughts, Thunder barely remembered where he was when a loud shriek pierced the air. He dropped to the ground in terror. Turning over, he was met by the glowing eyes of a crazed screech owl, its wings outstretched and its talons coming straight for his throat.

Instinctively, he flipped and curled into a ball. It came so close, Thunder could feel the whish of air from its wings, but he was not touched. He lay shaking for several minutes, gasping for breath. What did that mean? He'd been so sure of the signs, but now...

Gazing into the night sky. He thought of Mama Juba's claim that the ancestors were with them still, watching from the stars. For the first time in years, he felt the presence of his father. It had happened often when Papa had first died, but less over time. He grasped the leather bag with the sacred words inside.

What do you want from me? I am lost.

In the rustling breeze, he could have sworn he heard the words, "Be a man." But as the wind passed, he wasn't so sure. His eyes burning with emotion, he rose to his feet and continued on his way.

On the rutted road, the walking was easier, and his heart began to slow to its normal pace. Yet, he was surprised once again by the sound of wagon wheels and a horse coming his way. He leapt from the road into some brush. Looking at his light-colored homespun shirt, he tore it off and stuffed it beneath him with his gear. He prayed he'd not be seen.

As the wagon neared, he recognized Carlton's laugh followed by the chatter of Miss Rosabel Gatch. Without breathing, he lifted his head to watch the two ride by, her arm tucked beneath his. He sighed. Never would he understand the ways of these strange people.

Chapter Eighteen

Carlton woke but refused to open his eyes. The soft breathing beside him matched his own. He'd not felt such serenity since he was a lad, and he yearned for it never to end.

Replaying in his mind the drama of the previous night, he reached for Rosabel's hand and held it beneath the blankets. He thought of his relief when she'd appeared out of the darkness and, seeing him, ran toward the wagon. She threw a small satchel in the back and clambered on. He smiled at how she snuggled beside him on the seat, her delicate scent intoxicating. Had she always smelled like that?

Later, when he led her toward his bed, she gasped, not with fear but something else—anticipation? Giddiness? How different than the slave girl, Minda, or the false pleasure of the few whores he'd been with. He swept those images from his mind forever.

Once the two had consummated their union, tears rolled from eyes that still gazed at him with fondness. Carlton's heart swelled. So, this was how it was supposed to feel.

Now, with her warm body close to his, he felt comforted and safe in a way he'd forgotten was possible. He resented the morning light tickling his eyelids. The harshness of the day and what it could bring threatened this new-found happiness.

"Master Carlton, suh."

Ugh. Wilbur had let himself into their chamber. Rosabel awakened with a squeal as she yanked the blankets to her chin.

Once he sat up, Carlton noticed the sun was higher in the sky than he'd expected. It was already mid-morning.

"It's only Wilbur, darling," he told his new wife.

"Why is he in our room?"

He rubbed her cheek. "It is his duty to see to my needs, as it is now his duty to meet yours. You have risen in the world, my dear. You are no longer a mere farmer's daughter, but lady of the manor." He looked to his servant. "What is it?"

"You needed outside, Master Carlton. Right away. That fella, Mr. Reeve, is spittin' mad and askin', since he ain't to come near the Big House, you meet him at the barn."

"Good Lord, what next?" Loath to do so, he rolled out of bed. At least it wasn't Walter Gatch, as he'd feared. Wilbur bustled over with his clothes and helped him dress.

"Miss Rosabel," the old servant said, "Becca will bring yo breakfast directly."

"I'll be downstairs in a few minutes," the girl answered, still clutching the covers to her neck.

"No need, miss. Ya can eat right here."

"Oh my!" Confused, Rosabel looked to Carlton.

"My mother always took her morning meal abed." Her flushed cheeks and bright blue eyes brought renewed warmth to his heart. "Lady of the manor," he repeated. Once he'd put on his boots, he blew her a kiss and headed for the stables.

He'd nearly reached them when Johnny Reeve strode toward him, a scowl distorting his already-ugly face.

"We got us a real problem here." He couldn't stand still. Every nerve in his body seemed to scream.

His agitation was contagious. "Go on."

"I made sure everybody was up and working like you said. I done all I was s'posed to do, I want you to know that. You said stay away from the Big House and I done it!"

"Cut to Hecuba, man! What is it?"

"That big darky, Thunder, ain't nowhere to be found. We done searched high and low for that scoundrel to see if he wandered off in the night and fell in a ditch, but there ain't no sign of him. None at all."

Carlton's blood rose. His father had taken great pride that none of their slaves had run off as they had from other properties. There had to be another explanation. "Look again. You missed him. He's too valuable to leave bleeding somewhere."

Reeve gnawed on his thumbnail. "We can do that, sir. We sure can. But chances are, that lowdown cur is miles from here by now. We don't need to waste no time—"

Carlton waved him off. "Do as I say! He's here. Find him!"

He started toward the house. Was it possible Thunder had run away? It sickened him to think of it. Yet, those eyes at Joe Dillon's departure. A mixture of pain and rage. Perhaps he'd dismissed it too easily.

He turned back. "Stop!" he called to Reeve. "We'll get the dogs. In case."

Thirty minutes later, Carlton joined Reeve and Ketch, who were bringing his four hunting hounds out of Thunder's cabin. The dogs lunged from the ends of their leashes, keen on treeing their prey.

Ruth, Nan, and some others huddled outside the kitchen. The carpenter, Jeb, had his arms over the shoulder of Daniel while Little Oscar whimpered at the man's feet. Their distress was clear, but Carlton had no choice. In that moment, he despised both Thunder and Reeve for putting him in such a position.

Young Nolan brought his horse. Carlton mounted, then gave the nod for the dogs to be released. In a cacophony of shouts and barking and wails from the women, the dogs tore off behind Thunder's cabin.

Carlton was but a few yards behind them when the pack drew up short, sneezing and whimpering, turning this way and that in a state of confusion. When Reeve and Ketch caught up on foot, the overseer grabbed their leashes and dragged them away from the area. His alarm was clear. "What kinda person would harm these poor pups?"

Carlton's horse was skittish as well, reflecting his rider's rage. "Get them back to their pens. By God, I'll find out what wickedness is afoot here and there will be pain!"

❖

Carlton mounted the cabin's steps and flung the thin wooden door open, caring little if it flew from its hinges. It slammed against the wall and bounced back which allowed him to send it crashing once again.

Within the darkened cabin, Mama Juba huddled beside the hearth. A single opened shutter showed the day's light. The slave woman seemed shrunken with fear, wringing her withered hands.

Carlton approached, determined to increase her anxiety. "What have you done, you conniving witch?"

Avoiding his eyes, she kept her head down, "I ain't done nothin', suh. I'm a old woman. What could I do?"

He scanned the hanging herbs and shelves of jars. "Don't be so modest. You can do plenty." The opened shutter faced the area where his dogs were enfeebled. "What did you do to my hounds? Confess now! It's your only chance."

"Suh, I ain't done nothin' to them dogs. I look out my window, wonderin' what the fuss be about and seen them creatures stop dead, coughin' and sneezin'." Tears poured down her lined face in earnest. "I got to wonderin' what could cause such as that." Eyes widened, she peered into his. "I ain't had nothin' to do with it, suh. You gotta believe me."

"Do I?"

"The onliest thing I done then was to look up to my shelf and seen my jar that holds the hot foot powder, empty. It gone, Master Carlton. I got no idea who coulda done it, but it weren't me."

Carlton glanced at the row of jars. "No idea? You let anyone who pleases come in and steal powerful potions?"

"No, suh, I don't. All I can figure is when Thunder stopped by yestiddy."

"Thunder was here?"

"He lookin' for somethin' to ease his sorrow what with Joe Dillon leavin' and all. I give him a cup of sassafras tea I done brewed. But now I'm rememberin', before I give it to him, I had to leave for a bit. You know, to make water. It musta been then he took my itchin' powder."

"He took the jar?" It was of good size.

She shook her head. "I'd-a noticed that for sure. He coulda emptied the powder in a cloth bag, but there ain't no way for me to know." She covered her eyes with both hands. "Please don't whup me, suh. I'm just a old healer who means no harm to no one. Not man nor beast."

Could the nearly lame old crone have managed an exploit such as this? He doubted it. It was the guile of the African that enraged him. To be outwitted by a scheming, lowdown brute was unacceptable. He'd not be made a fool!

Carlton thrust his finger only inches from the old woman's face. "If this happens again, I'll look to none but you for my pound of flesh."

Having little idea which way Thunder went, Carlton, Johnny Reeve, and Ketch spent the rest of the day tracking him through forest, field, and swamp. To no avail.

✢

Joe Dillon sat beside the fire he'd built on the second night of his travels. He huddled close to the flames to ward off the brisk air as well as night creatures. He should have been almost there, considering the fine steed he was riding. But his heart was heavy, and he was in no rush to reach his destination.

He'd stopped on the edge of a swamp, far enough from the stagecoach road to avoid unwanted attention. What was Mr. Carlton thinking to send him on a quality horse like Hector? He was a target for any ruffian roaming the backcountry, as though dangers did not abound in any event.

As the katydids sang their night song accompanied by owls, bats, and one particularly hardy bullfrog, Joe could think of nothing but his beautiful wife. Would she ever forgive him? He could not imagine his life without her. His own heart ached at her pain which he felt helpless to prevent.

What if he were to go back on his word and return? Life could not be the same. They would be set on the road, beggared, in a cruel world where even friends and family were at each other's throats. He'd seen so many back in Ireland wither and die once they'd been evicted from their homes. Nan had seen them, too. Were they gone so long she'd forgotten their suffering?

A rustling snapped Joe to attention. Something was out there. Was it four-legged or two? He lifted his rifle and aimed in the direction of the sound.

"Show yerself!" he called out.

"Peace, brother," returned a voice. "Can I come in? My hands are raised."

"Aye, but slowly."

The barefoot stranger limped in from the dark. The firelight showed a haggard man in a torn coat with a musket slung over his back. As he'd said, his empty hands stretched out for Joe to see. "May I share the fire with you tonight? I mean no harm to anyone."

Joe lowered his gun. "Sit. What name do ye go by, then?"

"Mumford. John Mumford." He nodded toward Hector, tied to a tree. "That's a fine-looking steed you got there."

"I'm Joe Dillon. It belongs to me employer, Carlton de Barnefort, from Kilkenny Plantation. Near Red Hill."

"I'm hoping to head through there myself. Been gone too long." He laughed. "My wife's name is Patience, but I believe she's run dry of it."

Joe threw another small branch onto the fire. "I wish I was turning back meself. If I may, where ye coming from?"

The stranger shifted. "Well, you seem peaceable enough. I come from the fighting at Charles Town. It pains me to say we had to give it up."

"You with the king or against?"

"I hope I won't forfeit my place by the fire, but I fought with the rebels. The British have taken the city."

"I've no stake in this fight, man. I came to America to escape such things but am being drawn into it against me will." Joe handed the man some beef jerky from his satchel. "De Barnefort's sent me to fight with the Loyalists, but I hold no ill feelings toward ye."

John Mumford ripped into the meat like a starving dog.

Joe's heart beat faster. What had this man been through? What would he face at the battle lines? He could only pray the conflict was over. "What was it like?"

The man's face fell. He put the last of his jerky in his mouth and picked up a nearby stick to stir the fire. "I won't lie to you, friend. It was bad. Me and my men were ready for them. We built abatis outside the city, a barricade of sharpened sticks we wired together. Then we stationed ourselves within the walls as the enemy got nearer and nearer."

He sighed. "They surrounded us. Cut us off from our supply lines. Ammunition was scarce, but so was food. Some lost heart and fled to the other side. Each day, the Brits moved their lines closer and closer, tearing down our abatis and emptying the canal. We bombarded them with everything we had, but they just rebuilt their lines the next day. And the German Jaegers! Deadly. We dare not lift our heads from behind the parapet without getting them shot off."

Joe had fought with the Levellers in Ireland, but they had no firearms. Most of their attacks were in disguise and under cover of darkness. His stomach wrenched at the agony on the man's face as much as the intensity of the fight.

Mumford went on. "One fellow, Parker from Virginia, fought beside me. He lifted his head the slightest bit. I couldn't believe it. A rifle shot rang out and, in an instant, he crumbled at my feet, the top of his head blown off." He stirred the fire once again. "It was hell. We were blinded by dust and sand. Bullets whistled all around, it seemed. I can still hear the deafening roar of cannon fire as their balls bounced and sparked along our trenches."

"Ye needn't say more if ye'd rather not."

Mumford shook his head. "Over time, our gunners shot whatever they could find—hunks of iron, broken bottles, old axes, gun barrels. Even small rocks. Food got scarcer. Some of the men started ransacking the houses of civilians. Women and children without enough for themselves. I and the other officers threatened the severest of punishments, but they were so desperate."

"Yer an officer, then?"

"Captain in the militia. Some of my comrades quit. Just threw down their arms. Not I nor anyone else could convince them otherwise." His voice grew quieter. "Once the soldiers at Fort Moultrie gave up, it was only a matter of time. My heart broke at the news. Our misery was so great, faces everywhere were swole with lack of sleep. You could barely see their eyes. I suppose I looked the same.

"When the end came, I'm ashamed to say part of me was grateful. The Brits agreed we in the militia could go home on parole. We marched out the city past the British in our deplorable condition, few in number by then. I heard one of their officers call out, 'You've made a gallant defense of it. Of that there is no doubt.'"

Joe could think of nothing to say. He needed time to take everything John Mumford—Captain John Mumford—had told him.

The soldier laid down. "Do you mind if I call it a night? I'm still so very tired, you see."

"Not at all, sir."

Joe laid down as well, but sleep didn't come for some time. The mojo bag around his neck weighed heavily on his chest. He yearned to do the right thing. If only someone could tell him what that was.

✦

The sun creeping above the horizon flickered through the trees. As he lay on the ground, Joe took in the scents of black, moist soil mixed with the embers of last night's fire. Twittering birds and buzzing insects filled the air.

Joe sat up to see Captain Mumford in the growing daylight brush the debris from his tattered clothing. The man's drawn face wore the trials he'd described the night before.

"I must be on my way, Dillon. It was a pleasure to share your fire. I wish you...I don't know what I wish you, for I cannot hope for your success."

Joe stood, dusting his own clothes. "I confess, I'm not sure I hope for it meself. I am torn, Captain. In Ireland, I fought against the king and now I'm off to join me old enemy."

Mumford cocked his head to one side. "Life is never as simple as it should be, is it? I am now on parole, expected to sit out the rest of this fight. But can I honor that with a clear conscience? If not, then what of a man's word, which I've given?"

Joe's jaw clenched. He was furious at the villainy of Carlton de Barnefort, but also at life itself for creating these impossible choices.

"Listen," Mumford said. "I may be a fool, but I sense I can trust you. I don't know what's to come, but I'm going to Cracker's Neck, along the Savannah River. Not far from Silver Bluff. Like-minded men can be found there if your conscience sends you in a different direction. At least they were last I heard."

Joe shook the man's hand, almost resentful of yet another choice. "May yer travels be safe, Captain Mumford. And yer conscience clear."

He laughed. "Can one ever hope for such a situation? God be with you, as well." Hobbling, the weary soldier continued on his way.

Chapter Nineteen

Carlton rose earlier the following morning, anxious to resume his search for the runaway. His blood boiled every time he thought of the insult to him, but more to his father's memory. After all Thomas had done for the bloody ingrate! If he weren't recaptured, how many others would attempt it? A situation he could ill afford.

After a hearty breakfast, he returned to his chamber to kiss his wife good morning. He peeked into the room and there she sat, propped in their bed smoothing the coverlet. He smiled. She filled a hole in him he hadn't known was there.

Catching sight of her husband, Rosabel giggled. "What are you doing out there, hiding like a child?"

"Feasting on your beauty," he said as he approached her bed. "Good morning to you, my dear. What will you do today?"

"The weather is so lovely and warm, I'd love to spend time in the garden. I must learn all about it so I can keep it up as your mother has." Her eyebrows raised. "And I'll see to her, of course."

"Don't let her demands tie you down, love." He brushed her lips with his. "I'm off for the day. We must find Thunder before he gets much farther."

"You will succeed, Carlton. I'm certain of it."

Still basking in the warmth of her words, he reached the stables, riding crop in hand. Red-faced, Reeve was railing against Jimmy, who should have been at the cow pens.

"What's all this?" Carlton asked.

"Ah, this fella here claims two of our cows been slaughtered, their haunches cut off, then left to rot."

The rawboned cow-hunter stared at his feet, hat in hand. "That's right, Master Carlton. And I seen who done it. I was hidin' behind a tree and they ain't seen me, but I seen them."

"Go on."

He lifted his eyes. "Well, first I heard one of the cows bellowin' so I knowed he was hurt. I thought he might be stuck in some brambles and I hurried his way. That's when I saw the rustlers. They already had one carcass down and a man was carving his flank. There weren't but four of 'em. Why they need to kill that second one?"

Carlton crossed his arms. "Get to the point."

"Well, they was four white men so I dast not show myself. I hid behind a big tree, like I said. But I seen 'em clear. One was a swellup, orderin' the other three about."

With nervous eyes, Reeve glanced at Carlton, then back to Jimmy. "Tell us what he looked like. That's what we need to know."

"The one who act like the boss, he had a thick neck and big nose that was bent-like. Beady eyes, too. From where I stood, he didn't have no teeth to speak of."

"Ben John," Carlton said. "Had to be."

"It do sound like him," Reeve said.

"I couldn't see the other fellas' faces that good 'cause they was movin' around doin' what that beady-eyed one told 'em. But I heard him call one 'Matt' and the skinny one, I believe he call "Lijah.' I never heard the other one's name."

"I'll be damned," Reeve said. "That do sound like Ben and his bunch. They fighting against the rebels, like you be. Must need some food."

"Hogwash, man!" Carlton still smarted from their treatment at McHeath's two weeks back. "They're no more than vulgar louts who happen to be Tories. Any buffoon can claim to fight for the king as an excuse to rob and torture."

Reeve took a step back. "Now hold on there, Master Carlton."

"No, you hold on! Did they ask my permission, one who supports their cause, for meat to feed their troops? And what kind of barbarian kills to take only the best of an animal, leaving the rest to rot or draw predators? I won't have it! They're spitting in my face, that's what they're about."

"Now, them boys don't mean no harm, Master Carlton. You know that," Reeve said.

"Jimmy, tell Geoffrey I want the cattle kept as near the cow pens as possible, day and night. Have a couple of the fellas sit watch at night, guns loaded. If they see any cow thief sneaking around, they're to shoot. Do you hear me?"

"Yes, suh, Master Carlton. I'll tell 'im right away." Jimmy did not hesitate but ran from the barn like he'd been stung.

Reeve chewed on his lip. "Master Carlton, it's my job to see to that."

"So it is. First, Thunder is missing, likely run off, and now this. You're doing a hell of a job so far. As for the cattle thieves, I expect you to carry out my orders to the letter. I'll not have those rogues make a dupe of me!"

Upon his return, Carlton groaned at the sight of Walter Gatch's horse and wagon in front of the Big House. Still furious about the cattle, he stopped to collect himself before confronting his father-in-law. He hoped the man didn't expect Rosabel to return home. She'd been de-flowered, now suitable only as his wife.

Carlton found father and daughter huddled together in the parlor, tears streaming down Rosabel's face. He strutted into the room, determined to make a bold entrance. He would have preferred that Rosabel leap from her father's side and take her place next to him, but that did not happen.

Instead, Walter Gatch rose from his chair. He trained his eyes on Carlton with such loathing that it took every iota of strength for him to maintain his air of confidence.

"You have disappointed me, lad." Walter looked at Rosabel. "Both of you. I made my feelings clear, but you swept them away as no more than an old man's drivel."

"Oh, Daddy." Rosabel hung her head to cry.

Another voice startled Carlton. "What's done is done."

He spun to find Mrs. Gatch in a wingback chair in the corner.

She looked him in the eye. "When we woke in the morning to find Rosabel gone, I told Walter, 'That ship's left port.' And it has, ain't it, son?"

Her frankness disarmed him, leaving him grasping for words.

"See, Walter," the woman went on. "Your little girl is a woman now, and her maidenhead is one thing even you can't put back."

Walter turned red in the face. "Eleanor, would you shut your maw for once in your life!"

She crossed her arms. "Yes, I can. But that ain't gonna change a dang thing."

Walter Gatch once again turned his pained eyes to his daughter. "I give you 'til the end of the week to see the error of your ways. If you return by then, I'll forgive you."

"Good Lord!" Mrs. Gatch said, but Carlton kept his eyes on Rosabel.

She spoke in a small, childlike voice. "My place is here now, Daddy."

With difficulty, Walter tore his eyes from his daughter and turned to Carlton. "On another matter, Charles Town has fallen. The king's army is in command and will soon rid the rest of the state of this pestilence. Yet, we've got to stand strong 'til the end. I hope your support for our cause hasn't wavered."

Carlton's frustration at the slaughter of his cattle returned. "Some of these Tory yahoos have butchered my livestock, taking the prime cuts and leaving the rest to rot. All in the king's name, apparently. I cannot countenance that. I have ordered any thieves, in whoever's name they claim, to be shot."

Walter Gatch's lower jaw quivered. "Eleanor, I refuse to remain here another minute." To Rosabel, he said, "'Til the end of the week," and took his leave.

♦

For the rest of the day, Carlton, Reeve, and Ketch scoured the countryside for any sign of Thunder. As the sun began to lower in the sky, Carlton waved them toward the Big House.

"We'll make a new attempt in the morning."

"You know, sir," Reeve said, "chances are pretty high that darky headed straight to the British army. They been promising any slave who shows up he'll be free at the end of the war. And a lot of them believe it! Why, two of Phineas Odom's field hands took off last month and they ain't been heard from since. A lot more than that are gone, too."

"I know of that offer, but how would slaves way out in this wilderness ever hear of it?" Carlton asked. "Ketch? Had you heard of this?"

"No, suh," he answered. "That's news to me."

"I can't tell you how word is spread," Reeve said. "I only know it is." He sighed. "Just a thought, boss."

Later that night, Carlton was delighted to join Rosabel in bed and leave the frustrations of the plantation behind, at least for a little while.

"I'm sorry your father distressed you so, darling," he told Rosabel. "But I was pleased to hear you say your place is with me." He kissed her on the lips but was met with a cool response. He lay back on his pillow and stared at the ceiling.

After several moments, Rosabel spoke. "Carlton, I love you. You know that. But I'm afraid I've shamed my parents, and it breaks my heart."

"You'll not go back, will you?"

"No, I don't think so."

Carlton rolled over, his back to Rosabel. He could not risk her seeing the tears fall from his eyes.

Awake for hours, Carlton mulled over the problems he faced. Could Thunder be on his way to the British? Their offer to South Carolina's slaves was an affront. The gall of them, coming to their land and undermining the very bedrock of the upper crust's position and wealth. Without free labor—well, could it even be called free? Solid shelter, good clothing, and food a-plenty. All such expenses cut into his profits.

The betrayal of the African proved how his father's cosseting of the servants did not spare the de Barneforts. Likely, it emboldened the man into some sort of blind arrogance. Carlton pictured Thunder presenting himself to the officers, perhaps General Clinton himself. His declaration that he be from Kilkenny Plantation would undermine Carlton's dignity and prestige in the general's eyes.

His beloved's soft breathing beside him did not comfort him this night. The slave's affront, as well as that of the so-called Tories led by the troglodyte, Ben John, must be addressed! He refused to be seen as some backwoods milksop to be trampled upon.

The battle for Charles Town was over. He would travel to the lines in person and demand redress for the loss of his cattle and the return of Thunder, should he be among them. Joe Dillon would have reached them by now and Clinton, or at least Ferguson, would have received his splendid gift of Hector. He would be warmly greeted.

A concern niggled his brain. What if they demanded he stay, as Walter Gatch insinuated he must? And what of Kilkenny? Reeve could handle things for a few days, but was he to be trusted around Rosabel? If he sent her back to her father, would she ever return?

His stomach clenched into a tight ball. As he lay in the darkness, his breathing became ragged. There seemed to be no answer to his dilemma. Until there was.

Once again, he was genius. He would take the coach to Charles Town. He could hire Davey McTier to drive it. The man was a brute who could handle any attackers, and he was always in need of a few coins to pay off his account at McHeath's.

As for the brilliance of his plan, he would take Rosabel with him.

She would be safe from Reeve as well as her meddling father and—the very best part—he would find a minister there who would tie a marital knot that could not be undone. He filled his lungs with air and released with it his tension from crown to toe.

Unable to contain his joy, he woke dear Rosabel for a midnight celebration.

Chapter Twenty

Nan sat before the kitchen table, snapping early pole beans. It didn't take much thought, thank the Almighty, because she couldn't concentrate. Mellie was chopping bacon while Ruth mixed cornmeal into a pone. They would eat Limping Susan that evening, a favorite around the farm. Not that Nan had an appetite these days.

"I still can't believe Mr. Carlton set out for Charles Town just like that." Mellie snapped her fingers. "And takin' Miss Rosabel on such a journey with all them cutthroats and thieves on the road these days."

"They's always been that," Ruth said. "Only more of 'em now with the fightin'."

The mention of fighting caused runnels of tears to wend down Nan's cheeks. Any reminder of Joe caused her eyes to spill. Never had she been so weak-minded, more like a child than a grown woman. She swiped the wetness with her sleeve, hoping it escaped the notice of the others.

Fortunately, Ruth was gazing out the door. "There go Ketch again. Wilbur and Becca got that man runnin' back and forth like a confused rabbit."

"Without Thunder," Mellie said, "they got no choice." She shook her head. "I never thought ol' Lady Anne would live this long."

Ruth lowered her voice. "She too mean to die."

"That's the truth." Mellie scraped the chopped bacon into the large cast iron pan. "I can't think of one person, not even her son, who'll be sad to see her go."

"Best guard yer tongue," Nan mumbled.

The young girl sucked her teeth. "And who gonna hear me? Master Carlton? Miss Rosabel? All gone. That Johnny Reeve ain't allowed nowhere near us."

"Thank the Lawd for that," Ruth said, covering the dough with greens. "That man ugly as the rump of a goat. He need to keep away from here." She lowered the pan into the hearth's ashes to bake.

Turning around, she shoved Mellie toward Nan. "Girl, take the bowl of beans from that woman. Nan, you cryin' again?"

She touched her cheeks and chin to find they were wet. Tears had seeped from her eyes without her even noticing. "I've not slept," she told them. "Not since Joe left. I lay on me pallet listening to the night sounds and wondering where he be. Does he hear the same sounds? Is he safe?" And the one she couldn't speak aloud, Does he still love me?

"Honey, you in a bad way," Ruth said. "The master gone for who know how long. We got the supper cookin'. All yo chillen busy with they chores. Why don't you go back to yo cabin and rest. I'll send Mellie for ya when it be time to eat."

Nan knew she should argue but hadn't the will. All her muscles ached for sleep.

Ruth stood with arms akimbo. "Go on! Do what I tell ya."

"I thank ye both." More tears streamed down her face.

The other two looked at each other and clicked their tongues as Nan headed out the door to her cabin.

Once there, she dragged herself up the steps and inside, dropped to the pallet and curled into a ball. She pleaded with the Lord to allow sleep to take her, and He did.

A rough hand shook Nan's shoulder, its owner grunting. Not Joe. He had a gentle touch. Where was she? Was it night or day? She struggled to pry her eyes open as her arm was jerked this way and that.

Inches from her face, she saw the stringy hair, darkened eyes, and crooked nose of Johnny Reeve peering at her. His breath reeked of tobacco and rotten teeth. She opened her mouth to scream, but he muffled it with his hand.

He sneered. "You don't wanta do that, now do ya? It'll ruin all the fun."

Nan grabbed his hand, using all her strength to wrest it from her face. She twisted and kicked, determined to get away from the scoundrel, but he only laughed.

"I like my women with some fight in 'em." He straddled her hips, holding them down. Without uncovering her mouth, he used his free hand to yank up her blouse, exposing her breasts.

Nan screamed the best she could, but little sound escaped. Her pounding heart seemed louder than her attempts to cry for help. She redoubled her efforts to escape as the vermin kneaded her breast, which, before this, only Joe had ever touched.

She cried out for him in her mind, wishing somehow he could hear her distress and come running. But that would never happen. She kicked her legs, banging her bare heels on the floor in hopes that muted sound would draw someone near.

Reeve spread her legs, holding them fast with his knees as he unbuttoned his pants. Her terror only seemed to excite him further. She closed her eyes, for the sight of him was as devastating as his touch.

"No!" cried a graveled voice. Was it his? Or her own?

The pressure of Reeve on her body lessened. "What the bloody hell?" he growled, then fell to his side.

Nan untangled herself and rolled toward the wall.

"I'll save ya, Minda! I'm gonna kill ya. Ya'll never hurt Minda again."

Whomp! Whomp! Nan opened her eyes to see a black man beating Reeve with the iron fireplace poker. She screamed. The white man's face was smashed and bleeding, looking much like raw meat, but her rescuer continued his assault until she could stand no more.

"Stop! He's dead, to be sure."

She looked up at the man, whose shoulders were heaving as he panted. Ketch. It was Ketch.

She scrambled on her knees toward him and grabbed him about his legs. "Thank God ye came." She broke down in tears. "Thank ye, Ketch. Thank ye," she repeated 'til he tore her hands from his legs and dropped to the floor.

Sweat poured from his face and neck. "I killed him," he said. "I'll hang."

"Ye did no more than ye had to. He...he's a monster." They sat in silence, the mutilated overseer only feet away. Nan looked at him. "Ye called me Minda."

"I loved her, too." His eyes glistened. "I didn't never say nothin', is all."

She touched his arm. "I'm sorry."

As reason returned to her mind, she realized he was right. A slave killing a white man? No matter the reason, Ketch would be hanged. "We'll move his body. If we take it far enough away, no one will know how it happened." She looked at the mangled face. "Could have been a bear, even. Only you and I will know."

They rolled the corpse onto Nan's blanket and wrapped it inside. Using a loose end, they pulled it from the cabin, down the steps, and far, far into the trees.

Chapter Twenty-One

Jimmy walked his old mule through a wooded area a good distance from the cow pens. While he knew he shouldn't, he took his sweet time searching for lost calves. Mr. Carlton had been gone two days and Reeve was likely sleeping off a big night at McHeath's. He could finally breathe around this place.

"I don't know where Reeve at," Geoffrey had told him, "but we gotta have all them cows in the pen when he do show up. Look far and wide. No tellin' where thiefs leave they carcasses, though I'm hopin' them babies just lost."

It had rained all the night before and half this day, so Jimmy was late getting out. But after five hours of hunting calves, the sun was low in the sky. There wasn't much use looking any longer. He'd pulled the rope around the mule's neck to the left when he got a sniffer full of dead animal. Groaning, Jimmy headed toward the sickeningly sweet smell of rotting flesh.

As he got close, he had to stop and puke, the stench was so strong. Bending over, he saw it. A mottled blue-gray hand poked from a damp pile of leaves. He screamed as he stumbled backward.

Jimmy panted for several minutes, trying to decipher what he'd seen. Rising to his knees, he grabbed the nearest long stick. He stood and crept closer, then, with the stick, scraped the leaves from the putrid mound. There lay the mutilated face of Johnny Reeve.

His vision blurred. Heart racing, Jimmy turned his head, trying to clear it. Once he could see, he looked again. Flies and young maggots covered the overseer's torn flesh. His crown was smashed.

He should lift the dead man onto the poor beast but hadn't the stomach to do it. Instead, he took a rope he'd draped around the mule and tied it to the man's feet. Together, they pulled the foul remains back to the pens.

✚

At dusk, everyone gathered outside Kilkenny's barn as the cowherds dragged the body of Johnny Reeve into the quarters on a sledge. Nan's throat tightened at the sight of the fiend. She placed her hand on young Nolan's shoulder to steady herself.

As gruesome as Reeve had been when Nan and Ketch planted him in the woods, he looked even more grisly now. And the stink! Every one of Nan's nerves was frayed raw. She looked to Ketch, who stood with arms crossed over his chest, knee joggling. Reeve was not supposed to be found so quickly.

Geoffrey was saying, "Looks like some beast got him. A bobcat or even a wild dog. What he doin' way over in them woods?"

"And how long he been there, in them wet leaves?" Hercules asked. "The stiffness already startin' to ease."

"Let's go, Mellie. I'm about to lose my supper." Ruth led the crying girl back to their cabin. Becca scurried to the Big House as well.

Nan could keep her counsel no longer. "Get him out of our sight! Put him six feet below!"

Ketch glanced at her from the corner of his eye.

Geoffrey looked from one to the other. "I don't know what we s'posed to do. Master Carlton gone and this here man is dead."

Mary Edith and Baby held each other, crying softly. Daniel crouched in a ball behind his sisters' legs. Mama Juba shuffled down the lane, waving her hand. "You chillen go on home now. This ain't for young eyes to see."

Without a word, they obeyed.

"What you say we do, Mama Juba?" asked Hercules. "Did the man have fam'ly somewhere?"

Nan, along with the cluster of servants, shook her head. No one knew much about the cruel overseer.

"What 'bout that Gatch man?" Mama Juba said. "We could send for him."

Nan bit her lip. She dared not repeat her opinion. She might appear too eager to see him sleeping with the worms. Glancing at Mama Juba, she caught the woman staring at her with narrowed eyes.

Ketch lifted his head, chin out. "And who we gonna send for Gatch, or anybody else for all that? Anyone here got papers saying they can travel off K'Kenny? No. And there ain't no one here to write none, neither."

They mumbled, heads down.

"Which of you fellas gonna ride up to McHeath's Tavern," Ketch went on, "without no permission and tell them we out here with none but Lady Anne and a dead white man? No, suh. Not me."

No response.

Nan could stand no more. "Put him in the grave. Tonight. If anyone asks questions, let them dig him up. Though I can't imagine who would care that much for the lout."

She could sense the relief on the faces of the others. Mama Juba continued to watch her, head cocked to one side.

"Where?" Geoffrey asked. "Not with the fam'ly. Not with us, neither."

"Some place away from the rest of us," Ketch said, with a confidence Nan had never heard in him before. "Alone."

After sending Nolan to check on his sisters and little brother, Nan went to the loom house for some woven cloth to use as a winding-sheet. There, she sat for a time, letting her tears flow.

If only Joe was here. She could rail and scream, then bolt for the woods. Yet, for the first time in her life, the forest was not her friend. It was a misty, wheezing demon that held the secret of her crime, luring her to her own destruction.

✢

Thunder trotted down the stagecoach road, guided by the glow of a nearly full moon. While the lighted path allowed him to cover more ground, he felt exposed. The skin on his neck and back prickled as though unseen eyes watched his every step.

Was it his fourth night since leaving Kilkenny? Or his fifth? How the days ran together. He tried to count. The first morning, he'd built a small shelter of sticks and leaves behind a large tree, more to hide himself than protect him from the elements. The next day, he'd found an abandoned lean-to. He piled the open side with brush and lay in the darkest corner. It had rained all day, so he'd slept well there. The day after that, he'd had to travel a few miles away from the road, since he'd neared a village as the sun peeked above the horizon. That was where he'd caught a fish in a narrow stream. He ate it raw, reluctant to risk even a small fire. Tonight was the fourth, then.

Without warning, his skin bristled even more. He froze. Every pore in his body stood alert. Was he skittish or was something, or someone, there? He heard it clearly now. A low humming or singing.

With great care, Thunder moved off the path and behind a tree, straining to place the sound. As his ears became accustomed to it, his tension eased. The singing was comforting, al-most like—it couldn't be!

Like Joe Dillon's songs from his homeland that he sang to the sheep and for his children. Once in a while, he sang for everyone in the quarters, his heartfelt tones bringing comfort and, at times, tears of longing.

Thunder knew this one, "The Gaol of Cluain Meala." He lis-tened for the familiar words.

"And the dance of fair maidens," he heard, "the evening will hallow. While this heart, young and gay, lies cold in Cluain Meala."

He could barely catch his breath. How could he have caught up with Joe Dillon, who rode mounted upon Hector? Yet, who else could it be? Joe once told him he was locked up in that very gaol as a lad.

The voice began a new song, another of Joe's favorites, and Thunder crept toward the sound. The voice's pure notes clashed with croaking toads and the high-pitched howl of a fox. If he was wrong...

He inhaled the scent of burning wood before he glimpsed the small fire. Peering through some brush, Thunder's heart sang. There, hunched over, sat Joe Dillon, gazing into the low flames. A nicker drew his attention to Hector, tied to a nearby branch. He wanted to break out of his hiding spot and an-nounce himself but held back to be sure Joe was alone.

After several minutes, Thunder called under his breath. "Joe, my brother. I have found you."

Joe's head snapped up. "Odds bodkins!"

As Thunder stepped into the clearing, Joe leapt to his feet. "Could it be you? Sweet Jesus, 'tis! Yer an answer to prayer." He looked one way, then another. "Sit beside me, man, and help me finish these squirrels I've roasted."

Thunder did so, tearing into the small animal and stripping it of its meat. He told Joe all that had happened once he'd ridden away, keeping mum only about Nan's flogging. He described Nan's regrets for her stubbornness toward him.

A tear trickled down Joe's cheek as he tossed the squirrel bones into a pile. "Ah, she cares for me still."

Thunder, too, lobbed his cleaned bones into the small heap. "I could not stay dere at Kilkenny. Dat man, Reeve, is evil. He want to kill me."

"I tried to warn Carlton, didn't I?" Joe drew a large breath. "What's done is done, me friend. Ye'll not go back now. Ye must move on. Joining up with the British, then?"

"It be my best chance." Moonlight revealed a worn path from the fireside to a brush hut not far from Hector. "And what of you? You have been in dis spot a while. Why you here and not with de army in Charles Town?"

Joe's face fell. "I am stuck. If I go back, me wife and children could starve."

"And if you go on?"

Joe reached into his shirt and pulled the mojo bag Mama Juba had given him. "This small patch of leather holds a piece of everything that matters to me. Ye saw the bits of hair from me Nan and young ones. But there's more."

Clutching the sack like it held life itself, he opened his mouth to speak, but no words would come. At last, he swallowed and began his story, his voice little more than a whisper.

"Sometimes, it seems a lifetime ago. Others, like tonight, only a few days past. A black-hearted villain I thought was me friend led me through a meadow. A mission, he called it, against the rich bastards who held us down." He licked his lips. "There, a simple fellow named Jack surprised us, and the other fella stabbed him. The coward run off, leaving Nan's Uncle Nolan and the priest, Father Alistair Moore, blamed and accused by the king's men of murder."

Joe ran his sleeve across his eyes. "I visited Nolan in the Clonmel Gaol and declared I'd tell the truth to get him released, but he'd not hear of it. 'Yer a noble man,' he said, and asked me to care for Nan. Me, noble. When it was him who was hanged, an innocent man." Joe's voice cracked. "Last I saw him and Father Alistair, they was in a wagon, headless."

He held up the mojo bag. "As Nan and me left for America, we stopped by the churchyard where they lay. In me bag are handfuls of dirt from their graves."

Joe's torment was contagious, causing Thunder's own chest to ache.

"Their spirits lay on me heart like an anvil, anchoring me to this place. I vowed to Nolan, a man who'd treated me like a son, to do what he could no longer do. Care for his family. My family. But how? Betray Nolan Scully by fighting on the side of those who murdered and mutilated him? Or allow Nan and the children to become homeless and starve?"

"Ah," Thunder said, "dis is hard. But my people say, 'Patience can cook a stone.'"

Joe cocked his head to one side.

"Dis will take time to work out. I will stay with you tonight. In de day, I must hide."

"Ye can sleep in me hut. I'd be grateful for yer company, friend. Ye cannot imagine how alone I've been."

"Yes, tonight we will pray, each in our own way. Den we will see what your heart tell you."

In the pink-hued mist awaiting the sun's first peek, Thunder shifted his position before the dying embers. He grabbed some wood and threw it on the fire. Joe lay snoring in his small shelter but would have to rise soon. Thunder needed to take his place during the daylight hours since he dast not be discovered.

He'd spent much of the night praying for discernment on Joe's behalf. His friend's situation seemed impossible. Yet, Thunder's heart continued to cry out the old Fulani saying, "Patience can cook a stone."

He stepped away from the campfire to relieve himself and, once again, ran the situation through his mind. Joe feared ripping his family from their home. It would take little time to build a crude shelter, but what would they eat? Could they be safe? Was anyone safe these days? Joe and Nan Dillon were not slaves, but they were stuck, no more free than he was.

Returning, he watched Joe stretch his legs within the brush hut. I am wrong, he told himself. He is freer dan I be.

He called out, "Rise up, Joe Dillon. We will talk of how you can cook your stone."

Within minutes, Joe was walking back from Hector's saddlebags carrying a large piece of jerky. He tore it in half. "Here," he said to Thunder. "'Tis the last of it."

The two crouched before the fire. "Remember," Thunder said, "dis will take time. But you are a free man. You can walk away from everything. You can build your own home, plant crops, and even one day trade for stock. And you can do dis while Nan and de chiddren stay at Kilkenny, safe and sound."

He stopped to see Joe's reaction, but the man, looking down, only pushed coals around with a long stick.

He went on. "You can get de young ones and Nan when dere is a house with four walls and food to eat." Still no reaction. His heart sank. "I said it would take time."

"I gave me word to Carlton."

"And to de man, Nolan."

Joe finally looked up. "If I don't turn up in Charles Town? What then? Nan and the cubs are thrown to the dogs. I'd be better off dead."

Thunder sucked in his breath. "Never say such, Joe Dillon."

"I don't want to die, but even if they all thought I did, it would be better." He looked at Thunder, his eyebrows raised. "That's it. We could make them believe I died."

"How would dat work? And what of Nan? Her heart would—" He maneuvered his fingers as though crumbling bread.

Joe's face fell. "I must be mad. There is pain no matter which way we turn."

The two sat in silence, chewing their jerky. Joe stood and left to fill his canteen. When he returned, they both drank the water from a nearby stream. It tasted of iron.

An idea had been rumbling around Thunder's brain. It seemed fool-headed, yet he spoke anyway. "When I get to de army and tell dem I want to join, I can say I find you dead."

Joe's eyes widened. "No, not dead. Dying. Ye can bring them the letter from Carlton, proving who I be. And the horse!" He pointed to Hector, who munched on nearby grasses. "Take the horse as his gift."

"I am a runaway. How far will I get with a fine animal like dat? Can I hide him up a tree?"

"If I keep him, I'll be a thief. I ain't no thief!" Joe chewed his thumbnail. "Carlton was a dunce to send such a beast. A fine excuse to murder either one of us." He sighed. "I'll take the horse. Ye'd get killed a sight quicker than I would, and not a one will hesitate to hand me a muddy death."

He shook his finger at Thunder. "Ye tell 'em ye come across me wounded, but alive. Say I told ye some ruffians sliced open me gizzard and stole the horse. Then I give ye the letter and died. Ye scraped up a bit a dirt and buried me in the swamp. None will come looking."

The plan was taking form. "But what of Nan? She will hear of your death."

The sadness in Joe's eyes tore at Thunder's heart. "That part I cannot help," Joe said. "I can only hope upon learning I'm alive after all, in her happiness, she'll forgive me."

The two old friends spent one more day together before parting, likely forever. Once darkness fell, Thunder wended his way eastward through the forests and swamps. He'd take the stage road when he could, Carlton's letter tucked in his pack.

The following morning, Joe extinguished the fire for the last time and walked away from his Purgatory. He would seek out John Mumford at Cracker's Neck, a fine man who'd know what to do.

✣

As Nan headed to the kitchen, Mama Juba called to her from her cabin. Shoulders slumped, she trudged to the door and called inside. "What ye need, Mama Juba?"

"I needs ya to come inside and talk to me like ya got some sense."

Nan dragged her feet up the steps and into the darkened hut. The old woman sat beside the hearth. "Bring that there stool close to me."

The days were getting warmer, too warm to sit beside a fire, but Nan did as she was told. "I don't have long," she told the old healer. "There's work to be done."

Mama Juba leaned in close. "Ketch and the other fellas buried that old scoundrel by the light of a full moon. He lyin' there, a-rottin'. He can't hurt ya none."

Nan resisted the urge to flee the old woman's eyes that seemed to bore into her soul. She gritted her teeth, determined to say nothing. Yet, in a cruel betrayal, her own eyes burned with unshed tears.

"Somethin' goin' on here. Ya can't hide nothin' from me, Nan. Ya should know that by now. Tell me how that white man got kilt."

Nan struggled to find words that would free her from this invasion into her shame and guilt. Instead, the traitorous tears fell. "He tried to ravage me. He had no right. No right to touch me like that."

"No, sugar. No, he ain't." The old woman took Nan's hands and squeezed them. She did not let her go.

"I fought him," Nan went on. "As hard as I could fight. But he was stronger than he looked. I could only think of Joe. I...I'll never be clean again."

"How'd ya kill the dog?"

Nan pulled her hands back. "I didn't. Ketch killed him."

Mama Juba's face fell. She started to rock back and forth. "Oh, Lawd, no! Not my boy. He all I got!"

"He saved me, Mama. He's a good man."

"He'll hang, I know it. I can't lose my last one."

Nan's stomach churned. "Do ye think they'll dig Reeve up? He'll look even worse than he did going in. An animal ate him. That's what Geoffrey said and that's what happened."

Mama Juba grabbed Nan's upper arm. "And if they don't believe it, it was Thunder. You tell 'em that. It was Thunder come back and kilt that man. That boy a dead man anyway."

Dear Lord, could it come to that? "I will, Mama Juba. I'll tell them."

Chapter Twenty-two

Looking out the carriage window, Rosabel was amazed at the people of all types crowding the road. British soldiers in fine uniforms passed bone-weary men in shredded rags. More black men and women than she'd ever seen drove carts loaded with supplies, hauled bulky burlap sacks, or toted wide baskets atop their heads.

She could barely take it all in. There were few carriages like theirs. An occasional British military man, an officer likely, rode a magnificent steed in great regalia, but most walked or, more often, trudged down the roads. A few had carts pulled by mules or nags.

Near midday, the driver, Davey McTier, pounded on the roof of their carriage. "We'd best stop soon, Carlton. The roads are thick with fighting men."

"Fine," her husband said, his head stuck out the window. "There's a tavern ahead. Let's see if it's suitable."

As the coach pulled up, Rosabel read the wooden sign swinging before a white clapboard building: 8 Mile House Tavern.

"Eight miles from where?" she asked.

"From Charles Town itself." Carlton frowned. "I wonder how many of the city's grand taverns remain."

Many horses, carts, and mules were scattered before the building. Carlton opened their carriage door and got out before helping Rosabel disembark. "We'll stop for refreshment,

McTier. If it meets our needs, we'll stay the night." He flipped the driver a coin. "Don't go far."

Taking her husband's arm, Rosabel stepped into the darkened hall of the tavern. She gasped. Despite the bright sun outside, the room required numerous candlestick chandeliers and wall sconces. They wended their way through the trove of tables and chairs. Each was filled with men talking, women laughing. The sight filled her with wonder and excitement.

His hand on the small of her back, Carlton led her to an empty table for two in the corner. She nodded and smiled at the other patrons, but few even glanced her way. All were caught up in the busy-ness of their own lives, she figured.

A young woman in a mop hat came to their table and smiled. Carlton said, "Two bowls of your best stew and a mug of ale for each of us."

She raised one side of her mouth in a sort of smile. "The stew is the stew we got. Call it the best or the worst, it won't make no difference."

To Rosabel's surprise, Carlton laughed. "I'll call it the best, then, if it's all the same to you. If I can find a willing minister, this is our wedding day."

Rosabel's heart pounded. "Oh, Carlton! I don't know what to say."

His eyes brightened. "What is there to say? You've already said yes."

The barmaid pulled an empty chair from a neighboring table and set it beside theirs. She called out, "Reverend Jenkins, these two be looking for ye."

A red-haired man in a black cassock and white cravat half-stood as he finished his conversation with three men. He then approached their table and made a quick bow before dropping into the chair provided.

"And who might I be speaking with today?"

Carlton offered his hand. "I am Carlton de Barnefort of Kilkenny Plantation, located in the Orangeburgh District." He nodded to Rosabel. "This is my wife, or soon to be, if you are the man we seek."

"I am Reverend Edward Jenkins, Doctor of Divinity." He sighed. "It's a bit crowded in here, but I suppose we can work something out."

Rosabel's face fell.

"We have come a long way to marry in a church," Carlton told him. "Rosabel deserves the best I can give her. Within the current circumstances, of course."

"Yes." The minister turned to her. "And you do deserve that, my dear. Alas, I am an ordained minister of the Church of England without a church, of late having served Saint Michael's in Charles Town itself." He sighed. "I despair of seeing its condition today."

Rosabel took deep breaths as her eyes threatened to fill with tears. She would not cry!

The clergyman continued. "As you can see, with the fall of our dear city, the whole area is in disarray. We've been flooded with people swarming in to switch their loyalties to the British. A disgrace, really."

Her husband-to-be bristled over the priest's comment, but the man didn't seem to notice.

"The Redcoats don't know what to do with them all. Not yet, anyway. I've heard the Patriot militia was paroled solely to keep from feeding them. How long do you think it will be before those parolees have guns in their hands once again?"

Carlton's face became ruddy. He opened his mouth to speak but was cut off.

"The British are barbarians when it comes to houses of worship. You know they burned that splendid edifice, Sheldon Church, don't you? To the ground. The Lord's house!"

Carlton's eyes widened. "I worshipped there once as a lad. To what purpose?"

"Who can say? To destroy the spirit of the people? St. Andrew's Church, two miles down the road, was nearly destroyed when the British and their ilk came through. By the grace of the Almighty, it was spared."

"Two miles away? Would the pastor consent to marry us?"

"There's been no pastor at Saint Andrew's for seven years. The rich stopped coming, holding services on their estates. It's crawling with the king's men, but I might be able to get us in."

"Oh, could you?" Rosabel blurted. "If it's no trouble, I mean."

"It may be trouble. I can't say."

"I am prepared to pay well for the privilege," Carlton said. Rosabel wondered how she could love him any more.

Before long, the three of them were in the de Barnefort carriage heading to Saint Andrew's. The barmaid, Mary Ellen, came along to serve as a witness. Davey, who drove them, would be the second one.

Reverend Jenkins was right about the effects of the army on the area. As they pulled into the little churchyard, the grounds were torn up and littered with the debris of troops who'd recently camped there.

But that did not stop Rosabel's heart from swelling at the sight of the white brick building. She was more familiar with roughhewn structures without the sophistication of such beautiful double doors beneath a magnificent glass gable. Stepping from the carriage, she inhaled the saltwater aroma of the marsh, which she'd not experienced since a young girl. Her head and heart grew light as air.

Mary Ellen glanced at Rosabel, then took her hand. "It's like in a fairy tale, ain't it? And today you're a princess!"

The service passed in a blur of tearful happiness, with a few droplets reserved for her father and mother, whom she missed with all her heart.

✠

After an active wedding night, Carlton left Rosabel at the tavern. He leaned back in the seat of his carriage as Davey maneuvered his way toward the city. When asked how to find Major Patrick Ferguson, the folks at the tavern had given only vague directions.

Despite the stench of mud and smoke mixed with filthy bodies of the defeated and victorious alike, Carlton basked in the glow of his marriage. The proprietor and his wife had eagerly given up their own quarters when they saw the money he was willing to spend. Only the best for Rosabel. He reveled at her face bright with wonder at each new sight and experience, her radiance as she stood beside him, repeating her vow to remain with him forever.

His fortunes had turned. He would reap the harvest of prosperity and happiness he deserved. He'd lurked within shadows since before his father's passing. Now he would bask in life's sunlight.

His confidence surged at the prospect of meeting Major Ferguson. He pictured the man overwhelmed with gratitude for Hector, a worthy gift. He would nod at the justice of Carlton's request for Thunder's return and compensation for Ben John's thievery of his cattle. When all was said and done, a small token of the king's appreciation would not go astray. A seat on some council or another?

The road became so jarring, Carlton feared the carriage would break apart. Through the window, he pounded on the side of the door. "Stop here, man! Locate Ferguson on foot, and bring him here, if you can."

Davey McTier sighed, a bit too loudly. "Right you are. Sit tight and don't you move a muscle."

In the hour Carlton was forced to wait, he watched exhausted British soldiers herd prisoners of war through the muck, barking that if they were too stubborn to join the king's army, they could rot in the wormy hulks anchored in the harbor. The captives were haggard, nearly cadaverous, their eyes filled with rage, fear, or no life at all.

At one point, a man of some means stood within earshot, speaking to a British officer. Apparently, he'd scouted the vicinity to determine the dispositions of the area's first families.

"I told General Clinton they fall into four camps, if you will." He counted off on his fingers. "One recognizes the error of their ways and is anxious to return to the king's graces. Others had been avid rebels, but now realize the royal government is the only viable pathway forward. The third believes their cause was indeed virtuous but can no longer be maintained. Then, of course, there are the ones who will never succumb to reason."

"In what proportions would you say these categories of men fall?" the officer asked.

"Oh, the first three who are ready to return to the king's protection far outnumber the firebrands. I made that very clear to the general. Not that I spoke directly to the agitators. To what purpose? But we can assume they are few in number."

As the two men walked away, still chatting, Carlton remembered Walter Gatch making the same assumptions. In what category did Alden belong? Would he wind up at the end of a rope? A lump landed in his stomach. They were still brothers, after all.

At long last, Davey McTier returned. "They won't let me nowhere near Ferguson hisself. Some fellow named Crookshank said you can come to him."

"Of all the arrogance!"

"Men's running every which way, Carlton. I never seen nothing like it."

His mouth twitching, he climbed from the carriage. "Bloody hell! Lead the way."

After tramping through the mud for some time, Davey pointed. "There he be!"

Carlton headed toward a fellow who bawled out orders, pointing this way and that with his tricorn hat. He was clearly Loyalist militia in his fringed, deerskin hunting shirt and looked no older than Alden. Once the fellow saw him approach, Carlton could have sworn he rolled his eyes.

"You've come to sign up, sir," the man said.

Carlton smirked at the horse's arse. "Crookshank, is it? I've come to meet with Major Ferguson, not some snotty underling. You can tell him Carlton de Barnefort of Kilkenny Plantation has business with him."

"Looky here, Mr. Barney Fort. We got a hundred fellows like you coming in every day. The major can't take time out for every...man...who thinks he's important."

Carlton seethed. He was sure he heard Davey McTier snort behind him.

Crookshank went on. "See that fella behind the table yonder? He'll sign you up."

"I did not come to enlist. I've sent my replacement ahead—an Irishman, Joe Dillon. And if you can't remember him, you will recall the fine horse I sent as a gift for the major. A chestnut stallion with a faint star?"

"I ain't heard-a nobody named Joe Dillon and I ain't seen no stallion with a star."

"Allow me to speak to someone more knowledgeable. I'm also here about my runaway slave, a large African who goes by the name of Thunder."

Crookshank cocked his head to the right. "You can talk to Lt. Ryerson over there about the Negro recruits, but I can tell you, he ain't giving up no runaways."

Carlton looked in the indicated direction to see a ragtag mob of blacks about a hundred yards away. He squinted. A large dark figure with a familiar gait ambled in the direction of the rabble.

"There he is!" Carlton left Crookshank shaking his head and took off at a run toward Thunder. McTier followed. Before they could reach him, a small band of soldiers blocked their way.

"That's my man, right there!" Carlton called out. "I demand you return my property."

A tall, lanky fellow in a British uniform stepped forward. "That will not be possible, sir. All slaves who agree to join us are under our protection."

"How dare you! That's robbery, pure and simple. I demand my man's return."

"Sir, we have made a promise in the name of the king that cannot be broken. Those who serve well will be given their freedom."

"Thunder," Carlton yelled. "Get over here this instant! I order you."

Thunder turned toward him. The white man beside the slave nodded to Thunder, and they both approached Carlton.

The soldier said, "Lieutenant, here's another one demanding his slave back."

"I'll handle this." He dismissed the soldier. "I'm Lt. Ryerson, and you are?"

"Carlton de Barnefort of Kilkenny Plantation, this man's owner and master."

"Yes," Lt. Ryerson said. "Thunder arrived only a short time ago with a rather unusual story and I think it involves you." He pulled a sheet of parchment from his jacket. "Did you write this letter?"

Carlton took it. "I did. I sent it by my man, Joe Dillon. He came on my steed, Hector, a gift for the major."

"I regret to tell you, Mr. de Barnefort, neither your man nor your horse ever arrived. Thunder here was explaining to us that he came across Joe Dillon in the swamp. Shot by thieves, it seems, who stole the horse. Before he died, Dillon asked that Thunder deliver this letter to us by way of explanation. My condolences, sir."

Carlton's chest ached. "Joe Dillon, dead? Are you sure, Thunder?"

Lt. Ryerson said to Carlton, "I can see by your face that Joe Dillon was a good man. This war...too much death."

"He had a wife. And children." Carlton told him.

"I bury him in de swamp so no creature can eat him." Thunder's narrowed eyes bored into him. "You should never have sent so fine a horse."

The biting accusation in the African's tone and words slapped him across the face, leaving him speechless.

"You cocky black cur! You can't talk to Carlton like that!" Davey McTier raised his coach whip over his head.

Before he could strike, three soldiers wrestled the spitting, cursing driver to the ground. Carlton found his voice, insisting they release McTier. Once the man was subdued and his whip confiscated, Ryerson nodded. "Let him up."

Carlton turned to see Thunder's hard-bitten eyes continuing to drill into him.

Ryerson, too, glanced at the slave, his eyes widening. Surely not in admiration! "Go back to the others, Thunder," the Loyalist officer said, and he obeyed.

Carlton glared at Ryerson. "I see you have no intention of returning my property. In that case, I must demand compensation."

"That will not be possible, Mr. de Barnefort. We can barely feed the soldiers who have taken up the cause. There is no money to reimburse your loss. Consider it your contribution to king and country."

"To say nothing of my beeves that have been butchered, their carcasses left to rot. Am I to receive nothing for those as well? I am a loyal supporter of King George and this is how I am treated?"

Lt. Ryerson's jaw became set. "I'm sorry you feel that way. If you are willing to take up arms in defense of your country, please do. Otherwise, I suggest you return to your dear remaining beeves." With that, he turned on his heels and left.

"Sons of bitches!" Carlton paced back and forth. "Have they no regard for the well-born? This is an outrage!" To Davey McTier, whose whip was now returned, he said, "We will go back to the tavern, gather Mrs. de Barnefort and our belongings, and leave."

"Carlton, it's late. We won't get far."

"Every inch away from this place is an inch closer to Kilkenny. Get me out of this hell-hole."

✦

It was mid-afternoon when Carlton rolled up to 8 Mile House Tavern, yet there were plenty of patrons. The barmaid, Mary Ellen, informed him that Rosabel had gone to her room for a lie down.

When he woke her, Rosabel sat up immediately, distressed. "What is it, Carlton?"

"Nothing for you to fret about. It's men's business, but we must pack and leave right away."

"So soon? Is it the war? Did the battle start again?"

He ran his hand down her soft, porcelain cheek. "No, love."

"I hate to see the pain in your eyes. Go downstairs. Have a rum punch while I prepare to leave."

Her concern touched him, and he did as she suggested.

Before he'd finished his second glass, his new wife descended the stairs with a package wrapped in paper. She joined him at his table.

"Dearest, my new friend, Mary Ellen, has offered me these two novels. I would so love to have them. One is new from England. It's only been out for two years."

"Novels?"

"Yes." Her lips poked into a pout, she took a deep breath and laid her hand upon his. "I so love to read, and my father would never permit it. Would you please, please buy these for me?"

Although he suspected she flirted to get her way, giving her a gift her father had refused was satisfying. "Of course. Send Mary Ellen to me."

She leapt up, kissed him on the brow, and ran off. Carlton directed Davey McTier to carry the luggage to the carriage while he paid their tab and for Rosabel's prize books.

As they headed for the door to make their departure, the proprietor called out, "Raise your glasses to Madame de Barnefort."

To Carlton's shock, the entire establishment lifted their mugs, calling, "Here, here!" and "To your health!" and "Long life!"

Rosabel's cheeks burned red, but with a sly smile, she gave a short curtsey.

Once outside, Carlton asked, "What was that for?"

Without looking back, she said, "I have no idea. Mary Ellen must have told them we're newly married."

✦

Joe Dillon pressed forward as best he could, anxious to be among friendly faces. Particularly, Captain John Mumford. Joe had headed due south, his sights set on reaching the Savannah and continuing upriver. People thought him dead now, but if recognized, the tale of his death would likely become reality.

While being ever vigilant, he took advantage of Hector, who allowed him to travel at a strong, steady pace. This despite swampy areas where he breathed thick, stagnant air that smelled of rot. The water was often two to three feet deep, festering with venomous snakes and alligators.

Near the end of the second day, he arrived at the river and found a bluff over the Savannah on which to camp. While there were no guarantees, the area seemed deserted. Even though the nights had been getting warmer, he built a small fire so he could roast a fat squirrel he'd snagged.

Once wrapped in darkness, Joe became spellbound by the reflection of the nearly full moon on the river below. The soft chirping of crickets and occasional splash of a fish took him out of himself, as though he were one with the earth, the sky, and flowing water. He breathed easy for the first time in many days.

A rustling in the underbrush startled him out of his reverie. His heart stopped until he realized it was likely some small creature seeking its evening meal. Tears filled his eyes. What a fool! How could he have been lulled into any sense of peace?

Hector nickered, reminding him he was now a horse thief, a crime punishable by death. At least 'twas so in Ireland. Was he also a deserter of an army he'd never joined? A man with no home to return to? His family would soon be wracked in anguish at the news of his death. How many days before they found out?

His stomach wrenched, and he vomited what little he'd eaten earlier. Wiping his mouth on his sleeve, he lifted his eyes to the expanse of the heavens.

He could hear sweet Mary Edith's voice, cracking with emotion. "I'll look to the stars and pray for you every night."

What had he done? Would he never see those beautiful green eyes again? Or those of any of his children? His beloved Nan? Alone, stuck between heaven and earth, he rose to his knees and raised his hands toward the sky.

"My God, this is madness!" he called. "There is no way out! What am I to do?"

In the silence that followed, he wept, his sides aching with the power of his grief. When no tears were left, he dropped to the ground and fell into a deep sleep.

Chapter Twenty-three

Upon waking atop the river bluff, weariness weighed heavily on Joe Dillon. His eyes still stung from weeping the night before. He broke camp and, since no other plans had come to him while asleep, he rode Hector northwest along a pathway on the Carolina side of the Savannah River.

When the opportunity presented itself, Joe and Hector drank from a stream. While the horse grazed, Joe splashed cool water over his face but had no desire to find food for himself. Resigned to whatever Fate sent his way, his mind was empty.

Once the sun was high, Joe approached what appeared to be an earthen fort protected by thick, pointed branches. He reined in Hector, taking time to consider his position. While all seemed quiet, he had no idea who held the breastworks or how he'd be greeted. He approached slowly, hanging onto the option of escape for as long as possible.

Still yards away, Joe heard two distressed voices but could not make out what they were saying. Did they need help?

"Ah, bugger it!" He gave Hector a jab and rode up to the fort. Dismounting, he saw two men, one quite tall, pacing in distress.

"Those riders had to be the ones," said the shorter man who resembled the tall one. Likely brothers. "The question is, where is everyone now?"

"Damnation! We've got to find them!" shouted the tall red-haired one, flinging his arms into the air.

"Hallo!" Joe yelled over the breastworks. "Are ye in need of help?"

The men stopped. They looked from Joe to each other.

The shorter one raised his musket toward him. "Dismount and identify yourself."

Determined to avoid sudden movement, Joe swung his leg over Hector. His mind raced. Who should he say he was? Certainly not his own name. Why hadn't he thought of this before?

Reaching the ground, he blurted, "They call me Alistair Moore, fellas." The name of the priest he so admired as a young man. Was that blasphemous or respectful?

"I'm Lt. Tarlton Brown and this is my brother, Bartlett, come home from Charles Town. I went to meet up with him and I come back to this. Everyone gone."

"It was the fellas we saw ride past the house." Bartlett snorted. "We thought they were reinforcements for our guard here at the fort."

The veins in his neck throbbing, Tarlton Brown slapped his hat against his thigh. "The unprincipled, bloodthirsty tools! It's a slander to call them men."

"Calm yourself, brother. You're of no use if you lose your head."

Two more came riding toward them from upriver. Joe was stunned to recognize one as young Alden de Barnefort. His heart pounded as he pulled his hat lower over his eyes.

Tarlton Brown called out, "What the bloody hell is going on here, Levi? Alden?"

The two approached but did not dismount. The man they called Levi said, "Me and Alden were out foraging. Left about three hours ago. Coming back, we heard a commotion across the river. Shouting, cussing. About two miles or so from here.

We laid low 'til they was past, then came hot-foot back to the fort."

"They rounded up every blasted man and have taken them God knows where," Tarlton said. "I'll flay any Tory bastard that harms our father, Bartlett. I swear it!"

"We're wasting time," his brother answered. "Let's move out." He turned to Joe. "Will you join us, friend?"

Joe nodded but kept his head down. He could feel the blood pounding through every part of his body.

It was then Alden first glanced Joe's way. "Is that Hector? What...? Joe, is that you?"

Bartlett said, "He calls himself Moore."

Joe lifted his head. "'Tis, Mr. Alden."

Tarlton paced a few steps, then headed for his horse. "This can wait. Mount up!"

Alden had time for only one question before they lit out. "Is Carlton alive?"

"He is," Joe answered, then spurred Hector to catch the brothers who'd galloped off at a fast clip.

About a mile and a half upriver, they found a suitable spot to ford the Savannah. Joe was grateful for Hector's strength. The horse had to swim part of the way across while Joe held his gun above his head. On the other side, they stopped to make plans.

"Any ideas where they might be?" asked Bartlett.

Levi removed his hat, raked his fingers through his hair, and replaced it. "I heard tell of a body of Brits and Tories holed up at Harbard's Store. That's one possibility."

"It's only a mile from here," Tarlton said. "We'll try that first. Is everybody's powder dry?"

They all nodded and rode off.

Once the small log store came into view, the five of them stayed within cover of trees and brush, taking time to scout the situation. The men from the Burton's Ferry fort were on the ground outside the building, hands and feet tied. A large pen held more horses in one spot than Joe had seen in his lifetime. Several British regulars and Tory militia milled about the area, barking orders and harassing the prisoners.

With the din caused by over two hundred horses plus the cries of the prisoners themselves, Joe and the other would-be rescuers were in no danger of being overheard. They were, however, outnumbered.

"If we could somehow break them horses out," Levi said, "it could create enough of a fracas so's we could get our men loose."

For Joe, this tactic brought to mind his days in Ireland as a Leveller. With no guns nor horses to speak of, the rebels tore down the walls of the gentry in the dark of night, setting loose the rich man's livestock, his bread-and-butter. "I'm game," he said.

While plotting within the trees, the rumbles of galloping horses and roars of battle cries shook them from their plans. Joe was stunned at the sight of mounted and foot soldiers charging with bayonets flashing and guns exploding.

Caught unawares, the British and Tories were cut down by bullet and sword. Joe's companions gathered their wits and joined the attackers. Joe followed suit, racing on horseback from the trees. He aimed his gun, hoping to get a shot, but within the bedlam, he couldn't be sure where to fire.

Perhaps it'd be best to free the prisoners. He rode toward those seated on the ground. In the hail of lead, he prayed he'd make it unhit. Once among the captives, he dismounted and used his knife to slice the ropes binding their wrists and ankles. Grateful men joined in the fray.

Joe was still releasing some of them when a cheer of "huzzah" arose throughout the field of battle. Looking up, he saw that most, if not all, of the enemy was slaughtered. The splayed bodies of the dead and the writhing of those nearly dead sickened him. He had participated in fights before and had seen brutally tortured corpses, but never so many.

Amidst the celebration, Joe swallowed, and freed the last few Patriots from their bonds.

⊕

As the dust began to settle, Alden joined Lt. Tarlton Brown and Bartlett in their discussion with Col. LeRoy Hammond, leader of the Patriot assault. The colonel, with a beak-like nose and black, steely eyes, stood with arms crossed.

"We received intelligence early yesterday of the impending raid. Sorry we couldn't arrive earlier."

Tarlton Brown said, "We're grateful you arrived at all."

Alden shook the colonel's hand. "Some fine soldiering, sir. Real fine."

Mr. Billy Brown hobbled toward them. "This is my father," Tarlton told Col. Hammond.

The old man shook the officer's hand as well. "Ain't never seen nothing like it. Something to tell the grandchildren in my dotage."

Tarlton and Bartlett exchanged a look before Bartlett said, "Come on, Pa. Let's get you something to drink."

"Now you're talking," said Billy Brown as he limped away with his older son.

"I'll tell you, Lieutenant," Col. Hammond said, "what happened in Charles Town is a blow to our cause. A heavy blow.

Part of our delay was due to a meeting of us rebels in Augusta called by General Williamson."

"We'll fight to the last man," Tarlton said.

Hammond winced. "If only it were so. There was much disagreement as to where we go from here. General Williamson wants to return to his home in Ninety-Six, with the understanding that he and his contingent will regroup, if necessary, to keep the Redcoats at bay until help arrives. Others feel our cause is lost."

"What was decided?" Alden asked.

The colonel sighed. "Nothing. No decision was reached."

One of the rebel soldiers sidled up to Alden. Scowling, he whispered in Alden's ear, "We only learnt about Charles Town a day or two ago." He nodded toward Hammond. "Him and the general kept the news to themselves."

Alden didn't answer but looked at the man as though he were mad. First, to speak ill of his commanding officer in such proximity, but also at the contempt he wore. The man tipped his head, indicating that the two should speak further away from the officers. Curious, Alden followed.

"Joshua Spears," the man said by way of introducing himself.

"Alden de Barnefort. What are you insinuating about the colonel? Or the general, for that matter?"

"I was under Colonel Singleton and our term is damned near up. It's May, ain't it?"

"It is," Alden said.

"Then it's up. And the colonel told General Williamson so, that he's to discharge us. But instead of that, the old fool placed Singleton under arrest! Took his sword and everything."

"I don't understand."

"He don't want to lose none of us, but it ain't right. We can't trust him. Not with his suspicious ways. You know where the general gets his washing done?"

"How would I?"

"Williamson goes to some Tory on the South Carolina side. A Tory woman! And what do you think they talk about?"

Alden didn't like where this conversation was going. "Hopefully, that he should be more careful not to dribble soup onto his uniform."

"Ha! Or maybe she's passing him correspondence from some of them uppity Lobsterbacks."

"Spears, I fear your loose tongue might get you hanged." Alden resented the seed of doubt about their cause the soldier had sown in his mind.

"After this trip here, I'm heading home. So are the rest of the boys. We ain't fighting for no traitor." With that, young Joshua Spears joined a group of his compatriots who all wore the same disgruntled expressions.

Alden scanned his surroundings, his head spinning with the possibility that a general critical to their cause could be in bed with the British. He spied Joe Dillon seated with his back against the log store, head down and knees bent.

Joe's eyes widened with fear at Alden's approach. He, Nan, and the children were as close a family as Alden had ever seen. What series of events could have brought Joe here? And with Carlton's prize horse?

To ease Joe's mind as much as relieve his aching feet, Alden sat beside the Irishman. "I know you have a story, Joe. I can't imagine what it is."

✤

Joe's moment of reckoning had arrived. He'd stewed about how to handle his run-in with Alden, but decided his best course was the truth. Providence would determine his future.

Leaving out Thunder's role, he told Alden his story. Once finished, Joe said, "I'm no horse thief. I hope ye know that."

"I do, Joe. I regret the spot Carlton placed you in. This is a quandary, how we two old Kilkenny fellows are no longer welcome in our own home. And now, the British have overtaken Charles Town and most of our army. At this rate, we'll soon no longer be rebels, but traitors to the crown."

"I was hoping Captain Mumford would know what to do. He seemed to understand me struggles inside. I thought..." Joe felt a bit foolish now. What did he think?

"Mumford was killed, Joe."

"No, I spoke to him only days ago. He was on his way to his wife and then to the Cracker's Neck Boys."

"He was waylaid at the Morris Ford earthworks on the Salkehatchie River. Ben John and his boys, a nasty bunch, cut him down and left him for the buzzards. Some of our boys found him and buried him beneath a big pine there."

Joe's heart was heavy. Somehow, he felt lonelier. How could he feel so close to a person he'd known so short a time?

"I've never met the man," Alden was saying, "but he's well-spoken of by all who did."

"Aye. He was a fine one."

✦

After they'd buried the dead in a large, open pit, a small band of Patriot militia rode into the clearing. One of the men approached Col. Hammond, saluted, and gave him some sort of report. Alden couldn't hear a word, but the colonel's gestures displayed his disgust.

Moments later, Hammond approached Tarlton Brown. Alden, along with Bartlett and Levi, joined them to hear what he had to say.

"Them fellas come from Augusta. They left a few hours after we did. It seems the general took a poll." Col. Hammond stopped to gather himself. Alden could see the vein throbbing in his temple. "Only a handful of 'em want to fight on. The rest are ready to forsake all and return to their homes. The fall of Charles Town has stripped the fight out of too many."

"We're already considered traitors to the king," Alden said. "A crime punishable by death."

"Not exactly. They're offering parole to militia boys like you, provided you swear to never take up arms against them again."

"It would be the end of the American army in South Carolina," Tarlton Brown said. "We'd be finished."

"It looks like General Williamson has gone back to his plantation in Ninety-Six. They say they'll regroup if the call goes out," Col. Hammond said. "Blast it! Why not take the fight to North Carolina? That's my question." He pointed to the men who'd brought the information. "They're headed home. I suggest you boys get together and decide what y'all want to do."

They split the captured horses—about two hundred in all—and went their separate ways. The Burton's Ferry boys headed back to the South Carolina side.

Astride Hector, Joe Dillon caught up with Alden once they'd crossed the river. "I cannot keep this horse, Mr. Alden. 'Tis too fine a steed for the likes of me. A man in me old country would get hanged for owning a horse this fine."

"Keep him, Joe," Alden said. "It's the least our family can do. Or me, anyway."

"Ye don't understand. If me story got through of the theft of Hector and me resulting death, I can't be seen alive. And even if no one recognized me, but knew the horse, I'd be hanged for a thief. Either way, I'm a dead man if I ride Hector."

"I see your dilemma. Let me talk to Tarlton. Maybe you can take one of the horses we confiscated instead."

Back at the breastworks, the contingent decided to disband until further notice. Alden found it hard to believe the dream of freedom he'd first adopted under Charles Town's Liberty Tree was to fade away in so inglorious a manner. A dream he'd forsaken his family for, leaving him adrift in a hostile world.

Alden found himself following Billy, Tarlton, and Bartlett Brown back to their home at Brier's Creek. Levi and Joe Dillon rode along as well. There was much rejoicing at the safe return of all the Browns, especially Billy after his harrowing experience as a prisoner of war.

Seeing Suzanne, even more beautiful than before, caused Alden's heart to leap. He was dismayed to find time and distance had not weakened his attraction to her. Aware of the lieutenant's eyes upon him when his little sister made her appearance, Alden struggled to adopt a stoic demeanor. This was especially difficult when Suzanne's face lit up at the sight of him. He spun away.

Alden didn't dare join the others as a houseguest as he had in the past. Not that he'd been invited to do so. He made camp outside the house with Joe Dillon.

He thought of Levi inside, a part of the family, and grew hot with envy. If only Levi had been some sort of scoundrel, he could have gleefully hated him. But there wasn't a finer man in the entire squad, and if he'd detected the spark between Alden and his beloved, he gave no indication.

Alden may have hated him even more for this, but not glee-fully.

Chapter Twenty-four

Rosabel was tired and sore on the third day of their return journey from Charles Town. Carlton had been dour and irritable the entire way. In the roadside inns where they stopped, he tossed and turned at night, moaning incoherent complaints in his sleep. She'd asked him again and again what was wrong, but he'd brushed her aside more harshly each time.

The rugged trail through the woods was jarring, so much more unpleasant without an exciting destination to anticipate. The creaking wheels and snorting horses competed with buzzing mosquitoes, squawking birds, and bullfrogs as they plowed through swamplands. Humidity made it difficult to breathe. She thanked the Almighty for the woven fan Ruth had made.

Her mind wandered to the treasure Carlton had bought for her, two whole novels. She could barely wait to get lost in the story of Pamela, the poor servant girl who struggles to fight off her master's lustful advances. Also named *Virtue Rewarded*, Rosabel was sure she'd maintain her purity, but how?

She'd started the book a few years back, borrowed from her good friend, Maddie Welk. The two had giggled over the salacious parts, feeling righteous and naughty at the same time. Until her father found out. He'd forced her to return the novel, unfinished.

It was Maddie who'd taught Rosabel that fathers, and even mothers, need not know everything. With Maddie, Rosabel's dull, routine life became adventurous. Though once Mr. Welk was killed in the war, Mrs. Welk moved the family home to Beaufort. How proud her friend would be that Rosabel had wrangled her own copy of the forbidden *Pamela*!

The same yearning for adventure had convinced her to pick up a cloth at 8 Mile House Tavern and help Mary Ellen serve the patrons. The crowd loved how the mistress of Kilkenny laughed and teased with the soldiers and regulars of the establishment, giving as good as she got. She did have to slap one brute but had no trouble from wayward hands after that.

There were things husbands need never know, either.

They'd likely reach Kilkenny Plantation at midday. Rosabel dared not question Carlton again about his ill temper but thought of another way to lighten his mood. Sure that Davey McTier's attention was fixed on the trail, she slid her hand across Carlton's thigh toward his crotch.

Instead of the soft smile she anticipated, his eyes grew dark and glowering. "What the hell are you doing? Is this the whorish behavior that got you cheers at the tavern?"

Rosabel's jaw dropped. Her chest ached as though she'd been whacked with a club, and her eyes filled with hot tears of humiliation. She twisted her head to keep her husband from watching them fall. Heart pounding, she stared out the window for miles. She couldn't face him, demeaned and cheapened like that.

Not far from McHeath's Tavern, Carlton reached for her hand. She could not make herself respond.

"Forgive me, Rosabel. Please. I've been distraught." When she remained silent, he went on. "I learned something in Charles Town that I've not told you."

She faced him at last, only to see his own eyes reddened. "What is it, then?"

He swallowed. "Joe Dillon. He never arrived. Marauders stole Hector and killed him. Joe was found and buried in a swamp somewhere."

Rosabel gasped. She thought of the girls, Mary Edith and Baby, who worked in the Big House. On her visits, she often heard them speak of their da, as they called him, while they cleaned and polished. They had worshipped the man.

"I am heartbroken," Carlton was saying, "and can't imagine how to tell Nan."

"This is awful." Rosabel remembered how Maddie and her sister fell apart at the news of their own father's death. She felt sick inside.

"Joe was a good man, my dearest. He volunteered to fight in my stead so I could care for Mother. I told him not to do it, but he insisted. And now..."

Rosabel tasted the salt of his tears as she kissed each cheek. "We must be brave for them. I will stand by your side while you tell Nan."

He snatched her up in a desperate embrace, as though afraid to let her go. "No. I must do this alone."

♦

Carlton sensed tension the moment Davey drove onto Kilkenny. Something was amiss. As they rode through the quarters, there were no greetings. No one lifted his head as Carlton passed. Could they have somehow heard the bad news already?

He'd been tortured for the entire trip home at the thought of telling Nan about Joe's death. He wavered between guilt over his demand that Joe fight in his stead and the assertion that war brings death. It was God's will that Joe didn't survive. Either way, his stomach churned at the thought of Nan's anguish and, worse, that of the children.

One thing he knew for sure. Rosabel would not witness Nan's wretchedness nor the inevitable venom she'd spew Carlton's way.

Once Davey pulled the carriage up to the veranda steps, he was disconcerted to see a sullen Old Wilbur greet their arrival. After helping her disembark, he ordered his new wife inside. "See about Mother," he said. "Stay with her until I arrive."

He watched her scuttle up the steps ahead of Wilbur, turn back to him, then enter the Big House. He was remorseful for his treatment of Rosabel these last days, but he'd have to make up for it later. He settled with Davey McTier who took the carriage to the barn.

Little Oscar ran up to him with eyes the color of his own. "Hallo, Master Carlton. You back!"

"I am. What's happening here? Fetch Johnny Reeve immediately."

The boy's eyes widened. "Can't do that, suh."

"What? Why not?"

"Can't tell ya that neither. Becca say to keep my mouth shut."

Carlton rubbed his entire face with both hands. He looked up to see Ketch hustling toward him. Most of the servants had gathered around the courtyard but kept their distance. This was more than mourning for Joe. They looked fearful.

As soon as Ketch was within earshot, Carlton called out, "What is going on here? Where is Reeve? I demand answers!"

Reaching him, Ketch removed his hat and began wringing it in his hands. Panting, he said, "Master Carlton, we don't know what happen, but Reeve turn up dead."

Stunned, Carlton whispered, "Dead? Where?"

Ketch had broken into a sweat. "Well, suh, Jimmy come across him in the woods about a mile or so from here. He been missing more'n a day or two. Look like some big animal got him."

The others moved in closer, likely to hear Carlton's reaction. Ketch went on. "With no white folks here 'cepting yo mama, we didn't know what to do. Geoffrey and his boys made him a grave."

Carlton heard Nan's voice. "Dig him up if ye like. See for yerself."

Ketch flinched, as though struck.

Glancing Nan's way, Carlton was taken aback by her appearance. Her eyes were encircled by dark, sunken skin made even more ghoulish by her deathly complexion. The fiery spirit he dreaded seemed extinguished. This because Joe had left for war? What would become of her when she knew?

Bile rose into Carlton's throat. Whether from Nan's agony or the thought of viewing the rotting, stinking carcass of a man repulsive when alive, he didn't know. Truth be told, part of him was relieved to be rid of the vile excuse for an overseer.

"There's no need. Let the dead lie." He looked around. "Have you all done nothing in my absence, then?"

"It was Ketch," Ruth said. "He kept us going." The others nodded.

Carlton heaved a sigh of relief. "And he will continue doing so with my blessing. You will obey him as you would me. Is that understood?"

Head shaking and mumblings of "Yes, suh," spread through the group. His eyes once again landed on Nan Dillon, a shell of her former self, and he knew.

He could not tell her about Joe. He would not be the one.

▟

"Lawd-a mercy! Kingdom come. Don't tell me this. Please, Master Carlton, don't tell me none of this."

Sitting across from Mama Juba, Carlton tried to swallow through a clenched throat. Her tears wended their way through creases in the healer's worn, brown face, renewing his own grief.

"Trouble follow sin. Sure as fever follow a chill."

Her comment stopped him short. "What do you mean? Joe committed no sin." Surely, she dare not suggest he had.

Her hand cradled her head, seeming too heavy to hold itself up. "No, that sweet man done nothing wrong. He had the purest heart I ever seen." The tears surged once again. "God rest his soul, his beautiful soul."

Carlton struggled to sit before such open grief. But he had more to accomplish and could not leave.

"A pow'ful cross been placed on K'kenny, Master Carlton. Too pow'ful for me."

"What are you talking about?"

"A curse, a spell. First, yo daddy, then yo mama. I thought it might be just the fam'ly. But now that Reeve man's kilt. Worser, Joe Dillon be lying deep in a swamp. Alone." She wiped tears from her chin. "I'm too old. I can't bear no more."

He pounded the table. "A curse? Such ludicrous superstition!" Yet, dread shrouded him. "I'll not hear of it."

The pity in Mama Juba's eyes did nothing to ease his turmoil. He chewed his bottom lip, anxious to calm himself enough to do what he'd come to do.

Finally, he said, "I've decided it best for you to tell Nan what's happened. You will know what to say, how to say it."

She squinted, looking him in the eye. "It ain't gonna make no difference who tell her. She been mighty strong through a lot, but not this. He her whole life." She paused. "He was."

Afraid he might explode, Carlton stood. "Tell her," he demanded and left.

✦

Nan burst from Mama Juba's cabin and raced for the trees. Her mind thought of everything and nothing at all.

I can't breathe. I can't make it. I can't. I can't. Let me die.

She stumbled over roots and fallen logs, welcoming the pain but feeling none of it. Joe gone. It could not be. Please, God, don't let it be. I need to see him. Just once more.

She tripped again, landing on a rock that ripped open her arm. Blood gushed. She stared at it amongst the rotting leaves, vines, and twigs. A beetle crawled over the offending rock, now splashed red. Struggling for breath, she called out to the heavens.

"I love ye, Joe! My God, how I love ye! I'm so very sorry. For everything. Please, wherever ye be. Hear me!"

Wracked with pain, she rose and stumbled through the woods. She wept until her mind was emptied. When it began to refill, it was with a churning anger.

Wiping her arm across her skirt, she headed toward the Big House and those responsible. The de Barneforts.

Once reaching the veranda, she leapt up the steps two at a time. Crossing the porch, she flung open the front door and stormed past Wilbur, then Becca. They each spoke, called her name, but she had no idea what they said.

Looking from room to room, she found the family in the library. The bedridden old crone, the new wife, and the gutless coward. Mother and son wore widened eyes of fear, but the young girl showed only pity.

Nan wanted none of it. With a mama bear's roar, she leapt toward the lily-liver, eager to rip off his face. He shrank back amongst the screams of the servants, the wife, and even his mother. Becca and Wilbur tried to pull her back, but it was the sudden appearance of Ketch that saved Carlton. The others backed off as Ketch pinned her arms and dragged her away.

"Get this hag out of here!" screamed Carlton.

Ketch held her but did not remove her from the room.

"Ye killed me Joe, ye spineless prick! Not good enough to lick his boots, ye sent him to die in yer place."

Carlton glanced at Rosabel, then said, "His death is a tragedy. He was a good man."

Seeing Anne glare from her sickbed, Nan said, "Ye damned de Barneforts!" She faced the old woman. "First, ye set me poor ma on the road to starve, alone and with child. Then, Sir Richard murders me uncle—hangs him 'til dead before hacking his poor body to bits. Now Joe! The kindest, most gentle man on this earth. Bloody murderers, every one of ye!"

Rosabel rose and touched her on the shoulder. "He offered to go."

"Is that what he told ye?" Nan turned on Carlton with all her fury. "He never wanted to fight for ye and ye know it. Ye promised to leave us homeless and starving if he didn't. He died for me. For Mary Edith, Nolan, Baby and Daniel. All fatherless now, and with yer same blood running through their veins. There's not an ounce of shame in ye."

Carlton leaned forward. "She's talking out of her head. Get her out of my sight."

Nan looked to Lady Anne. "He doesn't know, does he?" To Carlton, she said, "We're cousins, you and me."

He laughed, then looked at his mother. Her downward gaze told the story.

"She knows," Nan said. "Sir Richard Lynche was me father. I may not have yer pedigree, but the blood is the same as yers."

Carlton's face grew scarlet. He picked up a small vase and heaved it. It smashed into her shoulder, then ricocheted onto

Ketch's head. "If you don't get this bitch out of here, I'll have you both killed! Now!"

Wilbur and Becca scuttled into the hallway, giving Ketch room to haul Nan from the library and through the back door.

Within the hour, the news came. Nan and her brood must remain out of Carlton's sight. By the following nightfall, they were to be banished from Kilkenny

Chapter Twenty-five

Though the morning sun was well above the horizon, Nan huddled in her cabin, defeated. Her children, Mama Juba, and Ketch surrounded her. Others in the quarters had come and gone.

Since learning of her eviction, she had not slept. Instead, she fluctuated between wailing in distress and wondering where to go. What to do. How to feed four children. Who she was without Joe.

"I was but a lass of fifteen when we met," she told Mama Juba.

The old woman shot a disturbed glance at Ketch.

"You told her that, Ma." Mary Edith took her hand.

"I did?"

"Many times."

Nan shook her head, hoping to clear her clouded brain. "I...I'm sorry." She squeezed Mary Edith's hand. "What'll we do, love?"

Nolan lifted his quivering chin. "I told you I'd take care of you."

"I know, son. I know." But he was a child.

Mama Juba pushed a bowl of something toward her. "We'll help all we can, Nan. But ya gotta help yoself. Eat."

She was so empty. Yet, if she jammed one spoonful into her mouth, she'd puke. "I will, Mama Juba. Later."

Daniel rose from his pallet where he'd curled into a ball. "I gotta pee."

Ketch took his little hand. "We'll go behind the cabin, boy."

"What if Master Carlton sees me?"

"Let me clear the coast so that don't happen." After stepping onto the porch and looking all around, he waved the child on.

Nan seethed at the fear on her little boy's face. Carlton was a cruel son of a bitch.

Watching on the porch for Daniel's return, Ketch called inside to her. "Jimmy out lookin' for a old, empty cabin somewhere. Not too far."

It was all so pointless. "'Tis kind, I know. But near or far, ye cannot come to us nor can we come here. We might as well be oceans away."

"Master Carlton gonna cool down and see the error of his ways," Mama Juba said. "Ya'll see." Her words were fine, but her troubled face told all.

Daniel scooted back into the cabin, eyes wide. "The new mistress coming!"

Ketch glanced down the lane. "Oh, Lawd. I shoulda kept better watch."

"God-a mercy, what next?" from an ashen Mama Juba.

Nan sat up, her stomach upset. She held her breath at the sound of footsteps upon her wooden stairs.

The form of Mistress Rosabel blocked the brightness of day from the room. She nodded to them. "I'd like you all to leave me and Nan. Mama Juba, take the children to your cabin. Carlton is locked in his study, so there's nothing to fear."

The children scrambled to their feet as the healer gathered them like chicks to a hen. Once Mistress Rosabel stepped inside, Ketch ducked out.

"Don't go far, Ketch. I'll be needing you."

"Yas'm."

As the children were leaving, Mary Edith held back. "I'll stay with you, Ma."

Tears of pride filled Nan's eyes. She dipped her head toward Mistress Rosabel. "Do what she tells ye, lass."

The mistress took a deep breath. "Sit on the steps outside."

A small splash of relief washed over Nan. Could it be such terrible news if a child were allowed nearby? She pushed herself to her feet and moved to the table.

Mistress Rosabel sat across from her. She reached out with soft, white hands. "My heart breaks for you," she said. "I've thought of little else since I heard. You don't know me well, but I feel like I know your girls. I've overheard their chatter while they worked, and the loving way they spoke of their father, their da."

Nan was curious to see tears fill the woman's eyes. How could someone who'd marry the likes of Carlton care about her? Or Mary Edith and Baby? Seeming to read her mind, the young woman—girl, really—looked at Nan and spoke softly.

"You're wondering how I could love Carlton. He seems harsh, I know. But he has a soft side. A tenderness. He doesn't always show it, but it's there. When we're alone...anyway, he is heartsick about Joe, I assure you."

Nan ached to lash out at this little fool but held her tongue.

"He has some of his mother's arrogance, but he carries Mr. Tom inside him as well. It must be confusing for him, to feel so strongly while fearful of appearing weak. That's what it is, you know. He's afraid. He thinks he must be harsh to be respected. My own father is partly to blame. His advice to Carlton...is wrongheaded. But we women are encouraged to be silent, aren't we?"

Joe's urges for silence were for her own good. He never put her off when she expressed her thoughts or feelings to him, such a rare and beautiful person. Unbidden tears returned.

"I hope I can depend on you never to repeat this. If you do, I'll deny it." She took a deep breath. "Carlton is weak. He is intelligent and a gifted farmer. Even his father used to say so. Unlike his mother, he has the capacity for lovingkindness. But, as I said, he is weak and, to compensate, he pretends toughness. Even cruelty, as I well know."

Nan looked up and found pain in the woman's eyes. Maybe there was something to this girl.

Mistress Rosabel sighed as she pulled back her hands. "I am saying too much. I wanted you to understand. It helps, I feel, to figure out a person if you want to—how shall I say it? To shape them, to mold them. No. Manage. That's the correct word. For their own good, of course."

Nan almost smiled. This little ninny was not as bird-witted as she appeared. "Do ye manage yer new husband, then?"

Her eyes brightened. "I'm a fast learner." She twisted her head toward the door, then back to Nan. "Today, I'm helping him with the pain he's caused, and the guilt he feels but won't admit. More important, I'd like to help you. Especially the children. I can't do much. If he suspects managing...well, you know."

"I don't suppose we can stay."

Her face fell. "No. That's not possible. But you can remain another week if he doesn't have to see you. Not like this, hiding in your cabin. But the girls can't work in the house. Tell your boys to hide when he's around. Can they do that?"

"Aye." A week. She didn't want to be ungrateful, but what then?

"Carlton will allow you to live on his property, but on the outskirts. Away from here. Ketch can get the fellows to build you a cabin. It won't be much. Enough to keep the rain off."

Nan stared at her hands. "Thank ye, miss."

The young woman's mouth drooped. "It was the best I could do. He refuses to set eyes on you or yours ever again. So, once you leave here, you cannot come back. Do you understand?"

She nodded.

"If you do, it will be on my head. I beg you to remember that."

Φ

Outside the Brown homestead, Alden moved closer to the fire. That afternoon he'd been bathed in sweat, yet dusk had cooled the air beneath the trees. He and Joe Dillon roasted the four fat turkeys Tarlton had caught for everyone's supper. Abundant and gentle as cattle, they could be run down on horseback.

While Joe ate with the others inside the Brown house, Alden gnawed his turkey leg alone.

The fire crackled. A steady chorus of crickets chirped while a nearby owl made its mournful appeals. They'd remained guests of Mr. Billy Brown the entire week since the skirmish at Harbard's Store, yet none of them were any closer to a plan on how to proceed. Joe was more and more skittish, fearful he'd be spotted and declared alive and a traitor.

"'Tis me family will pay the price," he'd said on more than one occasion.

None of them trusted the lull in the clashes between the Tories and the Patriots. The Loyalists would likely be emboldened by their great victory in Charles Town. The very air wheezed with tension.

Alden froze at a footfall in the leafy ground cover. Dropping his meat, he snatched his rifle and leapt to his feet. Girlish giggles stopped him cold.

"Silly! It's only me."

His heart continued to pound. "Suzanne, what are you doing? You nearly got yourself shot."

She moved in closer, her finger to her lips. "Hush. They don't know I'm out here."

A dizzying mixture of delight and trepidation overwhelmed him. "It's dangerous. You need to go back." Though, he wished she wouldn't. "What will your father say? Or Tarlton?"

It did not go unnoticed that Levi had left that morning to check on his parents and siblings. Damn Levi for invading his thoughts at this moment!

Suzanne moved even closer until inches separated them. Her scent was intoxicating. "Why won't you come inside and eat with us? Joe does."

"It's best I stay out here."

"Aren't you lonesome?"

She had to hear his heart hammering against his chest. "Someone has to keep watch." He tried to laugh. "Against intruders like yourself."

She took his hand in hers. "Must it always be you?"

Every impulse told him to grab her close, kiss her plump lips, inhale her womanly scent. And she looked so eager! In the moment, he cared little for Levi, Tarlton, or what anyone else would think of him.

Suzanne's eyes had closed, as though in anticipation, when he was slapped by an unwelcome thought. What of Suzanne's virtue? He took a step back. It would not be he who tainted her honor or brought her shame.

He brushed her hand against his lips, then whispered, "Go back, Suzanne."

Her eyes flashed. "I'm not a child."

"I'm aware of that."

A door squeaked open. Both froze.

"A good night to one and all," Joe called before the door slammed shut.

Suzanne's eyes grew round as coins before she spun on her heels and disappeared into the darkness behind the house.

His heart still racing, Alden lowered himself onto the log he used as a bench. Joe shuffled through the leaves to their camp and sat across from him.

"'Tis a shame yer not able to join us inside. I thought how much ye'd enjoy Mr. Billy's stories. The man can spin a dandy of a yarn."

Eager to cover his discomfort, Alden said, "I heard a song or two from you, didn't I?"

Joe laughed. "They seem to enjoy me ditties from the old country."

Alden grew serious. "I don't know how much longer I can stay here."

The Irishman nodded.

"We've got to make some sort of move," Alden said. "I've been thinking. Now that you've got Surefoot to ride, I should take Hector back to Kilkenny."

Joe gasped. "How would ye be doing that, then?"

"What you said struck me. With Hector supposedly stolen, who is safe to ride him? I could return the horse, claiming he was part of the herd we confiscated in Georgia." He chuckled. "Harbard's Store being a Loyalist stronghold would insinuate Tories were the murdering thieves. An irresistible poke at Carlton."

"Is it safe to show yer face?"

He sighed. "I don't know. But I'm drawn there, somehow." And away from the perilous Suzanne.

✣

Thunder sat in the back of Dr. Uzal Johnson's wagon with another runaway, Cuffee, a big man like himself. He was a fine enough fellow, despite his constant chatter. Dr. Johnson, a surgeon from the North, sat beside the driver.

As he rode, Thunder thought of the day a baby-faced man wearing a bloodied apron had dashed up to him and other new recruits. He jabbed his finger toward Cuffee and Thunder.

"Him...and him!" he called, then ran back where he'd come from.

Lt. Ryerson, looking a bit stunned, said, "Go. You're with the doctor now. Hurry!"

The two tracked the fellow to the hospital tent. The man waved them both to a low table where a soldier writhed and screamed so fiercely that hairs rose on Thunder's neck. The baby-faced one joined two others in similar aprons surrounding the patient.

"Hold this man still!" barked a short, bespeckled one, Dr. Johnson as it turned out.

The former slaves rushed over. Cuffee held one leg while Thunder braced the injured one. There was so much blood it was hard to say for sure, but it seemed to have been smashed above the knee. One of the assistants held the man's arms as the doctor began to saw through flesh and bone.

Thunder's muscles quivered from the effort, but he held firm.

The doctor spoke to him while his eyes never left his task. "You let that leg fall before I give the word, his bone will fracture. Ya hear?"

Once the leg was removed, a heated blade was used to seal the vessels. Thunder held firm, redoubling his efforts, even as the stench of cauterized flesh caused him to turn his head and vomit.

From that day, the two joined another black man and four runaway women who worked for Dr. Johnson with the sick and injured. Fortunately, no more limbs were cut off. Thunder helped mostly with the lifting and scrubbing blood and vomit from the treatment of fever victims. It was a relief to spend this day traveling to the docks of Charles Town.

The camp buzzed with activity as several regiments prepared to move out. Those who worked with the ill speculated that officers were anxious to escape the coast. The sickly season was fast approaching. Less crowds and pure inland air should be healthier, they said.

Some of the medical workers would be left behind with fevered soldiers and militiamen. Dr. Johnson and his crew would follow the fighting men, many of whom had already left. Thunder's stomach grew queasy with the realization that more amputations were in his future.

This jaunt to the harbor was to collect limes and pineapples from a sloop called *Providence* for the marching men. As they neared the waterfront and the salty smell of seawater, Thunder grew agitated. How long had it been since he'd been crammed into the belly of a creaky wooden ship, filled with the stench of unwashed bodies and vile fluids that go with them? Whiffs of sea air brought that misery flooding back.

Cuffee twisted his head and peered into Thunder's face. "What wrong with ya, man? Ya ain't never seen the ocean?"

The sight of ships' masts, with their spiderwebs of ropes made it hard for Thunder to breathe. "I seen it."

A light went on in Cuffee's eyes. "Ya rode on one of them boats, ain't ya? Like the old folk talk about. It bad like they say?"

Rivulets of sweat ran past his temples, but he didn't answer.

Cuffee put his hand on Thunder's shoulder. "If one of us gots to go on the boat, I'll do it. You tote the fruit to the cart."

Grateful, Thunder nodded. He yearned to go home, but to get on a ship? He didn't believe he could do it.

Once back at the hospital tent, Thunder saw Cuffee talking to the others. One by one, they turned to gawk. He was sure they mocked him. One young woman called Dolly stared even as the others went back to their tasks. While Thunder was grateful for Cuffee's offer to take his place on the sloop, he fumed.

Throughout the rest of the day and into the following morning, he caught the woman, Dolly, side-eying him. His temper rose until he thought he would explode.

Past midday, he could stand no more. He saw she was wiping a feverish man down with pluff mud that came from the marshes. Despite the rotting odor, the doctors claimed it relieved fever. He waited until she was finished to duck behind a tent she had to pass.

At her approach, he leapt in front of her.

Dolly sucked in her breath. The metal pan crashed to the ground, splashing mud over them both. "What ya doin', ya big oaf?" She leaned to pick it up.

He grabbed her arm, pulling her up to face him. "Why you look at me? You think I do not see you stare? Dat I am such a fool?"

She yanked her arm from his grasp. "Ain't no doubt you a fool. I look at ya 'cause...'cause ya remind me of someone, that's all!"

She attempted to get around Thunder, but he blocked her way. "Who it is I remind you? A coward?"

Dolly stopped to look him in the eye, her head tilted to one side. "A coward? Why would—? Because of what Cuffee say 'bout the boat? I was right. You is a fool!"

His jaw remained set, but he felt unsure.

A smile crept onto Dolly's face, lighting her eyes. "You come from Africa, like me. I come as a chile and don't remember much. But when I see you..." She stopped, then spoke in a whisper. "When I see you, I see my brother. He was older than me, so tall and strong." Sadness crept into her eyes. "He ain't get captured like me and another brother. He home, as handsome as ever, I reckon."

She smirked. "Don't go gettin' no big head. Y'ain't all that special."

Thunder swallowed, not sure what to say. "Were you Fulani?"

"I was. They name me Dalanda, but my master call me Dolly. My other brother was caught with me, but he die on the ship. I can't never forget that. When Cuffee talk about how you was at the harbor, it remind me even more."

Thunder nodded, grateful that someone understood.

"Now let me pass," Dolly said, shoving her way around him.

Not Dolly. Dalanda. She would always be Dalanda.

Chapter Twenty-six

Joe doused his head under the pump, clearing the dust from his face and the cobwebs from his head. Ready to face the day, he joined the other men at the corral outside Billy Brown's house.

"It's decided," Tarlton said. "Me and Bartlett can't sit here any longer, not while there's real fighting to be done back home in Virginia. We can oppose the crown's forces with our people up there. My father and Levi will protect life and property here."

Levi nodded.

Tarlton looked to Alden and Joe. "We'll head out for Charlotte as soon as we can get our gear together. Then we'll follow the foothills to our Virginia home, Albemarle. You fellows are welcome to join us, or you can go your own way."

Joe cleared his throat. "Lieutenant, I know Alden explained me predicament. I must find a way to provide for me family with none aware I walk among the living. For now, I'd like to stick with you and Bartlett, if ye'll have me."

"We'll be the better for it, Joe," Bartlett said.

Alden rubbed his chin. "If you're headed to Charlotte, you're likely to go right through my territory. That'll put Joe in a mighty bad way if he gets spotted through there."

"That's a fact." Tarlton turned to Bartlett. "What say we head up toward the Santee region and through the Waxhaws?"

Joe began to realize the spot he was putting the brothers in. "I don't want to cause ye no trouble."

"We'll get there just the same," Bartlett said. "What about you, Alden?"

"I've decided to take Hector back to Kilkenny." He laughed. "The horse is more a danger than Joe is. I don't know if I'll be welcomed or shot on sight, but if I survive, I'll join you down the road."

While the others were busy gathering their gear, Alden took Joe aside. "Would you like me to tell Nan you're alive, if I get the opportunity?"

Joe's stomach tied itself in knots. "I did nothing but think on it all night long. It would take a boulder off me heart to ease her grief, but 'tis her heart I fear."

"I'm confused."

"She wears it on her sleeve, as the saying goes. And when riled, caution is thrown to the four winds. Whatever pops into her mouth spews out. I dasn't risk it." He sighed. "Check on her for me, if ye will. Give her whatever hope ye dare, but the truth is best left unsaid."

Alden's face reflected his pity. "As you wish."

Soon, all the men shook hands, said their goodbyes, and left the comfort of the Brown home.

Joe's mind went where it always did. To Nan and the young ones. He prayed Alden would find them safe and well, that one day soon they would all be together again.

✦

Riding Enbarr while leading Hector on a rope, Alden's trepidation grew as he neared Kilkenny. Rain-laden clouds matched his mood. What did he hope for? He wasn't even sure why he felt compelled to return. His wistful observations of the Brown family life? He couldn't miss what he'd never had. More likely spending time with Joe Dillon...and Hector. When he saw the horse, he recalled the joy on Carlton's face when he'd ridden him.

Perhaps when he got close enough, Alden could set Hector loose. Surely the horse would wend its way back to the barns. Then he'd be free to catch up with the others. But he wouldn't do that. Whatever there was to face, he had to follow through.

Fat drops of rain splashed on his arms and legs when he reached the first cabins of the quarters. It had been weeks since he tore through there after his rift with Carlton. The first cabin he passed had belonged to the Dillons. No clatter of little children running across the porch. Of course, being late morning, they'd be occupied.

He passed other cabins. Had it always been so quiet this time of day? He saw Ruth carrying a basket of herbs toward the kitchen. When she spotted him, she stopped short.

"Mr. Alden? That you?"

"It is, Ruth. I've been missing your sweet bread."

"You a sight for my sore eyes. I gots some in the kitchen." She looked around. "Is ya staying?"

"I don't know." He tried to smile. "Is it safe?"

"The master don't know you coming?"

Alden shook his head.

"We'll soon see, won't we, suh?"

By this time, several others came out, calling their greetings. Even Mama Juba stuck her head from her cabin.

"Lawd, look who come back. There be hope in this world."

His confidence grew with the warm reception.

Then Mama Juba frowned. "That ol' Hector ya got there?"

"I found him, Mama," Alden called out. "Thought I'd bring him home."

The old woman's face fell. Without another word, she went back inside. The heads of other servants dropped as well. They all straggled back to their chores. Alden's spirit sank. They knew. Somehow, Joe's story had gotten back to them.

After taking both horses to the barn and leaving them in Amos's care, he inhaled several times. Gathering his strength, he headed to the Big House, climbed the steps, and knocked on the front door of what was once his home.

The door creaked open, exposing Wilbur. Alden wrapped the old man in a tight embrace.

"Mr. Alden, you home!" Tears rolled down his wrinkled cheeks. "We needing you so and here you be."

Alden's eyes burned. "It's so very good to see you, old man." He heard the patter of feet.

"Can it be?" came a female voice.

He looked around the old slave. "Rosabel Gatch!" He hadn't remembered her clear blue eyes and rosy cheeks.

"It's Rosabel de Barnefort now, brother. Come in!"

"Well, congratulations! Kilkenny was in dire need of sweetness and beauty." He stepped into the foyer and kissed her cheek, then whispered, "How is it living with the old dragon? Do you get any space to breathe at all?"

Her face fell. "You don't know."

"Know what?"

Carlton's voice cut through their murmurs. "Our mother is not well. She was befallen by apoplexy."

Alden bowed. "Brother." Carlton's face was unreadable. "I hope I am welcome. But if not, I will leave immediately. I mean to cause no trouble."

Carlton's nod was nearly imperceptible before he turned and headed to the library.

Alden followed. When he caught sight of his mother in her sickbed, he gasped. Did Joe know? If so, why hadn't he told him? She'd shrunken so, she about disappeared into the bedclothes. Her face drooped out of recognition. Mostly, she looked ancient, as though all life had seeped from her being.

"Mother," Carlton said. "Your son has returned." He stepped aside to allow Alden to come closer to the bed.

The crone turned to face her younger son. Alden saw the fires ignite behind her watery eyes, displaying an animal-like rage. She grunted, then growled.

"Mother? I'm sorry you're unwell."

At his voice, the intensity in her eyes heightened. She stretched her ghastly lips even further apart, emitting a gravelly, inhuman roar.

The hairs rose on Alden's arms as he stumbled backward, horrified. "I...I'm sorry. I didn't mean to upset you." He turned on his heels and sped from the room.

When Carlton joined him, Alden was still panting. "It's like she's possessed by demons. I don't know what to say."

His brother sighed. "We'll go to the study for a shot of McHeath's rotgut and some privacy."

Once seated in the very spots they'd inhabited for their last disastrous conversation, Carlton poured them each three fingers. They saluted each other with their glasses before Alden drank about half. He was surprised to see Carlton's measured sips.

Alden set his glass on the desk. "I brought Hector home."

"Yes. Amos called out to me as I headed to the house. I'm grateful."

Alden nodded. He was curious how his brother would explain the horse's disappearance.

Instead, Carlton asked, "How did you come to possess him?"

"I ride with a company of militia. We were engaged in a skirmish across the river in Georgia. He was among the horses in the corral of our adversaries. How he got there is a mystery I'd hoped you could enlighten."

"Loyalists had him?"

"They did. Our surprise attack enabled us to be victorious. Which isn't always the case, as you can imagine."

"I've learned some things about myself, Alden. One is that I'm not a fighter. I admire your ability to go to battle for your beliefs, such as they are, but I'm not made for it." His eyes begged for understanding. "I am a farmer. Like Father."

It took a lot for Carlton to admit a weakness, perceived or real. Alden's heart went out to him. "Father didn't like a fight either. Mother always said I was the one most like him, but perhaps it's you."

"Mother was wrong about many things."

Alden swallowed. "At the risk of sounding crass, how has she survived such a devastating illness?"

"Sheer meanness."

Alden started to chuckle at what he thought was a joke but stopped at Carlton's hard look. He cleared his throat instead. "Congratulations on your marriage, brother. Rosabel is the picture of a blushing bride."

"I had so many conceptions of who I am and how my life would go that have turned out wrong. I was oblivious to how happy Rosabel would make me. She's the best thing in my life."

Alden thought of Suzanne. "You're a fortunate man." He sighed, then got to the point. "How did you lose Hector?"

Carlton's face sagged. He looked tired. "Joe Dillon agreed to take my place in the Loyalist militia. I gave him Hector as a gift for the officer, Ferguson." His voice cracked as he said, "He never made it. Some thieves stole Hector and murdered Joe. Now they turn out to be my own side, Tories."

"There are abominations on both sides. I didn't see Nan or the children on my way in. Have they been told?"

"Nan took it poorly and tried to attack me. I had to send her off, to a spot near White Oak Springs. Ketch had the boys build a shelter there." He looked Alden in the eye. "I had no choice."

They sat in silence as rain pummeled the roof and porch. Alden felt sick to his stomach. All Joe did was for the safety of Nan and the young ones. He'd be devastated at this turn of events. Carlton's voice pulled him from his reverie.

"Did you know Nan's natural father was our cousin, Sir Richard?"

"No," Alden said, "I didn't." Although they'd visited Duncullen as boys, he had little memory of the man. Only that he kept to himself a lot.

"What do you think about that?" Carlton asked.

"So, she was Lynche's bastard. It doesn't surprise me Father would take care of her, knowing that."

Carlton spoke so quietly, Alden strained to hear.

"I can't look at her. Or the children." He guzzled the rest of his whiskey before picking up Thomas's old pipe. That he'd appropriated it as his own now seemed to Alden a petty complaint after all he'd seen. The familiar aroma instead brought Alden comfort.

"How Father grated on me the way he played this bloody conflict both ways." Carlton pulled on the pipe, then blew a cloud toward the window. "I see the wisdom in it now. I cannot in good conscience support either side."

Alden smiled. "Then we are no longer enemies."

Carlton's eyelids lifted. "Are you finding the same? Will you give up the fight, then?"

Alden sighed. "No. I cannot. Yet, we're no longer on opposing sides. That must count for something."

Carlton raised his glass. "It does, brother." He lowered it, chewed his bottom lip, and said, "When it's done, please come back. We can figure it out."

Alden stayed the night, all the while avoiding his mother's line of vision. Carlton's heavy hand on McHeath's whiskey bottle made for a pleasant respite from the upheaval colonial life had become. He floated in a haze of stories from childhood as well as wistful memories of their father.

Later, Alden lay on his childhood bed with tears rolling past his temples and into his ears. He had a family.

Chapter Twenty-seven

The following morning, Alden said his good-byes to his brother and Rosabel, then headed for the kitchen house. Ruth held out two warm loaves wrapped in an old piece of linen.

"These be for you, Mr. Alden." She lifted a basket containing four more. Holding them close to her, she looked at him from under her lashes. "If it don't be no trouble, can ya take these to Nan and her babies? We's worried about her near that swampy ground. She ain't got no garden or nothin'."

"I will be proud to do so." He reached for the basket, but Ruth drew it back.

"This gotta be 'tween us. If Master Carlton heared..."

"Why, Ruth, six whole loaves for me? You're too generous."

She gave him the basket. "You a blessin', Mr. Alden. May God keep ya safe from all this ugliness." As he said farewell to the other servants, he saw the cook wipe her eyes on her apron.

He swallowed, then went to the barn for Enbarr. After more good wishes from the men and a hug from little Oscar, he mounted. Nearing Mama Juba's cabin, he saw the old healer in her doorway, waving him over.

He halted at her steps.

In her hand was a small leather bag. "This here a mojo, Mr. Alden. Keep it on ya all the days and nights. I don't know if it's enough, but it's all I can do."

He frowned. "That doesn't sound like you, Mama Juba. I never heard you admit to something you can't fix."

Her sad eyes reminded him how ancient she must be.

"They's some pow'ful black magic up in here, Mr. Alden. Ain't no way to say for certain how things'll turn out." Without another word, she returned to the darkness of her hut.

A pall overwhelmed him as he headed out. He said a quick prayer that he'd find Nan the same feisty woman he remembered. Sad, even angry, but not defeated.

As he approached the dwelling on the far edge of Kilkenny, his heart dropped. It consisted of a few logs held together with more mud than wood. The roof was made of rafters covered with grasses and a hole for smoke to escape.

Nan appeared at the threshold, her hair a matted mess and eyes sunken into her gaunt face. She squinted before asking, "Who is it?" Then she cocked her head to the side. "Mr. Alden?"

He dismounted with a lump the size of an apple lodged in his throat. "It is, Nan. I've been to the Big House." He thrust the breadbasket her way. "Ruth sends these."

She received it like a treasure. "She's so good. They can't come here, ye know. Carlton forbids it."

"May I come in?"

She nodded and stepped aside. Alden found only a crude table and small stools set on a dirt floor. Straw was scattered in the corners where he assumed she and the children slept. Nan took a wooden cup and filled it with water from an old bucket.

"From the springs." She handed it to him. "Nothing to fear from it. Pure, they say."

Perched on an uneven stool, Nan stared at her folded hands and said nothing. Alden's anger grew, dissipating any warm feelings he'd felt for his brother. Joe risked all to protect his family and it had come to this. All for Carlton's blasted pride.

"I'm sorry." Such inadequate words.

"We're getting by," Nan said. "Nolan's been helping carpenters in the area. He brings home scraps for his efforts. The girls are at McHeath's Tavern. Kitchen and serving girls."

Alden's breath caught. "That's no place for young lasses like Mary Edith and Baby. The louts that—"

"I offered to work there meself, but McHeath wanted younger girls. His wife promised no harm would come to them." She frowned. "That woman ain't got no young'ns of her own, ye know. I think she's taken with little Daniel. He does this and that around the place. That's where they be now."

"But what of you, Nan? You don't look well." What should he do? Dare he break Joe's trust? How much worse could it be?

He knew the answer to that. Carlton could take back this shelter, primitive as it was. Then what? He had to get to Joe as soon as possible. His family needed him.

"They send me pig fat to make candles," Nan was saying. "I get a few coins for that. And I'll card wool during the season."

The rattle of wagon wheels and the bray of a mule startled them. Alden ran outside.

Charlie from the Mitchell Plantation pulled up in a cart with young Nolan beside him, shoulders slumped and face flushed. "He got the fever," the old slave called out.

Nan ran to the wagon and tried to lift her boy from the bench. "A blazing furnace, he is!"

"I'm sorry, Ma," Nolan mumbled. "They won't let me stay."

Struggling, Nan said, "Jesus in Heaven, not this. I can take no more."

Alden took the boy from her arms and carried him into the hut. It galled him that he had no more than a pile of old straw to lay the lad upon. Enbarr was treated better!

"I sorry, miss," Charlie said. "Wish I could do more."

Nan shook her head and waved as the old slave rode off.

Alden met her at the door. "It looks like the putrid fever. I've seen a fair bit of it riding with the militia."

Nolan moaned. "Ooh, my head. A pounding hammer's inside. Make it stop!"

Nan turned to Alden and whispered, "What'll I do? Me ma died from the fever. I can't do this again. I can't!"

The two turned at the sound of teeth chattering so badly, it seemed they would crumble to small bits. "Do you have a blanket?" Alden asked.

Nan grabbed a large woolen rag from a dark corner and threw it over her son. She wrapped it around him as closely as she could, then lay beside him and embraced his shivering body. The poor little fellow groaned and mumbled nonsense.

Helpless, Alden's chest ached. He'd do the only thing he could, ride like the wind to bring Joe Dillon back to his family. But before that, he'd get help.

"I'm off to Kilkenny," he said to Nan's back. "Mama Juba will know what to do."

✦

Rosabel heard boots stomping up the front veranda. After peeking out the window, she ran to the door to greet Alden.

"What brings you back?"

"The Dillon boy, Nolan, has the fever. A bad case. Speak to Mama Juba but remember she can't travel. You have to convince Carlton. He must swallow his pride and send help."

"He left early this morning. I don't expect him back before dusk. I'll see to the family myself. As he's fond of saying, I'm lady of the manor now."

"You're a good woman, Rosabel." He took a deep breath. "I have very important business to attend to, but I leave the situation in good hands." He bowed, ran to his horse, mounted, and sped away.

Rosabel wasted no time. Within the hour, Amos was driving her to the Dillon shack with a boneset tonic. Mama Juba's parting words left a chill on her heart. "There ain't too much we can do but pray. Pray for the boy's life soul, that it be strong enough."

Rosabel pulled back her shoulders as they neared Nan's new cabin, set in a small clearing within thick brush and swampy ground.

Amos glanced at her from the corner of his eye. "You wanna go back, miss?"

"Certainly not." She clutched Mama Juba's basket as, with his help, she climbed from the wagon. She could already hear the boy's cries and moans.

At the door, she waited until her eyes adjusted to the darkness inside. In the corner stood a white woman she'd never seen before. Nan was kneeling beside Nolan who writhed on the ground. A knotted string had been tied around his head, a cure some used for headaches. A rolled-up blanket served as the boy's pillow.

Nan turned toward her. "Miss Rosabel, you shouldn't be here. This fever could bring ye down as well."

"I've always had a strong constitution." She looked to the stranger. "This woman seems fine."

"That's me neighbor, Peggy Ogilvy," Nan said.

The woman had a nasally voice. "I got a bag of shit tied 'round my neck. What you got to ward off sickness?"

Rattled, Rosabel chose to ignore the Ogilvy woman. "Nan, I've brought Mama Juba's remedy. It's a potion made with boneset."

Peggy intruded once again. "I already brought a black chicken. My man brought me one last time he was by."

"Chicken?"

"A black one. I gutted it right where you standing. See? It's tied to that young'n's foot. That'll drain his fever sure enough."

Rosabel's eyes flew from the puddle of blood her beneath her left shoe to the limp carcass covering Nolan's foot. She suddenly wished to be feeding soup to Lady Anne while her mother-in-law passed gas.

"Nan, I will do what I can to make sure you have all you need until your dear boy is well. You are not alone."

Nan stood, approached Rosabel, and took her hands. "Pray for me son. He's a good lad."

Rosabel nodded and left the dark, cramped hovel that reeked of illness and death.

⚐

Alden had ridden about two miles before he was stopped by George Collins.

"We need every man, Alden! McGirth and his blasted ruffians are on a rampage up and down the Savannah River. He and his brutes are killing every man, woman, and child they find, loyalties be damned."

"What set him off?"

"Who's to say? They crossed at Summerlin's Ferry and are moving south along the Carolina side."

Straight toward the Brown homestead—and Suzanne!

"I gotta get more help." George spurred his horse and took off.

In a panic, Alden sped toward Brier's Creek.

McGirth was notorious up and down the Savannah River. Once a Patriot scout, a clash with one of his officers led to a brutal lashing for insubordination. Not severe enough according to people who'd since been robbed, beaten, or had loved ones murdered.

Afterward, he escaped to the British side seeking revenge. But he was no soldier. He and his gang of twenty or thirty marauders cared little which side they harassed.

Tarlton and Bartlett were gone. Only Levi and the old man remained. What havoc might these criminals wreak? With his heart in his throat, Alden tore through the countryside as fast as Enbarr would go.

⚜

Joe was amazed. What started as three men on a journey to Virginia grew to twenty-three on horseback or foot by the end of the second day. It seemed every five miles or so brought out more like-minded men and boys who saw no future in a British-led Carolina.

The small, growing band put Joe in mind of the Levellers he'd joined as a lad in Ireland. Their numbers had sometimes increased to two hundred until it was found smaller packs could sabotage the gentry with greater success.

Here, Joe felt safer as the party swelled. Like Tarlton Brown was a bit too fond of saying, they were liable to be butchered without mercy at any given moment. The more, the merrier.

Outside the town of Orangeburgh, three more fellows wearing grimaces of despair approached them on foot. Joe felt the usual twinge in his stomach. In the backcountry, clothing was scarce. The rags many wore barely covered them, let alone revealed which side they supported.

"Where you boys headed?" Bartlett called before they got too close.

A grizzled old man spit tobacco juice on the ground. "We's looking for men who ain't ready to lick the English boot. Hoping you'd be some of 'em."

A younger man squinted as he tightened his grip on his gun. "Careful, Zeb."

Zeb turned to his companions. "It don't matter, boys. I ain't going home 'til I'm dead or I'm free. No use in hiding it."

The two young men stepped back, raising their weapons.

Tarlton Brown lifted his hand in the air. "Hold on, now. Let's not get riled up for nothing. We're the fellows you're looking for, heading to Virginia. Plan to take up the cause there. Lower your guns and join us."

The two skittish ones looked at each other. One shrugged. They did as Tarlton suggested and increased the party's size to twenty-six.

Joe climbed down from Surefoot to give the old fellow a chance to ride for a while. His weathered face lit up at the offer.

As they walked, one of the young lads told him a band of Loyalists had attacked their small camp the night before.

"I seen one of 'em was my neighbor from a few years back. We growed up together. I called out, 'Hey, Noah. It's me, Jim.' He knew me, I could tell. But here he come a-charging anyway. I tripped him up and bashed his head in with my musket." He took a deep breath. "Don't that beat all."

Jim grew quiet after that.

Joe wondered what he was doing in this company. He didn't share the old man, Zeb's, passion for defeating the British. He never had. Even in Ireland, he wanted to be treated as a man in his own right, free to live and love in a just manner. Now, he was amid folks beating their childhood friends to death.

His mind reeled. Was what these fellows wanted any different? Is this what it took to be treated as a man? Part of him was frustrated. He felt he was moving farther and farther from his goal to care for his family once again.

Was this roundabout road the path he should be on?

⚙

Alden saw smoke blending into the overcast sky miles before he neared the Savannah River. He inhaled ash floating into his face. Gray-coated people stumbled toward him, kerchiefs covering their noses and mouths. Some had carts filled with possessions. Others clutched what they could carry their arms.

"McGirth," one gasped. "A monster."

A woman carrying a weeping child cried out to him. "Satan himself, he was, with his horde of demons! May they rot!"

Alden was torn. He hated to ride off from these destitute people, but what of Suzanne? He continued over miles of devastation without stopping.

Riding onto the Brown homestead at full gallop, the air drained from his lungs. Flames leapt from the house so recently filled with song and laughter. He jumped off Enbarr and ran toward it until the intense heat repelled him.

He shouted their names. "Mr. Billy! Levi!" Running this way and that, he was unsure where to look. "Suzanne! Oh my God, let them be alive."

The fence surrounding the corral had been knocked over. The livestock was gone. He moved toward it, not sure what he was looking for. Some sign of life?

In that, he was disappointed. There, on the ground, lay the body of Billy Brown sprawled in a pool of blood. Falling to his knees beside him, Alden flinched at the large gash in the old man's skull. He ached to keep his emotions in check. He must find Suzanne.

If only there were some sort of tracks to follow, but the yard was traversed with every kind of print. How many men and horses had come through here, stealing and slaughtering?

Had he heard something? A groan? Or was it the hiss of burning timbers? He continued to stumble outside the house, refusing to think of Suzanne inside the raging structure. And himself, unable to save her.

More groaning. He moved toward the sound, away from the house. From the edge of the woods, he spotted a man's boot. He rushed to the low brush where he found Levi Anderson. A wound had torn open his gut.

Alden gasped. An injury like that was fatal. Nothing could be done.

Levi moaned, then let out a whimpering wail.

Alden crouched beside him. "I'm here, Levi. Can you talk?"

"Papa?"

"No, it's Alden. What happened? Was it McGirth?"

Levi struggled to breathe. "'Bout thirty of 'em. Looking for McKay."

Alden had heard of McKay, a rebel along the Savannah across from Ebenezer, Georgia. What was McGirth doing this far upriver? "What about the women, Levi?" His voice cracked. "I can't find Sarah Brown...or Suzanne."

"The woods. I sent them."

Alden's heart lifted. "Which way? Do you remember?"

"Brier's Creek...small cave." His breathing grew heavier. "Find them."

"I will, Levi. I'm going for them now." He stood.

With a sudden movement, Levi snatched his ankle. Alden knelt back down.

"Tell Suzanne...I love her. Take...take care of her...for me."

Alden felt punched in the gut. Had Levi known of their attraction to one another the whole time? He felt drenched in shame.

"No, Levi. She's yours. I'm going to get her now and will bring her back to you."

He shook his head ever so slightly. "She wants...you."

Chapter Twenty-eight

Mary Edith walked into the kitchen house behind McHeath's Tavern. Their young slave, Lottie, was standing over a white baby lying on the wooden table. He was screaming to the rafters.

Susie, a slave from a nearby plantation, stood by, wringing her hands.

Lottie nodded toward the hearth. "Bring my pipe."

The infant's racket made it hard to think. Mary Edith picked up the corncob smoldering there and handed it to Lottie. "If Mr. McHeath comes in, we're all going to hear about it."

Lottie ignored her, speaking to the baby's mammy. "Susie, you sure you didn't let the teakettle boil while this here babe was in the room? That'll bring on the colic sure enough."

"I 'member what ya say. I always keep this little fella and my own chil' outside when the tea boils."

Things started to make sense to Mary Edith. Susie had her own baby to nurse, so she was the one to suckle her master's son.

"How 'bout rockin' the cradle when it empty?" Lottie asked.

Susie snorted. "Even I know better'n that!" The baby fidgeted so much, it was a struggle for her to remove his shift.

When she finally got it off, Lottie took a long drag of her pipe, filling her chest with smoke. She then leaned over the boy and blew it out, long and slow, across his soft, round belly.

Mary Edith smiled as the little fellow calmed, like a terrible itch had been scratched. She'd seen Mama Juba do this, but she never tired of watching a distressed baby's relief.

A grin spread over Susie's face as well. "Lottie, how'd a gal not much older than me come to know so much about remedies?"

"I done the same with my own boy back on the Jarrett Plantation 'fore I was sold off to the McHeaths."

Susie gathered her chubby package. "Well, I'd best take Montcrief back 'fore they whip me for takin' so long. I don't need none of their mess."

Once she'd left, Lottie took a deep breath. "I wonder how my little Henry doin'."

"Fine, I reckon," Mary Edith said. "Missing you."

The slave cook's eyes lit up. "Mrs. McHeath, she's teachin' me all about the Bible and how to read and write. When I can write good, I'm gonna send a letter to Mrs. Jarrett. She's kind-hearted like Mrs. McHeath. She'll read it to my boy and send me a letter back. Then I'll know for certain how he doin'."

"Now, Lottie, that's our secret. Remember?"

Mary Edith spun around. She'd not heard Mrs. McHeath come into the kitchen.

"My husband has given permission for your lessons," the woman went on, "but he is not in total agreement. Many folks around here would be upset if they knew you were becoming Christian. They say it ruins a good slave."

She picked up the ladle and stirred the pot hanging over the fire. "What's in today's stew?"

"Mos'ly rabbit and a little squirrel, miss," Lottie said.

"Anyway, we can continue only if your lessons remain a secret," the tavern mistress said. "I would not want our neighbors to put pressure on poor Mr. McHeath to stop them. His business depends on the goodwill of our friends."

"Mar' Edith won't say nothin'." Lottie stared hard at the girl.

"No, ma'am," Mary Edith said. "I won't say a word."

"I'm sure you won't." Mrs. McHeath looked around. "Where's Daniel?"

"I sent him to churn butter, miss," Lottie said.

Mrs. McHeath handed the ladle to Lottie and left the kitchen. To look for Daniel, Mary Edith assumed.

"That lady sure has a soft spot for yo brother," Lottie said. "I guess 'cause she can't have no chillun of her own. Before you Dillons started workin' here, she'd get the melancholy bad."

"But she's so cheery."

"Oh, she can get right glum. There been times we couldn't get her out the bed for the day. Mr. McHeath don't know what to do. I couldn't tell which would lose they mind first, him or her."

"Oh." Mary Edith tried to picture Mrs. McHeath like that but couldn't.

Lottie waved her closer and got quiet. "That's why he spoil her so. He can't take it when she like that. Say what you want, that man love his wife."

And no one else, Mary Edith wanted to say.

The two girls jumped when the lady burst through the door, wringing her hands. "I can't find Daniel anywhere. Something's happened to him, I'm sure of it."

"I'll hunt him." Mary Edith ran out before the lady could object. If he were up to some devilment, it was best she find him first.

She found no mischief, though. Only Daniel standing beside their sister, Baby Eveleen, who was spewing vomit the color of coffee behind the kitchen house.

"Holy Mother of God!" Mary Edith called out.

Baby sat back on her haunches and wiped her mouth with her sleeve. Tears rolled down her bright red cheeks. "My head is hurting. Everything. It all hurts."

Mary Edith touched her brow, which burned like hot coals. "You got the fever, Baby. We need Mama Juba."

"What's going on here?" Mrs. McHeath rounded the building, followed by Lottie.

The three Dillons said nothing.

Pulling her apron over her nose and mouth, the woman pointed at Baby with her other hand. "The fever! Get away from here. Leave now!"

On her hands and knees, Baby hacked and vomited again.

Lottie ran to the kitchen. In no time, she returned with a wet rag and handed it to Mary Edith. "For her brow."

Once Baby'd recovered from her nausea, Lottie and Mary Edith helped the poor girl to her feet. Mary Edith pressed the cloth against her head. They supported Baby as she shuffled toward the front of the tavern. Daniel followed.

"No, Daniel," Mrs. McHeath cried. "Not you. Stay with me. You live in enough filth without the risk of illness."

"He belongs with us, ma'am," Mary Edith said.

The woman's usually kind face twisted in disgust. "Your mother has enough to handle. If you loved your brother, you'd leave him here until the scare passes."

"I wanna go with you, Mary Edith," Daniel whimpered.

Mary Edith looked him in the eye. "Stay. Me or Nolan will come get you when Baby's better."

Mrs. McHeath heaved a sigh of relief. "I'll pray for you. All of you."

⊕

It didn't take Alden long to find the cave a mile upstream. The brush covering its opening was so haphazardly strewn, a child could have spotted it. Alden imagined their panic as they'd scrambled for safety.

Above him, clouds seemed close to bursting in the darkened sky. Burdened with only tragic news to share, he took a moment to gather himself before making his presence known. After placing his rifle on the ground, he began pulling the leafy branches away until he heard the quivering voice of Suzanne's mother, Miss Sarah.

"Levi, is that you?"

"No, ma'am. It's Alden de Barnefort."

From within the cave, he heard soft weeping and mumbled prayers.

Once enough branches were removed, he found Suzanne wedged into the small space. Arms and legs indicated the others squeezed behind her. He took Suzanne's elbow and helped her climb out.

"What are you doing here?" she said, her voice shrill. "Where are Tarlton and Bartlett?" The girl struggled to stand after who knew how many cramped hours.

Alden didn't answer. He helped her sister, Liza, Miss Sarah, and Tina, the cook, climb from the space.

The older woman looked drawn and pale, her legs and arms refusing to straighten. She clutched Alden's sleeve. "Tell me. What of Billy?"

"Things are bad. I'm sorry. Levi is alive, but barely. I promised I would bring Suzanne to him, but we have to hurry."

Without waiting for details, the old woman scurried through the woods toward their home. Liza steadied her over logs and through low brush. Tina followed, her arms tight across her chest.

Suzanne shoved Alden as he bent to retrieve his rifle. "Tell me what happened. Where is Levi?"

He looked away. "You should hurry."

With a squeal, the girl ran to catch up with her family. The rain held off until they reached the yard. Alden immediately led Suzanne to Levi through a light drizzle, but they were too late. The rain rolled off his ashen face like tears.

The other women clutched each other before the burning house, waiting for their next heartbreak. Alden asked them, "Are you sure you want to see Billy like this?"

Miss Sarah set her jaw. "Take me to him."

Head down, he steered them near the corral where Billy still lay, much of the blood already washed away with the rain.

Liza and Tina wailed at the sight of their father and master. His wife rushed to his side and crumbled to the ground. She ran her hand down his cheek and smoothed the hair on the side of his head that was still intact. All the while, she cooed, "Poor old fellow," over and over.

Alden didn't know how much more pain he could take. Tina pulled away from Liza. "Where the hands, Joseph and Cassius? Joseph be my man."

"I...I haven't seen them." Perhaps they'd run off in the fracas, he thought.

Suzanne left Levi to join her mother and sister in their grief for her father. Once their tears subsided, Miss Sarah looked to Alden.

"You spoke to Levi, then, before he passed."

Alden's stomach was in knots. "Yes, ma'am, I did. He told me where to find you." He struggled to meet their gazes. "He wanted Suzanne to know that he loves—uh, he loved her. He asked me to take care of her."

Miss Sarah's eyes flashed. "To take care of her?"

"That's right."

She smirked. "How very convenient."

Both Suzanne and Liza cried out, "Mama!"

Alden walked away. He searched for a shovel. Leaving the men exposed even one night would invite predators to further defile their corpses.

Returning from the outbuildings with a pick and shovel, two riders, unknown to him, came into the yard. He dropped the tools with thoughts of grabbing his gun when the women ran toward the newcomers.

As the men dismounted, they were accosted with hugs, tears, and questions. Alden learned they were neighbors, Adam Wood and his son, Jamie. They, too, had been ransacked by the murderous villains, their house set afire. Lucky for them, it was not consumed like the now-smoldering Brown home. Most of it was still habitable.

"We don't have much, so we didn't lose much." Adam looked around. "This here is a catastrophe. What happened to Billy and Levi—well, there ain't no explaining how hateful some men be."

"It's the same up and down the river," Jamie said, his own arm bandaged. "Henry Best and Old Mr. Moore was slaughtered, too. Levi's parents are gone. With what went on here, that's seventeen dead so far."

Tina spoke up. "Has ya seen signs of Joseph and Cassius?"

The old man shook his head. "Nope. Likely rounded up with the cattle and horses. Negroes fetch a pretty penny in Georgia."

"Leastways, they's alive," the cook said, her lower lip quivering.

The two men helped Alden dig graves for Billy and Levi. Mrs. Brown cried that she'd not even a yard of winding cloth in which to wrap her husband. She ripped the bottom of her skirts to tie his jaw shut before they lowered him into the ground.

The rain stopped in the late afternoon. Alden wasn't sure what to do. "Miss Sarah, let me take you and your daughters to Kilkenny. My brother and his wife will be glad to take you in, under these circumstances." He wasn't as sure as he sounded about Carlton, but Rosabel would never turn them away. "At least until Tarlton and Bartlett come back."

The distraught woman wagged her head back and forth. "I'll not do it. Your offer is kind enough, but I won't leave my Billy. This is my home."

"Mama, the house is nothing but embers," Suzanne said, glancing at Alden.

"I said it and I meant it. I'm not going anywhere. When my boys come home, they'll find me right where I belong."

They all looked from one to the other. Adam Wood said, "You stay at our place, Miss Sarah. It would be our honor to have you and the girls."

The woman looked at her neighbor with gratitude. "Thank you, Adam. You're a true friend."

Alden was torn between regret and relief. His pain was acute, making him unable to look at Suzanne or even stand near her. In his kindness, Levi had cursed him.

With nothing more he could do for them, he was determined to ride all the way to Virginia, if need be. He'd bring Tarlton and Bartlett back home, where they were sorely needed.

And Joe Dillon along with them.

✢

Thunder collapsed to the ground, grateful they'd arrived at their destination. For several days, they'd arisen hours before dawn and marched with their assigned corps through miles of forest and swamp. True enough, the early marches were cooler and less likely to arouse their enemies.

The sun was high when they'd finally reached Campbell's Plantation along the Santee River. All the talk was of British colonel, Banastre Tarleton's great victory. He'd surprised a body of rebels in a place called the Waxhaws. It was told when the colonel called for them to surrender, he was met with insolence. He and his men killed over one hundred Patriots, and many wagons of supplies were captured. British soldiers and officers alike whooped and cheered at the news. The traitors would submit now, they said.

Thunder was relieved the battle was so far away. He could only think how many graves were needed, how many amputations would be performed. He and his crew had come in behind the skirmishes along the route to perform these foul tasks.

Dr. Johnson, a decent man, made sure his staff, black and white, were given smallpox vaccinations. He cared little what side the wounded fought for, all were tended. But the Patriots were deemed prisoners and sent to Charles Town's disease-ridden hulks in the harbor. Few lasted long there.

Dalanda was the only bright spot in Thunder's new life—she and the promise of freedom. He felt drawn to her skill in treating the injured as well as her saucy tongue. So different than the shy sweetness of his beloved Minda. Part of him fought these new feelings as disloyal. He found himself avoiding Dalanda.

At dusk, Thunder and the others laid their pallets on the ground since the night was clear. Camp life's familiar evening noises lulled him to sleep.

In his slumber, he felt transported to a mystical place where a clean white glow enveloped him. Walking forward, he reached a group of people like himself, enjoying a large feast. In their midst sat Minda. His heart swelled, and he rushed to be near her.

Seeing him, she held up her hand. Her face glowed. "No, Thunder. You do not belong here."

It was torture to be so close without holding her once again. "I have missed you so."

"You see my happiness now among the ancestors."

Thunder only then realized his parents and others from his childhood surrounded Minda at the table. He cried out to them, but they did not seem to see or hear him.

Minda's eyes shone with love. "Go back. It's time for you to find happiness, too."

"I have met a fine woman," Thunder told her. "She is not as beautiful as you are, but she is good."

"Yes, I know. Go back now. It is well."

With that, Thunder was startled awake. Only a sliver of moon was visible amidst an explosion of stars. He once heard of a people who believed the ancestors became stars that watched over them. Could it be true?

As Thunder stared into the heavens, he realized. For the first time in many years, he was at peace.

Chapter Twenty-nine

Carlton felt his shoulder being shoved. Lifting his head from his desk, Rosabel's worried eyes were inches from his own.

"Are you unwell, my darling?" she asked. "You slept well past sunup and now I find you napping at midday."

He squared his shoulders. "I'm fine. The summer heat. Unbearable."

Rosabel kissed the top of his head. "Silly! It's still spring."

"Well, the beginning of June feels more like August. Hard to avoid a certain amount of sluggishness."

"Have you eaten? Becca said you missed the morning meal."

"Not hungry."

She flopped into the chair on the other side of the desk and removed the broad-brimmed straw hat she wore outside. She fanned away some flies before laying it on his desk. A white linen cap still sweetly framed her face.

Carlton shook his head as though clearing the cobwebs. He'd not even been aware she'd left the house. "Where did you go?"

With a sigh, her face darkened. "To the Dillons's cabin. I'm ashamed to say it's been two days since I visited. Things are much worse. The girl, Baby, is also abed with fever. And the lad is no better."

His chest tightened. "You cannot blame me for that."

Rosabel's head tilted. She tried to feign innocence, but Carlton could see right through it. "Why would anyone blame you for a fever? You've not been near the children for almost a fortnight and you're healthy as a horse. A bit tired, perhaps."

He flexed his fingers into and out of fists. "You can't fool me, my dear. I see in your eyes how you feel. But I had to send them off. You heard how she spoke to me. She tried to attack me like a wild beast, but I suppose that means nothing to you."

Her eyes filled with tears. "What are you talking about? I never once questioned your decision."

His stomach churned. She must see him as an ogre. If her eyes lost that luster of love, he couldn't bear it. "Send Oscar, my dear, to find Ketch. I will order him to check on Nan and her children each day."

Her eyes regained some of their light.

He leaned forward. "You must stay clear. I cannot risk your health for the likes of them. Promise me you'll not visit."

"You're a good man, my darling." She leapt up, snatched her hat from his desk, and flew from the study.

Carlton cradled his head in his hands. What would his father think? Carlton remembered the Dillon children laughing in the yard as Father sneaked them a sweetmeat. Now, they were crammed into a crude cabin, two of them laid low with fever.

He pleaded with his father's memory. "It's not my fault. The wench brought it on herself."

He lay on the desk, the spot still warm from his previous nap.

✛

Joe Dillon's blood ran cold. News came to their camp of the massacre of Patriot militia at the Waxhaws, led by British Colonel Banastre Tarleton. Over one hundred slaughtered, it was said, all while they waved the white flag. Joe shivered at reports of men, pleading for their lives, being chopped to pieces. Claims were made that even when the battle was over, the British plunged their bayonets into any man showing a whiff of life.

Now, even though the party had grown to sixty or seventy, a pall fell over the Patriots heading to Virginia. The leaders decided to wait a day or two before continuing.

"No need crossing paths with that butcher." Tarlton Brown spat. "A disgrace to the name."

While the decision was wise, it brought no ease to Joe nor the fellows around him. With every snap of a twig, he reached for his gun.

When night fell, so did a torrent of rain. Many scrambled to take shelter beneath large trees near the swamp. Joe was so wet, he might as well be lying in a shallow stream. Chilled to the marrow, sleep was impossible.

Sometime in the wee hours, the rain stopped. He heard only drips off the trees. Hot tears stung his eyes. He was raw, sodden, aching, exhausted. Few times in his life had he been more miserable.

At the edge of dawn, he heard men stir. Likely off to relieve themselves. He prayed for strength and, especially, patience for himself. But also for Nan and the young ones. If they could not be happy, may they be well.

More stirring. The hair on his arms rose. Something wasn't right. Joe lifted himself to his elbow and listened. Was the early morning mist giving him the fidgets?

He stood to get a better grasp of what was afoot when a ghastly shriek rang through the fog. To his horror, screaming men brandishing bayonetted muskets materialized from the mist.

The attackers' shrieks along with the clamor of frenzied men created bedlam. Thought was impossible. Joe snatched his rifle and, with no time to load, used its stock as a bludgeon.

He smashed one attacker in the face, turning it to a bloody mess. Without aiming, he swung the weapon at anything that moved. A spine-tingling clatter of crumbling teeth sickened him as the butt slammed into another man's mouth. The man dropped his weapon and collapsed to the ground.

Without warning, something like a sledge whacked Joe in his leg. An agonizing burn spread throughout. He sank into the muck. Far-off screams pierced the air. Sharp pain lit up his shoulder. Moving in and out of consciousness, he knew. He was dying.

⚜

Heavy clouds hung over Mary Edith as she poked the small fire outside their hut. If it rained, her efforts could be lost—or at least delayed. They had no time.

Nolan and Baby writhed on their straw pallets night and day, feverish and moaning from aches and throbbing pains. Neither Peggy Ogilvy's dead chickens nor Mama Juba's boneset potion were doing any good.

Mary Edith's brew had to work.

As the water inside an old tin cook pot began to boil, she stuffed several blades of pine straw inside. "Hurry," she told it, knowing her words were useless. Beside the fire lay holly leaves she'd blend with the pine tar, once it boiled out of the needles. The tea she'd make would not only relieve the sickness, it would ward off wicked spirits that threatened them. It must.

Inside the hovel, her brother cried out in agony.

"Mary Edith!" Her mother's shrill voice ran up the girl's spine. "We need more water. Now."

260 | M. B. GIBSON

The springs were a half mile away. Could she get there and back before the pine water boiled off, baking the resin to the bottom of the pot? She sighed. She had no choice. Grabbing the bucket, she ran through the woods to White Oak Springs.

While worried for her brother and sister, Mary Edith's stomach twisted with fear for her mother as well. Ma's face was sallow and drawn, her sunken eyes little more than black holes.

They were both tired. Sleep had been close to impossible. But this was more. Ma's skin sagged. The light had disappeared from her eyes. It frightened Mary Edith to see her so, but she was too exhausted to cry.

Upon her return, she carried her sloshing bucket past the cook pot to the door of their hovel. Their neighbor, Peggy Ogilvy, was tying five-pointed stars made from sticks around the door.

"Witch's marks," she said. "My granny swore by 'em if ya wanta keep ghosts and haints away."

Mary Edith's heart filled. "You're a good friend, Peggy." She carried the water inside and set it beside her mother.

"Ye been dawdlin' again." Ma brushed her stringy hair from her face. "Bring the ladle."

Mary Edith did as she was told, though anxious to get back to her pine tea. Her mother dipped the cold water and held it to Nolan's lips, then Baby's.

"The fever any better?"

Her mother choked back a sob. "Nolan's got a rash. Across his chest."

Peggy called from outside the door. "Some jasper's riding up."

Ma didn't move. "Mary Edith, see who's about. I can't talk to no one now."

She stepped outside to see Ketch pull up in a wagon. She almost cried with relief when he got down carrying one of Mama Juba's baskets. He handed it to her and lifted another filled with bread, vegetables, and even some jerky.

"This one be from Ruth." He nodded toward the one Mary Edith held. "Mama say you know what to do with that."

She looked inside. A white candle, chicken foot, and herbs—everything she needed for candle work, powerful conjure to rid themselves of the evil that seemed to be swallowing them up.

"They's some rabbit foots, too," Ketch said. "From one I trapped myself."

To place around Nolan and Baby's necks. More protection. Mary Edith felt some tension drain from her neck and shoulders.

"Where Daniel be? I don't see him nowhere."

"He's staying with the McHeaths 'til this fever's gone."

Ketch's face darkened. "Something bad about that tavern keeper."

"It's Mrs. McHeath who'll watch him. She's kind, mostly, and loves Daniel."

"Humph." He nodded to Peggy Ogilvy. "See ya got some witch's marks. Like them from the hill country."

Their neighbor smiled. "My granny was a mountain woman. I'd best get home in case my man come by. My auntie might send him on his way if'n I ain't around."

Ketch moved into the hut. Mary Edith went to check on her pine tar. Of course, it was ruined. Starting over, she listened to the conversation inside.

"Master Carlton say I can come each day to bring ya food and whatever else ya be needin'."

"His wife has him by the ballocks, I'd wager," Ma said. "'Twas no idea of his own."

Ketch laughed. "You right 'bout that. He do her biddin' without him even knowin' it."

"She's a fine person, Miss Rosabel. And so are you."

When Ketch came out of the house, Mary Edith ran to him. She hugged him so eagerly, she almost knocked him over.

"Well, well," he said, laughing.

It was then she realized. She'd never seen anyone hug Ketch before.

By midafternoon, the clouds had blown away leaving only a light sprinkle. Mary Edith finished brewing the pine tar and holly tea. When she brought it inside, she found Nolan and Baby had fallen into a fitful sleep. The tea could wait. Even better, Ma had nodded off for some much-needed rest.

She looked through Mama Juba's basket, anxious to begin her candle magic. To start, she brushed herself up and down with the chicken foot. She must thoroughly cleanse. Nolan and Baby's lives were at stake, and she'd take no shortcuts.

In a bowl, she mixed three precious spoonfuls of salt and three bay leaves with a tiny bit of rue into boiling water. She prayed with great passion over each ingredient. Since Mama Juba always warned her about the dull green rue, she handled it delicately. So powerful, too much of the plant could leave painful blisters on her hands.

While it cooled, she lay beside her mother and slept without dreaming.

It was still light when Baby's wails woke them all. "My back, Ma. Make it stop. Oh, my head."

Her sobs broke Mary Edith's heart. Still drowsy, she poured some of her tea into a wooden mug.

PATIENCE CAN COOK A STONE | 263

"Give it here, Mary Edith," Ma said. "You spoon some to yer brother."

When each of the children had all they could take—which wasn't much—Mary Edith poured more for her mother. "Take this, Ma. Drink it up." She grabbed two pieces of jerky from the basket, one for each of them.

After they ate, Mary Edith tested the bay leaf and rue wash. It was cool. She wiped down the candle with it. Everything must be cleansed. After it dried, she turned to her mother. "I have to wake it up now."

Ma nodded, too tired to argue.

She blew onto the candle three times before tapping it on the table thrice. Next, to call the spirits into it. Would the proper words come? Her heart thumped in her chest. In faith, she cried out to ancestors she never knew.

"To the uncle, Nolan, and grandmother, Eveleen. I've cleansed myself, prepared the way. We need you on this dark day. Send the pain and fever away. Wrap the sick in love. Like God Above."

Mary Edith stopped, panting from fear.

"Ye done good, lass," Ma said.

She nodded, then laid the candle on its side. After sprinkling red pepper sent by Mama Juba, she rolled the candle through it, away from her. She lifted the candle and rolled it away again. Sending the sickness, the pain, the fear far from them all. Under her breath, she begged God, Jesus, and the ancestors to remove the suffering from her family.

She stood the candle upright. After lighting a straw with her small fire, she touched it to the wick. After it flickered, it went out. She touched it with fire once again. For too short a time, a tiny flame held firm, but did not grow. When it fizzled, she lit the wick a third time. It quickly extinguished.

"Is it done, lass? Have ye finished the spell?"

Mary Edith kept her back to her mother. Her throat was clenched, making it hard to speak. But she knew. A candle that will not light means a block. Someone or something would not let the magic through.

"Mary Edith?"

Her voice cracked. "Aye, Ma. It's finished."

Chapter Thirty

Thunder sat beneath a large oak out of the noonday sun. There weren't many slow times working with Dr. Johnson. More skirmishes meant more injuries. Also, as they got further into the sickly season, fever flourished.

Looking up, his stomach fluttered at the sight of Dalanda gliding toward him. *May she sit by me under dis tree. Dat's all I ask.*

To his delight, she dropped to the ground beside him, close enough that their shoulders touched. "I see ya over here, Thunder." Her eyes cut sideways. "Lookin' like you wouldn't hit a lick at a snake."

"I would tie de snake in a bow for you, Dalanda."

She moved away and punched him on the arm. "Hush that sweetmouth of yours."

His heart beat so hard, he was sure she could hear it. Before thinking too much, he leaned over and kissed her on the cheek.

"Now, what you think you doin'?" Her tone was harsh, but her eyes danced.

"I give my friend a peck. Do not get de big head."

Dalanda drew back. "I ain't got no big head, but you sure do."

He crossed his arms over his chest. "It is de same one I give my mother."

Her laugh made him warm all over. "I ain't nobody's mama, least not yours."

Thunder scowled to see Cuffee heading their way.

He stopped about fifteen feet off and waved at them to follow him. "Dolly! You and Thunder need to come on. There
been some fightin' 'bout a mile and a half from here. Doctor
say to load up."

Grudgingly, Thunder dragged himself to his feet. Dr. Johnson tolerated no tarrying. He often said five minutes late could
be the difference between a man's life and death. Dalanda tore
off to their camp hospital. Her job was to gather supplies for
missions such as these.

Thunder and the other men loaded two wagons with a tent,
cots, sawhorses, and an old door to use as a table. Dalanda
placed the supplies in the wagon. A small space remained.

"You should ride dere," Thunder told her.

"I can walk as well as you can," she said.

Without another word, Thunder lifted her off her feet and
set her in the back of the wagon.

"I didn't run off from my master so you could tell me what
to do."

But Thunder noticed she stayed put. As the driver pulled
away, he allowed his lips to curve. His hand rested on the side
rail as he walked beside the wagon. Before long, it was covered
by Dalanda's, roughened by a lifetime of hard work. Warmth
washed through him.

The stench of sulphur, blood, and death assaulted them as
they approached the skirmish site. Locals were already picking
through the dead for anything they could use or sell. Some
bodies were stripped naked.

Thunder knew the people were poor and desperate, but it
smacked of grave robbing, even so. He was pleased to see a
woman carrying a bucket and ladle, offering water from one
man to the next.

Three of them set up the hospital tent while others began digging graves. Ten or so men lay on the ground. Some were sitting up, likely wounded. Dalanda and other nurses moved about the field to see who might be dead or alive. Thunder saw her stop to speak with the white woman toting water.

He spent the next hour carrying wounded to the hospital and the dead to the gravesites. One poor fellow was shot in the gut. He could not be saved, but he lay in the hospital until his inevitable death. Others needed stitching from deep gashes or bandages for powder burns.

Walking to check on one fellow slumped against a fence-post, he heard Cuffee shout from the edge of a wooded area. "There's some bad off over here."

When Thunder arrived, several bodies were strewn on the ground. Three were definitely dead, their faces bashed in, but the scavengers hadn't found them yet. He and Cuffee followed their procedure of sorting out the ones most likely to live.

"I don't know about this one here," Cuffee said.

Thunder came over to assess the filthy creature. Unconscious, the man's leg was smashed and blood oozed from a shoulder wound. "Maybe. He could live."

He turned to look at another man, moaning six feet away. But something stopped him. He returned to the first one and knelt before him. Removing the man's hat, Thunder gasped. It couldn't be. Joe Dillon!

He looked up at Cuffee. "I know dis man. He like a brother to me. Help me take him now!"

Cuffee nodded, without another word, the two lifted the damaged body of his most valued friend. They carried him to the hospital tent. Dr. Johnson was concentrating on another man, stitching an open wound over his eye with silken thread.

"Doctor," Thunder said.

The physician's head snapped up, mouth agape. "Who is this, Thunder?"

"It is my friend. You have to save him, my only family in dis land." He was embarrassed at the tears that filled his eyes.

The doctor nodded. "Put him on the table. I'm about finished here."

Joe moaned as they lowered him onto the wooden door that served as a surgery table. Thunder leaned over him. "You will live, Joe Dillon. I will make sure of it. You cannot leave us. Do you hear?"

Maybe he did, maybe he didn't. It was hard to say, but Thunder was sure his own doggedness would pull Joe through. "He has a wife. And four children who need him."

Cuffee nodded, then left the tent to tend others.

Thunder picked up a rag, dunked it in a water bucket, and blotted the blood on Joe's shoulder. He prayed with nary a pause. Once he could see the gash, likely a bayonet wound, he grabbed the fine linen reserved for officers. The consequences be damned.

As he wrapped the shoulder, Thunder looked up to see Dr. Johnson watching him. He said nothing about the good linen.

"You cleaned the wound, I see. Now, about this leg." The doctor inspected the smashed kneecap as Thunder's stomach churned. "It definitely must come off. Whether that will save the man, I cannot say."

"We must try." Thunder feared for an instant he'd been impertinent, but the doctor didn't seem to notice.

"We'll take it just above the knee. Hold the leg tight, Thunder."

Dalanda, who appeared out of nowhere, handed the physician a narrow strip of fabric. He wrapped it around Joe's leg about three times. Thunder winced. He knew this would guide the saw. The baby-faced man, whose name was Gerald, applied the tourniquet to his upper thigh and twisted until the blood was checked.

Then, the sawing began. Joe threw back his head and shrieked. A shiver ran up Thunder's spine.

Gerald stuck a chunk of wood into Joe's mouth. Mercifully, he lost consciousness.

Thunder grasped Joe's leg as though it were his friend's very life. He was unaware he was crying until drops fell onto the shin. He would not wipe them. He let them fall.

Once Dr. Johnson gave the nod, Thunder pulled the severed leg away. He took it outside the tent, to be later buried with the dead. After dropping the leg, something between a cough and a sob erupted from his throat. Gathering himself, he returned to the tent.

Dalanda was removing a knife from a small fire. She handed it to the doctor. Thunder saw what was to come and placed his hands on either side of Joe's head. Before the blade seared the sliced vessels, he whispered to his senseless friend, "You will live, my brother. I thank Allah for your life."

Once Dr. Johnson finished, he said to Thunder, "You realize he's a prisoner of war now. We must send him back to Charles Town."

"But he will be put in de hulks. He will die on de prison ship."

"I'm sorry, but the truth is, he may not even last the journey. It's out of our hands now."

As he and Gerald moved Joe to a cot, Thunder's mind raced. There had to be some way to save Joe from this fate. He turned to speak to Dalanda, but she'd run off from the tent.

"There are other men who need your attention now," the doctor told him. "We'll keep Joe as comfortable as we can while he's in our care."

Thunder moved about in a trance. He was once again twelve years old, powerless against the murder of his father by their people's leader. In his mind, he called out to Allah. "Why would You allow Joe to survive dis surgery only to let him die in a rickety cart? Or in dat hellhole of a prison hulk?" He knew he should humble himself and plead for help, but he couldn't. All seemed useless.

"Thunder!" It was Dalanda, running toward him with the water bearer. He waited.

Panting, Dalanda said, "This Miz Thankfull Williams. She want to help."

He looked from one to the other. "She help dem men who need water."

"No, with your friend." Dalanda regained her breath. "Miz Thankfull out here for her husband. He killed somewhere far off."

"Coming home to me from Charlotte." The pain in the woman's eyes was unmistakable.

"She say ev'ry sip a man take is for him," Dalanda explained.

Miz Thankfull's eyes glistened. "Each one, I may be paying some woman back for a kindness they give my Wendall as he lay dying."

"I told her 'bout Joe, how he got a wife and four young'ns. How they gonna send him back to Charles Town where he most likely die."

Thunder worked the muscles in his jaw. "There is no more to be done."

"But there is! Miz Thankfull willing to take Joe in and nurse him. She'll make sure he live!'"

The woman shook her head. "I'll do what I can but make no promises."

Dalanda grabbed Thunder's hand. "Come. We'll talk to the doctor."

"No," he said. "He must not know."

Thunder's hands were slick with sweat. How this night would end, no one could say.

As the sun lowered in the sky, Dr. Johnson tended the last of the injured. The diggers returned from the graves of the slain.

"Six rebels killed," the doctor said, "and three of our men." He sighed. "Let's break this down and return to the main camp."

Once they laid the four injured Loyalists in the back of a wagon, the physician climbed aboard and drove it back himself.

The baby-faced Gerald and Cuffee were to drive the second wagon carrying six injured rebels. When three of them were loaded, Cuffee called Gerald to redress one man's wound, a bandage he himself had pulled off.

"Look what he done to hisself, Mr. Gerald," Thunder heard Cuffee saying. "Don't that take the rag off the bush?"

While Gerald grumbled over his task, Thunder and Dalanda lifted Joe Dillon from his cot and hauled him behind the tent. They laid him on the sledge used to drag the dead and amputated limbs to the burial site.

Both sucked in their breath when Joe moaned. Thunder leaned over. It was dark, but he could see his friend's opened eyes. "You must trust me, my brother. Whatever you do, make no sound."

Dalanda stuck a shovel in his hand. "You be needin' this. If someone ask."

As he dragged Joe away, Thunder heard Cuffee's constant chatter, doing his part to allow Joe's escape. He was a good man. A true friend.

Passing the gravesites without stopping, he met with Thankfull Williams in the woods. As soundlessly as possible, he followed her to her house, a half mile away. Every hoot of an owl or snap of a twig caused his heartbeat to skip. Sweat rolled down his back. He forced away thoughts of what would happen were he found out.

Putting one foot in front of the other, he breathed a sigh of relief at the sight of a fire's glow through the window of a small cabin. Miz Thankfull rushed forward and held the door. "Quick. I fixed up a cot in the corner. Set him there."

Thunder lifted Joe and carried him inside. As he lowered his friend to the bed, Joe's eyes opened.

"What happened, Thunder?"

"You lost a leg, my brother. But you will live. Dis woman will care for you."

He winced. "It hurts like the blazes of hell." He grasped Thunder's hand. "Ye saved me life."

"Soon, you will return to Nan. You will see."

Joe tried to smile. "Aye. Patience can cook a stone, right?"

"It is what I have always heard." He brushed Joe's hair from his brow. "God is good. I was angry with Him, yet He answered my prayers."

Thunder couldn't tarry. He stood, his throat tight. "Be well, my friend. I may not see you again, but I carry you in my heart 'til the end of my days." He turned to Miz Thankfull. "What you are doing—may every blessing of Allah be yours."

The woman nodded.

Heartsick, he sped through the woods, hoping to return before the last wagon pulled away. When he broke into the open, he found the battlefield vacant, with little sign of the field hospital. Dread weighed down every muscle in his body.

He continued across the field, dragging the sledge through the dark of night. He didn't know what awaited him. Yet, he couldn't run off. To never again see Dalanda filled him with greater terror.

Once in the main camp, he sprinted through the soldiers' tents to where Gerald, Cuffee, and others were unloading gear from the wagons. Dalanda was nowhere in sight.

Gerald slammed a sawhorse onto the ground. "Where in blazes did you go? Dr. Johnson said if you showed your arse here, to go straight to his tent."

Cuffee kept his head down, but stole a glance Thunder's way, his eyes wide with worry.

Dropping the shovel and sledge, Thunder made his way to the surgeon's tent. As he got to the entry, Dalanda came out. With only the light from the doctor's tent, he saw her eyes close as if to blink, holding them shut a bit too long. What did that mean? He hoped it was to stick to their planned story.

Dr. Johnson met him at the opening and grabbed his shirt, dragging Thunder inside. He shoved him to the dirt floor.

"I demand an explanation! What in damnation did you do?"

Thunder kept his head down. "My friend is dead."

The surgeon lifted a cup of wine from his desk and gulped it down. "Dolly told me the man died. That you went off to bury him. But Gerald said you were nowhere near the graves."

"I did not want him dere with de arms and legs, like so much garbage. I take him to de woods. I dig a grave more fitting for such a man."

"God damn you! What gave you the right to make such a decision? Are you that great a fool that you actually believe you are free?"

The words slapped him. "No, suh."

"The British army owns you until this blasted war is over. If you make it that far!" He began to pace the tent. "Now I'm in a quandary. You are under my authority. I am responsible for you and the entire hospital crew. By rights, I need to have you flogged."

Thunder winced. Somehow, he'd avoided that penalty his entire life. Images of Nan's torn flesh came to mind.

"But," Dr. Johnson went on, "we don't have the luxury of waiting for you to recover from your lashes. You're the strongest back I have and a bloody hard worker."

Thunder maintained his humble posture as the physician walked back and forth, wheezing with rage. Awaiting his judgement seemed like hours instead of minutes.

At last, Dr. Johnson's breathing slowed. He stopped before Thunder and ordered him to stand. "You did come back. With the sledge, I assume?"

His eyes remained lowered. "Yes, suh."

"Be warned. I will not be made a fool of. If anything like this happens again, keep running. There'll be no quarter for you here. Now, get out."

Thunder headed back to his tent. Looking to the heavens, he muttered, "Allah is good."

Dalanda stood beside a nearby fire. "Well?"

He nodded. Her face broke into a rare smile as she ran to him and leapt into his arms.

"Yes," he thought. "Allah is very good."

Chapter Thirty-one

Leaning against the crude boards that made up her shack, Nan had wedged herself between Nolan and Baby upon their pallets. For no more than an instant, it seemed, her eyes closed as her head dropped to her chest.

"Ma."

She forced her eyelids open to find Mary Edith kneeling before her.

"He's gone."

Nan's mind felt weak. The words had no meaning. "What?"

Mary Edith's voice cracked. "Nolan, Mama. We lost him."

"He's right beside me, lass." She turned to her left. Her son's opened eyes were glassy. Slowly, Mary Edith's meaning became clear. "It can't be. I closed me eyes for an instant, no more."

She lifted his cooling body and drew it close to herself. "Come to me, son. Yer cold, is all. Let yer ma hold ye a bit." She rocked him back and forth as she had when first born, willing her own warmth into his clammy skin.

"Don't leave, Nolan," she whispered. "Stay with me."

Mary Edith stood by the door. "I'm sorry, Ma. I did all I could. I tried so hard, but..."

Nan lowered Nolan's lids and sang, as her mother'd once sung to her.

"That woe is me, poor child, for thee, And ever mourn and may. For thy parting neither say nor sing. Bye bye, lully, lullay."

She looked at Mary Edith, her heart pounding. "He's getting colder. What am I to do?"

Baby moaned. Mary Edith rushed to her side. Removing the cloth from her sister's head, she dipped it in the bucket, wrung it, and returned it to Baby's brow. Snatching the bucket, Mary Edith headed outside. "I'll go to the springs for fresh water."

Nan held her son and sang to him. She kissed his brow and told him all would be well. She would not let him go, of that she was sure.

Mary Edith's return startled her. Ketch followed the girl into the cabin. Had she heard him pull up in his cart?

"Lawd, Lawd," he said. "Poor fella. He in God's hands now. No more sufferin'."

He knelt beside Nan and petted Nolan on the head. "He was a good boy. Hard worker, like his daddy."

Nan gripped him tighter.

"Now, we need to send him on his journey home. I brung some windin' cloth with me, in case." Ketch turned to Mary Edith. "Get it out the cart for me."

Nan stared at her son's face, scared to look away. What if she forgot it, like she had her ma's face? The thought ripped through her heart like a bobcat's claw.

"Mar' Edith," she heard Ketch say, "come tell yo brother bye."

Mary Edith handed Ketch the bundle of cloth and kissed Nolan's cheek, then hurried outside. Nan could still hear her weeping.

"Now you, Nan. Ya gotta be strong."

She ran her fingertips over his features, to sear them into her memory. "Good-bye, sweet child. Ye brought nothing but joy." Without looking away, Nan said, "I've no place to lay him."

"We all been talkin' in case this happen. Me, Mama Juba, and the rest agree. We want Nolan with us, in our spot. Mr. Carlton don't never go near it, so he don't need to know."

Nan looked at Ketch, unable to speak.

"He need to be with fam'ly," he said. "And we his fam'ly."

"Nolan would like that."

Once his body was prepared, they placed her boy onto Ketch's cart.

"I'm coming with ye," Nan said. "I need to be with him 'til the end."

"Well, we got to sneak in the back way. I guess ya could ride along."

Nan climbed onto the wagon. "Mary Edith, stay with yer sister, lass. I shan't be long."

✟

Mary Edith went inside the cabin. Her eyes were dry, emptied of tears. Every muscle ached.

Baby had rolled to her side, her voice whispery. "Where's Nolan? Ma, where's Nolan?"

"He went off with Ma. She'll be back soon, Baby. I'm here."

Baby began to cry. "I'm scared. I want Da."

Mary Edith yearned to curl into a ball and be anywhere else. She headed toward the door for sunlight and air, hot and dank as it was. Mosquitoes buzzed around her head.

Baby moaned. "Don't leave me, Mary Edith. I told ya, I'm scared. Don't you go, too."

She slumped to the ground and laid her head against the jamb. "I'm right here."

✟

Before they'd gotten far, Nan climbed in back of the cart beside her shrouded son. She and Ketch rode in silence as they lurched over uneven ground. Across a pasture, Geoffrey and some of the cow-herders removed their hats and lowered their heads.

"What if Carlton sees us while he's out and about?" Nan called to Ketch.

He looked over his shoulder. "He ain't hardly outside his house at all these days."

Nan nodded and thought no more about it. Approaching the small plot set aside for slaves, she gasped at the sight of two holes ready to receive their tenants. A lump formed in her throat.

Ketch pulled up the cart and hopped off. He removed his hat. "We thought we'd make Nolan welcome. Don't mind t'other hole. God willin', it won't be needed, and we'll cover it right up."

With Ketch's help, she crawled down from the wagon. "I'm moving like Mama Juba these days."

"Ain't no one else can come," he said. "But don't you worry none. When the sun go down, we all be here to give Nolan a proper home-goin'."

♦

Baby was quiet for a while, but when the pain returned, she flailed in agony. The same rash that covered Nolan had spread to Baby's arms and legs.

Feeling helpless, Mary Edith swabbed her with cool water. Her heart ached at the sight of her sister's ghostly skin and sunken eyes. She filled the dipper and tried to pour water into Baby's mouth, but with clamped lips, her sister thrashed her head back and forth. Mary Edith slammed the ladle into the bucket. She crossed the one-room hovel as far away as she could get.

"Help me! It hurts so bad," Baby called.

Mary Edith spun, grasping her head. "I can't help you! I don't know what to do!"

Amidst her sister's groans, she heard a rustling in the room. When she turned around, she saw a cat had crept inside. Mary Edith froze. It was completely black without a single white hair. Before she could gather her wits, the creature stalked toward Baby's pallet and burrowed beside her.

A witch! Sent to suck her sister's breath.

Freed from her shock, Mary Edith ran to the pallet and snatched the cat from the straw. It screeched and waved its claws every which way. The rear leg ripped a gash in her arm.

She scrambled to the door, ran several yards, and heaved it into the woods. Returning to her sister, she was rattled with fear. Everyone knew a witch could become a black cat and work its evil. But what could be done?

Salt! Ma and Mama Juba agreed. Salt fended off witches. It was hard to come by since the start of the war, but Ruth had smuggled a small amount in her breadbasket. It was kept on the crate in the corner in case it was needed.

As she retrieved the small bag of crystals, Baby called out, "Sit by me, Mary Edith! I need you."

"I have to do something first." She raced for the door.

"No. Stay!"

Mary Edith yanked the bag open and stepped outside. "I'll just be a minute."

She heard her sister call for her as she raced around the house. She sprinkled their spare amount of salt as far as it would take her. Once the bag was emptied, she stopped to breathe. They were safe. No evil could touch them.

She went back inside, anxious to tell Baby what she'd done. "I'm back!" she called. Her sister was silent and eerily still.

"I told you I'd only be a minute." Mary Edith's stomach churned. It couldn't be. She grabbed Baby by the shoulders and shook. "I'm back!" She shook harder. "I'm back. I told you I'd be back!"

She lowered her sister to the straw. Baby Eveleen was gone. Mary Edith should have been there to save her, but she wasn't. She had left her all alone. Her only sister and best friend was dead.

✤

Riding for three days, Alden had too much time to think. Beneath a cover of pine, birch, and hickory trees, he listened to the chittering of mockingbirds and sparrows, the hammering of woodpeckers, and occasional hoot of an owl. It was the wren who amused him most. He imagined a tiny flutist warming up for a woodland concert.

The feathered choir was a relaxing alternative to the clump-clump of Enbarr's hooves over leaf-covered paths, or worse, the infernal buzzing of mosquitoes.

It also quieted the worry of what his future held. He was riding to return Joe Dillon and the Brown brothers to the destruction of home and family. Albemarle, Virginia, was a journey of hundreds of miles. How many, he didn't know. Four hundred? Five? God forbid it was six.

He quashed the next question: What if they weren't there?

He was headed toward Charlotte on the route they said they'd take. After that, he'd depend on local knowledge to steer him in the right direction. Yet, how many of those people would be friendly? How many were foes?

He had to dam this waterfall of crippling questions. "One hoof in front of the other, Enbarr," he said aloud.

After continuing for another hour, he heard the lively step of an approaching horse. With a hand on his rifle, he pulled Enbarr to one side of the path.

"De Barnefort! That you?"

Startled, Alden turned in his saddle to see George Collins trotting toward him. He'd not laid eyes on him since he'd sounded the alarm on McGirth's savagery.

Alden dismounted. "What in blazes are you doing here?" He grabbed the reins while George swung his leg over his mare.

"Hoping to find you."

Alden's stomach turned to pap. "What's happened?"

George's face fell. "I headed south from the Lower Three Runs after the ruination left by McGirth. When I got to Adam Wood's place..." He shook his head. "He told me what happened to Billy Brown and Levi. A bloody disgrace." He swallowed. "Same thing with my grandpa."

Alden remembered old Mr. Collins. He could not think of a more inoffensive man. "They killed him?"

"Standing on his porch, he was, calling out how he didn't cotton with either side. I could hear him from the field. I come a-running, but when I got there, he was already struck down where he stood." George wiped his sleeve over his eye. "And them spawn of Satan done rode off."

Alden clenched his fists. "An old man with hair as white as snow. What harm did he pose anyone?"

"Not a whit. Anyway, I laid him in his grave and rode off to see what other folks dealt with. That's when I learnt about Billy and Levi. And that you was heading to Virginia to fetch Tarlton and Bartlett." He removed his hat and wiped sweat from his brow. "I shoulda stayed back in case of more trouble. But God help me, I couldn't. I had to get away from there."

Alden placed his hand on George's shoulder. "You're welcome company, I assure you. I damn near started a conversation with a raccoon a while back." He hated to admit how close to the truth this was. "I'm sorry about your grandfather. May the black-hearted bastards rot in hell!"

He sighed. "No sense in me acting neutral no more."

"Guess not."

The two traveled until dusk, then camped for the night. Alden was pleased how much quicker two men could catch a meal—rabbit, this night—and have it skinned and roasted, hot and ready to eat.

Midmorning the following day, they rode through a fallow field, littered with the remains of battle. Branches of trees were ripped from bullets, sword, or hand-to-hand combat. Who could say? Tatters of uniforms lay beside a common man's rags. Musket balls. Flint. Splotches of blood, large and small, dyed the grasses. The stench lingered. Trails of flattened hay led to freshly dug graves.

Soft rain began to fall. "You think they come through here?" George asked in a whisper.

"Hard to say." Alden saw a lone figure a couple hundred yards away. As they rode toward him, he noticed the man limping in their direction. Once they got close, Alden and George dismounted.

"What happened here, friend?" Alden asked.

"A dust up 'tween some Patriot fellows passing through and the Redcoats moving west from Charles Town." He looked around. "Been three days. It's picked pretty clean now."

"We looking for some fellows that mighta come through here," George said. "Think it coulda been them?"

The man scowled. "How would I know that? Even if I'd-a been here, I doubt they was calling out their names."

The rain came down harder. "No harm meant. Guess we gotta keep going," George said.

The man's expression softened. He rubbed his bristled jaw. "A woman name of Thankfull Williams lives not far off. She might know more'n me." He pointed. "Through them woods a short ways."

Water ran off the brim of Alden's hat. He turned to George. "We've a long journey. We can't interview everyone within a five-mile radius who might have seen something." To the man, he said, "Thank you, sir. We'll be on our way."

"Suit yourself." The man limped back in the direction he'd come, then turned. "I guess ya heard the news."

"Can't say," Alden said.

"So-called Patriot General Williamson from Ninety-Six, he gone and done it. Turned himself over to the Lobsterbacks. Damned bloody traitor!" The man spit on the ground and walked on.

⚜

At Kilkenny's entryway, Rosabel allowed Amos to help her from the wagon. He was a gentle fellow who seemed to enjoy taking her places. Especially to the Dillon cabin, if one could call it that. The children always brightened a bit at his visit.

It was a difficult duty, but Rosabel demanded it of herself. The sad eyes of Mary Edith and Daniel paled at the pain-wracked features of Nan. To have lost two children in a single day! Rosabel could not conceive of such sorrow. She placed a hand on her belly. Especially now that she suspected a wee one of her own. Too soon to tell Carlton, she held the secret in her heart.

On this visit, the children had left to work at McHeath's tavern. Rosabel thought to cheer Nan by telling the story of Pamela from one of her treasured novels. She'd finally finished it to find the young maidservant had married Mr. B, who'd been pestering her. But Pamela's kind ways turned the cad from his depravity. Nan, however, had struggled to listen. Rosabel sighed as she climbed the veranda steps.

When she entered the Big House, Carlton stepped from his study. It pained Rosabel to see his eyes ringed with dark circles.

"Where have you been?" he asked.

"To see Nan Dillon where—"

His face darkened, scaring Rosabel. "You promised me you'd stay away from there. You lied to me."

Her heart pounded. "You asked me to promise, but the words never passed my lips."

"Is that how you intend this marriage to work? Through backbiting? Deceit?"

Oh dear. This was turning ugly. "No, my darling. If you knew what—"

"I gave the bitch a house because you asked it of me. At your request, I allow Ketch to ignore his duties to bring them food. I bid one thing of you. Only one, and you play this coquettish game. Get out of my sight." He returned to the study and slammed the door.

She supposed she should feel bad, but she was angry. He'd not allowed one word about the anguish Nan had suffered. Every time she'd tried to explain, he cut her off. Nolan and Baby were dead, yet he refused to hear it. She'd little patience for his trifling ways.

Not to worry. He'd have a few more whiskeys, then forget all about it. She allowed herself a sly grin. Once again, no promise had passed her lips.

Chapter Thirty-two

<u>JULY 31, 1780</u>
<u>SEVEN WEEKS LATER</u>

Mary Edith came back from the privy to find little Daniel building some stick-and-rock structure in the dirt outside their house. The sun was well up in the sky. "Come on!" she called out. "You know Mr. McHeath don't tolerate no late workers."

Her mother was finishing her last batch of candles. The McHeaths sent all their beef fat with hemp for wicks so Ma could do the hot, miserable work of dipping. All in exchange for a few of the tapers. Her mother's hair was saturated with sweat as a steady stream of it dribbled from her chin.

Daniel stood carefully to avoid toppling his creation. "I gotta give Ma a hug 'fore we go."

He tore full speed across the yard. Mary Edith opened her mouth too late as his big toe stubbed a rock. He spun, his arms grabbing nothing but air, until he crashed into the freshly dipped candles. They went sprawling across the open yard. Still soft and warm, they rolled in the dirt until coated with sand.

Ma cried out as though slammed in the gut. Hours of work, ruined in an instant. Mary Edith cringed at her mother's eyes, lit up like white-hot embers. Ma grabbed Daniel, yanking him up like an old sack of potatoes. With her other hand, she slapped the boy hard across the face.

"I'm sorry, Ma," he wailed, but she answered him with another slap. His cheek glowed red.

Daniel sobbed, apologizing again and again. But to Mary Edith, her mother had become a savage beast.

When Ma reared back for another strike, Mary Edith lost her own mind a bit. Without thinking, she snatched her mother's arm mid-swing. The heat in Nan's eyes fanned even hotter.

"Mary Edith, ye damned bloody brat!"

After receiving several blows, Mary Edith grabbed Daniel's hand and ran off toward the tavern.

It was funny. All the time her mother was pounding her, all she could think about was Ma's spit on her face when she hollered.

Daniel stumbled along the path past White Oak Springs to McHeath's Tavern atop Red Hill, named for clay as red as the evening sun. His face was awash with tears, so he didn't see the log he tripped over.

Mary Edith pitied the boy, but they didn't need another tongue-lashing from Old Man McHeath. She helped him up. "Daniel, you're near six years old. Too big to be blubbering like that. I got a beating, too, and you don't see me acting that a-way."

He stood on his own two feet and wiped his dirty, wet face with his sleeve. "I'm fine."

When the two arrived, they headed straight to the kitchen behind the tavern to help the cook, Lottie.

"Where you been?" the slave girl asked. Then she saw Daniel. "Lawd A'mighty, look at you. Yo lip's all busted up. What you do this time?"

She snatched some rags from the pile. Mary Edith took one and swiped at her face before throwing it back in the pile. She hoped Lottie didn't notice. That girl would scrub the dirt along with a layer or two of skin.

The slave cook seemed gentle with Daniel today, even though her words were rough. "You chillun know I don't have time to fuss over the likes of you. If Mr. McHeath knowed about this—"

"Lottie!"

A bolt of lightning ran up Mary Edith's spine. Mr. McHeath filled the doorway. He was on the small side, but his voice boomed like a cannon.

"I came to see how today's meal is coming and this is what I find. These two brats are more trouble than help. Catherine!"

His wife rushed in as though she'd been waiting outside. "Yes, John?"

He stabbed a stubby finger at Mary Edith and Daniel. "I told you this wouldn't work out. These two are nothing but a hindrance. You and Lottie spend more time coddling these little potato-eaters than running this tavern. We're a business, not an orphanage!"

Mrs. McHeath spoke softly. "John, the Good Book says, 'Inasmuch as ye have done it unto one of the least of these my brethren, ye have done it unto me.'"

"Well, our spots in heaven are assured!"

His wife sniffled and held her hand to her mouth.

The tavern keeper's shoulders slumped. "My dear, pay me no mind. Whatever makes you happy." He returned to the bar.

"Beg pardon, miss," Lottie said.

"Nonsense. What else could you do?" The woman took the rag and tended to Daniel herself, telling him, "Don't worry. No one will hurt you here." After dropping the cloth, she tousled his hair. "Run along, sweetheart, and do your chores."

Once he'd left, she glared at Mary Edith as though she'd been the one to hurt him. "The stage is due very soon. The two of you'd best get the dinner out on time."

The stagecoach, when it was able, stopped on its way from Charles Town to Augusta and back again. They often rested at McHeath's during their noontime meal. Since Red Hill was a small backcountry outpost, the McHeaths made a fuss over these customers. The few settlers had little money since the outbreak of war, and those who did stop in were mostly looking for news from the cities and the latest gossip.

Before leaving, Mrs. McHeath set out a stack of bowls. She studied them, then put half back. "If we have any customers at all, that is. That devil, Tarlton Brown and his accomplices are back in the area."

✦

Nan was in a dark place. How could she have treated poor Daniel so? Such a wee lad. She knew what it was. Like she'd always feared. The madness.

Instead of starting the candles over, she returned to her pallet and curled into a ball. The sun rose in the sky, bringing a scorching heat to the small hut. The damp, close air made for labored breathing, but she stayed put. Life wasn't worth living.

Who knew how much time had gone by when she heard the familiar squeak of Ketch's wagon wheels? Still, she didn't move.

"You ailin'?" Ketch said from the doorway.

Her back to him, her eyes burned with unshed tears. "Aye, I've a sickness. 'Tis one I caught from me father and his mother before him. A raving lunatic, he was, and I hated him for it. Now, I'm no different."

Her breath caught in her throat as she was yanked to her feet.

Ketch shoved her through the door. "Get out this oven first."

She blinked at the bright sunlight. "Holy Mother of God, leave me be!"

"Sit down there." Ketch pointed to the tree stump she used as a stool. He squatted before her. "Listen here. Y'ain't sufferin' from no madness. Ya in a deep well of sorrow. Ain't no one can blame ya neither. A few months ago ya had a family of six. Now they's three."

"I can't sleep. I can't stay awake. I can't think. I can barely breathe!" Tears crept down her face as she saw the candles strewn in the dirt. "I beat them. Me young'ns. They didn't deserve it. A wild woman, I was."

"I's sorry for that. You in a bad place. But it ain't one ya can't get clear of." Ketch drew a circle in the dirt with his finger. "Seems ev'rybody scared all the time these days. 'S like we's walkin' over a rattlesnake pit on a ladder. One wrong step, we slip 'tween the rungs to our death."

"Every step feels wrong."

"Them chillun need ya anyways, Nan. Ya can't give up now."

"I don't want to give up," she said. "But without Joe, I'm lost."

Ketch went on like she hadn't spoken. "I'm rememberin' when my old master sold all us slaves. He done gone broke or somethin'. Next thing I know, I's on the auction block. Mama Juba in a pen nearby, waitin' to get herself sold. It seem my whole life was over. I wouldn't never see my mama again."

I'll never see Joe, Nan thought. He's gone.

Ketch brought her a ladle of water, then returned to his spot. "I can't forget how scared I was, lookin' at all them men holding they money. After Mr. Tom bought me, I don't know where I got the courage, but I ask him to buy Mama, too. 'She old and feeble,' I tol' him. 'Won't cost too much. And she know the root. Good at healin' folk.'

"He look me in the eye. Not many white folk do that. Maybe he seen my sorrow 'cause his own eyes got soft. And blamed if he didn't buy her. There ain't nothin' I wouldn't do for that man. I know how the others talk 'bout me, but I didn't never stop bein' thankful."

"He was a kindhearted man."

"Then he up and died. Now we gots Carlton. I thought to treat him like I did his daddy 'til he brought on that mongrel, Johnny Reeve."

Heat rose in her neck. "May he rot in hell."

Ketch lifted her chin. "That's why Thunder run off. Reeve had his sights on that African. I heard Carlton say he seen him with the British army in Charles Town. I hope he stay free." He swallowed. "I coulda run, too, but I got Mama Juba to think about. And you and the others. We can't count on Carlton like we done Mr. Tom. We gotta count on our own self."

He shook his head. "Even Carlton in a bad way, so I's runnin' things. But I don't do it for him. I do it for us—me, you, Mama, Ruth, Geoffrey, Hercules—all us. That's what it mean to be a man. Some white man call me boy? Them's his words. Inside me, I know I's a man. I don't need that fool to know it."

Nan peeked from under her lashes. "I know it."

He took Nan's hand. "And you a fool, callin' yoself crazy. You ain't crazy. You sad. But it's time you be brave. Put yo sorrow in a corner and do right for Mar' Edith, Daniel, and yoself.

You want to run away or disappear off the face of the earth? I say no."

He stood and pulled her to her feet "Sure, Thunder brave. But sometime it take courage to stay and keep on livin'."

Nan looked into his eyes. "I don't know if I've got courage."

"You does, inside," Ketch said. "For Mar' Edith and Daniel, you'll find it."

✦

At dusk, Rosabel closed her book. She rose from the garden bench and headed for the house, stopping a moment to take in the beauty of the setting sun. Lately, she'd been grasping at whatever bolstered her spirits.

As Carlton's gloom deepened, she feared telling him about the baby. If he expressed the least disappointment, Rosabel would be crushed. Laying her hand on her stomach, she marveled that a child was forming inside her. She already loved it so deeply.

Turning from the orange and red-streaked sky, a vicious scream reverberated through her body. In horror, she spun to find the fierce yellow eyes of an enraged owl, wings spread wide and razor-sharp talons appeared to head straight for her belly.

She threw herself to the ground to protect her unborn child. When her head slammed onto the slate flagstones of the garden path, she tumbled into blackness.

✦

Carlton's head bounced off his chest as he fought sleep. He'd been at Rosabel's bedside since Amos had carried her, unconscious, from the garden. It had been dark. The gash above her left ear indicated she'd taken a hard fall. Why had she stayed in the garden so long?

As the morning sun rose, he silently begged her to wake. On cue, her eyes opened. He grasped her hand. "Thank God, Rosabel," he said. "Thank God."

With trembling lips, she whispered, "Did I lose it?"

"What, darling? Your book is on the table. It's you I care about."

She took her hand back. "The baby. Did I lose the baby?"

Carlton stood, then fell back into his chair. He turned to Becca who sat in the corner of the room.

The servant rushed to Rosabel's bedside. "Master Carlton, you best step outside."

Feeling helpless, he obeyed. Becca closed the door behind him. Gathering his wits, he noticed little Oscar crouched in the hallway.

"Find Ketch. I want to see him immediately."

Once the boy took off, Carlton went outside and paced the veranda. After several minutes, Ketch ran up, panting. Carlton sent him for Silas O'Bannon, the closest they had to a doctor. His heart in his throat, he returned to Rosabel's chamber to find the door reopened.

Becca waved him in. "There ain't no sign she lost a baby."

"Leave us," he said. Once they were alone, he kissed Rosabel on the brow. "My heart is filled."

To his shock, his wife broke into sobs. He remembered Phineas Odom saying that a woman's spirits rose with her blood. Not knowing what else to do, he sat in silence until her weeping ended.

She sniffled and took the handkerchief he offered. "I was so afraid."

"As was I, but you are well."

"No." She brushed the tears from her cheeks. "I was afraid you would be angry. About the baby."

"Angry? What must you think of me?" He smiled. "Imagine, me a father." As soon as the words left his lips, the reality hit him. Was he ready?

⊕

Joe lay on his cot in the dark of Thankfull Williams's cottage. As they often did, his thoughts drifted to Nan. While his leg was healed, he could still feel it at times. He should make his way home, but he was afraid. What would he find?

He and Nan had left each other under terrible circumstances. It was months ago but felt like years. What if he were to hobble up, one-legged, on the crude crutch made by Thankfull's neighbor, Paul White? Would Nan be happy to see him, a cripple who'd lied about his death? Or would she despise him? The thought was more than he could bear.

Thankfull was a tender, caring woman. She had the gift to make her small cottage a home where Joe could be happy. For each small task he did for her, she lived up to the full virtue of her name. He felt special here.

The widower, Paul White, also noticed Thankfull's nurturing ways. He'd set his sights on her for his next bride. More than once, he'd side-eyed Joe saying, "One must move forward."

"He needs a bit more time," Thankfull would say.

Paul only grunted, not daring to cross the woman.

As it had so many nights before, a searing pain ran up and down Joe's gullet. Unable to sleep, Joe's fears grew with the pain in his craw. He rolled this way and that, looking for relief. Finding none, he moaned, hoping it didn't wake Thankfull. To no avail.

She whispered in the dark. "Joe, you hurting?"

"A bit. Me stomach again."

She spoke so softly Joe could barely hear her. "I could lay beside you if that would help."

Had he heard right? She'd never said anything untoward before. "I'm sorry I woke ye, Miss Thankfull. Go back to sleep, if ye will."

Unwittingly, he moaned again. His heart pounded as he heard the woman's bare feet pad across the wooden floor. She pulled back the cover and slid beside Joe. He could barely breathe. He should send her away, but he kept silent.

"Roll to your side," she whispered. "This used to put my Wendall to sleep."

He obeyed. Her breath tickled his back, and he went weak. Soft hands ran up and down his spine, across his shoulders, and down his sides.

He feared for himself and for Thankfull, but still no words came. He demanded his mind recall Nan's face, but she refused to appear. He begged himself to be strong, but there was no vigor to be had.

He should stop her. For both their sakes. But he knew he wouldn't.

Chapter Thirty-three

S ilas O'Bannon came and left, assuring Carlton that Rosabel was well.

"It might be best she stay abed a day or two." Silas had laid a hand on his shoulder and nodded toward Becca. "We'll keep an eye on her for you. I'll return later in the week."

Carlton waited until his wife was sleeping soundly before leaving her in Becca's care. He stepped outside and filled his lungs with air.

A son. He would have a son. His heart swelled with pride. He imagined the little fellow standing beside him, gazing up in admiration. The way he looked to his own father at that age. He grew sentimental at the memory. How he'd loved Thomas as a boy, so tall, so kind-hearted and patient. And intelligent!

Father explained all aspects of plantation life to him from the time he could remember. The soils and what they could grow, the trees and plants and their many uses, what grasses made for the healthiest livestock. Carlton listened and soaked it all up like life-giving water.

I love this land. And now I can pass that love onto my own boy.

He knew he should tell his mother the news but decided against it. He'd not permit her to ruin his happiness with her derisive facial expressions.

He'd been holed up in his study for too long. It was time to renew his love for Kilkenny and take his place as its caretaker. He headed to the barn and ordered Amos to saddle Hector.

Waiting, he remembered the innovations his father developed, many that improved their crops. Thomas would set aside an acre or two for testing and take Carlton with him each day to monitor his experiments' progress.

How had he forgotten the smell of the soil, the thrill of new growth? Intoxicating! It was what he'd yearned for, to show his father that he, too, had ideas that could take their production to new heights.

Once Hector was ready, Carlton mounted his steed and set off to see what had become of his property while indisposed. He passed the servants' quarters. The vegetable gardens looked healthy. Unlike the previous year, there'd been sufficient rain.

Next, he'd ride out to the cattle range. It wouldn't hurt to catch Geoffrey off his guard. From there, he'd check on the cedar shingle enterprise he'd started.

Passing through a stand of trees that bordered the cow pens, he glanced to his right. His eye caught two rectangles of red soil covered with a spattering of grass. He pulled up on Hector's reins. The slave burial ground. Curious, he rode closer. On top of each mound lay several offerings, as was the slaves' custom.

He dismounted to find straw dolls, flowers, and an embroidered cloth on one. The other held a carved toy hammer, some nails, and a small box. It hit him like a sledge—the two Dillon children were dead and buried on his property.

He grabbed Hector's reins to steady himself. Yes, they'd been feverish, but no one told him they'd died. His heart ached. He'd been furious with Nan, but never wished for this.

In his mind's eye, he could see the two as tots laughing and playing outside the kitchen. Nolan, as a lad, took such pride in his carpentry. He remembered Baby Eveleen, giggling behind doors with her sister, Mary Edith. This wasn't his fault!

How did they come to be buried on Kilkenny? He leapt onto Hector and raced back to the quarters. Climbing Mama Juba's steps, he stood in the doorway.

"No one told me."

The old healer rose from her seat. "Come on in, Master Carlton. Ain't no one told ya what?"

He stood inside and waited for his eyes to adjust to the darkness. "The Dillon children, right? Buried with y'all. Nolan and Baby, I assume."

"That's so, suh. They passed weeks ago. The fever took 'em." As Carlton sat on a stool, Mama Juba did the same. "I b'lieve yo wife try to tell ya, but ya wouldn't let her."

Was that insolence? Carlton didn't care. "Maybe."

"Now, don't go blamin' Ketch for burying them chillun with us. It was all us decided. They belong there, Master Carlton. We all the fam'ly they got."

His next words surprised even himself. "You're right. They're where they belong, as much a part of Kilkenny as you are. Or even me." A pall blanketed him. "How have things gone so wrong, Mama Juba? I was remembering my boyhood. With my father, everything seemed possible. Now, all is suffering."

She placed a hand on his knee. "I tol' ya, son. A bad cross been placed on K'kenny. A curse. Like I said when we learnt about Joe. I done all I could to uncross us, but it didn't do no good." Mama Juba stopped. She took back her hand and stared at it. He knew something was on her mind.

"Speak," Carlton said. "You know you want to."

"I do got somethin' to say." She rubbed hand over hand as she spoke. "When all my spells and magic gone for naught, I prayed. I prayed to the ancestors and I prayed to Jesus. And one thing I learnt." She paused.

"Well, tell me."

"You gotta do it. You the onliest one who can break this evil we wrapped in."

He looked her in the eye. "What do I know of your superstitious mumbo jumbo?"

"I can't explain it. Somehow you know where this curse come from and only you can break it."

His temper started to rise. "That's ridiculous!"

"It seem like it should be, but it ain't. Search yo heart, Master Carlton. Truth's pounding on yo door and it won't be turned away. Listen to Truth. Then do what it tell ya to do."

The air became thick, suffocating. Without another word, he left.

✦

After throwing every shutter open wide, Carlton poured himself a glass of madeira. He plopped into the parlor's upholstered wing chair. His study now felt like its own kind of prison. All the way back to the Big House, in his mind, he railed against Mama Juba's words. But he knew. Truth had been hammering at him for some time. He dreaded where it might take him.

He sipped his wine, trying to clear his brain. Yet, his father came to mind. The man his twelve-year-old self had so admired. The one who slipped him a sweetmeat before popping one into his own mouth when Mother wasn't looking. Just as he had for Nolan and Baby. When did that fondness turn?

Memories floated through him from his youth. He thought of a particular social gathering when he stood on the outskirts of a group of men. Phineas Odom and Walter Gatch were there. Carlton could remember his pride as Father shared with them his newest discovery. It would make their wheat crop increase by half. The other men nodded, showing great interest as they interrogated him for details.

Once his father had left to join another conversation, however, the mood changed. No one noticed Carlton when they began to mock his father.

Walter Gatch said, "He can make all the changes he wants to his farming techniques—and he does have a knack for it— but until he stops being so delicate with them slaves. Well, let's say no farming tricks gonna make up for lazy, impertinent workers."

"He's like a soft, old woman with them drudges," another said.

They were laughing at him! Carlton's face burned with humiliation as he slunk away. Worse, when he confronted Thomas with the behavior of his peers, his father chuckled. "Small minds, son. Pay them no attention."

But Carlton couldn't ignore it. Upon each occurrence, his anger and disdain for his father grew. The man wouldn't even defend himself! The respect he'd had for Thomas melted away.

He tossed back his wine and refilled his glass. Look at things now, he thought. The men who'd mocked his father were fools. It sickened him. Father had been right. Small minds.

His mouth dropped at a flash of insight. The opinions of neighboring plantation owners may have been the harvest, but the seeds had been sown long before.

By Mother.

His chest sank. Truth had broken down the door. And it was ugly.

While drinking several more glasses of madeira, memories flooded Carlton of sly comments his mother'd made of Father's foolishness, his weakness, or lack of virility. At the same time, she told her son how much smarter and more competent he was than Thomas. More of a man. Oddly, in the end, it only served to weaken him.

Mama Juba said he knew where the curse originated. Only he could break it. It was true. All this had to end, and he, Carlton, must end it.

Ensuring he would not be interrupted, Carlton stepped into the library where his mother lay, asleep. He closed the door and locked it.

Shaking her shoulder, he woke the woman who gave him life. Unhappy at her disturbed nap, she sneered at him. He pulled out his handkerchief and wiped away the drool beside her mouth.

"Hello, Mother. I've done some thinking, and I've come to realize you've always treated me like I'm stupid." She frowned. "But I'm not. I'm only slow."

He lowered himself onto the chair beside her bed. "It's taken me a long time to work you out. Too long. You—are a thief."

Her eyebrows raised.

"Yes. A thief. You've stolen from me the opportunity to be my own man, make my own choices. You've stolen my pride in myself. You've robbed me of a brotherly relationship with Alden. Or even of a mother with the maternal instinct God gave a woman, to wish for her children's happiness over her own. And in the truest sense of the word, you stole my father from me."

She snarled and looked away from him. He grabbed her jaw and twisted her head until she faced him again.

"I know what you did. I've always known though I couldn't bear it." He took a deep breath. "Somehow, you lured Father into your room, into your bed." The thought disgusted him, and he was sure it showed on his face.

"Then, you cold-hearted bitch...well, you waited until he slept, I suppose. The wisest man I ever knew was a fool to trust you, wasn't he? But he did, so you placed a pillow over his face." He removed one of the pillows from beneath her head.

Her eyes widened with fear and she let loose a growl as loud as she could manage.

"You don't want to make so much noise, Mother. I'll have to silence you." His voice cracked. "Like this."

Carlton choked back a sob as he lowered the pillow over his mother's nose and mouth. Only her eyes remained uncovered. He forced himself to peer into them. In a whisper, he said, "It is you who brought this curse onto all of us. And there is only one way to remove it."

With that, he clamped the pillow down with all his strength. His mother's eyes went wild as her body writhed.

"Is this what it was like for Father? I admire your strength that you could pull it off, a testament to your cruel determination. You always said I was strong, like you."

He stared as she continued to struggle. "You will not destroy me."

At last, the movement ended. He removed the pillow and searched for signs of life. There were none. He replaced the pillow beneath her head.

Carlton sat and contemplated his mother's dead body, waiting to feel something. And he did. The air seemed less oppressive despite the late summer heat. And something else. A release. He felt free.

Mama Juba had been right. Only he could lift the cross, and Truth would tell him how. Finally, the tears came. Tears of relief.

Chapter Thirty-four

Mary Edith groaned. Walking into the tavern from the back door, the first person she spotted was that ogre, Ben John. A foul-smelling monster of a man with rotted teeth. The bulge in his cheek from a large wad of tobacco made him look all the more vile.

He spewed slimy brown juice onto the floor. One more thing for her to clean up.

He and Mr. McHeath seemed wound up about something. They huddled at the end of the bar whispering and waving their hands in the air. Mary Edith wiped tables as far from the two men as possible. They looked like they needed an old dog to kick, and she would do in a pinch.

But the more tables she cleaned, the closer she was forced to move toward them. Without wanting to, she heard a name—Tarlton Brown. No one could get McHeath and his Loyalist cronies more riled. Keeping her head down, she glimpsed Mr. McHeath leaning across the bar only inches from Ben John's ugly face.

"Get that towering monstrosity," he hissed. "Whatever it takes!"

Ben John was gone in the blink of an eye.

By the noon hour, the tavern filled with stagecoach travelers and locals looking to wet their whistles while soaking up the latest gossip. Mary Edith ran from the kitchen with bowls full of Lottie's stew, returning with empty ones to be wiped out and refilled. She rolled her eyes when the Watkins brothers, two mean and ugly drunks, settled themselves onto a bench. Frank, especially, could be vicious.

"Is this what ya call service 'round here?" Lester Watkins shouted. Heads turned as he walked to the bar and slapped several coins onto the counter. "See? We got money this time." They strutted to a table and sat.

Mr. McHeath filled two mugs of ale. "Take these to our friends, girl," he told Mary Edith. "And fetch them some stew."

When she returned with the bowls, Mr. McHeath was already refilling their mugs. "Drink up," he told them.

They didn't need encouragement. Before long, between swigs they were shouting, belching, and cursing the travelers. Mrs. McHeath, who flitted from one to the next as she often did, scowled at her husband.

Mary Edith avoided the two men as long as she could, but Mr. McHeath nodded that she needed to clear their empty bowls. Sure enough, once her arms were filled with dirty dishes, Frank stuck out his nasty foot and sent Mary Edith sprawling. Clay bowls and cups smashed beneath her.

The two louts bellowed with laughter while the tavern keeper yelled, "Get that cleaned up. Now!"

Mrs. McHeath bustled over to her husband. "Those two must leave."

Mr. McHeath's face dropped at his wife's displeasure. "Be on your way," he told the Watkins boys. "We don't cotton to that behavior here."

With an apron full of shards, Mary Edith rushed outside the tavern. She dumped the clay pieces in the trash pit and returned to the kitchen. Before she stepped through the door, Lottie handed her a teapot. "Take this and fill up the cups."

"I ain't going back there." Mary Edith thrust her bloodied hands toward the cook. "Look!"

"Them scratches? Dip 'em in this here bucket and go on."

She dragged her feet on the way back to the tavern. Once inside, she steeled herself, determined not to spill a drop. Her eye caught Mrs. McHeath seated with a man of the cloth. Such men were rare in these parts, likely passing through. Mary Edith used what her ma called "big ears" to catch the man's words.

She jumped out of her skin when he called, "You, there."

"Mary Edith," Mrs. McHeath said, "Father Samuels is speaking to you."

Had she been caught eavesdropping? "Sir?"

"Are you hurt, my child?"

The tavern grew quiet. Alarmed as the center of gawking faces, she hung her head and mumbled. "Just scratches. Tea?"

He covered his cup by way of refusing and returned his attention to the mistress of the tavern. "How good of you to take in one of God's children."

Mary Edith scooted to a far corner table, but not before hearing Mrs. McHeath say, "Two of them. There's a sweet boy, Daniel, who cleans out the animal pens."

Anxious, it seemed, for all the customers to hear of her Christian charity, she spoke too loudly. "It's awful, Father, the squalor they live in. After her husband deserted them, the mother pleaded with us for help. Of course, we do all we can."

Mary Edith burned with shame, but no one seemed to notice. They'd returned to their own conversations. Mrs. McHeath lowered her voice, but Mary Edith's ears only grew sharper. The woman was describing the deaths of Nolan and Baby.

"The most amazing thing was the mother never shed a tear. Neither did the girl." She nodded in Mary Edith's direction. "When she told us about their deaths, she might as well have been saying it would rain tomorrow. As I'm sure you know, those people don't have feelings like we do."

Against her will, Mary Edith's head jerked up. Her eyes met those of the preacher. She couldn't read him. Was he embarrassed by those harsh words, or did he agree? For Mary Edith, they were a bitter bile she was forced to swallow. How could Mrs. McHeath be so coldhearted? Was she there when Ma's sharp wails cut into the night? Her cries so heartsick, at times it felt like the end of the world. She glared at the woman, but Mrs. McHeath didn't even notice.

"...and she mistreats her children so. Father, I would never blaspheme. But why would someone like that be blessed with babies while I go childless?"

The preacher placed his hand atop Mrs. McHeath's. "'Who hath known the mind of the Lord,' Madam?"

Father Samuels had the decency to throw a flustered glance at Mary Edith who simmered with rage.

✝

Alden climbed the steps to George Collins's cabin. Since their return from Virginia a week before, the two shared the Collins home. "Well, I've dug up some potatoes and found this fat squirrel in your trap." He held up the gray, furry carcass.

"We'll carry that with us." George was in full riding gear, rifle in hand. "Tulius come by. Tarlton says Ben John and them been spotted by Red Bluff. They's in a fishing cabin there. Likely likkered up. We can grab 'em easy, he says."

"Meet them there?"

"Nah. Tarlton says to gather at his old place. We can strategize then."

Alden gritted his teeth. Since their return, he'd avoided any contact with Suzanne. Her mother's accusation about Levi remained a raw wound. Of course, he'd told Tarlton and Bartlett

306 | M. B. GIBSON

of the tragedy when they met up in Virginia. Most of it, anyway. He'd left out Levi's dying request that he watch over Suzanne. Sarah Brown's veiled accusation that he'd let the man die, or worse, was not something he cared to relive in Tarlton's eyes.

Now they were to meet at the remains of the Brown homestead with Billy Brown and Levi's fresh graves only yards away. He and George rode to Brier's Creek in silence.

Once they arrived, Alden's jaw tightened at the scene of the disaster. The house was no more than the heaviest beams, now frail, charred versions of their former selves, jutting from a cold pile of ash. The outbuildings were tumbling or partially burned. Thank the Lord, time had washed away the acrid stench now seared in his memory.

Bartlett, Tulius, and a few of the fellows were talking by the crumbling corral. Alden and George rode over to join them when Tarlton called out from beside the graves.

"Alden! A word."

A lump solidified in his stomach as he steered Enbarr that way. He dismounted and wrapped the reins around a tree branch.

"Lieutenant?"

"You told me of this." He waved his arm to indicate all the destruction. "My blood boiled in my veins." He blinked his eyes. "But it wasn't quite real until I saw it myself. It's hit me hard."

"I imagine it has."

Tarlton's head drooped. "We never shoulda left. I'll regret it 'til my dying day. I can't help but feel it wouldn't have gone this far if me and Bartlett had stayed behind."

"Tarlton, there were at least thirty of those brutes. I feel the same way, but looking at it in the daylight, we have to admit two or three more of us couldn't have made that much difference."

"Maybe, maybe not." He sighed. "You told me you spoke with Levi before the end, but my mother told me things you left out. He asked you to watch over my sister for him."

"He...he did. But you're here now."

"Mama has a generosity and kindness about her that's rare. But she's hard beneath that dear heart. Likely from years of living in this wilderness trying to keep my daddy and brothers in tow." He smiled. "And a feisty sister I could mention."

He shook his head. "I'm going on and on. What I'm trying to say is Mama'd like a word with you. If you're willing, ride by Adam Wood's place for a spell and catch up with us after. I want us all on this raid together."

His stomach ached. "Sure, Tarlton."

Now what? His efforts to avoid this very thing were in vain. When he arrived at the Wood place, he found Sarah Brown sitting alone on a bench beneath a large oak. He glanced around for a glimpse of Suzanne, but no one else was about.

After tying his horse to the hitching post, he approached Miss Sarah, hat in hand.

"So you came," Miss Sarah said. "Sit."

He took his place beside the woman and lowered his head. "You're looking well, Miss Sarah. Again, I offer my condolences."

"Thank you. Some mornings I wake up and turn to Billy, only to remember he's gone. The pain's as fresh every time." Her eyes weakened as she struggled to hold herself together.

Alden waited, working his hands around the brim of his hat.

"I asked you to see me because, well, I'm ashamed of myself."

He frowned as he studied her face.

"You did all anyone could ask after those vermin did their worst, and I have not shown proper gratitude. I regret that." She paused. "But more than that, I cast ugly aspersions on your motives that are beneath you and, frankly, beneath me. So, I am humbled, and I beg your forgiveness."

Tarlton was right. Sarah Brown was a proud woman. It was clear she did not offer apologies easily. "There's nothing to forgive."

She pushed an errant strand of hair back into her mop cap. "Looking back, I can't think of anything you've done that was dishonorable. I'm not as confident about Suzanne, but that's another story." She looked him in the eye. "I believe you, sir, about what Levi said. He gave you and Suzanne his blessing, and if that's still where your heart is, I must do no less."

"I...I'm at a loss."

"Tarlton has a high regard for you, Mr. de Barnefort. He feels the same about it as I have come to feel."

Unsure of what should follow, Alden stumbled for words. "Thank you, ma'am. Your faith in my honor means everything to me." He stood, searching for somewhere to look. "I'd best be on my way."

Sarah Brown's eyes saddened. "I imagine you should. Y'all stay safe. We women can't bear to lose anyone else."

Chapter Thirty-five

The raid on the fishing cabin had been a disaster. Ben John's mob was there, but they weren't fishing. They were lying in wait. Whoever'd brought them the report of the Tories' whereabouts was a bloody traitor.

During the ambush, it had quickly become clear the enemy had the upper hand. Tarlton ordered a retreat to Adam Wood's place. Everyone got out as best they could.

Alden wiped blood from his eye. During the fighting, he'd bashed his head into a tree. George Collins had been shot in the arm and shoulder, losing a good bit of blood. He was right dazed. Once they were clear of danger, Alden looked behind him to find George slumped against his horse's neck. He went back and grabbed its reins.

Oh, damn. Don't fall off.

George was two or three inches taller than Alden and a good stone heavier. If he tumbled from the horse, Alden doubted he could lift George, let alone put his dead-weight back on his mare.

"Not much farther," he said aloud, unsure if George was conscious.

At the house, he found Obie Heape with his right hand already bandaged. Alden helped George into the house to be doctored by Sarah Brown and the other women. He caught Suzanne's eye, which widened briefly. She brought him a wet rag and pressed it to his head.

He touched her cheek. "Just a scratch. See about George. I'm afraid for him."

Adam Wood burst into the house. "Who's seen my Jamie? He's no more than a lad. He had no business on a strike like this."

Sarah went to him and laid her hand on his arm. "He'll be right, Adam. They get to an age, you can't stop them. Neither Tarlton nor Bartlett is back. He'll be with them."

The man rubbed his face with his roughened hand as though he could wipe away his fears, then went outside. Alden soon heard more horses approaching. He and Obie went to greet their comrades, Hiram and Jamie Wood, who were grimy and blackened.

Adam ran over and wrapped his boy in his arms. "Lord be praised!" He petted the hair of his son, who looked relieved in the safety of his father's embrace.

Suzanne dried her hands on her apron as she stood in the doorway. "Any sign of Bartlett? Or Tarlton?"

Alden turned to her. "When the shooting started, they took us by surprise."

She frowned. "I know what ambush means. Obie told us that already." Her lips pursed, she went back inside. Hiram followed, holding his left arm. While the wound wasn't life-threatening, he'd been grazed, leaving an open gash.

Within the hour, Bartlett came in. He was unharmed, but his hat had been shot clear off his head. He scowled. "Too close. Where's Tarlton?"

"No sign yet," Alden said. "Wasn't he with you?"

"We split up and the half dozen following us all chased him." He laughed. "Went for the easy target with that red hair of his. If I know Tarlton, he'll run 'em all off a cliff!"

The next morning when there was still no sign of Tarlton, Suzanne took Alden aside. "Bartlett keeps telling us not to worry, but when will y'all look for my brother? I'm frightened. We all are."

Before Alden could form an answer, an eleven- or twelve-year-old boy trotted up on a small horse.

"I'm looking for Alden de Barnefort," he called out.

Suzanne clutched his arm, but Alden removed her hand. "I'm de Barnefort."

"Mr. Carlton paid me good money to find ya. He says to come home for a spell. Your ma's dead."

Φ

Mary Edith and Daniel arrived at McHeath's Tavern mid-morning to find Lottie singing a tune in the kitchen. Ever since she'd told Mary Edith about her secret reading lessons, she was like spring water, eager to bubble out all she'd learned.

"Now, that Noah fella was somethin'," she said. "Uppity folk just laughed and laughed at that man when he built the ark. But he was doin' the Lawd's business and he didn't pay them no mind."

"What's a ark?" Mary Edith asked.

"Why, it's a big ol' boat—for the flood. A flood that covered the whole world with water and Noah was the only fella to build a ark. The rest of them fools drowned."

"Why didn't Noah let 'em on his boat—I mean, ark—if it was so big?"

"'Cause he filled it with two of ev'ry kind of animal they was. So the world could go on after the flood."

Mary Edith struggled to imagine it. "I bet that ark was rank."

"Now, don't you blaspheme," Lottie said. "That's Noah you talkin' 'bout and he didn't keep no foul-smellin' ark."

Mrs. McHeath burst into the kitchen. "They've got him! That crafty old devil has been caught."

"Who, Miss?" Lottie asked.

"Ben John and his soldiers with the help of McGirth from Georgia," she answered. "I've never seen Mr. McHeath so happy."

"I thought they was friends," Mary Edith said. "Why is he glad Ben John got caught?"

Mrs. McHeath giggled like a child. "No, no. They didn't get captured. They did the catching. And their prisoner is none other than Satan himself—Tarlton Brown!"

Lottie wrung her hands. "My, my. Tarlton Brown."

"Yes," said Mrs. McHeath. "He'll finally hang, as he should have long ago."

"Where he at?" Lottie asked.

"Out front, tied to his horse," the tavern mistress said. "Before they execute the traitor, Mr. McHeath is treating the men to a well-deserved celebration."

Lottie's eyes got big. Mary Edith grew nervous as well.

"Not to worry," Mrs. McHeath said. "He's well-guarded, I assure you. Mary Edith, the tables have not been wiped down. Mr. McHeath wants it done immediately."

Once the woman left, Lottie looked at Mary Edith. "I don't feel too good about a man like that so close to the tavern. They need to hang him first and celebrate later."

Mary Edith grabbed a wet rag and entered the back door of the tavern, avoiding Tarlton Brown altogether. Laughter and shouts blasted from the Great Room. Mr. McHeath was pouring whiskey like water, not even caring how much he spilled.

The men toasted each other, Mr. McHeath, England, and King George himself. They were already tipsy which worried Mary Edith. Ben John was a brute when he was drunk. Then she spotted someone scarier. A man with heavy whiskers and bushy eyebrows hawked a big wad onto the floor.

"I kilt his daddy," the man called out. "I kilt his brother. I burnt his house to the ground. Now I got the man himself!"

Ben John laughed like a barking dog and slapped the man on the back. "A clean sweep, McGirth. You're wiping out the whole family."

"Them grimy Patriot scoundrels will wish they'd never laid a whip on ol' Daniel McGirth," he boasted. "I've made 'em pay ten times over."

The Tories burst into song. The hatred on their faces sent a chill up Mary Edith's spine. She wiped tables faster than she'd ever wiped before. "Get me out of here," she prayed.

"Come listen a while and I'll tell you a song. I'll show you those Yankees are all in the wrong..."

The words were slurred. Spittle flew from their lips.

"The state is rotten, rotten to the core. 'Tis all one bruise, one putrefying sore."

As she neared the back door, the man named McGirth pointed at her. "Who's this little hussy sneaking about?"

Mr. McHeath said, "A local girl. Her father was killed on his way to fight for Ferguson."

"By lowdown Tories," she mumbled. Thunderstruck at her blunder, she shrank under the stares of the men.

McGirth growled. "What you say?"

"Nothing." She tried to leave, but Ben John blocked the door.

"I heard her loud and clear," said the man named Elijah. "She called us lowdown Tories!"

She wagged her head back and forth. "No! The men who killed my da were lowdown."

"You got a rebel spy working for you, McHeath." McGirth, spit flying from his mouth, jabbed his finger toward the tavern keeper. "For all we know, you're a spy yourself!"

It got quiet as a tomb. All eyes were on Mr. McHeath's brick-red face. Veins throbbed in his neck. Danger hung in the room like thick smoke.

Ben John's barking laugh broke the spell. "Come on, now. John McHeath's as true as they come. And if this puny girl is all the spy the rebels can come up with, we've got time for another round."

McGirth looked at Mary Edith, shook his head, and laughed. The men cheered and held out their mugs for refills. Mr. McHeath poured with a face of stone.

Without warning, Mary Edith was yanked from her feet, steered out the back door, and flung into the grass. For a delicate lady, Mrs. McHeath had the strength of a grown man.

"What were you thinking?" she screeched. "You almost got us killed!" Her wild eyes were scarier than her words. The woman walked over and kicked Mary Edith in the thigh, hard. "Stay away from the Great Room. Don't come anywhere near us!"

With that, she burst into tears and ran inside.

Mary Edith's thigh and arm were aching, but she didn't care about that. Mrs. McHeath had never raised her voice toward her. Not once. Her own eyes filled up.

"Come on, girl." Lottie was standing in the kitchen doorway. "Get up. Dust yoself off. I'll give ya a sip of buttermilk."

Buttermilk was for paying customers only, but she followed Lottie into the kitchen and accepted the gift. "I meant no harm, Lottie. Honest, I didn't."

The slave sat on a bench. "The way I see it, people 'round here been skittish for some time. That's how white folks get when things ain't goin' too good." She shook her head. "Mean. I seen the same thing at my old plantation when the young master was havin' all his troubles."

Lottie leaned forward. "And who them folks gonna blame? They own selves? Why, that'd only make things worser. So, it's the likes of me and you gets kicked 'round like scabby ol' dogs." She stood and patted Mary Edith on the knee. "You finish that buttermilk, girl. Don't waste it. And no more frettin'. I got a pretty good tonic my mama always used. It'll take the fidgets right outa Mrs. McHeath."

Once Lottie stepped outside, Mary Edith drained her cup. Feeling better, she almost laughed. Buttermilk must be some kind of tonic itself.

Leaving the kitchen, she saw Lottie in the garden gathering roots of nightshade. Daniel was mucking out the barn and tending the Tory horses. Mary Edith had nowhere to be. She wasn't needed in the kitchen and was forbidden from the tavern.

She slinked off to her secret place, one not even Daniel knew about. The west side of the tavern, beyond the hitching post, was wooded. In the middle of all the saplings, vines, and brush stood a tall, proud oak. Its branches were so thick and wide that not much grew beneath them. It was like Mary Edith's own private room where, on the rare opportunity, she escaped.

As she rounded the tavern's chimney, she dove back out of sight. Tarlton Brown! She'd forgotten the feared fighter was trussed up in front of the inn. She tried to slow her breathing and think.

A high, whiney voice hit her ears. "They's in there boozing and having a big ol' time while I'm stuck out here with the likes of you."

It was true. Mary Edith could hear the singing and shouting inside. She peeked from beside the chimney. A dirty, scraggy fellow was pacing back and forth, waving his arms in the air. The guard.

"I always miss out on all the fun," he was saying. "It ain't right. I'm blamed sick and tired of it."

A calm voice said, "What good are you doing out here, anyway? With my legs tied under the horse like this, I'm going nowhere."

"Shut up, you! I ain't listening to no rebel fool. You a dead man, soon enough. But by then, the party'll be over. It ain't right."

"Suit yourself," said the calm voice.

Mary Edith risked another peek. A large horse was tied to the hitching post and atop it sat one of the tallest men she'd ever seen. His legs were so long and thin that the Tories had tied his feet together under the horse's belly. The man's arms were bound behind his back.

His head turned. He caught sight of Mary Edith and winked. She leapt back so fast, she cracked her head on the chimney.

Could the red-headed man be the villain they were so afraid of? He had a look of kindness. And why was he so calm? Didn't he know what Ben John and the others were fixing to do? That ruckus inside wouldn't last forever.

"I ain't a-putting up with this," the guard said. "With your arms and legs tied up like that, you ain't going nowhere. I'm a-going in." He gave all the ropes one more tug to make sure they were tight, then off he went.

Mary Edith heard him inside the tavern. "Hey, boys! Pour one for me."

She hung back, waiting for the oaf to be thrown out on his ear, but soon his voice fell in with the whooping and hollering and singing.

Once she was sure it was safe, she ducked into the woods. The prisoner sure wouldn't sound the alarm. She wriggled through the brush to her special place. Her safe place. She breathed in the warm, moist air that smelled of greenery and dirt. Birds whistled and bugs hummed just for her. For a spell, no troubles could touch her.

But she couldn't avoid thoughts of the tall man who'd soon be swaying from the end of a rope. Tarlton Brown was nothing like the McHeaths said. He'd winked at her! Would a demon of a man do that?

What if Da had been tied up on a horse? Maybe someone watched when he was killed, but they hid out in the trees. Shouldn't she do something? Yet, if any of those men in the tavern found her talking to their enemy, they'd kill her, too. Maybe even Daniel. Ben John would smack his lips at the chance, like a dog drooling over a bowl of lard.

Also, what of Mrs. McHeath's kindness to her and Daniel? Or her cruelty a short while ago, she reminded herself. A man's life was the most important thing. This was Mary Edith's chance to make up for what happened to her father. She had to try.

She crawled back through the brush until she was only feet from the hitching post. Beyond a curtain of vines, branches, and leaves sat a man who would die without her help. She wanted to say something, but the words stuck in her throat. She wasn't sure she was breathing.

"Watch out, inn girl."

Mary Edith felt dizzy. Tarlton Brown spoke so softly, she wondered if she was dreaming.

"You don't want your master to catch you around me," he said. "Don't you know who I am?"

He'd definitely spoken. "You're Tarlton Brown. Satan himself, they say."

He chuckled. "Ah, you risk a conversation with the devil. What's your name?"

"Mary Edith. Mary Edith Dillon."

"Dillon? Like the Irish fellow, Joe?"

"You knew my da? He died in a swamp." Her throat clenched. The pain was still fresh.

The man hesitated, like he wanted to say something, but he didn't. "I'm sorry to hear that."

Her heart thumped. The brutal men inside the tavern would soon send this man to his Maker. She knew what she had to do. There wasn't much time. She crawled on her belly through the brush and under the hitching post.

Keep looking at his tied-up feet, she told herself. Nowhere else. It wasn't far, but it could have been a mile.

"Don't risk it," Tarlton Brown said.

Her heart thundered in her chest so loudly, she barely heard him. Fear threatened to crush her while, under the horse, Mary Edith tackled a knot made by a grown man. Lottie or Daniel could round the tavern at any moment, hunting for her. Or the drunks inside could pour out, ready for blood. Not only Tarlton Brown's. Hers, too.

She pulled and tugged at the knot. After what seemed an eternity, it loosened a bit. Where she got her power, she'd never know. But the binds slacked bit by bit until the rope dropped to the ground. She scrambled to free the horse.

"Leave my hands," Tarlton Brown whispered. "I can guide Castor with my knees until I'm clear of this place."

In no time, she untied the horse, but the man made no move to leave. Mary Edith looked up at Tarlton Brown and saw his eyes brimming with tears. "You're free," she said.

A tear splashed onto his leg. "I'll never forget you, Mary Edith Dillon. In all my battles, I've never seen such courage."

She cocked her head to one side, unsure what to make of him.

"I'll stay until you get clear of here," he said.

She gave the man one last look and ran.

For the next hour, her nerves were jangled, wondering when the tavern would explode with the discovery of their missing prisoner. In the kitchen with Lottie, she dropped or spilled one thing after another.

Lottie frowned. "What on God's green earth is wrong with you, Mar' Edith?"

She shrugged and cleaned up the spilled flour.

His chores done, Daniel moped in the doorway. "Wanna hear a riddle?"

"Sure." Mary Edith wasn't listening.

Daniel's face lit up. "Clink, clank, under the bank, Two against four. What is it?"

Before Lottie and Mary Edith could claim they didn't know, an earsplitting cry froze them to their spots. Within seconds, heavy footsteps pounded in all directions at once.

"Check the stables." It was McGirth. "You two—comb the bushes. Search all the way down to the creek."

Mary Edith struggled to breathe at the sound of grunts and footsteps running off.

"But his horse is gone, too," from the whiny guard.

"That could be a trick, you chowderhead!" McGirth thundered. "You ain't got the brains of a flounder. You better hope

Ben and them others catch up with that slippery eel, or we gonna hang you for treason."

"But, Ben, I checked them knots and checked 'em again. There ain't no way he got 'em loose."

Mary Edith froze as the forms of McGirth and the guard darkened the doorway.

"And which of these three do you peg as the one what freed them knots, Rufus?" McGirth shook his head and spit on the ground. "Them tight knots made by a big strapping fella like you? The slave woman, the puny girl, or that runt of a boy?"

As Rufus chewed his lips, McGirth nodded toward Lottie. "What you been up to, ya black wench? You find yourself in front of the alehouse for some reason?"

Lottie stared at the floor. "No, suh. I been right here."

"What about you, Spy Girl? You been skulking about, prying where you got no business?"

His bushy eyebrows hung over dark, fearsome eyes. Mary Edith opened her mouth to speak, but no words came.

"Her and the boy been with me the whole time," Lottie said. "We been mixin' some tonic for Mrs. McHeath. She feelin' poorly."

McGirth scanned the kitchen. The herbs, pots, and spoons seemed to satisfy him. "Any of y'all seen a ugly red-haired giant running around here?" He bored his fierce eyes into Daniel.

Daniel shook his head so hard, it could have flown off.

"No, sir," Mary Edith said, hoping to take the heat off her brother.

"We ain't seen no devil like that," Lottie added. "If'n we do, we'll come hollerin'."

McGirth grunted and left, Rufus trailing behind. All three in the kitchen melted as the tension seeped from their bodies.

Lottie's shoulders slumped. She puttered through the kitchen as though sapped of all spirit.

Looking at no one, she said, "Mar' Edith, I don't know what you been doin'. I don't wanta know. But if it ever gets out that I did not tell all the truth, I be whipped 'til there's no skin left on my back. Maybe no breath left in my body."

Both Mary Edith and Daniel started to speak, but Lottie held up her hand. "No. That's it. I ain't never gonna talk 'bout this no mo'." Head hung low, she scrubbed her pot.

Chapter Thirty-six

Joe refused to look in Thankfull's eyes. When he had, he found a willingness, an openness to something that could never happen. She'd reached out for him many times, a soft touch on his arm or shoulder. While loath to hurt her, at last he'd had to remove her hand from his arm.

Thankfull's face reflected the pain he'd dreaded. "We did nothing wrong," she said. "A woman brought comfort to a man in distress. I rubbed your back, no more."

The image of Nan that refused to come in the night had arrived by morning and was haunting him still. "Yer a gift from God, Thankfull. I'd have died without ye."

To his horror, she grasped his hand and dropped to her knees. "Stay with me."

Without hesitation, he lifted her to her feet. "Don't."

Joe rushed outside, avoiding her as much as possible. Then there was Paul White. Although Joe tried to act as though nothing had changed, Thankfull's admirer had glanced from one to the other, brow furrowed. He knows, Joe thought, which sickened him even more.

It was time. He had to leave. But how? He had no idea how far off Kilkenny was. He'd racked his brain to remember the distance he'd ridden before the battle near the Santee River. To walk back with one leg and a crutch was overwhelming.

The next day, Paul arrived driving a rickety cart drawn by a mule. He took Joe aside. "This here's for your journey home."

Joe nodded. "It'll take days to get back to me family. How will I return this to ye?"

Paul's eyes drilled into Joe's. "I don't need this old cart so much nor this mule neither. I need you gone."

The unfounded accusation was a punch in his gut.

"Today," Paul said.

Joe brought Thankfull the news of his departure under Paul's watchful eyes. He regretted he couldn't display his genuine affection for her. Aside from Paul's scorn, he could not risk her confusion about his feelings. He kept his thank-you crisp.

Thankfull's eyes narrowed and her bottom lip quivered. Then, throwing caution to the wind, she threw her arms around Joe and kissed his cheek. After giving him food, water, and a blanket roll, she wordlessly returned to her cabin. Paul gave him one last look and followed her inside.

Joe would never see her again. It saddened him, but it was for the best. His stomach twisted as he turned his sights toward Nan. If she sent him away, he couldn't bear it.

☦

When Mary Edith returned to the tavern with Daniel the following day, a pall loomed over it. While relieved to learn Tarlton Brown remained on the loose, she cringed at the thought of facing Mrs. McHeath. Yet, the tavern mistress was nowhere to be seen.

"She still abed," Lottie told her. "Ain't been up since she tossed you out. She got that melancholy again. Worse'n last time." She handed Mary Edith a bowl of soup. "Take this upstairs and see if she'll eat. Feed it to her if ya have to."

Mary Edith felt quivers over her whole body. "No, Lottie."

The cook frowned and gave her a shove. "Now, if ya wanta work here, ya gotta face her. The sooner the better."

Mary Edith crept to the tavern and dragged herself upstairs to the mistress' chamber. She found the woman curled up like a child.

"Mrs. McHeath? I brung some soup."

When the lady rolled toward Mary Edith, her face was covered in fresh scratches and cuts. "Go away," she mumbled and turned back.

Stunned, Mary Edith set the bowl on a side table and rushed back to the kitchen. "Where she get them cuts to her face?"

"Oh, Lawd, I shoulda told ya," Lottie said. "She may sleep all the day long, but last night she be wanderin' 'round without nobody knowin'. Me and Mr. McHeath heard a scream that'd stand yo hair up. There she was, a-lyin' in a heap in front the tavern. She done fell over that stump out there and landed in all them sticker bushes. Her shoulder and arm messed up, too, under that gown. This mornin', I tried to read some of the Bible like she showed me. She use a word I ain't never heard no lady say."

It called to mind Mary Edith's own ma. "I know about the sadness. Why don't you give her some of your tonic?"

"Oh, I can't do that, chil'. Mr. McHeath seen me feedin' her some and throwed the cup right out the window. He say that flim-flam the cause of all her troubles." Lottie shook her head. "That man's 'bout lost his own mind."

Lottie was right. The tavern keeper looked like an old man. His eyes drooped and his body sagged. Mary Edith felt sorry for him, something she never thought she'd do. In the next hour or so, Mr. McHeath himself came to the kitchen.

"She's asking for the boy," he said.

"Daniel?" Lottie asked.

He nodded. Mary Edith fetched her brother and they sent him to her chamber with a full glass of buttermilk. He didn't come back. In fact, he stayed with her the entire afternoon. Mary Edith did Daniel's chores, but she didn't mind.

Late that afternoon, not long before it was time to head home, Mary Edith stepped into the tavern. It had been a quiet day, but now the ogre, Ben John, was back with McGirth and a man named Matt Birch.

She stood as still as a block of ice, not wanting to hear any more of their business. She knew too much already. But the tavern keeper spotted her and waved her in.

"Empty these spittoons," he said.

Gathering the little brass barrels, she cursed her sharp hearing. "We lost Tarlton Brown because of Rufus!" she heard Matt Birch whisper. "I tell ya, I saw that fool with my own eyes talking with a no-good rebel all private-like down by Turkey Creek."

They stayed quiet while, with cold hands, Mary Edith slipped the spittoon from beneath their feet. What if they knew it was her who set their captive free? Once she crossed the room, McGirth spit on the floor and mumbled, "Rufus is done. Take care of it, Matt."

A shiver ran up her spine. She wrapped her arms around the stinking spittoons and ran them out the door.

⊕

At Kilkenny, Alden was once again beside his brother in the family burial ground. The nearby stream trickled into Turkey Creek. Two small graves of their lost brother and sister lay beneath the large oak next to their father, Thomas.

"So much has happened, Carlton. I still can't believe he's gone. I miss him so, especially now."

Clouds filled Carlton's eyes. "I didn't appreciate him like a son should. If only I could have another chance, I..." He choked back a sob.

Alden put his arm over his brother's shoulder. "He knows. I feel it in my soul, brother. He's with us still."

Carlton forced a smile. "You sound like Mama Juba now."

"Some of these more primitive people, I believe they are closer to the spirit world than we allow ourselves to be. For all our devotion to reason."

"Perhaps."

"And Mother...why is she buried so far from Father?" Alden looked at his brother. "I'm not criticizing, you understand. Just curious."

Carlton stiffened. "There are things I've never told you, Alden. I question whether I should share this with you now."

"Go on."

"After Father's sudden demise, you expressed suspicion about his manner of passing. I, too, had my doubts, but I swallowed them. It was something Mother said before you arrived."

"What did she say?"

"She said, 'I saved you.' That's how she put it. It makes my skin crawl even now."

Alden waited for his brother to continue.

"She said Father had told her that very night he wanted the two of us to share in the inheritance of Kilkenny. Then she said she saved me. I didn't want to believe she could do anything so vile, but she was cold as a dead fish." He looked his brother in the eye. "Truth knocked. When I didn't answer, it forced down the door. She killed him, Alden."

Alden's breath caught in his throat.

Carlton nodded toward his mother's grave. "I couldn't subject Father to an eternity beside her, but no one knows the real reason. Only you. I told the others she never liked darkness, so

I placed her in the sun." He turned to his brother. "Not as hot as where she is now, though."

The ache in his chest surprised Alden. He was sure he'd reconciled his feelings about his mother. "And the black drape over the cross?"

Carlton grinned. "She did despise that color."

They shared an awkward laugh.

Walking back to the Big House, a familiar lad on a small horse galloped up the lane.

"Mr. Alden!" he called. "Another message." Handing it to him, the boy said, "From a lady."

Taking it, he said, "Have you a coin for this fellow, Carlton? This is a profitable enterprise for you, son."

The boy pocketed Carlton's coin. "Sure is. Do you have an answer for me to deliver?"

Alden laughed. "I've yet to read this." He opened the note.

"Dearest Alden," it said, "My brother Tarlton has returned unharmed. Be sure you do the same! With the highest possible regards, Suzanne"

"No return note today."

After the boy rode off, Carlton said, "How about we take a ride over the farm? I can show you what I'm working on."

"Sure." For the first time in months, Alden felt at home.

They made their way to the barn, mounted their horses, and headed out. Once they reached the road, they shared a look that set them racing along the two-lane track. First one would lead, then the other by a nose. When they reached the curve that had always been their finishing line, it was Carlton who crossed first.

Alden congratulated him, and they both laughed. "You got lucky once again. Next time!"

As they walked toward the field of new indigo plants, he said, "You seem better, Carlton. I mean more relaxed. Happier."

His brother looked at him, his eyes glistening. "I'm going to be a father. Can you believe that?"

"I do. It often follows marriage. I'm pleased for us both. I'm to be an uncle!"

"I'd known I was to marry Rosabel, but to be honest, I didn't even understand what that meant. Some bird-witted ninny for me to bed, I figured." He snorted. "If I thought that much about it. But she's so much more." Feigning seriousness, he said, "This may surprise you, but I can engage in the art of priggery from time to time."

"You? Can't picture it."

Carlton raised his eyebrows. "Oh yes. The thing is, Rosabel loves me even so." They rode a few more paces. "When she disapproves, she lets me know in her restrained, but forthright manner." His eyes softened. "But she cares for me, Alden. Truly and without limitation. I didn't know a woman like that existed." He pulled Hector up and turned. "It makes all the difference."

Had his brother ever spoken to him in such intimate terms before? If so, Alden had no memory of it. Carlton gave all the credit to Rosabel, but it was something more. Their mother was gone, and a wall had been breached.

"I've met someone as well," Alden said. "From Brier's Creek not far from Burton's Ferry."

"Is that so?"

"A saucy little thing named Suzanne Brown. I plan to marry her when the time is right."

"How will you know when that is?"

A good question. Alden had no answer, so he shrugged. The two continued their tour, dismounting to inspect the cedar shingles that had been made.

"When the war is over," Carlton said. "I'll send a load to Charles Town. Hopefully a market for cedar will still exist."

"As long as termites like to eat, there'll be a market for cedar shingles." It was one type of lumber the pests avoided.

They climbed onto their horses and headed to the cow pens. Alden was anxious to see Geoffrey and the others there.

As they rode, Carlton cleared his throat. "When you're ready to start your family, I'd like you to consider returning to Kilkenny. Like Father wanted."

Surprised, Alden stared at his brother, but said nothing.

"Don't say no right away," Carlton continued. "Think about it. There's room for you and your bride in the Big House until you build your own home nearby."

"What would I do here?" he asked. Or anywhere, for that matter. It occurred to Alden he'd deserted his chosen career.

Carlton said, "I have Father's gift with animal husbandry, and I can grow things." He sighed. "I don't know people well. I listened to the wrong men about how to handle our servants, Alden. I realize that. But I don't have Father's knack for striking a chord, so to speak. I don't know how to say it, but there's another side to this life that requires a deftness with others, be they peers or underlings. I don't have it. You do."

Alden held up his hand. "Enough, Carlton. I know what you're trying to say. This war is far from over, despite recent British victories. We don't know what the future will bring. But that you've invited me home—for in my heart, Kilkenny is still my home—fills a void."

A void more vast than he'd realized. In what could be a calm before the storm, Alden decided to spend the next days at Kilkenny. At her first opportunity, Rosabel took him aside.

"I must say," Alden told her, "marriage to you has done wonders for Carlton."

"I love him, Alden. I know his faults, but I believe I can influence him to bring out his best."

Alden smiled. "I agree. What would you like to talk to me about?"

"Nan and her poor children. I have urged Carlton to bring them back to the fold, where they belong. But with this, he's been quite stubborn. I'm hoping you can speak to him. They're part of Kilkenny's family and they belong here."

"You give me too much credit. All my attempts to impact Carlton have come to naught."

"Yet, the Dillon family struggles. What have we to lose?"

Alden put his hand on her shoulder. "You're a tenderhearted woman. I'll do what I can."

Later, when Alden broached the subject, Carlton grew cold. "How do you expect me to look upon her contemptuous face day after day? I send Ketch almost daily to see to their needs. That will have to be enough." The subject was closed.

Chapter Thirty-seven

For the next two days, it became part of Daniel's tavern chores to spend time with Mrs. McHeath. The lady remained bedridden and mostly slept by day but wandered about at night. Mr. McHeath was beside himself with worry. He snapped at Lottie and Mary Edith for minor and even imagined flaws.

Mary Edith had seen neither hide nor hair of the woman herself since she'd brought her the broth. Walking home, she asked Daniel, "What's she like?"

The boy frowned. "She's puny looking, Mary Edith, her skin all white and pasty. Her hair is falling 'round her face, but she won't do nothing to fix it right." He picked up a stone and chucked it. "Sometimes, she starts hugging me and crying. I don't know what the dickens to do."

"Well, what happens?"

"I stand there and wait 'til she turns me loose."

"Lord A'mighty," Mary Edith said as they approached their hovel. Her mother was talking with their neighbor, Peggy Ogilvy, who looked upset.

"My girl knows about healing," Ma was saying. "We'll see what she thinks."

"My auntie is a-burning with fever," Peggy said, wringing her hands. "Ain't there something ya kin do for her?"

"Have you tried a wild onion poultice?" Mary Edith asked.

The woman scoffed. "This late in the summer?"

"The bulbs are on top of the plant now. I know where some are growing. Me and Daniel'll fetch 'em. And some white root, too," Mary Edith said. "Ma, she should drink white root tea."

"I'll get the cloth ready for the poultice," Ma said, "and set the water to boiling for the tea. Peggy, go on. Be with yer auntie. We'll bring the cures as fast as we can."

It warmed Mary Edith's heart to see her mother's usual spirit.

Peggy's eyes watered. "I'm mighty grateful for neighbors such as y'all with my man away. I never know when he'll be by." She hurried off.

"Always talking of her man," Ma mumbled, "but never says his name. I wonder if there even is a fella." She waved at her children. "Off with you two. No tarrying!"

White root plants were easy to find. "I'll get these," Mary Edith told her brother. "You go on and look for the onions. The little bulbs will be laying on the stalk in bunches. Holler when you find some."

Her brother ducked into the brush while she started digging out the roots. Insects buzzed around her head as she yanked the plant from the ground. Without much trouble, she wrenched the root from the stalk. Pulling up her apron to make a sling, she dropped the tuber inside, then uprooted two more. Better to have too many than not enough.

At the sound of a garbled scream, she shot up like an arrow. Daniel! Letting the roots fall to the ground, Mary Edith scrambled toward the outcry. About thirty yards away, she found him staring skyward with a look of horror.

At first, she was annoyed. The boy didn't seem hurt. Then, a rancid stench smacked her square in the face. She lifted her now-empty apron to cover her nose while following Daniel's gaze.

From a sturdy branch about a dozen feet above them hung a bloated, decaying body. The eyes were closed and the mouth gaped as flies flew in and out and around its head.

"Rufus," Mary Edith said aloud. She wasn't sure how she recognized him in such a state, but it was Tarlton Brown's guard, the one they claimed was a traitor.

Gagging, she turned to her brother. "Daniel?"

He peered at her with wide, haunted eyes. When she reached out to pet his head, he bolted, gasping and retching as he beat a path through the brush.

Mary Edith called his name and raced after him, but he was small and quick through the undergrowth. In no time, she lost him. Then a long, high-pitched scream turned her blood cold. Stumbling in her haste, she struggled to stay on her feet.

When she came to him, he'd collapsed in a hollowed-out tree trunk, under attack from a murderous swarm of wasps—and he was losing.

With no thought whatever, Mary Edith grabbed her brother's arm and dragged him with all her might from the yellow jackets' nest. The furious wasps did not back off. They chased both children through the thicket. When Daniel could run no more, she slung him over her shoulder and plowed on. The heat, the underbrush, and evil droning of their attackers threatened to undo Mary Edith. Only two words clanging in her head kept her going: Save Daniel!

As the last of them gave up, she set her brother down on the path. The sight of him took her breath. Countless welts spotted his ashen face, neck, and arms. His eyes were swollen shut. He struggled to get air past his puffed lips and bloated tongue. He fainted dead away. The pain must have been too much.

"Daniel," Mary Edith said, "don't die." Like Baby Eveleen.

Swooping him up like he was no more than a babe, she started back to her house. But his gasping breaths horrified her. She could not let him die.

I need Mama Juba, she thought, although Kilkenny was too far away. Lottie had healing ways almost as good. She'd take Daniel to the tavern. With no time to lose, she hauled the boy through the woods as fast as she could go.

"Sweet Jesus in heaven!" In one move, Lottie swept the table clean before taking the child from Mary Edith. She laid him on top. "Hang on, boy. Lottie's gonna make things right."

She threw Mary Edith a rag. "Fill the bucket with cool water from that there rain barrel. Then swab him down good. Don't stop 'til I tell ya."

Lottie grabbed a bundle of wild leeks from the rafters. "Mr. McHeath, yo stomach trouble gonna have to wait."

While Mary Edith wiped him down again and again, Lottie chopped the roots and fried them in a pan of grease. When it was done to suit her, she took it off the fire to cool. Once ready, she brushed Mary Edith aside and rubbed the salve into Daniel's chest.

"This gonna help you breathe again," she told him, as though he were awake to hear it. Pointing to a small bucket, she told Mary Edith, "Go on down to Turkey Creek for some red clay." She nodded toward the hearth. "Over there be the last of my tobacco, but we gonna use it to heal these bites."

Mary Edith grabbed the bucket and headed to the door but was stopped short by the sight of Mrs. McHeath still in her shift. Seeing Daniel on the table, she shoved Mary Edith aside and rushed to the lad's side.

"Lord, have mercy! Lottie, this is no place for the boy in this condition. Bring him to my room. I'll go ahead to prepare a pallet for him. Also, he'll need comfrey tea for this swelling." She turned and spotted Mary Edith. "Get that clay as you were told. Now!"

The sun was lowering in the sky as she filled half the bucket with clay. Upon her return, Lottie was working on the tea Mrs. McHeath had called for. Following the cook's directions, Mary Edith mixed the tobacco into the clay.

"Now," Lottie said, "take that paste up to Mrs. McHeath's chamber and spread some on ev'ry one of that boy's bites. Use plenty now. And Mar' Edith—" She put her hand on the girl's head. "Use the rest for y'own bites."

Mary Edith looked at her arms and legs. She was dumbfounded to find herself speckled with red welts. She had no memory of the wasps stinging her.

Climbing the stairs to the lady's chamber, her shoulders drooped at the sight of Mr. McHeath standing at the top. But his expression was not the bitter one she was used to; his eyes were warm. Entering the room, she saw why. Daniel was lying on a soft straw pallet beside Mrs. McHeath's bed. Next to him was the lady herself, fully dressed. She put Mary Edith in mind of her old self, the "Mistress of the Tavern."

"Bring that poultice here," she told Mary Edith.

Daniel wasn't breathing easy, but he was better. His face was still red and swollen out of shape, but he was calm. Mary Edith helped the lady cover the welts with the tobacco and clay paste. She, too, began to calm down. Her brother was going to live.

"Mary Edith." Mrs. McHeath's tone put the girl on guard. "Where's your mama?"

Every one of her muscles grew taut. She remembered the woman's disdain for her mother and knew to choose her words well. "She's caring for a sick friend."

336 | M. B. GIBSON

Who, she realized, she'd completely forgotten. But it couldn't be helped.

"I see." The woman looked at her husband and rolled her eyes like Mary Edith wasn't in the room. "John, we can best help Nan by keeping Daniel here at the tavern until he recovers. It's the Christian thing to do. As the Good Book says, 'And whoso shall receive one such little child in my name receiveth me.'"

"Of course, Catherine." He wore the most oily smile Mary Edith had ever seen.

Yet, she was glad to hear the words herself. Mrs. McHeath's sudden recovery seemed like one of those miracles Lottie had told her about. More important, between Lottie and Mrs. McHeath, Daniel would be well-tended. Memories of Baby crowded her mind. If they lost Daniel, too, under her care— well, she couldn't bear to think on it.

Mrs. McHeath interrupted her thoughts. "Go to the kitchen, girl, and bring back the comfrey tea. It's as good for easing pain as it is for swelling."

Once Mary Edith reached the kitchen, Lottie said, "It's about done." She set out two cups.

"He's breathing easy now," Mary Edith told her. "We covered him up good with your poultice."

Lottie stopped what she was doing and looked her in the eye. "How come you ain't put none on yo bites? I told ya to use some on yoself."

"Mrs. McHeath wants to save it. Daniel might need it later."

Lottie clamped her lips together as she ladled tea into the cups. "That woman give all the love to one chil' and forget about t'other."

"What?"

"I ain't said nothin'. Take this tea to yo brother. Then come back and drink this other cup. We'll put plain ol' mud on yo bites. That'll help some."

Daniel was awake when she returned, but her relief didn't last long. Worry gnawed at her. What they'd done to Rufus was what awaited her if they knew she'd let Tarlton Brown loose. She'd saved one man's life, but another got hanged for it. Would they string her and Daniel up if they learned she knew of the murder?

When Mrs. McHeath left the room to speak to her husband in private, Mary Edith jumped at the chance to talk to him. "You gonna be fine, Daniel."

"Yeah." His tongue and lips were still swollen, so speaking was difficult.

"Have you talked to Mrs. McHeath?"

"She talk. Told me hush."

Mary Edith could see why. It looked like it hurt bad, and she could barely understand him, anyway. "She's right. Don't talk now. But when you do, be careful what you say."

He nodded, so she went on. "Don't say nothing about what we seen in that old tree. None of it. Understand?"

Daniel stared so hard into her eyes, she was afraid the reminder of Rufus's rotting body was too much. Then he pushed the words out of his mouth. "I know."

⊕

Nan sat on the stump poking her outdoor fire. The pot with which she'd brew the white root tea waited on the children's return. She'd also laid out the cloth for the onion poultice and a mallet to smash the little bulbs. They shouldn't be much longer.

Her mind wandered. Poor Peggy. Without Aunt Betsy, she'd have no one. The ache of loneliness returned to Nan's bones. It helped to think of others rather than herself, but the agony of her own loss always returned.

She tried to think of happier days growing up with her mother. With only Uncle Nolan nearby, her family was small, but she and Ma were close. Now, as a mother herself, she wondered how Ma had kept her wits about her as often as she had. When neighbors mocked them as a trollop and her bastard child, Eveleen held her head up and dragged her away. Nan was forbidden to return the taunts, which angered her so. Why should she have to keep mum when others were free with their cruelty?

But Ma would say, "A kind word never broke anyone's mouth, Nan."

"'Tis not their mouths I want to break," she'd respond, only to get a swat on the back of her head. Ma would frown, but her eyes were laughing.

Nan listened to the songbirds and crows in the surrounding woods. She stirred the fire with a stick. The coals were about perfect. The children needed to hurry along.

How she missed her mother's calm wisdom during times like these. Nan had inherited none of it. She had always craved revenge. If she couldn't make people change, she could at least make them pay for their wickedness.

Nan laughed to herself. She'd started sneaking out at night, settling scores with unsuspecting neighbors under cover of darkness. That was not quite true. They suspected her but could prove nothing. It was then her mother's eyes quit laughing.

Now, her youthful pranks seemed all the more foolish. Who must pay for the deaths of her hard-working son, Nolan, growing so straight and tall? How he'd admired his Da! And Baby, always finding a laugh in every situation. Who was Nan to see about them?

She knew who to blame for Joe, but her attack on Carlton only led to their plight. Her hollow heart ached in her chest. Could she ever be happy again?

Her ma, Eveleen's voice sounded clear as a bell in her head. "Patience is the poultice for all wounds."

"No!" she called aloud. "No amount of patience can heal me."

She imagined her ever-gentle mother shaking her head. "Ye've two children among the living who cherish ye. Think on them."

Once again, Ma managed to shame her from across the ocean and within the grave. She must not lose sight of her remaining blessings in Mary Edith and Daniel.

Where were those two? They'd been gone far too long.

Nan's hands and feet grew cold. It was not like Mary Edith to be trifling, especially with Aunt Betsy's life at stake. If Nan found they'd been dawdling, there'd be the devil to pay. She got up to search for them, plowing through the underbrush. When had it become so difficult to make her way through the thicket?

She knew where white root grew and suspected Mary Edith had headed there. When she got to the area, her stomach twisted at the sight of harvested roots strewn on the ground. Something happened. Nan called out their names in a tone even she heard as shrill.

She ran in one direction, then the next, her heartbeat throbbing in her ear. Then the sickly-sweet odor of death reached her nostrils. She forced her feet to carry her toward the stench, whimpers escaping her throat.

Lord, don't let them be kilt. Take me, but let me babies live.

At the humming of flies, Nan forced her head upward. In a tree, she saw a swollen, green-tinged corpse that was not one of her children. She dropped to her knees and struggled to catch her breath. But her relief was short-lived. Did Mary Edith and Daniel stumble upon this horrifying sight? Did they flee in panic?

A more distressing thought occurred to her. Did this man's killers take them and—do what? Nan ran throughout the woods, looking for any sign of where someone, anyone had been. She found broken twigs and followed that track, only to fear she'd strayed off in the wrong direction. She tried several paths, all in vain.

Perhaps they were home, wondering where she'd gone. She made her way to their house, but they were nowhere in sight. Not finding her there, did they go to Peggy's house?

Panting, she approached Peggy's door. "Mary Edith ... Daniel ... are they here?"

Her friend's face twisted in anger. "Ain't no one here, Nan. Not a-one of ya come by with all your talk of remedies for Aunt Betsy. She died, ya lowdown hussy!"

Nan shoved Peggy, causing her to stumble backward. "Me children are gone. There's a dead body hung from a tree not far from here and me babies are missing! To hell with ye!"

The sinking sun brought a veil of darkness. What'll I do? Nan asked herself as she ran from Peggy's porch. While she'd always found comfort in the night, how would she find them with no clue where to turn?

The tavern! Would they have gone there? Nan didn't know, but at least the McHeaths might be of some help. She made her way to Red Hill through the lengthening shadows.

As she approached the front steps, her jaw dropped at the sight of Mary Edith walking from behind the inn. She ran to her. "Mary Edith! Thank you, dear Jesus. Are you hurt? Where's Daniel?"

Her daughter hung her head. "I'm sorry. He fell in a wasps' nest. He's all swelled up. He can't hardly talk." Her chin quivered. "He wasn't breathing right, Ma. I...I didn't know what to do. Lottie helped him." She blinked her eyes. "He's gonna live."

Nan held her daughter tight. "I was scared. So very afraid."

"I know," Mary Edith said. "I couldn't let Daniel die, too."

"Too?"

"The way I left Baby to die."

"Mary Edith, stop talking foolishness. Where's me boy? I want to see me son."

The tavern keeper came to the front door. "Mrs. Dillon? Your boy is upstairs in my wife's chamber. She's offered to keep him here until he's more stable. Come inside. I'll take you to him."

Nan stepped through the door and followed McHeath toward his staircase. She was stunned to hear a woman's harsh voice at the top of the stairs.

"She can't come up here. These are our private chambers."

The tavern keeper spoke softly. "Catherine, she's his mother. She wants to see Daniel."

The woman stood on the top step holding clenched fists against her mouth. "Come back tomorrow. Better yet, we'll send word when you can come."

Mr. McHeath grabbed a candle and holder from one of the Great Room's tables and lit it. When he climbed the stairs, the flickering flame illuminated the tavern mistress' features.

Nan tensed at the woman's eyes, so like those of her father, Sir Richard Lynche, when he'd go raving mad. She looked again, and Mrs. McHeath seemed fine. Nan took a deep breath. Her mind was running wild.

"Please, madam, I'm grateful for all ye've done for me boy. I only want to see him, alive and well."

Without a word, Mrs. McHeath walked away. The tavern keeper waved Nan and Mary Edith up.

"I don't know what happened to me children, Mr. McHeath. But there's a dead man hanging from a tree near me house. Danger is about."

Mary Edith gasped. The man's jaw tightened, but he said nothing.

When they entered the room, his wife stood beside Daniel with her arms clenched across her chest. Nan's throat caught at her son's puffed eyes and lips. She knelt beside him and petted his head.

"Daniel, yer ma's here. Are ye awake?"

He opened his eyes as best he could. "Ma?"

"Ye need rest, son. Do what this lady and Lottie tell ye. I need me little man home."

A tear squeezed from his eye. "Don't go."

"Ah, I must. I promise I'll be back tomorrow, sweet boy."

He couldn't move too well, but he shook his head. "Take me home."

"Daniel," Mrs. McHeath said, "don't you want to stay with me? You know you'll be loved here."

Heat flashed across Nan's face. "He's loved at home."

Mr. McHeath jumped in. "Of course, he is. Come back in the morning. We'll watch him like he's our own."

Nan kissed Daniel's brow. "Sleep well. I'll be back before ye know it." She stood, fighting a rising rage. "I appreciate all yer doing but make no mistake. I'll take me son home, likely tomorrow. Come, Mary Edith."

She held her head high as her mother had so many years ago and strode from the tavern.

Chapter Thirty-eight

Joe pulled his cart up to the water's edge. He took a deep breath. Toby Creek. Though he only need ford the shallow stream to be on Kilkenny once again, he wavered between joy and dread. To see his children's fresh faces was almost a wonder to him now. His comely wife who'd filled his dreams was less than a mile away.

Yet it was Nan who caused him to hesitate. If she rejected him, his heart would be ground to powder. There was also the question of Carlton. Would he throw them off his land when Joe turned up alive? He hardly cared about that now.

Have courage, he told himself and forged ahead toward the plantation's quarters. As he rolled his rickety cart across the pastureland, he became uneasy at the sight of a lone mounted figure outlined in the dusk. It was unusual for anyone to work this time of day.

The figure rode toward him at a steady clip. To his relief, Geoffrey, the cow pen manager, pulled up beside him with a rifle tucked under his arm.

"I'm a friend, Geoffrey. At least, I hope so."

The old slave leapt from his horse. "Joe Dillon? Could it be you, come back from the dead? Glory be!" He ran over and threw his arms around Joe, who remained in the cart. "A miracle, sure 'nough."

He stepped back, his hand clamped to his forehead. "Ya done lost a leg, I see. No matter. You alive!"

Joe felt some of his tension melt away. "Yer a fine sight, I'll tell ye. I'm glad to be home if yer welcome is any sign."

Geoffrey cocked his head to one side. "Ain't nothin' the same. First, Nan ain't here no mo'. Once she hear you dead, she lost her mind and set on Carlton right bad, they say. He didn't whip her that time, just put her down near White Oak Springs in a little shack."

Joe's chest tightened. "What shack?"

"One me and the boys put up. I'll take ya there. I's s'posed to be watchin' for poachers, but it been quiet." He climbed on-to his horse and led the way across the field, telling Joe all that had happened.

His old friend was holding back, though. Joe could feel it. He wanted to press Geoffrey, but fear stopped him. He learned that bastard of an overseer was dead. Carlton had married and would have a child by and by. Ketch took over and was doing a damn good job, Geoffrey told him.

Soon through the shadowy trees, Joe saw the slave ceme-tery. Geoffrey dummied up so quick, Joe knew the hidden in-formation lay there. He pulled up on the mule's reins. "What is it?"

Geoffrey stopped and swallowed. "I didn't wanta be the one to tell ya. The fever come, Joe. It took two of yo chillun. They be over here with us."

Joe followed Geoffrey to the graveyard. This outstripped his greatest fears. Two of his treasures, gone. Why had he ever left? The pain was brutal.

As they approached, he saw two mounds covered with sprigs of grass and offerings left by the others. He grabbed his crutch from the back of the wagon and climbed down. He should ask who he lost, but, in a way, it seemed pointless. No matter who, the anguish would be the same.

"It's Nolan, Joe," Geoffrey said, standing beside him. "And Baby."

He slunk to the ground. "My poor, wee babes. With their father off on a fool's errand. I'm so sorry, my son. My sweet Baby."

He remembered the morning he left. "What if I never see you again?" Baby had asked. He promised she'd never be rid of him. Little did he know it was she who would leave. He'd suffered much sadness in his life, but this agony was crushing.

Geoffrey placed his hand on Joe's shoulder. "We gots to leave. It'll be my hide if I miss one of them poachers."

Joe pushed himself up with his crutch and returned to the cart. "Let's go."

They traveled until the hovel came into view. "That be the one. I best head back to the cow pen," Geoffrey said. "God bless ya, Joe. You a sight for my poor eyes." With that, he rode away.

Joe sat in his wagon for several minutes, watching the house. His heart fluttered at the sight of Mary Edith walking outside and toward the woods. He was home.

✢

Back in their cabin, Ma told Mary Edith that Aunt Betsy had died. "Peggy's addled. She blamed us for not bringing the remedies, but they'd have done her aunt no good so close to the grave."

Mary Edith agreed. "Does she have anyone to help lay Aunt Betsy out? Get her ready to be buried?"

Ma seemed weary. "I don't know. We must see to our own troubles before helping Peggy with hers."

"I'd better have a wee before it's too dark," Mary Edith said. She stepped outside. The night noises were comforting after such a horrible day.

After finishing her business, she headed back to their door. She balked at a rustling in the trees. Heart thumping, she moved faster.

"Are ye well, lass?"

She froze, not daring to breathe. A voice from the brush was eerily familiar. But to hear it, she must be among the dead. "Da," she whispered. "What do you want of me?"

"I ain't no ghost. I'm in the flesh." Her father stepped into the clearing, his face gaunt, his eyes sad and a little fearful. She saw he was leaning on a crude crutch. Empty breeches hung where his leg had been. Her brain was muddled. What she was seeing couldn't be real.

Did ghosts lie? Though afraid, Mary Edith inched toward him. He seemed in solid form, but she was so tired. Her mind could be playing tricks on her. She gazed at him and realized she didn't care. If he was a ghost, let her be with his spirit. Casting caution to the winds, she ran to her father and flung her arms around his lean waist. Recognizing he was flesh and blood, a squeal escaped her lips. She would never let him go.

He laughed the way she remembered, only softer. "Careful, lass. Ye'll knock yer old man on his rump."

Her head against his chest, his heartbeat was more beautiful than any music. "They told us you were dead."

"I'm a tough old Irishman." He removed her hands from his waist. "Darlin', I heard about Nolan and Baby. How is yer ma? And Daniel? Are they inside?"

At the same moment, her mother stood in the doorway. "Mary Edith! Where are ye? I'm all a-dither as it is."

"Nan. As beautiful as ever." Her father hobbled to Ma as fast as his crutch would take him.

"Joe?" Her mother fell against the door jamb. "It can't be possible."

Mary Edith ran past Da to her mother's side. "He didn't die. It was all a mistake. He's here." Her own mind struggled to believe it.

Her father reached them, dropped his crutch, and swept Ma into his arms. So much crying! All Mary Edith's feelings jumbled together. Wonder, relief, joy. But, strangely, also grief over all they'd been through.

Her father asked Ma, "Are ye speaking to me yet?"

"Ye bloody bastard," Ma said. "I guess I'll forgive ye." She pulled away and looked him up and down.

The fear in Da's eyes grew. "I'm ashamed to tell ye, Nan. Truth is, I feared coming back to ye like this. A beautiful woman like yerself, so full of spirit, needs a strapping man to care for her."

Ma looked Da in his eyes. "I didn't fall in love with yer right leg, ye old fool!"

Da exploded with laughter, stumbled back, and fell on his buttocks. Ma grabbed her father's hand, pulled him up, and led him into the cabin. Once inside, Mary Edith turned away while they kissed for a very long time.

"Is little Daniel asleep?" Da asked, looking around.

"He's been stung up bad, Joe, after falling into a nest of yellow jackets," Ma said. "The McHeaths and their slave are nursing him at the tavern. 'Til tomorrow, at least."

Da frowned. "I've heard of bad goings-on at the tavern. Are ye sure he's safe?"

Shouting from outside the house interrupted them. "Nan! Come out here. I need to talk to ya."

Peggy.

Hoping to give her parents some peace, Mary Edith rushed outside. "We're real sorry 'bout Aunt Betsy."

Mary Edith barely had the words out of her mouth when she saw one of Ben John's mob, Matt Birch, sitting beside Peggy on a horse-drawn cart.

"So, she found ya," Peggy said. "Daniel, too?"

Mary Edith's mind was a jumble. There sat the man McGirth had sent to take care of Rufus. Did he mean for Matt to hang the scraggly guard?

"What ya gawking at?" Peggy asked. "My man is back. That's what I come to tell your ma. He's helping me with Aunt Betsy. Where's Nan?"

"Inside," Mary Edith mumbled. "My father's alive, Peggy. He wasn't never dead after all."

"Well, heavens above! What ya think of that, Matt?"

Eyes narrowed, Matt grunted.

"He just got back." Mary Edith nodded toward the cabin. "They need time alone. And Daniel ain't doing well. Ma will stop by your place tomorrow."

"Let's go," Matt Birch said.

"Tell her I come by and what I told ya," Peggy said as the wagon rolled away.

Mary Edith waved, a queasy feeling in her stomach.

◈

Upon awakening, Alden felt it immediately. The mood at Kilkenny had shifted. Becca hummed as she passed him on the staircase, and Old Wilbur stood a bit taller. Could the loss—dare he say riddance—of his mother have lifted spirits to this extent?

When he sat at the breakfast table, he noted Ruth's bright eyes as she served his porridge. "Something's happened, hasn't it?"

The cook broke into a wide smile. "Ain't ya heard? Joe Dillon done returned from the dead, Mr. Alden." A tear rolled down her cheek. "Praise the Lawd!"

He was stunned. Of course, they'd all assumed he was killed in the skirmish near the Santee River, but no one had witnessed his death. "Have you seen him?"

"Not me. Geoffrey seen him in the pasture last evenin' and took him to where Nan stay. He say Joe just got one leg."

That made more sense. Joe had been wounded, not killed.

Carlton came in and sat across the table. Ruth set his steaming bowl before him.

Alden said, "Joe Dillon is alive. He's lost a leg, but he lives." Even as the words left his mouth, they seemed fanciful.

Ruth raised her hands in the air. "Ki! It's a miracle, Master Carlton." Wiping her eyes with her apron, she darted back to the kitchen.

Carlton blanched, then stared into his porridge. "Thank God," he whispered.

"I'm going to see him." Alden stood. "Come with me, brother."

"I can't."

Alden watched him for a moment. His brother never lifted his head, so he left the house.

✦

Mary Edith woke at the break of day. She spun in her pallet to be sure the impossible had happened. It had. Da was alive and lay beside her mother. Her heart and brain couldn't take it in. He was awake, whispering to Ma as he petted her rust-colored hair.

"Hush now, old man," Ma said. "Ye need yer rest."

Da chuckled. "Don't stifle me. I've a lot of talking to catch up on."

Her mother rose and stood by the door. The glow on her face warmed Mary Edith from head to toe. Candles seemed to flicker behind her eyes, the most beautiful thing Mary Edith had ever seen.

The sun was well above the horizon when, with her mother, Mary Edith led Da through the woods to McHeath's Tavern. She was surprised how well he could hobble on one leg.

"Daniel may not be ready to come back," she was telling her father. "Them wasps swelled up his face so bad, his eyes are no more than slits. His lips are two fat pillows under his nose. He couldn't hardly breathe, Da."

"He looked bad, Joe," Ma said. "The McHeath's slave knows the healing ways, but if he's able, I want him with us."

Da sighed. "We'll see what we see, then do what's best for our boy."

As they reached the inn's clearing, Mary Edith sensed something wasn't right. The stillness of a graveyard hung over the place.

"Do ye think they're asleep this time of day?" Ma asked.

"Let's go to the kitchen. Lottie'll know." Mary Edith ran to the back of the tavern, but as she rounded the corner, her blood turned cold. No smoke rose from the chimney. No pots rattled. No aroma of baking bread floated through the air. The door hung open.

Her parents walked up behind her. "How could this be?" she asked them. "Looks like they up and left." It made no sense.

Da ran into the tavern through the back door while Mary Edith flew to the stables. No wagon. The two horses and their gear, gone.

Where would they go? Did they take Daniel or was he lying upstairs all alone? With legs like lead, she followed Ma and Da into the tavern. She shouted her brother's name.

"He's not here, Mary Edith," Da called from the second floor. He hobbled down the stairs with Ma right behind, reaching out with help he didn't need.

"Their clothes are gone," Ma said. "Bedding, too. What'll we do, Joe? Our son's been stolen."

Da spoke in a whisper. "Would they hurt him?"

"Mrs. McHeath dotes on him," Mary Edith said. "And Mr. McHeath dotes on her."

She remembered the cruel words about Ma the woman spoke to the priest, her craving for her own child. If she begged her husband to run off so she could keep Daniel for herself, would he do it?

Mary Edith's heart sank. He would.

✚

When Alden arrived, he was bewildered to find the Dillon cabin deserted. He dismounted and looked around. It was clear they hadn't been gone long. Fresh tracks led toward White Oak Springs.

He climbed astride Enbarr and headed that way. When no one was at the springs, he remembered the children worked for McHeath and rode to the drinkery. Out front, he found Joe looking dejected while Nan spouted off, waving her arms. She stopped at his approach and ran toward him.

"Mr. Alden, they got me boy!"

He leapt from his horse. "What?"

Joe shuffled over with his crutch, his face pained. "The McHeaths were watching over Daniel, but they've cut and run. Who knows how long they've been gone?"

Nan's strident voice caused his muscles to tighten. "They stole me child! What are we to do?"

Mary Edith rounded the tavern from the back. "I found something in the kitchen."

They followed her to the outbuilding. Once inside, Mary Edith pointed to the table in the middle of the room. "There's some kind of scrawl on here. Like writing."

Charcoal marks had been scratched into the wood. "Can you read, Mary Edith?" Alden asked.

The girl shook her head.

"That's strange. This seems to be written to you." He read the message aloud, allowing for poor spelling. "Mary Edith, gone to Florida. Good-bye old friend. Lottie." He looked at the girl. "Who's Lottie?"

Mary Edith chewed her lip. "Their slave. Mrs. McHeath was teaching her in secret to read and write. She only wanted to send word to her boy on the Jarrett Plantation she was well. She meant no harm."

"Harm?" Alden said. "I'd like to kiss her. Now we've some idea which way to go. Joe, if I get you a horse, are you up for the journey? You still look a bit puny."

Joe swelled his chest. "The entire British army couldn't stop me."

Alden nodded. After a quick look around, he suggested to Nan and Mary Edith they remove as much of the merchandise McHeath had left behind as they could. "The rebel cause can benefit from his hasty departure. At least we can keep the liquor out of Ben John's hands."

"Use the mule and wagon I rode home in," Joe said. "Move it all to our place 'til we find a better spot."

Mary Edith nodded. "I been thinking. Mrs. McHeath's blood near curdled when this man name of McGirth called Mr.

McHeath a traitor. That's what brought on her melancholy. You think that run them off?"

"Reason enough to get clear of this place," Alden said. "McGirth is a cruel and dangerous man."

Alden bolted to Kilkenny to borrow a horse for Joe. They would ride to Brier's Creek and enlist the help of Tarlton and Bartlett Brown, as well as any other rebels they could muster. He was furious. How dare they kidnap a helpless child! God be his witness, they'd bring that boy back.

Upon arrival at Kilkenny's stables, Alden told Amos to prepare a swift horse for Joe Dillon to ride. No time must be lost.

✦

Carlton was drinking tea in the library when boots pounded across the veranda and into the hall. He leapt from his seat and ran out to find Alden, highly agitated. Rosabel was hastening down the staircase.

"Step carefully," he warned her before turning to his brother.

"Joe is back, as we were told," Alden said. "He's one-legged, but otherwise healthy. The McHeaths have disappeared overnight, Carlton. And they've taken little Daniel with them."

Carlton's mouth dropped. "Damnation! What in blazes is going on?"

Rosabel's hand flew to her mouth.

"I don't know. Joe and I are going after them. I've asked Amos to ready one of your horses for him, with your permission."

"Of course! Go."

Alden turned on his heel and flew to the stables.

Still trying to take it all in, Carlton turned to his wife. "The McHeaths gone? In the dead of night?"

"And stealing a sweet boy from his mother as they go." Rosabel's face burned bright red.

"It's an outrage." He pointed to the settee. "Sit down, my dear. You'll become overwrought."

"I'm not a child, Carlton." She sat, dabbing her eyes with a handkerchief. "The best day of Nan's life so quickly turned to disaster."

Out the window, he watched Alden ride off, leading one of his mares. Joe had somehow survived. Carlton had spent the morning thanking the Almighty for the wonder of it. And now the Dillons's little boy snatched away? This was beyond the pale.

"Rosabel, I'm going with Alden."

Her head snapped up. "Yes, Carlton. We must do all we can. Just promise you'll return unharmed."

"What I promise is not to give up until we get Daniel back."

Rosabel stood and kissed him with a passion that spilled into his own heart.

Chapter Thirty-nine

After Carlton galloped off on Hector, Rosabel sent for Amos.

"I'm sure you've heard that little Daniel has been stolen from his mother. Carlton has joined the men in the rescue. I will go to Nan's cabin and offer my support."

Amos removed his hat and lowered his head. "I don't know 'bout that, miss. I's sure Master Carlton want you here, safe 'n sound."

Rosabel sat up straighter. "I have made my wishes known, Amos. I expect you to obey."

Amos wagged his head back and forth. "Yas'm."

When he pulled the wagon in front of the house, she stepped outside. As usual, Amos's flintlock rifle lay in the cart's bed. "Amos, bring an extra gun."

"Miss Rosabel, I can't shoot but one at the time."

"We don't know what we'll find. Bring one for me."

A smile crept onto the servant's face. "These here rifles too heavy for a lady like you."

"I've not grown up in some fairytale tower. I'm the only child of a frontiersman, living where danger comes in the form of men, animals, and slithering snakes. I can handle a rifle, I assure you."

Amos sighed. "Yas'm."

Once they reached Nan's place, no one was about. Despite Amos's irritation, Rosabel insisted they continue to the tavern.

There, she found Nan and Mary Edith rolling a keg to an unsteady cart.

"Place those heavy items in our wagon," Rosabel called out. "Amos will help you."

"Miss Rosabel, what're ye doing here? 'Tis not safe for the likes of ye," Nan said.

"Fiddlesticks!" she called out. "I'll not be lifting any barrels, but I can still be of help." She looked around. "Where do you plan to move these items?"

"Joe said to hide them in our cabin," Nan said.

"They're rather large and difficult to hide." Rosabel shook her head. "I'm skeptical. Word must be out about the McHeaths's disgraceful midnight flight. Your cabin will be vulnerable to thieves. Or shall I say, fellow plunderers. I don't know how well the four of us can ward them off."

Nan and Mary Edith looked at each other.

Mary Edith said, "I know a good hiding place." She described her private spot spread beneath the large oak tree. "We'd have to roll these barrels and other stuff through the thicket, then cover our tracks."

"Amos, let Mary Edith show you this spot."

Once they crawled out of the underbrush, Amos said, "This here place be good as any. If we's careful 'nough, won't no one find this stuff."

Rosabel nodded. In the August heat, the others began the exhausting work of transferring the items of value. They took a variety of pathways to the clearing, hoping to mask their scheme.

Once finished, Rosabel directed Amos and Nan to put the carts and animals in the stables. "Should anyone choose to come by," she said.

Within a short time, that precaution proved prudent. At the sound of neighing horses, all four hid in the barn behind the large wagon. Rosabel lifted her gun and nodded to Amos to do the same.

Heavy boots could be heard clumping around the tavern. After what seemed like an hour, they heard two voices nearer the barn.

"You was right," one said. "McHeath musta lit outa here like a scalded dog."

Mary Edith's eyes grew round. "Frank Watkins," she whispered.

"After I seen Rufus swinging from that oak, I knowed they wasn't staying long. McHeath's a coward at heart."

Mary Edith mouthed the name Lester.

"That musta been a sight," said Frank's voice. "Rufus was right ugly before they strung 'im up." They both laughed.

"Ya know," said Lester, "McHeath would skin a flea for its hide, but I'll be durned if I kin figure how he hauled all that likker off with 'im." He paused. "Think it coulda been that inn girl and her maw. Weren't nobody at their place."

The men grew quiet. The four in the stables barely breathed. Had they left?

"Wait," Rosabel heard Frank say. "You check the barn?"

"You smart!" Lester said. "Must be why your head so big."

Rosabel tensed as she steadied her gun across the edge of the wagon. Amos did the same. The barn door screeched as it inched open. Once the outlines of the men became clear, Rosabel squeezed the trigger. The blast rang in her ears.

Both men dropped to the ground. "What the hell?" one called out.

The other climbed to his knees. "Pert near blew my ear off!"

"You'd best be on your way," Rosabel called out. "The next one'll go between the eyes."

"That a woman?" the first one said. "Lester, you was 'bout kilt by a woman."

"Damned right," Rosabel said. She snatched the rifle from Amos. "Unless you get moving, Frank, the next shot will hit between your legs."

Both men looked like giant bugs as they scrambled from the stables. Those inside the barn went to the door to watch them run.

"Miss Rosabel, you some good shot," Amos said.

She smiled. "I don't think they'll be back. That's not to say there won't be others. Now that we've hidden the goods, I'd best go home." Cocking her head, she considered Nan and her daughter. "You should come with me. If your hut is too dangerous for contraband, it's too dangerous for you."

Nan tensed. "I'll not cross Master Carlton after he's helped bring me son back."

"I'll handle Master Carlton," Rosabel said, hoping she sounded more confident than she felt.

"I appreciate yer kindness, miss." Nan swallowed. "It may seem foolish to ye, but when they bring Daniel back, God willing, they'll come through here first. I want to be here when they do. Me and Mary Edith will stay upstairs." She took her daughter's hand. "We'll be well."

Rosabel sighed, then handed Amos the gun. "After Amos takes me home, I'll send him back. He can stay with you." She looked to her driver.

He smiled. "I's a right good shot myself."

Nan took her hand. "Yer a fine woman. Mr. Carlton is a lucky fellow."

Rosabel smiled. In her heart, she agreed.

✦

Alden and Joe flew to Brier's Creek. Alden was in awe of the uncommon determination, even desperation with which Joe rode, affliction be damned.

In the two days he'd been gone, Tarlton and Bartlett Brown had built a crude shelter near the remains of their home. The brothers were making repairs to their corral as the two approached.

Joe dismounted to the astonishment of both Tarlton and Bartlett. He took his crutch from where he'd tucked it in his waist belt and walked over to the men. Alden joined them.

"We thought you were dead," Bartlett said. "We'd never have ridden off if we'd known you were still alive."

Joe raised his eyebrows. "I know that, boys. Me story is long and complicated, but, right now, me son is in danger."

Alden explained their crisis. "We've no idea when the McHeaths left, or how much of an advantage they have on us. They're somewhere in Georgia, I reckon. Are any of the fellows around?"

Wasting no time, Bartlett jumped on his horse to round up who he could.

Tarlton placed his hand on Joe's shoulder. "I met your daughter. Mary Edith, I believe."

"Where?" Alden asked.

"I was captured by McGirth and Ben John. They had me sure enough, and I was destined for the hanging tree. But the fools couldn't resist a celebration compliments of John McHeath."

"So ye saw her at the inn," Joe said.

Tarlton's face grew serious. "I did more than see her. While those murdering fiends were soused inside the tavern, she risked her life to untie my legs and release my horse. How did she even do that? I've never seen anything like it, Joe. She saved my life."

Alden was dumb-stricken. He'd known Mary Edith since her birth, but never guessed she was made of sterner stuff.

Joe's face showed a mixture of pride and fear. "She done good, then." He hobbled away, and, with his back to them, pulled out a handkerchief to blow his nose.

At the sound of horse's hooves, Alden looked up to see how much help Bartlett had found. His heart stopped. It was Carlton astride Hector, with a rifle and sword in his scabbard and a cartridge box strapped across his chest. He rode to Joe Dillon.

"They've got your boy," he said, "I'm ready."

Joe seemed at a loss for words. He covered his eyes with one of his chapped hands. In little more than a whisper, he said, "Thank ye."

Carlton then walked Hector to Alden and Tarlton. "I'm assuming you could use an extra gun."

Alden said, "This is my big brother, Carlton de Barnefort."

Tarlton extended his hand. "Glad to have you."

Within the hour, six more men arrived, including Adam and Jamie Wood, George Collins, and Obie Heape.

"Which way we heading out?" Obie asked. "Word is McGirth's marauding on the Georgia side of the river. No idea where or how many he's got with him."

Noticing Joe stiffen, Alden said, "If you want to chase down McGirth, no one can fault you, but Joe's boy's in a bad way. We need to see to him now."

"As thirsty as I am for vengeance against McGirth, today I'll get greater satisfaction returning this lad to his family," Tarlton said. "My only question is, should we cross the river at Summerlin's Ferry or Burton's?"

"The McHeaths have a good-sized wagon," Alden said, "with four people in it and likely all the supplies it can hold. My guess is Burton's. The barge is bigger."

"Let's go," Tarlton Brown called, and they set off.

◆

Joe was humbled that ten of his brothers were risking their skins for Daniel and, in a sense, for him. That Carlton chose to ride with them was the greatest shock of his life, but a welcome one.

Not long after noon, they reached Burton's Ferry. Old Tom and his boy had to cross from the Georgia side to pick them up. Joe watched Carlton pull out his money bag and pay the man for their crossing.

His emotions threatened to get the better of him, but he put Daniel foremost in his mind. He'd ponder these other things later. Leaning on the ferry's rail, he listened to the water lap against the sides of the barge. The mumblings of the other men swirled around him, but he could hardly focus on their words.

He did hear Tarlton asked the ferryman, "You seen a wagon come 'cross here with a woman, slave girl, and sick boy in the back?"

Joe turned to hear the answer and saw the man's eyes brighten. "Sure did. I was dead asleep when young Tommy here woke me up. The sun was hardly up and here this fella wants to cross. He looked rough, like they travelled all night."

Tommy pushed the pole through the water. "He was making such a racket, I don't know how ya slept through it. A crazy man! But he paid good, so we took him over."

His father nodded. "It don't surprise me none you mob are after him. Sure looked like a man running from something. Most folks carrying all their worldly goods move at a snail's gallop, but once we reached the Georgia side, this fella never even stopped to rest. Just took off like a shot."

"Which way?" Bartlett asked.

"The inland road. Mumbled something about keeping away from the river." He rubbed his jaw. "Can't blame him. McGirth and his dogs been tormenting people all over this area."

Alden mumbled to Tarlton. "Joe's girl said McGirth had the man scared."

"How was the boy?" Joe asked the ferryman. "Could ye tell?"

"No. Mighta been sleeping. Heard a few grunts, is all."

Joe nodded. At least Daniel was still alive.

Once they hit the opposite riverbank, Old Tom said, "If I was y'all, I'd head southwest down this road as fast as I could go. Once they reach the Ogeechee, no telling which direction they'll take."

They thanked him and went on their way. Tarlton shook his head. "I never heard that man talk so much."

They rode as hard as they could without overheating the horses. When forced to rest, Joe paced back and forth on his crutch.

"We're on horseback, Joe," Carlton said. "They're likely in an overloaded wagon. They can't outrun us."

Joe nodded but couldn't sit still.

Adam Wood made a point of asking anyone they came across whether they'd seen the McHeaths. Several had. They were on the right track.

Judging from the sun, it was between three and four o'clock when they approached the Louisville-Savannah Road along the Ogeechee. Joe's heart was in his throat. While they watered their horses, Obie Heape rode east on the road to Savannah.

In no time, he was back. "I spotted them 'bout half a mile off."

Joe mounted and started down the road.

"Wait," called Tarlton. "We need to go as a unit. If we overwhelm them, perhaps we can prevent any gunfire. We have women and a child to consider."

The eleven men headed down the road. Riding slowly to the wagon, they surrounded it before McHeath was aware there was trouble.

"McHeath," Tarlton called. "Halt!"

The wagon came to a stop and Joe pulled up beside his son. The slave girl sat beside him with a small bucket of water swabbing the boy's swollen face. "Son?" Joe said. "Daniel, can ye hear me?"

The girl Mary Edith called Lottie cocked her head. "You his daddy?"

"I am."

"You s'posed to be dead."

"So they keep telling me," he said. "I've come for me son. I'll be taking him home."

Spinning in her seat, Mrs. McHeath let out a wail that rose the hair on the back of Joe's neck. "You can't take him! He's my boy now. No one watched over him. No one loved him. Only me!"

Her husband's face crumbled at his wife's anguish. "We tried, Catherine. We have to let him go back."

The woman leaned over Daniel, sobbing. "Only I love you. Only me!"

Even Joe's heart went out to her. He couldn't bear to look at her horrified, tear-stained face. He just took his son's hand and tried to comfort him.

☥

Carlton trotted to the front of the wagon next to McHeath. When the tavern keeper caught sight of him, he sat up straighter. "Carlton de Barnefort? I never expected to see you with this raff. I thought you paid men to fight your battles."

Without forethought, Carlton slashed the man's shoulder with his riding crop. McHeath cried out and grabbed his upper arm. Blood seeped between his fingers.

Carlton's face burned. "I have my faults, but I won't take that from you. You want to stand by the king? I respect the principle. But you perched behind your damned bar day after day with the likes of McGirth—the Son of Perdition Himself—and his toad-eaters whom you sent to steal, rape, and plunder the guilty and the innocent. Now, you've stolen a child!" He held his crop up. "Speak to me like that again and I'll jam this down your gaping hole."

Adam Wood told McHeath, "You do got a big mouth for a man-a-hanging like you be."

At that moment, the whip was shot from Carlton's fist. He looked down to find the heel of his hand torn and bloody. Over the next seconds, it grew from numb to agonizing.

Whoops and hollers of battle came at them from all directions, it seemed. Carlton wasn't afraid. He was angry. Pulling his sword from its scabbard, he turned Hector toward the cries and started slashing at any who came near. There was no time to think. Only action.

Bullets whizzed past his ears. Those with him had pulled their rifles and returned fire. He glimpsed behind him to see Catherine McHeath crouched at her seat covered by her husband. Joe Dillon had leapt from his horse and lay in the wagon atop Daniel and the slave girl.

When his brain began to function, he saw there were only a few attackers. At least, only a few left. Two or three lay on the ground, dead or injured. A hairy monster of a man came toward him, reloading his gun. Carlton didn't wait. His sword extended, he signaled for Hector to gallop toward the fiend.

As the man raised his loaded gun only feet from Carlton's face, Alden leapt from his horse and tackled the man to the ground.

His brother rolled a few feet away while the monster rose to his feet. The man swung his gun one way, then the other, apparently shaken from his fall. At that moment, Tarlton Brown raced over and jumped from his horse.

McHeath lifted his head and called, "That's McGirth! Kill the bastard!"

Tarlton's face took on a fierceness that stopped Carlton cold. While others battled what men McGirth had left, he watched Tarlton Brown slam his fist into the brute's face again and again. McGirth's gun fell from his hand. Carlton could see he was reaching in his boot, likely for another weapon. Blood, spit, and sweat flew from the two warriors.

McGirth pulled out a blade. He seemed to get the upper hand as the pair rolled across the grass. Carlton slid from Hector's back while Alden scrambled to his feet. Shirt torn, Alden staggered toward the brawl.

The monster lifted the blade. Carlton and Alden ran toward him. Carlton reached him first, placed both hands on the hilt of his sword, and plunged it into McGirth's back. He placed his foot on the man and yanked his weapon from the body. McGirth wheezed, then gurgled as though choking on blood.

Alden shoved the man off Tarlton Brown, who was himself gasping for breath.

Two remaining wretches who'd come with McGirth ran into the woods.

"Save them for another day," Bartlett called out. "We got the head. The body will die on its own."

McHeath was sitting upright beside his wife, looking ten years younger. "That son of a bachelor will roast in the fires of hell where he belongs!"

"And what of you?" Joe asked, as he climbed from the bed of the wagon. "Ye'd take a child from a woman suffering the loss of two others. To say naught of the death of her husband, as she believed. Where should the likes of you end up?"

"I was doing her a kindness," Mrs. McHeath blurted. "She couldn't keep herself together, let alone Daniel."

Joe's eye twitched. "A strong woman of tender heart, but ye were too selfish to see it. If it weren't for yer young slave there..." He caught his words too late.

Carlton wondered what he meant, but he was soon to find out.

"Lottie? What did you do?" Mrs. McHeath asked.

Alden said, "Since the cat is out of the bag, you might as well know. Lottie wrote a message to Mary Edith in charcoal. It was on the kitchen table."

"Damn you, Catherine! I warned you about teaching her, didn't I?" McHeath said, his jaw set. "Take Daniel and that traitorous wench, too. We ask only that you spare our lives. I beg you, let us continue on our way."

The woman was pitiful. Carlton wondered at the wisdom of hanging McHeath only to leave his wife alone and unprotected.

Tarlton Brown looked from one man to the other. None seemed to have an appetite for vengeance. Joe Dillon said, "I have me son. Let them go."

"We'll accept your offer," Tarlton said. "We'll have the slave girl and one of your horses, too. Be warned, if you return to the tavern, or dare cross the Savannah, for that matter, there'll be nothing for you but the noose."

Chapter Forty

Mary Edith sighed. Was there anything worse than waiting? How long had she been cooped in the upstairs chamber of the inn with her mother and Amos? Minutes felt like hours and hours went on for days.

They chatted about old times when Mr. Tom was still alive, laughed about the antics of Carlton and Alden as boys, or recalled the days when the slave quarters were alive with song and dance. For a time, they were able to keep doubts and fears at bay. But soon, the talk would fall away and they'd each live within their own thoughts.

Mary Edith's heart was full at the knowledge of Da alive and home again. It was funny. While she'd been surrounded at Kilkenny by a large and loving family, it was Da who made her feel safe. Now that he was home, could she find that peace of mind again?

That led to an emptiness inside her. Her only remaining brother was God knows where. What if they never found the McHeaths? Could he end up in a distant land like Florida, lost to them forever? What if, when trying to rescue Daniel, Da were killed? Could he be taken from them twice? It seemed too cruel. She prayed like never before. It was all she knew to do.

Few people came by the tavern. Word must have spread that the tavern keeper had fled. After the first night alone, the stagecoach pulled up at midday. Finding no one, they left in short order. The three upstairs sat frozen until the sound of the coach's horses and wheels had drifted away.

In the early evening, Mary Edith and Amos went to the barn to see about Da's mule. Mary Edith gave it some hay and water while Amos kept guard. Before heading back to the prison-like tavern, she petted the creature. The Dillons had never owned an animal before.

"I'm gonna name him Hero," she told Amos, "'cause he brung my father home."

"It ain't no him," Amos said. "Mules can't be hims or hers. They just its." He sniffed. "You smell something burning?"

"I do," Mary Edith started to say when Amos waved his arm, cutting her short. They hid behind the wagon as before, Amos's gun at the ready.

Once again, Mary Edith heard the grating voices of Frank and Lester Watkins. What were they doing here after they nearly got shot up last time? Every muscle in her body tensed.

The sound of their footsteps headed toward the kitchen. "I don't know why ya gone and done it, is all," Lester was saying.

"To get shed of that trifling, thieving widder and her brats once and for all, that's why!"

"Frank, you was just burning green wood for kindling. Them Dillons weren't coming back nohow. Not after cleaning out the tavern like they done."

"I don't care a hate!" Frank said. "It was a perty fire any way ya look at it."

"You right about that," Lester said. "My backbone's a-rubbing my belly. You sure there's victuals here?"

"I thought I saw some in the kitchen. Them fools couldn'ta stole everything."

Mary Edith's legs ached from staying so still, yet she dasn't move. Please, Ma, she prayed, don't come looking for us now. She was grateful they'd already taken plenty of food to the McHeaths's chamber.

After several minutes, they heard the two mongrels again, chewing like a pair of wild dogs chomping on a dead animal. Mouth full, one of them mumbled, "Let's get the hell out of here 'fore someone 'cuse us of thieving."

After several minutes of silence, Amos poked his gun out the door and looked around. He motioned for Mary Edith to stay put while he checked the tavern for any sign of those slimy worms.

Had the two of them burned their house? Out of pure meanness?

Amos returned and waved her out. "They gone. But Mar' Edith, yo house be burning. Look there."

Billowing black smoke poured into the northern sky. From that distance, it had to be their cabin. Where would they go now?

Upstairs, Ma was gazing out the small window in the direction of their home. She turned toward them, tears rolling down her face. Without a word, her mother moved to her makeshift pallet and curled into a ball. When or how long she finally slept, Mary Edith didn't know.

In the morning, Mary Edith and Amos sneaked out to feed Hero and carry cold water from the pump to their room. When they returned, Ma said very little. She refused to join in on the old Kilkenny stories Amos told to distract them.

It was almost noon when Mary Edith heard someone pull up in a wagon. It was Ketch carrying Miss Rosabel who, chin up, had tucked a rifle under her arm.

Mary Edith ran downstairs to greet the newcomers.

After Ketch helped her off the wagon, Miss Rosabel told him, "Put the horse and cart in the barn. No need to draw unnecessary attention. And bring the basket when you come."

Mary Edith opened her mouth to speak, but Miss Rosabel placed a hand on her shoulder. "I've terrible news. Your cabin, it's burned to the ground."

"It was them fellows you shot at the other day," she told the woman.

"They've been here?"

She nodded. "We hid like before. I heard them say it was 'cause we stole the liquor."

Miss Rosabel snorted. "Before they had a chance to. I'm so sorry, child." She looked around. "I suppose there's been no sign of the rescuers."

"Not yet. We best get inside. What if the stagecoach stops?"

"Of course." They both went upstairs and joined Ma and Amos.

Miss Rosabel ran to a bleary-eyed Ma and grasped her hands. "Nan, your home is gone. But we'll figure it out, don't you worry."

Ketch joined them with a large basket. After setting it down, he hugged Mary Edith, then her mother. "This an evil world. That's all I know to say."

Miss Rosabel lifted her eyebrows. "Let's all have a picnic—an indoor picnic. I've brought lots of good food from Ruth." She reached into her basket. "And mojos from Mama Juba. She's using all her skills to ward off more sorrow, dear woman."

Mary Edith held her mojo in her hand. It was hard to explain after all they'd been through, but this small kindness from Mama Juba breached a dam holding back her distress. Her father's miraculous return, the near-death, then loss of sweet Daniel, the threat of the Watkins boys, and destruction of their meager home.

She broke into tears, saying, "It's a little bag of hope."

Looking around, everyone's face was wet. Even Ketch.

◆

It was early afternoon. Despite the kindness of Miss Rosabel, Ruth, Mama Juba, and the men, Nan could not shake her sense of foreboding. Like Mary Edith, she held onto her mojo bag, but it brought no relief.

She had heard people say waiting was the hardest part, but not for her. The news that her son was lost and her husband dead, that was the hard part. A part she was sure was coming.

She remembered the morning Joe had left her. Her hardheartedness toward him tortured her still. They'd had a few hours together since his return, but he'd done all the talking. And there was much she needed to say—how her love for him was endless, larger than the ocean they'd crossed, the expanse of sky overhead, the cruelty of those around them. Her love overshadowed everything. If he was already gone, would he somehow know how she felt? Or was it all too late?

Hoofbeats pounded outside the tavern. Ketch and Amos scooted to the windows to see who was astir.

"Ki!" Ketch called out. "They here. It be them!"

"Who?" Nan asked, afraid of the answer.

The others jumped up and headed down the stairs.

Ketch took her hands and pulled her from the floor. "It's Joe, Nan." His lower lip quivered. "He made it."

Her legs gave out from under her. Ketch held her up as they went down the stairs. Once they reached the bottom, she saw him atop the horse.

Her beautiful man, looking as strong and handsome as the day they met. His eyes met hers and his whole face lit up. Sliding from his mount, he grabbed the crutch from his belt, and hobbled her way.

"We got him, Nan," he called. "Daniel'll be coming along. He's well and in a wagon with Alden."

The haggard woman from upstairs disappeared. She was Nan Scully of Lurganlea, in County Tipperary, running to meet her true love. Leaping into his arms, his crutch gave way and she knocked him to the ground.

He grabbed her face and kissed every part of it again and again. The rest of the world melted away.

Her eyes blurred with tears. "I love ye, Joe Dillon. With every fiber of me body. For all me life and beyond."

Joe brushed her hair from her face. "Our son is safe and on his way home."

Around them, Carlton had dismounted. Rosabel stood beside him, fussing over his bandaged hand. Tarlton Brown walked around the tavern, looking for the Lord knows what. The others stood by, Ketch with his arm over Mary Edith's shoulder.

Joe looked into her eyes. "The lad's still swole some, but he's well. Once we crossed into Carolina, we found a wagon for him. Alden and Bartlett Brown are behind us. They won't be long."

"They burned our house, Joe."

"It don't matter," he said. "Nothing else matters. We're together."

Mary Edith knelt beside them. "All of us."

✥

Once Mary Edith and the others brought the remaining food to the Great Room, all sat down and ate with hearty appetites. It warmed her heart to see Ma gobbling food she hadn't touched before.

"It looks like the goods have been stashed," Tarlton Brown said with a chicken leg in his hand. "Did it burn along with your cabin?"

"I found a better place," Mary Edith said.

After she described her hideaway, Tarlton said, "You're a shrewd little Patriot. Though I've been the beneficiary of your gumption before."

"The wagons are here," Amos said.

Running outside, Mary Edith sped to the cart Alden was driving. Beside him sat a pretty young black-haired woman. Looking in the wagon bed, she stopped in her tracks.

"Lottie!"

Her friend leaned over Daniel, telling him, "We here."

Daniel rose up on his elbow and, with much-shrunken lips, formed his best smile. "I'm better, Mary Edith."

"You can talk a bit, but you gotta go slow." Her heart full, she kissed his brow. "Thank you, God. My brother is home."

Ma ran to the wagon and held her son against her chest. "To see yer dear face again is all I can ask."

After another round of hugs and good cheer, they went inside to eat. Amos had dragged a keg of ale from its hiding place so they could have a proper reunion. Even Daniel had a watered-down cup of the brew.

When Mary Edith left the table, she was surprised to see Tarlton Brown heading her way. He took her aside out of earshot of the others.

"I saved you," she told him. "Now you saved Daniel. I guess we're even."

The tall man shook his head. "There is no even. You gave me my life. What you did cannot be repaid." He swallowed. "I heard that guard, Rufus, was hanged, and you found him."

The memory drained the contentment from her body. She hung her head.

"You think Rufus died because of what you did for me? I know for a fact Rufus met with Patriots while he claimed to be a Tory."

"He did?"

"He played a dangerous game, Mary Edith, and he lost. His death had nothing to do with you or me." Tarlton Brown smiled and ruffled her hair. "Although my escape didn't help him any."

Mary Edith nodded. A stone had been lifted from her heart.

More Patriots arrived, bringing wagons. Alden announced he knew of a cave where no one would find the contraband. Then he smiled at the black-haired woman named Suzanne, who was Tarlton Brown's sister. Mary Edith could see they were sweet on each other.

Amos showed the half dozen men who'd joined them where the whiskey and other goods were hidden. They proceeded to haul the contraband from Mary Edith's secret place and load it on the wagons.

Mary Edith sat beside Lottie and watched her ma hold Daniel in her lap, stroking his hair. "He looks so happy. Both of them do."

"Ha!" Lottie said, "You need a peep at y'own face. It shines like a full moon."

She laughed, but noticed Lottie chewing her thumbnail. Laying her hand on her friend's arm, she asked, "How are you?"

Lottie shook her head. "Oh, I's right. Wonderin' what's to become of me, is all."

Alden stood close enough to hear. "Lottie, you're the savior in all this. Let me talk to the others."

He walked across the yard to where the other men stood. Lottie stared at the group as if that could help her hear what was said.

Mary Edith struggled for words of comfort to offer but found none.

At last, Carlton, Alden, Bartlett, and Tarlton Brown walked over and stood before Lottie. Her eyes widened. Mary Edith's parents joined them, along with Miss Rosabel. Lottie stood to face them.

Tarlton spoke. "Lottie, without you, this family would not be celebrating today. McGirth would be alive, with him and his ilk free to torment Loyalists and Patriots alike up and down the Savannah River. Our fight is far from over, but because of you, today is a fine day."

"We can't never repay ye. Ye saved me son's life, which means ye saved me," Ma said, holding Da's hand with both of hers.

Carlton said, "Both the Browns and I would be pleased to add you to our households. We have decided, due to your heroism at great risk to yourself, you should be the one to tell us what you want."

Lottie's mouth hung open a little as she listened. She looked to Mary Edith, who shrugged. For a moment or two, the McHeaths's now-former slave studied the ground. When she looked up, her face showed an earnest expression Mary Edith had never seen her wear. Taking a deep breath, she spoke.

"I been doin' what white men tol' me my whole life. Nobody ain't never asked me what I want. This be my chance, don't it?" She took a deep breath. "I want to be free."

Those around her gasped, but she stuck out her chin and spoke on. "I don't mind workin'. I can cook and I know healin' ways." She looked at Carlton. "I want to work on K'Kenny with my friend, Mar' Edith. But I want to be free, like her and Daniel."

"We don't live on Kilkenny, Lottie," Mary Edith whispered. "We don't live anywhere right now."

No one spoke. Mary Edith's heart pounded.

"They asked me," Lottie said, "and I told 'em."

When the silence became near unbearable, Rosabel poked her husband. "Tell her. Tell them all. The answer is yes."

Carlton glared at his wife, then turned to Lottie. "The answer is yes." He looked to Joe. "If you're willing, Kilkenny would welcome all of you home. I would welcome you home."

Waiting for her father's reply, Mary Edith held her breath. But he did not answer. He looked at Ma and said, "Nan?"

"We been through a lot," her mother said. "But it's time to go home."

Da nodded. "We accept, sir."

Mary Edith squealed with happiness. She grabbed Lottie and twirled her around. "We'll be like sisters!" she cried.

⊕

Alden had never been so proud of his brother. After Rosabel shocked everyone by kissing him square on the lips, he shook Carlton's hand. "Well done, brother."

"Finish the picture," Carlton said. "Come home."

"I'll give it some thought." Alden left to stand beside Suzanne who had kept her distance from the goings on.

"It's been too long," Suzanne said, "since we've seen such happiness. That's why I wanted to come along—to see the joy of parents getting their son back alive. And they did not disappoint me."

"Life doesn't bring enough days like this."

Suzanne peered into his eyes, making him a bit uncomfortable, before she leaned in and kissed him on the mouth.

Stunned, Alden glanced around, but no one was watching. "You're a bit of a hussy."

She raised her eyebrows. "If I didn't do it, it wasn't going to get done."

Alden kissed her back, experiencing a passion he'd never felt with any other woman. With her brothers in mind, he forced himself to pull back. Cocking his head to one side, he said, "Now, I'll have to marry you."

Suzanne grinned. "Yes, you will."

While he kept his own counsel, Alden knew he'd one day build a family on Kilkenny with this stunning woman.

⚜

Carlton knew the war was far from over, but on this day, he felt comfortable within himself. He glanced at Rosabel's barely swelling belly. Perhaps he could be the father his child deserved.

Bartlett Brown along with Adam and Jamie Woods were placing grasses, brush, and small branches at various spots around the tavern. He walked to Tarlton Brown.

"What are you planning here?"

"Making sure McHeath has no reason to come back, no matter what side wins this wretched war. It won't hurt if some of his foot-lickers receive the message, as well."

"You're burning the tavern?"

"Yes, we are," he told Carlton. "I know you don't subscribe to our politics, but you killed McGirth. A great service to both sides. My only regret is I was unable to run him through myself."

Carlton said, "I don't consider myself a rebel. At the same time, my zeal for the king's men has waned. While it seems an impossible needle to thread, I hope to emulate my father. I will not fight with you, but I'll not work against you either."

The two men shook hands.

Soon, the wagons were loaded, and the tavern was prepared for its fate. Everyone stood before the old inn, waiting for Tarlton to give the nod. When he did, a few of the men went around the building with torches, lighting the tinder placed along the foundation.

The witnesses stood by in silence, waiting for the sparks to do their job. A flicker became a flare, which grew to a flame. From there, the blaze radiated at a steady pace. Before long, they backed away from the scorching heat as fire consumed the tavern.

Alden gave the signal to the men in wagons. He and Suzanne climbed aboard their cart and led the others, fully armed, to the contraband's new home.

Tarlton stayed a bit longer. "A beautiful sight," he said of the burning tavern. Then, he mounted Castor and, with one last wave, left for Brier's Creek.

Wood cracked like gunshots, as the structure crumbled to ashes. Carlton took a deep breath. He placed his arm around Rosabel's shoulder and took in the remaining people—Joe and Nan Dillon, their children, Mary Edith and Daniel. Ketch, Amos, Lottie. It came to him. He was a fortunate man.

"Well, family," he said, "Let's head home."

Chapter Forty-one

The air was finally cooling under a stark blue September sky. Mary Edith walked into Kilkenny's kitchen. Ruth clasped her hands and held them against her chest.

"I won't never get tired of seein' ya back where ya belong. Come over here."

Ruth wrapped her arms around Mary Edith like she was a big bundle. Letting go, the cook took down a jar only she was allowed to touch. "Don't tell nobody," she said, reaching inside.

After pulling out an almond sweetmeat, she looked at Mary Edith and reached in again. Taking out a handful, Ruth shoved them at her. "Take all these. Now git out my kitchen, ya hear?" Her eyes red, she turned her back to Mary Edith and puttered over her pot above the fire.

Mary Edith looked in her hand. Four pieces of marzipan! Ruth had gone mad. She opened her mouth to protest, but the cook waved her hand behind her.

"Go on. Git!"

Stepping from the kitchen, she knew what to do. Dropping the sweets in her apron pocket, she ran from the quarters into the woods to the slaves' graveyard. At the resting places of Baby and Nolan, she placed a sweetmeat on each mound.

"I'm sorry," she said aloud. "I done what I could to save you—each of you, but nothing worked. I thought I knew how to ward off the evil that overrun us, but I didn't. I shoulda stayed by ya, Baby. You begged me, but I wouldn't listen. I won't never stop being sorry for that.

"Da says I shouldn't be sad for you two. He says you're with Jesus now and there ain't no better happiness." She sighed. "But it's fine to be sad for myself, he says, 'cause I miss you so bad." Her throat clenched as she watched an ant climb atop Nolan's sweetmeat. "I'm mighty sad for myself."

She reached into her apron's pocket. The sticky sweetmeats were melting a bit. She thought to give Baby and Nolan a second one when another notion hit her.

"I gotta go. I'll talk to y'all two tomorrow."

As fast as she could, she ran to the family cemetery. Panting, she stood before Mr. Tom's grave.

"I'm back," she told him. "And I finally brung you something you might like in your new world." She reached into her apron and pulled out another sugary treat. "People brung you whiskey and tobacco and cornbread, but I bet no one thought to bring you no marzipan." She knelt, then looked around to be sure she was alone. "I have to sneak it to you 'cause that's how it's done, right?"

After laying her gift on the grave, she stood and stared at it, feeling warm inside. She had no doubt Mr. Tom was pleased.

One more piece. Mary Edith glanced a few yards away at the newer plot of Lady Anne and pulled out the sweet.

With a smile, she popped it into her mouth.

About the Book

The War for American Independence continued to be brutal for many months to come. On October 19, 1781, British General Cornwallis surrendered at Yorktown, Virginia. As things grew dire there for the British, they cut most of the escaped slaves loose to survive as best they could. The magnitude of their suffering and death is unknown but thought to be extensive. If this book were to continue, fictional characters Thunder and Dalanda would be among the few former slaves taken to New York City, then transported to Nova Scotia as free people. Descendants of such people reside in Nova Scotia today.

The British were finally forced to evacuate Charles Town on December 14, 1782, celebrated today as Victory Day.

The book's setting of Orangeburgh District in 1780 encompassed at least seven present-day counties. Kilkenny Plantation, a real place, was in what is now Barnwell County, South Carolina. The boundaries of that estate as portrayed are not factually precise. Red Hill and McHeath's Tavern were in today's Fuller Park Hill area of the city of Barnwell. White Oak Springs now lies beneath Lake Edgar Brown, created from Turkey Creek in the 1960s.

Burton's Ferry was in present-day Allendale County where US Highway 301 crosses into Georgia. King's Creek is to its south. Summerlin's Ferry, along the Savannah River, is now known as Brown's Landing. Tarlton Brown and his family lived nearby on Brier's Creek. The Cracker's Neck camp was in now-Aiken County.

While all characters connected with Kilkenny Plantation are fictional, several others in the book were actual people. These included Tarlton Brown and his parents, Billy and Sarah, his brothers Bartlett and Manden, and sister Elizabeth (Liza). Suzanne Brown is fictional. Tarlton Brown wrote a memoir in his later years, and many of the events in this book come from these recollections.

While the timeline as depicted should be taken loosely, the episode concerning the Cracker's Neck Boys chasing down and killing a man named Richardson was reported by the Patriot, Tarlton Brown. The attempt by Tories to enter the Brown homestead, leading to the death of brother, Manden, is also recounted in the memoir.

Brown did, in fact, join the King's Creek militia at his father's suggestion. He and the others mentioned in the story, except for Alden, went on a mission to recover jugs of rum at Hershman Lake in present-day Screven County, Georgia. The results were as portrayed in the book.

The militiamen at King's Creek, including Billy Brown, were rounded up by the enemy and taken about two miles to Harbard's Store in Georgia. Colonel Leroy Hammond got wind of the operation and came to the rescue, slaughtering the British and Tories as described. Patriots at that point were in disarray in the way Hammond explained.

The soldier, Joshua Spears's suspicions regarding General Williamson, were recorded years later as part of his pension application. At the time, General Williamson's actions toward the British were controversial. Even today, some claim he was the "Benedict Arnold of the South" and others call him the country's first double agent.

Tarlton and Bartlett did leave the area for Virginia after the fall of Charles Town, yet the skirmish depicted near the Santee River in which Joe was injured is fictional. However, similar episodes did occur along their way.

While they were gone, Daniel McGirth led a party of marauders on a killing spree of seventeen people, including Billy Brown. The family home was burned to the ground as described. The Brown women survived by hiding in the woods until danger had passed.

The description of that atrocity is mostly accurate, but I regret to report the part where McGirth is killed by Carlton de Barnefort is fictional. Though it was satisfying to write, McGirth and his thugs continued to cruelly harass people throughout South Carolina, Georgia, and Florida for years to come. He finally served time in an east Florida prison which wrecked his health but did not kill him. His end is not clear, but he likely sneaked back into South Carolina where he lived quietly into his fifties. A good article about him can be found at https://allthingsliberty.com/2016/08/daniel-mcgirth-banditti-southern-frontier/.

According to a woman named Harriet Moore who grew up near White Oak Springs, Tarlton Brown was captured by the Tories and taken to McHeath's Tavern. She told of the early celebration that his guard insisted on joining, enabling the Patriot's escape. Though found in *Village of Barnwell* by William Hansford Duncan, Tarlton Brown did not include this in his memoirs.

The descriptions of the horrors of Charles Town's siege recounted by Captain John Mumford, an actual person killed as described, were found in *A Gallant Defense* by Carl P. Borick.

Dr. Uzal Johnson did exist and kept a detailed journal of his time in South Carolina. Much of what's described of Charles

Town after its fall and what Thunder encountered as part of the British army came from Dr. Johnson's writings.

Many other minor characters actually existed, and Tarlton Brown experienced more exploits than are told in this story.

For those who'd like to learn more, Tarlton Brown's memoirs are posted at https://www.sciway3.net/clark/allendale/tbrownmemoirs.htm.

They can be purchased in print from the Barnwell County Museum. Contact information can be found at https://www.bcvm.org/barnwell/museum/index.htm.

Acknowledgements

While only one name appears on the cover of this book, many more people helped make it happen. I can only name a few, but I am aware and thankful for all of them.

For the research required with a story like this, re-enactors are a passionate, well-informed source. I thank those who allowed me to pick their brains at Camden, South Carolina's Revolutionary War Days and North Augusta, South Carolina's Living History Park. Thank you to Owais Kahn for generously sharing information about his Muslim faith.

As always, the Barnwell County Museum has embraced me throughout this project. The support of the board and staff are unmatched in their dedication to the advancement of history and the arts in the county.

The Aiken Chapter of the South Carolina Writer's Association has been stalwart in its support of my writing endeavors. I am blessed not only by their literary expertise, but also by a camaraderie that fulfills me. The Assassin's Guild members Candace J. Carter, R. George Clark, Steve Gordy, and Sasscer Hill have been godsends in their diligent evaluation of my work. I'm privileged to be part of a community that's embraced my writing as though it's their own.

Thank you to Carol Fox, Wendy Gibson, Milton Harden, Evie Kelly, Tim Kelly, Jerry Morris, Brenda Richardson, Norma Rockwell, and Lynne Seaha for taking the time and effort to go through *Patience Can Cook a Stone*. Your thoughts and suggestions have been invaluable. Book lovers like you are why I write.

I cannot adequately express the gratitude I feel toward my friends and readers since I've begun this journey as an author. You've made my dream come true. I am indebted to my family whose love and support are extraordinary.

Finally, to my husband. My first reader. My most ardent advocate. My greatest friend.

ABOUT THE AUTHOR

M. B. Gibson is the author of the award-winning Duncullen Saga. She is a lifelong learner and teacher, eager to share her passion for history and story to celebrate the dignity and value of all people. She and her husband enjoy the quiet life in rural South Carolina.

Find M. B. Gibson at
mbgibsonbooks.com